D0044590

Project
Pope

Project
Pope

CLIFFORD D. SIMAK

A Del Rey Book

BALLANTINE BOOKS • NEW YORK

A Del Rey Book
Published by Ballantine Books

Copyright © 1981 by Clifford D. Simak

Manufactured in the United States of America

Prologue

THOMAS DECKER WAS HALF AN HOUR FROM HOME WHEN
Whisperer stopped him in his tracks.

—Decker, said Whisperer, speaking inside Decker's mind.
Decker, now I'll get you. This time I will get you.

Decker swiveled about on the game trail he had been following,
his rifle raised, held away from his body, ready to snap to his
shoulder against the first sign of danger.

There was nothing in sight, nothing stirring. The heavy growth
of trees and brush came down close against the trail on either side.
It all hung motionless. There was not the slightest breeze, no
flicker of a bird. There was absolutely nothing. Everything was
frozen, as if eternity had clamped down.

—Decker!

The word was inside his mind. There had been no sound, nothing spoken. The only sound was in his mind and he had never
been able to decide, in all his previous encounters with Whisperer,
if there *had* been a sound inside his mind. He just knew the words,
lodged there in that area of his brain in the front of his head, just
above his eyes.

—Not this time, Whisperer, he said to the other, speaking to it
as it had bespoken him, no words uttered, but forming the
thoughts and words inside his mind for Whisperer to read. Today
I'm not playing any games with you. I've played the last game
with you. There won't be any more.

—Chicken, said Whisperer. Chicken, chicken, chicken!

—To hell with your chicken business, said Decker. Come out
and show yourself and see if I am chicken. I've had it with you,
Whisperer. I'm up to here with you.

—You are chicken, said Whisperer. You had me in your rifle sights last time and you did not pull the trigger. Chicken, Decker, chicken.

—I have no reason to kill you, Whisperer. Actually no wish to. But, so help me God, I'll let you have it just to get rid of you.

—If I don't get you first.

—You've had chances at me, said Decker. You must have had a lot of chances. So let's quit this bickering. Let us stop this horse-play. You don't want to kill me any more than I want to kill you. You just want to keep on playing. I'm sick of your silly games. I'm hungry and I'm tired and I want to get on home. I don't want to play hide-and-seek with you, chasing you up and down the woods.

By now he had figured out where Whisperer was located, and he shifted slightly in the path to face the spot where Whisperer was hidden in the underbrush.

—You had good luck this time, said Whisperer. You found a lot of gems. Maybe even diamonds.

—You know damn well I didn't. You were with me. You watched me all the time. I sensed you.

—You work hard, said Whisperer. You should find diamonds now and then.

—I'm not looking for diamonds.

—What do you do with what you find?

—Whisperer, why all these silly questions? You know what I do with them.

—You give them to the captain of the ship to sell at Gutshot. He steals you blind. He sells them for three times what he tells you that he gets.

—I suspect he does, said Decker. But what the hell? He needs the money more than I do. He's putting together a stake to buy that place on Apple Blossom. Why this sudden interest, Whisperer?

—You do not sell him all?

—That is true. I keep the better pieces.

—I could use some of your better pieces.

—You, Whisperer? What would you want of them?

—Shape them. Carve them. Change them.

—You are a carver, Whisperer?

—Not an accomplished carver, Decker. Just a hobbyist.

Now he knew exactly where Whisperer was located. If he made the slightest move, he would let him have it. Whisperer wasn't fooling him with this talk of gems and carving. It was just a lot of talk to throw him off his balance.

He might as well, Decker told himself, put an end to it. For months now, this hidden clown had been pestering him, trailing him and watching him, jeering at him, threatening him, getting him to play the silly game, making an utter fool of him.

—I could show you, in a stream not far from here, said Whisperer, a place where there are many gems. There is one piece, a large chunk of jade, I want very much myself. Get the jade for me and you can have all the rest.

—Get it yourself, said Decker. If you know where it is, get it for yourself.

—But I cannot, said Whisperer. I have no arms to reach, no hands to grasp, no strength to lift. You must do it for me. After all, why not? We are friends. We have played games enough to even be old friends. We've been at it long enough.

—Once I get my hands on you, said Decker. Once I get you in the sights again. . . .

—What you had in your sights, said Whisperer, was not me. It was a shadow, a shape I made that you would think was me. When you saw the shape and did not shoot, I knew you were my friend.

—Friend or not, said Decker, shape or not, shadow even, next time I'll pull the trigger.

—We could be friends, said Whisperer. We've spent an infancy together. We have romped and played together. We've grown to know one another. Now that we have matured . . .

—Matured?

—Yes, Decker, our friendship has matured. No more play is needed. It was only a rite. Perhaps it was foolish of me to inflict the rite upon you. A rite of friendship only.

—A rite? You're crazy, Whisperer.

—A rite you did not recognize, did not understand, and yet you played it with me. Not always willingly, not always in good temper, often cursing and frothing and thirsting for my blood, but you played it with me. And now that the rite is done, we can go home together.

—Over my dead body will we go home together. I'll not have you cluttering up the cabin.

—I would not clutter greatly. I would take little room. I could squeeze into a corner. You would not even notice me. And I need a friend so greatly. I must pick a friend so carefully. I must find one that is tuned to me—

—Whisperer, said Decker, you are wasting your time. Whatever the hell you are driving at, you're wasting your time.

—We could be good for one another. I would carve your gems and talk with you on lonely nights and sit before the fire with you, and there would be many tales we could tell each other. You, perhaps, could help me with Vatican—

—With Vatican! yelled Decker. What in the name of Christ have you to do with Vatican?

Chapter One

JASON TENNYSON, FLEEING FOR HIS LIFE, CAME IN LOW OVER the precipitous mountain range that lay to the west of Gutshot. Immediately after he caught sight of the lights marking the town, he pressed the ejection button and felt himself flung upward with a greater violence than he had expected. For a moment he was enveloped in darkness; then, as his body spun, he saw the lights of the town again and thought that he also saw the flier. But whether he saw the flier or not, he knew, was of slight importance. It would continue over Gutshot, angling slightly downward over the ocean that hemmed in the tiny town and spaceport against the towering mountains. Some fifty miles out to sea, if his calculations were correct, the flier would go into the water and be lost. And lost as well, he hoped, would be Dr. Jason Tennyson, lately court physician to the margrave of Daventry. The radar at Gutshot space base undoubtedly had picked up the flier and would track it on its course across the water, but at its low altitude, the base would soon lose contact with it.

His fall was slackening and suddenly, as the chute popped open to its full extent, he was jerked sidewise and began swinging in wide arcs. An updraft caught the chute, forcing it back toward the looming peaks and slowing the swinging; but in a moment it slid out of the updraft and was floating smoothly downward. Tennyson, dangling at the end of the lines, tried to make out where he would land; it seemed toward the south end of the spaceport. He held his breath and hoped. He threaded his arms through the chute straps and clutched his medical bag, holding it close against his chest. Let it go well, he prayed—let it continue to go well. So far it had gone surprisingly well. All the way he had held the flier low, rocketing through the night, making wide circuits to avoid feudal holdings, where radars would be groping skyward, for in this vicious world of contending fiefs, a close watch was always kept. No one knew at what time or from what direction raiders might come swooping in.

Peering down, he tried to gauge how close he might be drifting to solid ground, but the darkness made it impossible to judge. He found himself tensing, then consciously willed himself to relax. When he hit, he had to be relaxed.

The grouping of lights that marked the town was some distance to the north; the spatter of brilliance that was the spaceport was almost dead ahead. A blackness intervened to shield out the space-port lights and he hit the ground, knees buckling under him. He threw himself to one side, still holding tightly to the bag. The chute collapsed and he struggled to his feet, pulling on lines and shrouds.

He had landed, he saw, close to a group of large warehouses at the south end of the port. It had been the bulk of the warehouses that had cut off the spaceport lights. Luck, he realized, had been with him. Had he been able to plan it, he could not have chosen a better landing site.

His eyes now were becoming accustomed to the night darkness. He was situated, he saw, near an alley that ran between two of the warehouses. He saw also that the warehouses were set on pilings; a foot or so lay between the ground and the foundations of the build-ings. And there, he thought, was where he could hide the chute. He could bundle it together and push it as far into the space as he could reach. If he could find a stick of some sort, he could even push it farther. But all that was needed was to push it far enough that it would not be spotted by a passerby. This would save him considerable time. He had feared that he might have to try to dig a hole or find a clump of trees in which to hide the chute. All that was necessary would be for it not to be found for several days; hidden underneath the warehouse, it might not be found for years.

Now, he thought, if he could find a ship and, somehow, get aboard. He might have to bribe some member of the ship's per-sonnel, but that should not be hard. Few of the ships, most of which were freighters, that touched down at Gutshot would visit the port again for a long time, perhaps for years; others of them might never come this way again. Once on the ship, he would be safe. Unless someone found the chute, there would not be any evidence that he had ejected from the flier.

The chute safely hidden, the bag now unstrapped from about his waist and carried in his hand, he made his way down the alley between the two warehouses. At the mouth of the alley, he stopped. Out on the port, directly opposite where he stood, was a ship. The gangplank was down and a long line of people—all of them aliens of various sorts—were being herded up the plank and into the ship by a small group of ratlike creatures. The line extended some distance back from the ship, and the ratlike guards were yelling at the aliens in the line, waving clubs at them to hurry them along.

The ship would be taking off soon, Tennyson told himself, puzzled at what kind it was. Few passenger liners came down at this port, and this one did not have the appearance of a liner. It was a dumpy old tub, blackened and disreputable. Its name was painted above the port and it was some time before Tennyson could make out that it spelled WAYFARER, for the paint was flaking and there was much rust upon the hull. There was no smartness to the ship. It was not the sort of craft that any self-respecting traveler would choose. But, while he looked at it with some distaste, Tennyson reminded himself that he was not in a position to be discriminating. The ship apparently would be leaving soon, and that was far more important than knowing what kind it was. If he could manage to get aboard, that would be good enough. If his luck still held for him. . . .

Tennyson edged out beyond the alley's mouth. To his right, beyond the warehouse, a splash of light flared out across a walk that paralleled the perimeter of the field. Walking out cautiously a few feet farther, he saw that the light came from a small bar.

Some sort of altercation had arisen at the bottom of the gangplank. A spiderlike alien, all arms and legs, was arguing with one of the ratlike creatures that were superintending the boarding. As

Tennyson watched, the spidery alien was pushed out of the line, with one of the rat beings following, prodding it with a club.

The front of the warehouse lay in deep shadow and Tennyson edged along it rapidly. He came to the end and stood still, looking at the bar. His best course, he figured, would be to get beyond the bar and approach the ship from its forward end. Huddling in its shadow, he might be able to approach the gangplank and wait for a chance.

The last of the line of passengers were snaking up close to the gangplank. In a few more minutes, the boarding would be completed. The ship might not take off immediately, but he had the hunch that if he was going to get aboard, he would have to act quickly.

To get past the bar, he decided that he would simply walk past, moving confidently, as if he had the right to be there. Someone might see him but probably would pay no more than passing notice of him. The spidery alien had disappeared and the guard had returned to a position near the gangplank.

Leaving the corner of the warehouse, Tennyson set off down the walk that passed in front of the bar. Beyond the bar, deep shadows again lay in front of another warehouse. If he could reach that warehouse without being challenged, he probably could make it to the ship. On a secondary port such as this one, security measures were not tight.

Now he was passing in front of the bar. Looking in one of the three windows from which the light poured, he glimpsed a coat rack standing beside the door. He paused in midstride, riveted to attention by what he saw. Hanging on the rack was a blue jacket, with the word WAYFARER stitched in gold thread across one breast. Above it rested a cap that matched the jacket.

Acting on impulse, Tennyson swung toward the door, went through it. A mixed group of humans and aliens were sitting at tables at the back; a few were lined up at the bar. The barkeep was busy. A couple of people lifted their heads and looked at him when he came in, then went back to what they had been doing.

Swiftly he reached out to grab the jacket and the cap, then was out the door again, his shoulders hunched, expecting an outcry behind him. But there was none.

He slapped the cap onto his head, shrugged into the jacket.

The line in front of the ship's gangplank was gone; apparently everyone had boarded. Only one ratlike creature remained standing at the gangplank's foot. Swiftly, purposefully, Tennyson strode across the field, heading for the ship.

The one ratlike guard might challenge him, but he doubted it. The jacket and cap should be sufficient disguise. More than likely the guard would not recognize him as an intruder. Few humans could recognize any particular alien; to them all aliens looked alike. The same was true of aliens, who ordinarily could not distinguish one human from another.

He reached the foot of the gangplank. The ratlike creature made a sloppy salute.

"Welcome, sir," it said. "Captain has been asking after you."

Chapter Two

AFTER A TIME, ONE OF THE RATLIKE CREWMEN FOUND HIM in the small, closetlike equipment hold where he had squeezed himself to hide. The crewman hauled him out and took him to the captain, who was alone in the control room, sitting at his ease in one of the three chairs. At the moment nothing needed to be done; the ship was running on its own.

"What is this you have?" the captain asked.

"Stowaway," the rat creature said. "Dug him out of a small aft hold."

"Okay," the captain said. "Leave him here. You can go."

The rodent turned to go.

"My bag, please," said Tennyson.

The rat turned around, still holding the bag.

The captain said, "Give the bag to me and then get out of here. Get the hell out of my sight."

The rat turned over the bag and left hurriedly.

The captain examined the bag thoughtfully, then lifted his head and said, "So it is Jason Tennyson, is it? M.D.?"

Tennyson nodded. "Yes, I am a doctor."

The captain set the bag down on the deck beside him. "I've had a few stowaways in my time," he said, "but never a doctor. Doctor, tell me, just what is going on?"

"It's a long story," said Tennyson, "and I'd prefer not going into it."

"You'd been in that hold for hours," the captain said. "I suppose you sneaked on at Gutshot. Why did you wait so long?"

"I was about to come out," said Tennyson. "Your rat-faced friend beat me to it."

"He is no friend of mine."

"My error," said Tennyson.

"There aren't many humans out here," the captain said. "The farther out you go, the fewer you will find. I have to use this kind of scum to man the ship. And I have to haul loads of other scum out to End of Nothing and—"

"Out to the end of what?"

"End of Nothing. That is where we're going. Don't tell me you weren't headed there?"

"Until this moment," Tennyson said, "I had never heard of it."

"Then it must be that you were intent on leaving Gutshot."

"That, Captain, is a fair assumption."

"In some sort of trouble there?"

"I was running for my life."

"And popped onto the first ship that was taking off?"

Tennyson nodded.

"Sit down, man," the captain said. "Don't stay standing there. Would you like a drink?"

"That would be fine," said Tennyson. "Yes, I could use a drink."

"Can you tell me," the captain asked, "did anyone see you duck into the ship?"

"I don't think so."

"You're fairly sure?"

"Well, you see, I went into a bar. One of the spaceport joints. When I left, it seems that somehow I got hold of the wrong jacket and wrong cap. I was, if I remember, in somewhat of a hurry. . . ."

"So that's what happened to Jenkins's cap and jacket. Jenkins is my first mate."

"I'll return the jacket and the cap," said Tennyson. "I left them in the hold."

"I find it strange," the captain said, "that you did not take the pains to find out this ship's destination. You, apparently, have no wish to go to End of Nothing."

"Anyplace away from Gutshot," said Tennyson. "They were closing in on me. Well, maybe not, but I had the feeling that they were."

The captain reached for a bottle that was standing on a table beside him and handed it to Tennyson.

"Now I'll tell you, mister," he said, "I am convention-bound to quote the rule book to you. It says in Article Thirty-nine, Section Eight, that any stowaway must be placed in detention and returned thereafter, as speedily as possible, to the port where he had stowed away, there to be delivered up to the port authorities. During the intervening period, while he is on board the vessel on which he stowed away, he is required to do such tasks, however menial, the captain may assign to him to help defray his passage. Are you aware of these provisions, sir?"

"Vaguely," said Tennyson. "I know it is illegal to stow away. But I must tell you—"

"There is, however, another matter which I feel compelled to consider," the captain told him. "I have the feeling, knee-deep as I am in alien scum, that humans, under whatever circumstances, should always stick together. We run fairly thin out here and it is my opinion that we should be supportive of one another, overlooking transgressions if they be not too odious. . . ."

"Your attitude does credit to you," said Tennyson. "There has been something I've been trying to tell you and haven't had the chance. You see, sir, I am not a stowaway."

The captain turned steely eyes on him. "Then tell me what you are. If you're not a stowaway, what are you?"

"Well, let us say," said Tennyson, "that I was simply pressed for time. That I did not have the time to arrange for passage by going through the formal channels. That, for compelling reasons I have revealed to you, I couldn't afford to miss your ship, so came aboard in a rather unorthodox manner, passed on board by an unsuspecting alien crew member who mistook me for the mate and—"

"But you hid away."

"Easy to explain. I feared that you might not give me the time to explain my situation and be so conscientious as to heave me off the ship. So I hid and waited until there seemed little chance you could do anything but continue on your way."

"By all of this, do I understand you to be saying that you stand prepared to pay your passage?"

"Most certainly I do. If you'll only name the figure."

"Why," said the captain, "most willingly indeed. And I'll charge you not one tittle above the regular fare."

"That's considerate of you, sir."

"Dr. Tennyson," the captain said, "please go ahead and drink. You have not touched the bottle to your lips. It makes me nervous to see you sit there and merely fondle it."

"I'm sorry, Captain. I didn't mean to make you nervous." Tennyson tipped the bottle, took a generous swallow, then lowered it again.

"Marvelous," he said. "What is it?"

"It's a concoction called Scotch," the captain told him. "It first was brewed on Mother Earth."

"You mean Old Earth?"

"That's right," the captain said. "The home planet of us humans."

"I have a great curiosity about Old Earth. Have you ever been there?"

The captain shook his head. "Few humans have ever set foot upon its sacred soil. We are scattered far and thin in space, and few of us go on that pilgrimage we always promise ourselves that someday we will make."

"Ah, well," said Tennyson. He tilted the bottle once again.

"To get back to our arrangement," the captain said. "I fear I have to tell you that I have no place for you. The cabins, the few that I have, are filled. Even my own quarters are rented out to a horde of scaly horrors who are pilgriming to End of Nothing. At the end of the voyage, I shall have to fumigate the place before I can move back in, and it may be years before I am rid of the stench of them."

"Why let them have it, then?"

"Because of money," said the captain. "This particular band of scum is filthy rich and they must have my best accommodations without regard to cost. So that is how it is. I charged each of the bastards a triple fare. Although I think now I may live to regret my greed. The mate and I are sharing his quarters, turn and turn about. The mate is a devoted garlic eater. Thinks it keeps him healthy. Only dire necessity forces me to crawl into his bunk."

"The mate is the only other human?"

"Ordinarily, yes. Just the two of us. The crew is made up of rat people, like the one who found you, and other assorted unsavory beings. The passenger hold and cabins are filled with nauseating pilgrims."

"If you dislike aliens so much, why are you in this business? Surely you could operate in freight."

"Five more years of this," the captain said. "Five more years is all that it will take. There's no real money in freighting. But hauling these damned pilgrims is profitable if you can stand it. And I can stand it, just barely, for another five years. For, by then, I will have money enough to retire. Back to a pink planet, name of Apple Blossom. Silly name, of course, but it's perfect for the planet. Have you ever been on a pink planet, Doctor? There are not many of them."

"No, I never have."

"Pity," said the captain.

A tap sounded from the direction of the open door.

The captain swung about in his chair. "Oh, there you are, my dear," he said, obviously pleased.

Tennyson also swung about. A woman stood in the doorway.

She was statuesque, with broad shoulders and hips. Her eyes crinkled in an expressive face. Her mouth was generous and soft, her hair a halo of gleaming gold.

"Come in, please," said the captain. "As you see, we have picked up another passenger. Four humans aboard on a single trip. I believe that to be a record."

"If I am not intruding," she said.

"You are not," the captain told her. "We are pleased to have you. Jill Roberts, this is Dr. Tennyson. Dr. Jason Tennyson."

She held out her hand to Tennyson. "I am glad to see another human. Where have you kept yourself?"

Tennyson froze momentarily. Turning her head, the woman had exposed her other cheek. Across it, from temple to jaw, covering almost the entire right cheek, was an angry, ugly slash of red.

"I am sorry, Doctor," she said. "It is the way I am. It has horrified my friends for years."

"Please forgive me," said Tennyson. "My reaction is inexcusable. As a physician . . ."

"As a physician, there is nothing you can do about it. It is inoperable. No cosmetic surgery is possible. Nothing. I have to live with it; I have learned to live with it."

"Miss Roberts," said the captain smoothly, "is a writer. Articles for magazines. A long shelf of books."

"If that bottle has not grown fast to your hand," said Jill Roberts to Tennyson, "how about letting loose of it?"

"Certainly," Tennyson said. "Let me wipe it off." He scrubbed its neck on his shirt sleeve.

"It appears there are no glasses aboard this bucket," said Jill Roberts. "But I don't really mind. Drinking out of a bottle after someone else is only another way to trade around some germs."

She took the bottle and sat down in the one remaining chair.

"Where are you putting up?" she asked Tennyson. "I recollect the captain told me all the cabins are filled. He hasn't put you down in steerage with the alien cattle, has he?"

"Dr. Tennyson," said the captain primly, "was a late show. I have nowhere to put him. He turned up unexpectedly."

She raised the bottle to her lips, lowered it, looked inquiringly at Tennyson.

"Is that true?" she asked.

Tennyson grinned. "The captain is trying to be polite. Actually, I was a stowaway. As to accommodations, neither of you should worry about it. I can curl up anywhere. I'm just glad to be aboard."

"That is not quite right either," said the captain. "He did stow away, but now he offers to pay his passage. Technically, he no longer is a stowaway."

"You must be starved," Jill said, "unless you brought along a lunch."

"I never thought about it," said Tennyson. "I was in too much of a hurry. But I could do with a steak."

"You'll get no steaks on this tub," said Jill, "but there's guck to fill the gut. How about it, Captain?"

"Surely," the captain agreed. "Almost immediately. I'm sure something's left."

Jill rose and tucked the bottle underneath her arm. "Send the food to my cabin," she told the captain, then turned to Tennyson. "Come along, you. We'll get you washed up and your hair combed and see what you really look like."

Chapter Three

"NOW FOR SOME GROUND RULES," SAID JILL. "ON SUCH short acquaintance, I'm not about to crawl into bed with you, but I will share the bed—or, I suppose, the bunk, for it's really not a bed. Like the captain and the mate, we'll take turns in it. You can use the can—on board such a ship as this, I think it's termed a head. We'll eat our meals together and we can sit and talk and play my music crystals. I'll ignore a pass or two, being naturally good-natured and more kindly than is good for me, but if you get too heavy, I'll heave you out."

"I shall not get too heavy," said Tennyson, "however much I may be tempted. I feel something like a stray dog someone picked up."

He used half a slice of bread to mop up his plate, sopping up the gravy left over from the stew.

"In my ravenous hunger," he told her, "this meal was tasty, but it had a strange tang to it. Stew, of course, but a stew of what?"

"Don't ask," she said. "Just shut your eyes and eat. Holding your nose helps, too, if you can do that without strangling. There is a deep, dark suspicion that when one of the pilgrims die—and some of them do, of course, packed into steerage as they are. . . ."

He waved a helpless hand at her. "Please, Jill, desist. My body needs the food and I'd like to keep it down."

"I would not have thought a doctor would have a queasy stomach."

"Doctors, my dear," he said, "are not total brutes."

"Put the plate away," she told him. "You've mopped it shining clean. I still have the captain's bottle—"

"I noticed. You just marched off with it."

"It's not the captain's bottle. He simply pilfers it and the consignee looks the other way. He hauls in several cases on every trip, I understand. Special-order shipments for the gnomes at Project Pope."

"Gnomes at Project Pope? What in hell have gnomes to do with it, and what is Project Pope?"

"You mean you don't know?"

"Not at all," he said.

"Well, I guess they're not really gnomes, although it's a term that is often used for them. Some of them are humans, but the most of them are robots."

"That's no real answer," said Tennyson. "Tell me what you're talking about. It sounds mysterious and—"

"What about you, my friend?" she asked. "What's all your mystery? The captain said you stowed away and then you paid your passage. And if you don't know about Project Pope, why are you heading out for End of Nothing? There's no reason to go there except for Project Pope."

"So help me," said Tennyson, "before I set foot on this ship, I had never heard of End of Nothing or of Project Pope. What is this End of Nothing?"

"In due time," she said, "I shall be glad to give you all the details that I have. But you give first. I took you in, remember. I am sharing with you. Now, let's each have a drink, then you start."

They each had a drink. He wrested the bottle from her and took another one, then handed it back.

"You know," he said, "that stuff has authority."

"Give," she said.

"Well, first of all, I really am a doctor."

"I never doubted that. I had a peek into your bag."

"You know about Gutshot, the planet that we took off from."

She shivered. "A horrid little place, although I was glad enough to get there. It was the last stop on the way to End of Nothing and, working my way out, there've been too many stops. I never dreamed, of course, that I'd have to put up with such a filthy ship to get there. I asked around. Would you believe it, this is the only ship between Gutshot and End of Nothing. This captain of ours has the pilgrim trade tied up."

"About the pilgrims . . ."

"Nothing doing. First you talk of Gutshot, then I'll talk of gnomes and popes and pilgrims."

"It's simply told," said Tennyson. "Gutshot, as you may know, is a feudal planet. A lot of nasty little fiefs headed by crews of dirty people—some of them human, but a lot of them not. I was court physician to the margrave of Daventry. Human, as you may have guessed. A human doctor trained in human medicine would be of little use to aliens. It was not the job I would have picked, but at the time I considered myself lucky to get it. A young physician fresh out of medical school ordinarily finds it hard to get started in his profession unless he has some money. I had no money, of course, and there didn't seem to be too many clinics that were looking around for fresh new talent; besides, it costs a fortune to set up a practice of your own, after which you'd sit around for several years, slowly starving, until people began coming to you. Once the initial shock of Gutshot wore off, I became somewhat accustomed to it. Like you can grow accustomed, after a time, to an aching tooth. So I stayed on. The fees were good. In fact, to me, they seemed princely. The margrave was not a bad guy. Not good, but not bad either. We got along together. Then the bastard up and died on me. Nothing wrong with him. Just tipped over. Heart attack, I'd guess, although there hadn't been any indication he was heading for one. I didn't really have a chance to determine cause of death and—"

"But no one could blame you. It was not your—"

"What you can't comprehend," he said, "is the kind of politics there are in any feudal setup. A pack of wolves held in restraint by one man. Loose the leash and they're at one another's throats. I'd not consciously been involved in any politics, but I had sort of been the margrave's lieutenant and advisor, unofficially of course, so considerable resentment was aimed at me. Almost immediately the rumor sprang up that the margrave had been poisoned, and before it got well started, I was on my way. I had no real power base and knew it. I would have been a pigeon for almost anyone. I gathered up most of my ill-got earnings, which I had been careful to keep in a handy place and in highly transportable form, stole a flier, and was out of there as fast as I could manage. Night was coming on and I flew low and crooked to keep out of any radar range. I knew there was no place on the planet where I'd be safe—"

"So you headed for the spaceport."

"Right. I knew I didn't have much time. I figured there were people about three jumps behind me. So I had to find a ship and find it fast. One that would be out in space before the posse hit the port."

"So that's it?"

"That's it," he said. "What worries me most is the captain. I had to tell him some of it. I should have lied, of course, but had little time to think up a lie and . . ."

She shook her head. "You don't need to worry about our precious captain. If he's questioned, he'll swear he knows nothing of you. He's not looking for trouble. He's got this End of Nothing monopoly all tied up and doesn't want to lose it. It's a gold mine for him. He hauls a load of pilgrims out, dumps them off, packs in the ones he hauled on the previous trip and takes them back to Gutshot."

"They all come from Gutshot? I never heard of any pilgrims there."

"Probably none from Gutshot, which is just the port of entry to End of Nothing. They come from all over this sector of the galaxy, flying in from everywhere, gathering and waiting for the ship to End of Nothing. Then our captain herds them aboard and flies them out to Project Pope."

"You're not a pilgrim?"

"Do I look like one?"

"No, you don't. How about the loan of that bottle for a moment?"

She handed him the bottle.

"I don't know the entire story," she said. "I'm going out to have a look at it. It should provide material for several articles. Perhaps even a book."

"But you must have some idea, which is more than I have."

"Just the basic rumor. Just the tangled stories that one hears. Actually rumor may be all, but I think not. There must be something out there, with all this pilgrim traffic. I tried first to track down where the pilgrims were coming from, but that proved a dead end. There is no concentration of them. A few come from one planet, a few from still another, one or two from yet a third. All of them nonhuman—maybe specific kinds of aliens, although of that I'm not sure. Apparently all members of obscure cults or sects. Maybe each sect has a different faith—if you can call what they have a faith—but all of them are somehow tied in with this Pope project. That doesn't necessarily mean they know anything about it. It may just be something on which they can base a shaky faith. Creatures of all kinds reaching for a faith, willing to grab at almost anything just so it's mysterious or spectacular, preferably both. The thing that bothers me, the thing that sends me out, is that the whole business has a human ring to it. The site of Project Pope, as I understand it, is called Vatican-17 and—"

"Hold up a minute," said Tennyson. "That *does* have a human ring. There was a Vatican on Earth . . ."

"There still is," she said. "The center of the Roman Catholic faith, which still exists on Earth and on several other human planets, is still headed by a pope and is still as strong as ever, perhaps stronger, its people still as devout as ever. But I doubt that this Vatican-17 has anything to do with the one on Old Earth. It sounds like some sort of take-off. For one thing, there are robots—"

"What would robots have to do with an Old Earth religion?"

"I don't know and I don't think it *is* an Earth religion. Someone, perhaps the robots, borrowed the terminology . . ."

"But robots?"

"I know. I know. That's what I'm trying to find out."

"And End of Nothing?"

"End of Nothing," she said, "is out on the Rim. Among the Rim stars, of which there are not many. A lot of space. Not much of anything else. At the very edge of intergalactic space. So far as the planet is concerned, I know nothing except that it is Earthlike. No trouble for humans to live there. This ship, I am told, gets there in a standard month or less. How many times the speed of light that is, I have no idea. The old crate is equipped with an inertial drive, which one would not suspect in such a wreck. No great danger involved. It mostly crosses empty space. The ship makes six round trips a year, which spells out to an awful lot of pilgrims hauled. The captain is an enigma. He probably could have command of one of the proudest interstellar liners; he has the required status. But here he is, running pilgrims he despises."

"But making a barrel of money. Told me five more years and he can retire to a planet named Apple Blossom."

"Yes, he told me that, too. Apparently he tells everyone. I don't know how much to believe."

"Perhaps all of it," said Tennyson. "Men do strange things to cash in on their dreams."

"Jason," said Jill, "I like you. Do you know why I like you?"

"My honesty and trustworthiness," he said. "My humanity, my compassion, my integrity . . ."

"No, none of those. I like you because you can look at me without flinching. You don't pull away. People, to start with, always pull away and flinch. I have come to terms with it myself; I wish other people would."

"I scarcely notice," he said.

"You're a cheerful liar. You do notice it. No one could help but notice it."

"The shock, what initial shock there is," he said, "comes from the fact that otherwise you are so beautiful. Without the cheek, your features are classic. One side of your face arrestingly appealing, the other side marred."

"You can even talk about it," she said, "and make it sound all right. No pity for me. Not even sympathy. As if it were quite normal. And that helps a lot. To be accepted as I am. I tried so hard. I went to so many different clinics. I was examined by so many people. And always the same verdict. Capillary hemangioma. Nothing to be done. One specialist—can you imagine it?—suggested I wear a mask, a half-mask covering the bad side of my face. He assured me that one could be molded and fitted—"

"If it's a mask you are looking for," he said, "you have the best one that there is—your self-acceptance."

"You really think so, Doctor?"

"Of course I do."

"The bottle, please," she said. "Let us drink to that."

They drank to it, solemnly, in turn.

"One question," he said. "Not to change the subject, but a practical question. Once we get to End of Nothing, what kind of accommodations will we find? What kind of place to stay?"

"I have reservations," she said, "at a place called Human House. I don't know a thing about it except that it's expensive—if that's any criterion."

"When we arrive, may I take you to dinner that first evening? To take the taste of this ship out of our mouths."

"Why, thank you, sir," she said. "That is thoughtful of you."

Chapter Four

THEY SAT IN THE CONTROL ROOM, SPRAWLED OUT IN THE chairs.

"Don't make the mistake," the captain warned them, "of thinking of the robots of Project Pope as happy little servitors. They are high-powered electronic contraptions. Some people think they have managed to construct organic brains for themselves, but this I somehow doubt. Such a thought stems from the prejudicial viewpoint of a biological being. There is no reason to believe, once you think of it realistically, that a technological thinking and reasoning apparatus, given the present state of the art, need be one whit inferior to a human brain, or, actually, any kind of brain. These robots, for centuries, have been continually upgrading their capabilities, improving themselves in many different ways, as a human mechanic will keep on dinging up an engine to make it run better."

"How well are you acquainted with them?" Tennyson asked.

"Normal contacts only," the captain replied. "The necessary contacts for the conduct of my business. I have no friends among them, if that is what you're asking."

"I'm sorry if I seemed to question you," said Tennyson. "I was simply curious. It seems I'm being plopped down into a situation I know nothing about. I'd like to find out as much as I can."

"I have been told," said Jill, "that the robots have humans working for them."

"I don't know if the humans are working for them," the captain told her. "Maybe they are working together. There are humans, a rather large corps of them. But my contacts never have been with the humans. I see only the robots and then only when they want to see me. Project Pope is a big operation. No one outside Vatican really seems to know what is going on. One story has it that the robots are trying to build an infallible pope—an electronic pope, a computer pope. There appears to be an idea that the project is an outgrowth of Christianity, an Old Earth religion."

"We know what Christianity is," Jill said. "There still are a lot of Christians, perhaps more than ever before. True, Christianity no longer looms as important as it did before we began going into space. This, however, is a relative thing. The religion is still as important as ever, but its seeming importance has been diluted by the many other faiths that exist in the galaxy. Isn't it strange that faith is so universal? Even the ugliest aliens appear to have a faith to cling to."

"Not all of them," said the captain. "Not all of them by any means. I have run into alien areas, into entire planets, where no one had ever thought of religion or of faith. And, I must say, that they were not the worse for it. Sometimes, I thought better."

"Constructing a pope," said Tennyson, "is a strange task to set oneself. I wonder where the robots got the idea and what they expect the end result to be."

"You never can tell about robots," the captain observed. "They are a funny lot. Spend enough time in space and you quit worrying or wondering about why anyone is doing something or what they expect from doing what they do. None of these rummy aliens think the way we do. They're a bunch of zany bastards. Compared to most of them, robots are downright human."

"They should be," said Jill. "We are the ones who dreamed them up. No other culture did. There are those who will tell you that robots are extensions of ourselves."

"There may be some truth in that," the captain agreed. "Screwy as they may be at times, they are still several cuts above any alien I ever met."

"You don't like aliens," said Tennyson.

"You aren't just whistling through your teeth. Who does like the scummy bastards?"

"And yet you use them on your ship."

"Only because I can't pull together a crew of humans. Out here, there aren't many humans."

"And you haul the aliens out to End of Nothing, then haul them back to Gutshot."

"Someone has to haul them," said the captain, "and I get well paid for doing it. I haul them, but nothing says I have to associate with them. It's not only that I dislike them, which I do, but we humans have to stick together. If we don't, they'll overwhelm us."

Tennyson studied the captain. There was nothing of the look of the fanatical bigot about him. He was of indeterminate age—a young-old man—his profile resembling a hatchet. There was no humor in him; he was all deadly business. A strange man, Tennyson told himself—one of those twisted men found in lonely places. More than likely the captain was lonely. For years he had ferried alien pilgrims between Gutshot and End of Nothing, and all the time, out of his loneliness that cried out for humanness, his contempt and horror of his passengers had grown until it now was tightly woven into the fabric of his life.

"Tell us about End of Nothing itself," said Jill. "We've talked about it ever since I came aboard and not once have you told me what kind of planet it is. I have no idea if it's farmland or—"

"It's not farmland," said the captain. "The project does have some gardens and fields, the robots laboring in them, to grow food for their biological brothers. But other than that, it is all wasteland, the environment untouched, standing as it always has. It has not been exploited; there are not enough people in its economy to exploit it. The only exploiter that I know is a man by the name of Thomas Decker. Decker is a strange character. He lives alone in a cabin at the outskirts of the settlement."

"You are a friend of Decker's?"

"Not a friend. We have a small business arrangement. Almost every trip he brings me a small sack of semiprecious stones. You know the kind—garnets, aquamarines, amethyst, topaz. Nothing very rare, seldom really valuable. Low-grade opal now and then. Once a couple of emeralds we did rather well on. No great deal. No possibility of great wealth. I have a feeling he doesn't do it for the money, although I may be wrong about that. A man of mystery. No one knows a single thing about him, although he's been there for years. I think he does his gem hunting for the fun of it. He brings me the gems and I sell them to a contact I have in Gutshot. He pays me a ten-percent fee."

"Where does he get the stones?" asked Tennyson.

"Somewhere out in the wilds. He goes back into the mountains and picks them out of streambeds, working the gravels."

"You said you doubt he does it for the money," said Jill. "What does he do it for, then?"

"I'm not sure," the captain responded. "Maybe it's just something to do, a hobby to keep him busy. One thing I didn't tell you. He does not bring me all the gems he finds. The better pieces he holds out. Some of them he carves. There is one good-sized piece of jade. All by itself, it would be worth a lot of money. The way he has carved it makes it worth a fortune. But he won't let loose of it. Says that it's not his, that it doesn't belong to him."

"Who else could it belong to?"

The captain shook his head. "I wouldn't know. Perhaps no one. It's just his way of talking. Lord knows what he means. You must understand that in many ways he is a strange man—a strangely private person and old-fashioned, as if he'd stepped out of another age, as if he did not quite belong in the present. The funny thing is that I can say this, but I can't tell you why I say it. It's not anything he does or the way he talks; it's just a feeling that I get. I say he's strange and even tell you in what ways he is strange, but I can't cite a single example of behavior that would make me say that."

"You must be a close friend of his. To know this much about the man, I mean."

"No, not a close friend. No one is a close friend of his. The man's pleasant enough, in many ways he's charming, but he does not associate with the other humans at End of Nothing. By that, I don't mean he repels them, or even that he avoids them, but he does not seek them out. He never joins the crowd at the bar at Human House; he almost never ventures into town. He's got an old beat-up vehicle, one of those cars that can cover tough terrain. He bought it off someone in the settlement. I don't remember who, if I ever knew. He does some traveling around in that, but always by himself. When he goes back into the wilderness to hunt for gems, he doesn't take it. He walks. It's as if he needs no one, as if he has all he needs back there in the wilderness and in his

cabin at the edge of town. I've been at his cabin once—that's when
I saw the carvings he had made. I wasn't invited, but I went and
he seemed glad enough to see me. He was friendly. We sat in front
of the fire and talked, but there were times when I thought he
wasn't really there, that he wasn't with me, that he scarcely was
aware of me. As if—and this may sound strange—that while he was
talking with me and listening to me he also was talking with and
listening to someone else as well. Once again, there is absolutely
nothing I can put a finger on, but the impression was there. He
told me, when I left, how glad he was I'd come, but he didn't ask
me back and I've never gone back. I doubt I ever will."

"You say," said Tennyson, "he does not join the crowd at the
bar at Human House. I suppose mostly humans are there."

"Yes, of course," the captain said. "The aliens have places they
can go, but Human House is human. No alien would think of
going there."

"How about the humans at Vatican? Do they go to Human
House?"

"Well, now that you mention it, I don't think they do. No one
sees too much of the Vatican people, either robot or human. They
stay pretty much up on their hill. My impression is that they
don't mix with the people in the town. I'm not talking about a lot
of humans in town. There aren't too many of them, and they're a
close-knit group. Most of the humans in the town have jobs of
one sort or another that are tied in with Project Pope. I don't
mean Vatican stuff, but jobs that have some association with the
Vatican. When you come right down to it, End of Nothing *is* Vatican. It's the only thing that's there. There are some aliens in the
town. They cater to the pilgrims. Most of the pilgrims, as you
know, are alien. I've never carried a human pilgrim. As a matter
of fact, scarcely ever a human of any kind at all. Last trip in, the
one before this, I did carry a human, but he wasn't any pilgrim.
He was a doctor. It seems to me, of late, that I'm getting a run on
doctors."

"I don't understand," said Tennyson.

"This one, this other doctor, was going in to join the Vatican
staff. His name was Anderson, a young fellow, kind of cocky

chap. He sort of grated on me, but I got along with him the best I could. It wasn't as if I would be saddled with him for too long a time. He was going out to replace the Old Doc—name of Easton—who'd been at the Vatican for years, taking care of the human staff, of course. Robots don't need doctors. Or maybe they have their own, I don't know. Anyhow, Easton finally died and Vatican had no doctor. Vatican had been trying to get another one for years, knowing Easton was getting old and wouldn't live forever. I suspect it's hard to attract anyone to End of Nothing, which is not the sort of place a doctor or anyone else would really care to live. Some months after Old Doc died, here was this whippersnapper of a medic showing up at Gutshot. I hauled him out, of course, but I was glad when I could wash my hands of him. He's the only Vatican staff member who ever traveled on my ship. There's not much going back and forth."

"This matter of only aliens being pilgrims bothers me," said Jill. "Vatican must be oriented to the human idea of religion. It's run by robots, and robots by and large are surrogate humans. Then the terminology—Vatican and Pope. That's straight out of Earth. Would it be a sort of bastardized Christianity?"

"That might be the far-back basis for it," the captain said. "I've never got it straight. It may basically be Christianity, but interwoven with no one knows how many alien beliefs and faiths, all of it twisted out of human recognition by the perversity of robotic thinking."

"But even so," Jill continued, "there should be some human pilgrims, some human interest—outside the project itself, I mean."

"Maybe not," said Tennyson. "While a lot of the humans who left Old Earth all those millennia ago also left Christianity behind them—or shucked it and probably other Earth religions as well, after a few centuries in space—the average human, almost any human, still would know something about it and have a sort of instinctive feeling for the religion his ancestors had left behind. They could spot a phoney faith and would have nothing to do with it."

"That may be right," the captain said. "Aliens, on the other hand, having no background to judge the concept of Christianity—however twisted that concept might be—may find themselves at-

tracted to it. I suppose that it is from the aliens that the project
gets its support. Some aliens are fabulously wealthy. That bunch
of creeps now occupying my quarters practically stink of money."

"I asked you about the planet," said Jill, "and you haven't told
me. We got off on something else."

"It's terrestrial," said the captain, "with some minor differences. The Vatican colony is the only settlement. All the rest
is howling wilderness that's never been properly mapped; a few
quick fly-overs by a survey ship and that is all. Only one settlement, as you know, is not unique. Many frontier planets boast
only a single settlement, near the spaceport—both the planet and
the settlement sharing the same name. Thus, Gutshot is the desig-
nation of both the planet and the colony surrounding the port,
while End of Nothing means both the settlement and planet, as
you choose. The thing is that no one except Decker knows anything about the planet farther than a few miles beyond the settlement, and I can't think Decker has traveled any great distance into
the mountains. Gutshot, of course, is better known. It's littered
with dinky little feudal holdings, but, even so, much of it is still
wild and unexplored.

"As far as End of Nothing is concerned, it is virtually unknown. We suspect there is no intelligent creature native to the
planet, although that is an assumption. No one has looked for an
intelligence, and there just might be one, or more, tucked away
somewhere. There is animal life—herbivores and carnivores that
feed on the herbivores. Some of the carnivores, according to what
one hears in the colony, are ferocious brutes. I asked Decker
about them once and he shrugged me off. I never asked again.
Now," the captain said to Tennyson, quickly changing the subject,
"how much time did you spend on Gutshot?"

"Three years," said Tennyson. "A little less than three years."

"You got into trouble there?"

"You might say I did."

"Captain," said Jill, "it is unseemly of you to be prying. No one
saw him get on the ship. No one knows he did. It's no skin off
your ass."

"If it will ease your conscience any," said Tennyson, "I can tell you that I committed no crime. I was a suspect. That was all. On Gutshot, being a suspect is enough to get you killed."

"Dr. Tennyson," said the captain primly, "when we land at End of Nothing, you can get off the ship with the understanding that I have never talked with you. I would think that might be the best for both of us. As I've said before, we humans stick together."

Chapter Five

THIS WAS THE TIME OF DAY THAT HE LIKED THE BEST, Decker thought—supper done and the dishes cleared away, a good fire blazing, the world shut outside the door and Whisperer at the table in the corner, working at shaping the piece of topaz they had brought home on the trip of the week before. Decker settled more comfortably in the chair, kicking off his moccasins and putting his stockinged feet on the raised hearthstone. In the fireplace a log burned through and settled on the other logs in a shower of sparks. New tongues of flame leaped up and ran along the burning wood. The chimney throat mumbled and was answered by the moaning wind that nosed along the eaves.

Shifting in his chair, he looked toward Whisperer's corner, but there was no sign of him. Sometimes you saw Whisperer, sometimes not. Set on one corner of the table was the intricately carved piece of pale green jade. A piece of work, Decker told himself, that was hard to make out. It was confusing because there was too much in it, much of which was unhuman, nuances that had no parallel to the way a human thought or saw; start to follow the lines of it and one soon lost oneself. The line that first manifested itself became something else and the pattern that the viewer thought he'd puzzled out became another pattern and then another and another, each one more confusing than the last. There was no end to it. A man probably could spend the rest of his days sitting in front of it and staring at it, trying to puzzle out and resolve the flowing of it and in the end always getting lost.

On the front of the table stood the large topaz crystal, and there had been some progress in its shaping since the day before, although he never had been able to catch the actual shaping of anything that Whisperer did. In each instance, the piece changed from time to time and that was all. It wasn't carving, for there were no chips, no material that had been cut away to effect the shaping, and yet, despite this, it was not molding either, for the finished parts had sharp lines as if the material had been cut away—not rounded edges as if it had been molded. Whisperer used no tools, of course—there was no way in which he could use tools. He was as close to nothing as one could imagine. And yet he got things done. He talked mind to mind, he changed the shape of gems, he slithered in and out; he was, seemingly, everywhere at once.

Watching, Decker saw the slight flicker of the diamond dust that was Whisperer, hovering above the topaz crystal.

—You're hiding again, he said in his mind to Whisperer.

—Decker, you know well I do not hide from you. It's that you do not see.

—Can't you occasionally brighten up a bit? Can't you shine a little more? You're always sneaking up.

—Now you needle me, said Whisperer. I never do any sneaking up. You are aware of me. You know when I am here.

And that was right, thought Decker. He did know when he was here. He sensed him, although how he sensed him, he had no idea. It was just knowing he was there. An impression, knowing that this little puff of diamond dust (although he was certain there was much more to Whisperer than a puff of dust) was somewhere very close.

And the question—always the question—of what he was. He could have asked him, Decker thought, could even ask him now, but somehow it had always seemed a question that was inappropriate. He had wondered at first if his simply thinking it, wondering about it, might not be equivalent to asking, speculating that whatever lay in his mind might be apparent to Whisperer. But over long months, it had become apparent that it was not, that this strange being either could not, or would not, read his mind. To communicate with Whisperer, he had to bring the words up into a certain segment of his mind and there expose them to Whisperer. This constituted talking to him; thinking was not talking. But how he talked with him, how he communicated with Whisperer or read what he in turn should tell him was still a mystery. There was no explanation, no human explanation, of the process that made it possible.

—We didn't do too badly on the last trip, Decker said. The topaz made it worth our while. And you were the one who nosed it out. You showed me where to find it. There was nothing showing in the gravel. Not a single glint. Just water-worn pebbles. But you showed me where to reach in and find it. Damned if I can figure how you do it.

—Luck, said Whisperer. No more than luck. Sometimes your luck, sometimes mine. Time before, it was you who found the ruby.

—A small one, Decker said.

—But of the finest water.

—Yes, I know. It's a beauty. Small as it is, it is still perfect. Have you decided yet if you want to do something with it?

—I am tempted, yes. I'll have to think some more upon it. It would be so small. So small for you, I mean. You'd have to use a glass to see the beauty of the shaping.

—Small for me. Yes, of course, you're right. Small for me. How about yourself?

—To me, Decker, size is relative. Almost meaningless.

—We'll hang on to the ruby, said Decker. I have more than enough to hand over to the captain.

He no longer could see Whisperer. The small glitter of diamond dust was gone. Perhaps, he thought, it was not because of anything Whisperer had done. Rather, it was due to a subtle shift of light values in the cabin. He knew Whisperer still was in the cabin, for he sensed him. And what was it that he sensed? What was Whisperer, what kind of thing was he? He was here in the cabin, of course, but where else might he be? How large was he? How small? A tiny mote dancing in the firelight or an essence that spanned the universe?

An incorporeal being, not always invisible, but incorporeal, a drifting next-to-nothingness, perhaps, that was linked to this planet, or perhaps only to a sector of the planet. Thinking of that, Decker was certain, however, that the linkage was at Whisperer's discretion. For some reason, he wanted to be here. More than likely there was nothing to prevent him from going wherever he might wish—to exist in the upper atmosphere, or beyond the atmosphere, in space; to domicile inside a glowing star; to sink into the granite of a planet's crust. All space, and all conditions of space, must be the natural range of Whisperer. Or could it be, Decker asked himself, that the Whisperer he knew was only one small facet of a more encompassing Whisperer? Could the total Whisperer be a huge, sprawling presence that existed in all of space, and possibly in all of time as well, a true creature of the universe?

More than likely, he told himself, he would never know, or knowing, would not understand. Which probably was at least one of the reasons he had never asked. Why ask for information that was beyond his understanding, unresolved information that would plague him all his days, that would rouse him, sweating, from his sleep in the dead of night, that would never let him be, that would set him apart, an alien creature, from the universe?

Whisperer spoke to him again.

—There is tragedy in the forest, he said. Three members of Vatican are dead.

—In the woods? You must be mistaken, Whisperer. Vatican people don't venture into the woods. They stay close to home.

—These ones were hunting the Old One of the Woods.

—No one in their right mind would hunt the Old One. In the woods, it is well to pray most earnestly the Old One does not come hunting you.

—One of these was new to Vatican. He was full of arrogance. He had a powerful weapon that he thought was a match for anything. It was not a match for anything.

—And they found an Old One.

—No. The Old One found them. He knew they were hunting him.

—And now they're dead. All three are dead?

—Yes. Dead most horribly.

—When did this happen?

—Short hours ago. Vatican does not know as yet.

—Perhaps we should notify Vatican.

—Why? asked Whisperer. There is nothing can be done. In time, when they are gone overlong, others will set out to seek them and will bring them home.

—But the Old One will be there and waiting.

—Perhaps, said Whisperer, but he will not harm the seekers. They'll not be hunting him.

—He kills only those who hunt him?

—Yes. Did not you know that? You've tramped the woods for years.

—I've been lucky. I've never seen an Old One. I have never had to face one.

—Old Ones have seen you, said Whisperer. Many, many times. They do not bother you because you do not bother them.

—To bother them, said Decker, is the last thing I would do.

—You carry a weapon. What you call a rifle.

—That's right. I very seldom use it. Occasionally to get some meat to put into the pot.

—And not often even so.

—No, not often, Decker said.

He picked up a poker and engineered the fire, settling logs into more compact space for better burning. The chimney mumbled at him. The wind moaned underneath the eaves. The fireplace flames sent shadows chasing up and down the room.

—Vatican, said Whisperer, is very much excited.

—Because of the Old One?

—No, not because of the Old One. That is not known as yet. Something, it seems, has been found by a Listener.

—The Listeners are finding something all the time.

—But this finding is a special finding.

—Special in what way?

—I know not as yet. Everyone is excited. Some jubilant, some skeptical, some shocked. If true, I gather, something of very great import. The index of faith is running very high. An increase in devotion.

—They have their little triumphs, said Decker, and their small defeats. The place is in continual uproar.

—The triumph in this instance, said Whisperer, cannot be classified as small. There is great hope; many tellings of the beads.

Chapter Six

THEY STOOD ON THE LANDING FIELD, STARING IN SOME DISmay at the small grouping of nondescript buildings that made up the colony of End of Nothing. On a low ridge behind the town rose a sprawling structure, or a group of structures—from this distance it was impossible to tell—all gleaming white, stately despite the lack of height, with a comfortable, down-to-earth appearance despite the stateliness. And, behind the structure, a backdrop to everything, reared up mountains purple in the distance, with the hint of white-capped peaks seeming to float in the air above them.

Tennyson pointed at the structure on the ridge.

"Vatican, I take it."

"I would think it might be," said Jill.

"I've seen photographs of the Old Earth Vatican. That looks nothing like it."

"You're taking the name too literally," Jill told him. "It's nothing but a name. I doubt it has any real connection with the Vatican."

"But a pope?"

"Well, maybe some connection. An imagined connection. But I doubt there's anything official, nothing that the Old Earth Vatican would officially recognize."

"And you propose to storm those heights?"

"Jason, you're being dramatic now. A bit consciously dramatic.

I'm not storming anything. There is a story here and I intend to get it. By going through channels. By marching up there in all politeness and saying who I am and what I want to do. And while I'm getting this story, what do you propose to do?"

"Honestly, I don't know. I've not even thought about it. I've been running and I guess here the running stops. I can't go back to Gutshot, not for a while at least."

"You sound as if you intend to keep on running."

"Well, not right away. This is as good a place as any to stop and rest awhile and have a look around."

The long line of pilgrims who had disembarked from *Wayfarer* were snaking down the field, apparently going through a visitor checkpoint.

Tennyson nodded at them. "Do we have to go through the same procedure, do you know?"

Jill shook her head. "I think not. No papers are required, not for humans anyhow. End of Nothing officially is listed as a human planet and there are certain courtesies extended to humankind. It's a small place, too, and apt to be informal. A few days from now you may find yourself having lunch with the police chief, or the sheriff or the marshal, whatever the man is called, who will ask you some polite questions and will look you over well. I'm not sure about here, but that's the way it usually works in small human colonies."

"Well, that sounds not too hard."

"You'll have to explain no luggage. The people at Human House may be curious. I think it would be best to explain that you had to run for the ship at Gutshot and somehow lost the luggage."

"You think of everything," said Tennyson. "Your mind is devious. What would I do without you?"

"I sort of have taken care of you, haven't I?" said Jill.

"This evening I'll start paying back," Tennyson promised. "Dinner at Human House. Candlelight and a clean cloth on the table, china, shining glass, silver, a menu with some choice, a bottle of good wine . . ."

"Don't get your hopes too high. Don't fantasize too much. Human House may not have that kind of dining room."

"Well, whatever it may be, it'll be an improvement on that cubbyhole aboard the ship you shared with me."

"That cubbyhole aboard the ship was kind of nice," said Jill.

"I think," said Tennyson, abruptly changing the subject, "someone is finally driving out to get us."

Chapter Seven

THE DINING ROOM AT HUMAN HOUSE WAS FAIRLY CIVILIZED. There was a clean white cloth on the table, shining glass and china, the menu had five entrees, and the wine was passable.

"It is all so enjoyable," Jill said to Tennyson. "I hadn't expected the food to be so delicious. I suppose that after the month we spent aboard the ship, anything at all would be something of a feast."

"Tomorrow you start work," he said. "Will I be seeing you fairly often?"

"As often as possible. I should be back here every night. Unless, of course, Vatican throws me out or won't let me in."

"You mean you haven't previously contacted them?"

"I tried to, but I couldn't. I sent several letters, but received no reply."

"Maybe they don't want publicity."

"We'll see about that. I'll talk with them. I can be fairly persuasive if I have to be. And what about you?"

"I'll look around. I'll get a feel of the place. If there's no other physician here, I may set up a practice."

"That would be fine," she said. "Jason, would you really like it?"

"I don't know," he said. "I said it on the spur of the moment, I guess, without a lot of thought. There is a doctor at Vatican and he may take care of the humans here in town. A new practice might be hard going for a time. The town looks like a pioneer town, but it can't be. If what the captain told us is right, the robots have been here for almost a thousand years."

"The town probably is not nearly that old," she said. "The robots might have been here for quite some time before the town actually got started."

"I suppose so, but it still must be old. Although it's quite apparent little progress has been made. Maybe that's because it is dominated by Vatican. Everything and everyone here must revolve about Vatican."

"That might not be all bad," said Jill. "It would depend on what kind of people—robots and humans—make up Vatican. They might welcome someone with fresh viewpoints and new ideas."

"I'll wait and see," he said. "There isn't any hurry. I'll know better what is here for me, if anything, within a week or so."

"You sound as if you plan to stay. For at least a while."

He shook his head. "I don't even know about that. I need a place to hunker down for a spell. I don't imagine the people back in Daventry will ever guess I made it to the End of Nothing ship."

"Chances are," she said, "they think you were lost at sea. The Gutshot radar must have tracked your flier. There is no way, is there, they could tell you got out of it?"

"Not unless someone found the chute. I think that's unlikely. I pushed the chute as far under the building as I could."

"That should make you fairly safe. Would they be so enraged at you—so anxious to apprehend you they would track you here?"

"No, probably not. The whole episode was more or less political. It would have helped some people if they could have hung the margrave's death on me."

"They were looking for a scapegoat."

"Exactly," said Tennyson. "And they probably can use my disappearance to hang it on me, anyway. So everyone is pleased. But, at the moment, what happens back at Gutshot is not important. How about you? You must have a fair amount of money invested in this trip."

"Some, but in my business, that's a chance you take. The cost won't be all wasted in any case. If I can get the story, I think I may have something that will be really big. If I can't crack Vatican, I still have something. Not so big, of course, but something."

"Jill, how do you figure that?"

"Well, look, I travel here and they won't let me in. They won't talk to me. They give me a total brush-off. They might even, if they feel violently enough about it, throw me off the planet. So why won't they let me in? Why won't they talk to me? Why did they throw me out? What's going on? What's going on at this big, secret-religion institution that can't stand the light of day? What have they got to hide?"

"Yes, I see," he said. "Yes, that would make a story."

"By the time I got through with it, it would make a book."

"How did you run into it in the first place?"

"Things I picked up here and there. Over several years. I kept hearing things. Funny little whispers. None of them too important, some of them with little information in them. But, pieced all together, they got more and more intriguing."

"So you've been digging at it for years. Trying to pick up clues."

"That's true. I worked hard at it. Not all the time, of course, but whenever I had a chance. I did a fair amount of thinking. The more I thought about it, the more the facts seemed worth going after. I may, as a matter of fact, have hypnotized myself with my thinking on it. It may turn out there is little here, no more than a bunch of silly robots embarked on a nonsensical enterprise."

Both of them fell silent for a moment, giving their attention to the food.

"How is your room?" asked Jill. "Mine is quite satisfactory."

"So is mine," said Tennyson. "Not the lap of luxury, but I can get along with it. One window gives a view of the mountains."

"There aren't any telephones," said Jill. "I asked about it and was told there are no phones at all. A phone system has never been set up. There are electric lights, though, and I asked about that. I said how come electricity but no phones? No one seemed to know."

"Maybe no one ever felt the need of phones," said Tennyson.

"Pardon me, sir," said a voice. "Pardon the intrusion, but it is important. . . ."

Tennyson looked up. A man was standing at his elbow. He was tall, somewhat beyond middle age, with a craggy face, smoothed-back hair, and a bristling, neat mustache that was turning gray.

"I understand," said the man, "that you are a physician. At least, I am told you are."

"That's right," Tennyson replied. "I am Jason Tennyson. The lady with me is Jill Roberts."

"My name," said the man, "is Ecuyer. I'm from Vatican. Our physician was killed several days ago in a hunting accident."

"If there is some way in which I can be of service. . . ."

"You'll pardon me, ma'am," said Ecuyer. "I dislike to interrupt your dinner and take away your partner. But we have a very ill woman. If you'd have a look at her. . . ."

"I have to get my bag," said Tennyson. "It's in my room."

"I took the liberty," said the man from Vatican, "of asking the manager to have it brought down for you. It will be waiting in the lobby."

Chapter Eight

THE WOMAN WAS OLD. HER FACE RESEMBLED A WITHERED apple, the mouth pinched in, the puffy cheeks showing an unhealthy, hectic pink. The black button eyes stared at Tennyson with no sign that she had seen him. She struggled for breath. Beneath the sheet, the body was shrunken and stringy.

The gray-garbed nurse handed the chart to Tennyson.

"This woman is important to us, Doctor," said Ecuyer.

"How long has she been this way?"

"Five days," said the nurse. "Five days since . . ."

"Anderson should not have gone on his hunting trip," said Ecuyer. "He told me she'd be all right; rest was all she needed."

"Anderson is the man who was killed?"

"He and the two others. They tried to talk him out of going. He was new here; he did not recognize the danger. I told you it was an Old One of the Woods, did I not?"

"No, you didn't. What is an Old One?"

"A huge carnivore. Bloodthirsty, ferocious. Attacks a man on sight. The other two went along in an effort to protect the doctor—"

"The temperature has held for the last three days," said Tennyson to the nurse. "Has there been no break?"

"None at all, Doctor. Small fluctuations. Nothing that could be called significant."

"And the respiratory difficulty?"

"It seems to be getting worse."

"The medication?"

"It's all on the chart, Doctor."

"Yes, I see," said Tennyson.

He picked up the woman's scrawny wrist. The pulse was rapid and shallow. The stethoscope, when he held it against her chest, communicated the rasping of the lungs.

"Food?" he asked. "Has she taken nourishment?"

"Only the IV the last two days. Before that a little milk and some broth."

Tennyson looked across the bed at Ecuyer.

"Well?" asked the Vatican man.

"I think pneumonia," said Tennyson. "Probably viral. Have you facilities for making tests?"

"We have a laboratory, but no technician. He was with Anderson and Aldritt."

"All three were killed?"

"That's right. All three. Perhaps you, Doctor . . ."

"I do not have the expertise," said Tennyson. "All I can do is treat the disease. You have medical and pharmaceutical supplies?"

"Yes, a wide range of them. Ordinarily, we do not run so thin on medical staff. We did have two technicians, but one resigned several months ago. We've not been able to replace him. End of Nothing, Doctor, apparently is not the kind of place that attracts good people."

"My best diagnosis," said Tennyson, "is some type of viral

pneumonia. It would help to know the type, but without trained personnel, that's impossible. There are so many new viruses, picked up and transmitted from planet to planet, that it's hard to pinpoint one specific agent. Within the past year or two, however —or so I read in medical journals—a new broad-spectrum antiviral substance—"

"You mean protein-X," said the nurse.

"Exactly. Do you have it?"

"Some came in on the last trip *Wayfarer* made. The trip before this one."

"It could be effective," Tennyson said to Ecuyer. "Not enough is known about it to be sure. The substance specifically attacks the protein coating of a virus, destroying the entire virus. We'd be taking a chance using it, of course, but we have nothing else."

"What you are saying," said Ecuyer, "is that you cannot guarantee . . ."

"No physician can make a guarantee."

"I don't know," said Ecuyer. "Somehow or other, we must save her. If we don't use the protein . . ."

"She still may live," said Tennyson. "Her body will have to fight against the virus. We can give her some support. We can help her fight, but we can't do anything about the virus. She has to beat that herself."

"She's old," said the nurse. "She hasn't much to fight with."

"Even with the protein," asked Ecuyer, "we can't be sure?"

"No, we can't," said Tennyson.

"About the protein agent? You want to think about it further? The decision is up to you. But I'd judge we haven't too much time. What is your recommendation, Doctor?"

"As a physician, if the decision were mine alone, I would use the protein. It may not help. But so far as I know, it is the only thing with which to fight an unknown virus. I have to be honest with you. The protein could conceivably kill her. Even if it helped, it might not help enough." He moved to Ecuyer's side, laid a hand on his arm. "This woman means a great deal to you?"

"To all of us," said Ecuyer. "To all of us. To Vatican."

"I wish I could help you more. I'm in no position to insist on anything. Is there something I can do or tell you that would help you in reaching a decision?"

The woman on the bed moved, raising her head and shoulders from the pillow, fighting for a moment in an attempt to raise herself even further, then falling back again. Her face twisted and her lips moved. Words came from her. "The towers," she cried. "The great and shining staircase. The glory and the peace. And the angels flying . . ."

The face untwisted, relaxing. The words shut off.

Tennyson looked at the nurse. She was staring at the woman as if hypnotized.

Ecuyer was pawing at Tennyson's shoulder. "We use the protein," he said. "We will use the protein."

Chapter Nine

THE SUITE WAS LARGE AND WELL APPOINTED. THE LIVING-area floor was covered by thick carpeting, the furniture stopped just this side of elegance; in a huge fireplace that took up half of one wall a fire burned. Off to one side was a dining area, doors opened into a kitchen and a bedroom; gilded mirrors and tasteful paintings hung upon the wall, intricate carvings of what appeared to be ivory were positioned on the mantel.

"Sit down and take it easy," Ecuyer said to Tennyson. "Make yourself at home. I can guarantee that chair over there is comfortable. And what are you drinking?"

"Would you have some Scotch?"

"You have good taste," said Ecuyer. "How did you run into Scotch? It's virtually unknown. Only a few old human hands . . ."

"The captain on the ship," said Tennyson, "introduced me to it. An Old Earth drink, he told me."

"Yes, the captain. He keeps us well supplied. Several cases every trip. We have a standing order from a planet called Sundance—a human planet, as you might guess. It is the only place within a thousand light-years that stocks it. The cases always seem to be a little short. The captain pilfers them. We make no comment on it. It is, we figure, a legitimate kickback."

Ecuyer brought the drinks, handed one to Tennyson and settled himself with the other.

"Drink up," he said. "I think we may have something to drink to."

"I hope so," said Tennyson. "The patient, even this soon, seems to be responding to the protein. We'll have to keep close watch of her."

"Tell me, Doctor, do you always show this much devotion to your patients? You stayed at Mary's bedside until she showed signs of possible improvement. You must be tired. I will not keep you long. You should get some rest."

"If you have a place for me. . . ."

"A place for you? Dr. Tennyson, this is your place. It is yours so long as you stay with us."

"My place? I thought that it was yours."

"Mine? Oh, no. I have a suite much like this. But this one is for guests. For the moment, it is yours. We understand you lost your luggage, and we've arranged to supply you with a wardrobe. It will be here in the morning. I hope you do not mind."

"It was unnecessary," Tennyson said stiffly.

"You persist in not understanding," said Ecuyer. "There is nothing we can do that would properly repay you. . . ."

"You can't be sure of what I've done. Mary still may not make it, even with the protein."

"But there was improvement."

"Yes, the pulse is better. She seems a little stronger. The temperature dropped a bit, but not enough to be significant."

"I have faith in you," said Ecuyer. "I think you'll pull her through."

"Look," said Tennyson, "let's start by being honest. You've talked with the captain, or some of your people have talked with him. You know damn well I didn't lose my luggage. I brought along no luggage. I had no time to pack. I was on the run."

"Yes," said Ecuyer smoothly. "Yes, we know all that. But we

were not about to confront you with it. We don't know what happened, and unless you want to tell us, we don't want to know. We have no need to know. I know you are a doctor. I wasn't even absolutely sure of that to start with, but now I know you are. With you there is a chance Mary will live; without you, what would have been her chance?"

"Probably no chance at all," said Tennyson. "Unless that little nurse had decided on her own. . . ."

"She wouldn't have," said Ecuyer. "She had no way to know. And she would not have dared."

"All right, then. Say I saved the patient. Hell, man, that's my business. That's what I'm trained to do. Save all I can; I cannot save them all. You are not in debt to me. A simple fee would be all I ask. Maybe not even that. I left my credentials behind. At the moment, I couldn't prove I am a doctor if my life depended on it. And I'm not sure at all of my legal right to practice here. There are such things as licenses."

Ecuyer waved his hand. "No need to worry on that score. If you say you are a doctor, then you are a doctor. If we let you practice here, then you have the right to practice."

"Yes," said Tennyson. "If Vatican says so. . . ."

"On End of Nothing, if Vatican says so, then it is so. There is no one to dispute us. Were it not for us, there'd be no End of Nothing. We *are* End of Nothing."

"All right," said Tennyson. "All right. I'm not arguing with you. I have no wish to argue. One of your people is sick and I treated her. That's what I'm supposed to do. Let's not build up a case about it."

"By now, Doctor," said Ecuyer, "you should have grasped the situation. We have no doctor. We very badly need one. We want you to stay on as our resident physician."

"Just like that?"

"Just like that," said Ecuyer. "Can't you see? We're desperate. It would take us months to get another doctor. And then, what kind of doctor?"

"You don't know what kind of doctor—"

"I know you have devotion to your patients. And you are hon-

est. You are honest about how you happen to be here, and when I
asked about your treatment, you'd give no guarantees. I like that
kind of honesty."

"Someone may come storming in here with a warrant for my
arrest. I don't think it will happen, but . . ."

"They'd play hell serving it," said Ecuyer. "We protect our
own. If you really are in trouble, Doctor, I can guarantee your
safety here. Be you right or wrong, I can still guarantee it."

"All right, then. I don't think I'll need protection, but it's nice to
know it would be there. But what about this setup? What would I
be getting into? You call this place Vatican and I've heard stories
about a Project Pope and all of it being headed by a band of robots. Can you tell me what's going on? This old lady, Mary,
talked of angels. Is that just an old lady's dream, a somewhat pre-
mature deathbed vision?"

"No, it's not," said Ecuyer. "Mary has found Heaven."

"Now," said Tennyson, "say that slow again. 'Mary has found
Heaven.' You sound as if you mean it."

"Of course I do," said Ecuyer. "She really has found Heaven.
All evidence points to her having found it. We need her further
observations to try to pinpoint it. Of course, we have her clones—
three of them, growing up. But we can't be certain that the
clones—"

"Evidence? Clones? What kind of evidence? If I remember
rightly, Heaven is not a place. It's a condition. A state of mind, a
faith . . ."

"Doctor, listen. This will take some explanation."

"I would suspect it might."

"Let's first try to put the whole thing into perspective," said
Ecuyer. "Vatican-17, this Vatican, began almost a thousand years
ago with a band of robots out of Earth. On Earth, the robots had
not been members—had not been allowed to be members—of any
faith. I think in some places it is different now. Robots can become communicants—not everywhere, but in certain areas, on certain planets. A thousand years ago this was not true; robots were
considered beyond the pale of any religion. To be a member of
any religious faith, to profess oneself to any faith, one must have a

soul, or the equivalent of a soul. Robots had no souls, or were thought to have no souls, so they were barred from participating in any religious experience. How well are you acquainted with robots, Doctor?"

"Really not at all, Mr. Ecuyer. In my lifetime I may have spoken to half a dozen of them, seen a few more than that. I did not come from robot country. There were a few in medical college, but humans and robots did not associate there. I've never really known one. I've never felt the urge—"

"What you have just said is what ninety-nine out of every hundred humans would say. They're not involved with robots, not concerned with them. Probably they think of them as metal humans, as machines trying to ape humans. I can tell you they are a whole lot more than that. At one time they would not have been, but today, here on End of Nothing, they are more than that. In the last thousand years, the robots here have evolved; they have become creatures that stand apart from men. In the process of evolving, they have never forgotten, however, that they are the creations of men, and they do not resent, as you might think they would, that they are created beings. By and large, they still feel a close relationship to humans. I could talk all night telling you what I think the robots are, what these robots here are. They came here because they had been denied religious experience elsewhere, had been read out of that part of human life that had a strong appeal to them. You have to know a robot well to understand his instinctive drive toward religious experience. It may be no more than an overcompensation—a deep instinct to model himself as closely to the human race as possible. He is denied so many things that a human has; there are so many limitations placed upon him by his very nature. A robot cannot weep; he cannot laugh. He has no sexual drive—although he does create other robots. At least here our robots do create other robots, building them with refinements that the human creators never thought of, probably would not have included in a robot's makeup even if they had thought of them. Here, on End of Nothing, a new race of robots has arisen. But I am getting ahead of myself."

"I can understand a religious drive as an overcompensative impulse," said Tennyson. "Religion could be a mystery they could share with the human race."

"That is right," Ecuyer told him. "There is a lot of history I could recite to you—by what thinking and what steps that small band of robots came a millennium ago to End of Nothing and set up their own religion. But we will let that go for the moment. We can discuss that some other time. If you are interested, that is."

"Of course I'm interested. If you can find the time."

"So the robots came out here," said Ecuyer, "and established their Vatican. They based it upon an Earth religion that had a deep appeal to them—not so much because of its teaching. Rather, I would suspect, because they admired its organization, its hierarchy, its long tradition, its dogma. In this Vatican you'll find much of the liturgy and ritual of Old Earth Vatican, which served as a model, but there was no attempt, I am convinced, to follow slavishly, or even closely, Earth's Catholic faith. The robots have never made any pretense that their religion is an Earth religion transplanted to the rim of the galaxy. If it were given any serious study, which it has not been, it would probably be labeled a synthesis of religions, for the robots have borrowed many aspects of alien faiths, or what passes for alien faiths."

"Actually what they have done," said Tennyson, "is construct their own faith, borrowing widely from whatever appealed to them?"

"Exactly. A robotic faith—which does not make it any less a faith. It all depends on your definition of religion."

"Mr. Ecuyer—or should it be something else than mister?"

"Mister is good enough. My first name is Paul. Call me Paul if you wish. I would be pleased if you did. I have no title, really. I'm not a member of the faith."

"I was about to ask you how you fit into all of this."

"I'm the coordinator of what we loosely called the Search Program."

"That I've never heard of."

"It's not much talked about. It's a part of Project Pope. I sometimes think that Project Pope now may have become little more than an excuse for the continuation of the Search Program. I would appreciate it if you did not mention this to the good fathers. Many of them remain quite pious."

"It all sounds confusing to me."

"It's all rather simple," Ecuyer said. "And logical, in a way. The idea of a pope, of a supreme pontiff to head the faith, had a great appeal to the founders. But where would they find a pope? There was a feeling that to make a robot a pope would be sacrilegious. They could not use a human, even if they could have laid hands on one, which, at the time they came here, they could not. A human would be too short-lived to serve as a pope for a robotic church, the members of which, theoretically, could live forever. With a little proper care, that is. In any case, aside from this severe limitation, a human probably would not have been acceptable. An ideal pope, to their way of thinking, should be immortal and all-knowing—infallible beyond the infallibility of a human pope. So they set out to make a pope—"

"To make a pope?"

"Yes. A computer pope."

"Oh, my God!" said Tennyson.

"Yes, oh, my God, Dr. Tennyson. They are still building him. They build him and improve him year by year. Over the centuries he expands. He is crammed with additional data almost every day, and as the years go by, he becomes more infallible."

"I can't believe it. It is—"

"You do not need to believe in it. Nor do I. It is enough that the robots believe it. After all, it is their faith. And if you sit down quietly and think about it quietly, it can begin to make a lot of sense."

"Yes, I suppose it does. Faith is based on instant and authoritative—infallible—answers. Yes, come to think of it, it makes a lot of sense. The data, I suppose, comes from the Search Program."

Ecuyer nodded. "That is right," he said. "And just because I have told you all of this matter-of-factly, perhaps even lightly, don't think that I am a total nonbeliever. I may not be a true believer, but there are some things I can believe in."

"I'll reserve my opinion. But the data. How does your Search

Program collect the data? You are here; the data, the data you must be after, is out in the universe."

"We use people we call Listeners. Not too good a term, but it serves."

"Sensitives?"

"Yes. Special kinds of sensitives. We comb the galaxy for them. We hunt them down. We have recruiters out, working quietly. The robots have developed methods and supports that enhance their abilities. Some of our results are unbelievable."

"All humans?"

"All human, so far. We have, at times, tried to use aliens. But it has never worked. Perhaps someday we'll find how to work with them. It is one of the projects we are working on. Aliens probably could provide us data humans never can."

"And this data you get is fed into the pope?"

"A good part of it. Of late we have become somewhat selective. We make some value judgments. We just don't feed in all the raw data we get. But we do keep complete files. We have it all down on—I was going to say on tapes, but it's not quite tape. But, anyhow, we have it all. We've built up a library that would astound the galaxy were it known."

"You don't want it known."

"Dr. Tennyson, we don't want the galaxy to come crashing in on us."

"Mary is a Listener. And she thinks she has come on Heaven."

"That is true."

"And you, a part-time believer, what do you think?"

"I'm not discounting it. She is one of our most efficient and trustworthy Listeners."

"But *Heaven?*"

"Consider this," said Ecuyer. "We know we are not dealing in physical space alone. In some instances, we don't know what we're reaching into. Let me give you one rather simple example. We have one Listener who has, for years, been going back through time. And not only through time, not haphazardly through time, but, apparently, following his own ancestry. Why he is taking this direction we do not know, nor does he. Someday we may find out.

He seems to be following his ancestry, his remote ancestry, tracing out his blood and bone. Step by step down through millennia. The other day he lived as a trilobite."

"A trilobite?"

"An ancient Earth form of life that died out some three hundred million years ago."

"But a human as a trilobite!"

"The germ plasma, Doctor. The life force. Go back far enough . . ."

"Yes, I see," said Tennyson.

"It's fascinating," Ecuyer said.

"One thing bothers me," said Tennyson. "You're telling me all this. Yet you don't want it known. When I leave End of Nothing—"

"*If* you leave End of Nothing."

"What's that?"

"We hope you'll stay. We can make you a most attractive offer. We can discuss the details later."

"I may decide not to say."

"Only one ship ever comes here," said Ecuyer. "It shuttles between here and Gutshot. Gutshot is the only place it can take you."

"And you're gambling that I don't want to return to Gutshot?"

"I had the impression that you might not want to. If you really want to leave, I doubt we'd try to stop you. We could, of course, if we wanted to. One word to the captain and he'd find himself lacking room to take you. But I think it would be safe to let you go. Even if you repeated what I told you tonight, I doubt that anyone would believe you. It would be just another space myth."

"You seem to be sure of yourselves," said Tennyson.

"We are," said Ecuyer.

Chapter Ten

IT WAS STILL DARK WHEN TENNYSON AWOKE. HE LAY FOR long minutes in a fuzzy, comfortable, woolly blackness, not sleeping, but still not quite awake, not entirely aware, remembering nothing of what had happened, thinking hazily that he was still in Gutshot. The room was dark, but there was a hidden light somewhere and through half-open eyes he could make out the darker shapes of objects in the room. The bed was comfortable, and a sense of delicious drowsiness filled him. He shut his eyes again, willing himself to sink deeper into sleep. But he felt that something was different, that he was not in Gutshot, nor in the ship. . . .

The ship! He sat upright in bed, jerked out of sleep by the thought. The ship and Jill and End of Nothing. . . .

The End of Nothing, for the love of Christ! And then everything came tumbling in upon him.

A terrible stillness lowered over him and a stiff rigidity, and he sat stricken in the bed.

Mary had found Heaven!

The light, he saw, came from a door that opened into the living area. The light flickered and wavered, brightening and fading, dancing on the walls, reaching forth and falling back. It came, he realized, from the fireplace, still burning. The fire, he told himself, should have burned to embers, drowned in gray ash, long ago.

In one dark corner of the room, a shadow moved, separating itself from the other shadows. "Sir, are you awake?" it asked.

"Yes, awake," said Tennyson, through stiff lips. "And who the hell are you?"

"I am Hubert," said the shadow. "I have been assigned your batman. I will do for you."

"I know what a batman is," said Tennyson. "I ran across the term some years ago in the reading of an Old Earth history. Something to do with the British military. The phrase was so strange that it stuck in my mind."

"This is exceptional," said Hubert. "I congratulate you, sir. Most people would not have known."

The batman moved out of the deeper shadows and now could be seen more clearly. He was a strange, angular, humanlike figure with an air of mingled strength and humility.

"Rest easy, sir," he said. "I am a robot, but I will do no harm. My one purpose is to serve you. Shall I turn on a light? Are you ready for a light?"

"Yes, I am ready. Please, a light," said Tennyson.

A lamp on a table against the farther wall came on. The room was a match for the living area he had seen earlier, its furniture solid and substantial, metal knobs gleaming, old wood shining darkly, paintings on the walls.

He threw back the covers and saw that he was naked. He swung his legs out of bed and his feet came down on carpeting. He reached for the chair beside his bed where he had draped his clothes. They were no longer there. He pulled back his hand, ran it through his hair and scrubbed his face. The whiskers grated underneath his palm.

"Your wardrobe has not arrived as yet," said Hubert, "but I managed to obtain a change of clothes for you. The bath is over there; the coffee's ready in the kitchen."

"Bath first," said Tennyson. "Would there be a shower?"

"A shower or tub. If you prefer the tub, I can draw your bath."

"No, shower's fine. Faster. I have work to do. Is there any word of Mary?"

"Knowing you would wish to know," said Hubert, "I visited her about an hour ago. Nurse tells me she is doing well, responding to the protein. You'll find towels, toothbrush and shaving tackle laid out in the bath. When you are finished, I'll have your clothing for you."

"Thanks," said Tennyson. "You're proficient at your job. Do you do it often?"

"I am Mr. Ecuyer's man, sir. He has two of us. He is loaning me to you."

When he emerged from the bath, Tennyson found that the bed had been made and his clothes laid out on it.

The robot, he realized, now really seeing him for the first time, was a close approximation of a human—an idealized, shiny human. His head was bald and his polished metal was quite frankly metal, but other than that, he was passing human. He wore no clothing, but his entire body had a decorative look about it that gave the illusion of clothes.

"Will you wish breakfast now?" the robot asked.

"No, only coffee now. Breakfast can come later. I'll look in on Mary and then be back."

"I'll serve the coffee in the living room," said Hubert. "In front of the fireplace. I'll stir up the fire and have it blazing well."

Chapter Eleven

TENNYSON FOUND THE GARDEN IN THE REAR OF THE BUILDING where the clinic was housed. The sun was coming up and to the west the mountains loomed close—perhaps seeming much closer than they were, he thought—a great wall of blue shadow, with the blueness changing tone and character, darker at the base, lighter near the mountaintops, with the whiteness of the icy peaks glittering with a diamond brightness in the first light of the sun. The garden was formal and well kept and, in this early-morning hour, had a softness to it. Brick-paved walks ran through it, the walks bordered by low-growing shrubbery and neatly laid-out beds of flowers, many of which were in bloom. Looking at them, Tennyson was unable to find one with which he was familiar. Far to his right, at the other end of the garden, three figures in brown robes strolled slowly, apparently in deep reflection, down a path, their gleaming skulls bowed forward, metal chins resting on their breasts.

The chill of the night was rapidly disappearing with the rising of the sun. The garden was a quiet and pleasant place, and Tennyson found himself thinking how fine it was to be there. At an angle where three paths ran together, he came upon a bench of stone and sat down upon it, facing the blue loom of the mountains.

Sitting there, he was astonished to find within himself a quiet, warm pride of competence he had not felt in years. Mary was doing well—perhaps beginning the road to full recovery, although it was still too early to be sure of that. The fever was abating and her pulse was stronger. The breathing was less labored. He had seen, or imagined he had seen, a faint flicker of latent consciousness in her eyes. She was old, of course, but in that pitifully shrunken body, he had sensed a willingness and a power to fight for life. Perhaps, he told himself, she might have much to fight for. She had found Heaven, Ecuyer had said, and that was patent nonsense. But having found Heaven, or what she thought was Heaven, the wish might be strong within her to learn a great deal more about it. That, at least, had been the sense of what Ecuyer had told him the night before—that Mary's life must be saved so she could learn more of Heaven.

There was no logic in it, he told himself. Someone was mistaken —either that, or it was some sort of joke, some sort of in-joke in Vatican or, perhaps, in the Search Program. Although Ecuyer, telling him of it, had not sounded as if he might be joking. He had told Ecuyer, and sitting there on the garden bench, he now told himself again, that Heaven, if it in fact existed, was not the sort of place that could be found. Heaven is a state of mind, he had said to Ecuyer; and Ecuyer had not disputed that, although it had been apparent that Ecuyer, a self-confessed not-quite-believer in Vatican itself, had held some sort of faith that Heaven could be found.

Nonsense, he told himself again. There was not a scrap of logic in it. And yet, he thought, more than likely this Heaven business was not one isolated instance of nonsense, but an extension of centuries of nonsense. No logic in it, and yet a robot, if it was distinguished by any character at all, would be known for its logic. The very concept of robotics was based on logic. Ecuyer had said that the robots had worked on self-improvement, were far better mechanisms than they had been when they first had come to End of Nothing. It did not seem possible, on the face of it, that the process of self-improvement would have lessened the quality or the scope of the logic that had served as the cornerstone of their creation.

He was missing something, he thought. Within all this array of apparent illogic, there must be some factor, perhaps a number of factors, that he did not recognize. Vatican-17 was not an institution that could be dismissed lightly. Ten centuries of devoted effort had gone into it, with the effort still continuing—the effort to establish a truly universal religion, to construct an infallible pope, the search to discover and understand all the facets that could be, or should be, incorporated into a universal faith.

He was trying too soon to evaluate it, he thought. Perhaps a human lifetime would not be sufficient to reach an evaluation that had some color of validity. He'd have to go along with it, watch and listen and question where he could, cultivate a feeling for what was happening in this place, get to know the personalities who were connected with it.

And thinking this, he was astonished to find that, unbidden, he had reached a decision, while thinking of something other than decision. For if he was to watch and listen, to question when he could, then the assumption must be that he would be staying here.

And why not? he asked himself. To get off this planet, he would have to return to Gutshot and, within the foreseeable future, that was the last thing he wanted to do. It was not bad here—not what he had seen of it, at least. Staying here he'd have the opportunity to practice medicine, perhaps a rather leisurely practice, watching over the health of the humans associated with Vatican, and probably occasionally caring for some of the human colony not actually associated with Vatican. He'd have good quarters, with a robot to look after him, more than likely interesting people with whom he could spend time. When he had fled Gutshot, he had been looking for sanctuary of any kind, and here he had found a better sanctuary than he had thought possible. A strange place, but he could become accustomed to it. Primitive in many ways, although no more primitive than Gutshot.

He sat on the bench and scrubbed the toe of one shoe back and forth along a crack in the bricks of the walk. He had come to a decision, he thought, much more easily than he had anticipated. Perhaps he would tentatively have accepted Ecuyer's offer the night before if the man had not thrown in the implied threat that Vatican held the means to keep him here. The threat had been uncalled for; why had Ecuyer felt impelled to make it? Threat or not, Tennyson told himself, staying on made sense. He had no place else to go.

He rose from the bench and strolled slowly down the walk. In a little while, he'd go back to the suite, where Hubert would have breakfast waiting. But he realized that this was precious time, that when the sun finally came up, this early-morning garden would become something different. The soft, gentle magic of the moment would be gone and might never come again—perhaps for someone else, but not for him. Here he had caught the needed moment to come to terms with himself, to decide, without rancor and with no guilt, that he would remain in this sanctuary.

Ahead of him the path took a sharp angle which was masked by a small group of purple-flowered shrubs, somewhat higher than most of the others. Rounding the curve, Tennyson stopped in mid-stride. Squatted on the walk, working with a pair of pruning shears on an array of bushes, was a robot. The bushes sprouted magnificent blooms of red, the velvet petals of the flowers jeweled with morning dew.

The robot looked up.

"Good morning, sir," he said. "You must be the physician who arrived last night."

"Yes, I am," said Tennyson. "But how do you come to know of me?"

The robot wagged his head. "Not I alone," he said. "Everyone has heard of you. There is nothing happens here that is not known to everyone at once."

"I see," said Tennyson. "But tell me—these are roses, are they not?"

"Indeed they are," the robot said. "A flower out of ancient Earth. We have many of them here and we prize them greatly. They do not have wide distribution. You recognized them; have you seen other roses?"

"Once," said Tennyson. "Long ago."

"You know, of course," the robot said, "that we ourselves came from Earth. The ties have long since been broken with the Mother Planet, but we cling tightly to the heritage. Will you tell me, sir, have you ever walked on Earth?"

"No, I haven't. Not many humans have."

"Ah, well," the robot said, "I only thought I'd ask." He clipped a single, long-stemmed blossom and held it out to Tennyson.

"Please, sir," he said, "accept from me a piece of ancient Earth."

Chapter Twelve

ENOCH CARDINAL THEODOSIUS HAD THE APPEARANCE OF A little man well muffled, almost overwhelmed, by the purple vestment that enveloped him. But the metallic gleam of his face, beneath the scarlet skullcap, betrayed him as a robot. Although, Jill Roberts told herself, betrayed was not the word. Cardinal Theodosius—or any of his fellows—was not seeking to masquerade as human. Perhaps, she thought, they might be proud of being robots. If what they had done here on End of Nothing was a true measure of their skill and capability, they had reason to be proud.

The functionary who had escorted her to the cardinal's study now closed the door behind her and placed his broad back against it, standing with his feet spread and his hands behind his back. The study was dim, with only a single candle burning on the desk beside which the cardinal sat. And why a candle? she wondered. With electricity and electric lights, why should there be a candle? Perhaps nothing more than window dressing, she decided. In this place, there was a lot of window dressing.

Red and gold drapes hung on the walls, and if there were windows, they also were covered by thick draperies. The floor was carpeted, perhaps in red as well, although she could not be certain. In the faint light, it appeared to be black—and who would install black carpeting? Furniture was placed haphazardly about, but in the dim light the furniture was only humped-up shadows, like resting monsters that at any moment might stretch their paws and come to life.

Slowly she walked toward the cardinal, trying to remember all the protocol on which she had been briefed in the anteroom. Kneel to kiss his ring, then don't rise until he lifts you up, then remain standing until he bids that you be seated. Address him as "Your Eminence," although after the first greeting, "Eminence" would suffice if she wished to use the shortened form. There might have been more, but if there had, it had slipped her mind. But she'd get through it, she assured herself; she had muddled through worse than this many times before. And what did it matter? If she slipped up on a point or two of etiquette she'd probably be excused. After all, they would tell one another, she was nothing more than a stupid bitch who meant no harm.

She moved slowly, hoping that slowness might signify some measure of dignity, although she had doubts it would. More than likely, the cardinal would lay it to the fact she was shaking in her pants. And she wasn't shaking; this robot cardinal on an obscure world at the edge of the galaxy meant very little to her. The cardinal sat quietly, waiting for her, probably sizing her up as she walked across the room.

She reached a spot some three feet in front of him and halted. She bent a knee and the cardinal extended a hand. There's the ring, she thought. She kissed it. He took away the hand and made a motion for her to rise, so she rose.

"Miss Roberts," said the cardinal, his voice low and deep.

"Your Eminence," she said.

"Please be seated."

She saw the chair that had been placed for her, at one corner of the desk.

"Thank you," she murmured, sinking into it.

For a moment silence held in the muffled room, then the cardinal said, "I would suppose good manners should lead me to express the hope that you had a pleasant voyage. But knowing the ship, I'm sure that was impossible. So may I say I hope it was not too bad."

"It was not too bad, Your Eminence. The captain is a good man. He did what he could."

The cardinal reached out to the desk, picked up folded sheets of paper that were lying there. The papers made a crinkling sound.

"Miss Roberts," said the cardinal, "you are a persistent person. We have here several letters from you."

"Yes, Your Eminence. Which you failed to answer."

"Our failure," said the cardinal, "was deliberate. We answer few letters. Especially we do not answer letters such as yours."

"Which means, I imagine, that you do not want me here."

There, she thought, I did it! I forgot to call him Eminence.

The cardinal, if he noticed, did not seem to mind.

"I do not know," he said, "how I can explain our policy without seeming rude."

"Then, Your Eminence," said Jill, "please that you be rude. For I want to know."

"We have no wish," said the cardinal, "to be publicized. We do not wish our existence and our work exposed to public view."

"You could have told me that before I made my trip, Your Eminence. You could have written to discourage me. I would have listened to reason. I might even have accepted, perhaps have understood, your posture. But you hoped, of course, that ignoring me would be discouragement enough."

"We had hoped it would, Miss Roberts."

"Your psychology, Your Eminence, did not work. A frank disclosure of your policy, as you call it, would have served you better."

The cardinal sighed. "Is this defiance that I hear?"

"I'm not sure," Jill replied. "Ordinarily, I'm not defiant of authority. I never set out to be. But it seems to me that I deserve better of you. I was frank in my letters. I told you what I planned to do, what I hoped to do. I asked your cooperation. You could, Your Eminence, have granted me the courtesy of telling me not to come."

"Granted, we could have done that," said the cardinal. "It would have been more fair to you and more considerate of us. But our thinking was that such a move on our part would have placed undue emphasis on the work we're doing here. A refusal of your request might have made it seem we were working undercover, as it were, and have made us seem more important, perhaps more sensational, than we are. We operate with an extremely low profile and wish to keep it that way. We have been laboring the last ten centuries and in that time have accomplished something of what we set out to do, but not as much as we had hoped. We may need many more millennia to achieve our goal, and to achieve that goal, we must be allowed to work without interference. We do not want the galaxy to begin moving in on us."

"Your Eminence, each year you have thousands of pilgrims moving in on you."

"That is true, but these thousands are a mere handful to the numbers that would move in or attempt to move in if a journalist of your competence and reputation were to write of us. The pilgrims come from many planets, most of them members of obscure faiths that have heard of us. But because the faiths are obscure and scattered over many planets, and not too many visit us from any single planet, the impact is not massive and awareness of us is diluted. We do not proselyte, we do not try to bring our message to the galaxy, for, as yet, I doubt that we have a message. Someday, some century, we will have a message, but not yet. However, we cannot close our doors to those who, in full faith, seek us out. We are honor-bound to do what we can for them and, in all honesty, I must admit that the contributions they make to our cause are welcome, for we have no financial backing. . . ."

"Let me write of your work, Eminence, and you will have the backing. All the backing that you need."

The cardinal raised his hands out of his lap and made a negatory sign. "The cost would be too great," he said. "We still have far to go, and we must walk that road in our own way and our own fashion. The pressures that would intrude from the galaxy, were we better known, would defeat our purpose. We still must labor, holding tight to the humility of a task little more than started. Seeming success, any sort of adulation, would work very much against us. We must hold to our dream of a universal religion and we must spare no effort. Worldliness would undermine our purpose. Do you understand?"

"I think I can, Your Eminence," said Jill, "but, surely, to accomplish your purpose you need not work in obscurity."

"But, Miss Roberts, that is exactly what we must do. Were we not obscure, we would be subjected to much interference, some of it well meant, some of it not so well intentioned. Even now . . ."

He paused and stared at her owlishly.

"Even now, Eminence?" she prompted.

"Consider," he said, "that we have something the galaxy could well use but which, in all conscience, cannot be put to use until we know the whole of it, or at least can glimpse an outline of the whole of it. There are, I am sure, unscrupulous forces in existence that would try to steal from us, to wrest our knowledge from us, for purposes of their own, ignoring the total structure that we try to forge. We do not fear this for our sake, but for the sake of the galaxy, perhaps the universe. Our structure must remain unflawed. It must, when completed, be whole, a consistent whole, built on a logic that cannot be denied, that is apparent to all who may look upon it. It cannot be picked apart by vultures. It cannot be riddled by the worms of self-interest. Pieces of it must not be wrenched away and put in the marketplace for the limited benefits these pieces would represent. We have recognized this danger from our beginning; recognition of the peril has been impressed upon us through the years. We fear that even now, even in our obscurity, there may be burrowers nibbling at us. We do not know who they are or what they are or how they nibble or even the purpose of their nibbling, but we feel sure that they are there. This small nibbling we perhaps can withstand, but if we were open to the galaxy, in full sight of the galaxy, if you should write of us . . ."

"You want me to leave," she said. "You want me to turn about and go away."

"We have tried to be honest with you," said the cardinal. "I have tried to reason with you. In reasoning with you, I may have said too much. We could have refused you admittance, refused to talk with you, but we realize that, in your heart, you mean no harm to us, that you did not even dream of the implications of what you propose to do. We regret the trouble and expense to which you have been put. We could wish you had not come, but since you have, we feel we must accord you a certain courtesy, cold though it may seem. We hope that you will think about what I have told you. I believe you are stopping at Human House."

"Yes, I am," said Jill.

"Please," said the cardinal, "would you be our guest? A suite can be assigned to you, for as long as you may wish to stay. Naturally, all expenses that you have incurred or are likely to incur as a result of coming here will be repaid by us in full. Plus a per diem to compensate for the time you've wasted. Would you do at least this much for us: Accept our invitation to be our guest and give yourself the time to think on what I've said."

"Your offer is generous, Eminence," said Jill, "but I do not intend to let it go at that. I do not accept your blanket refusal. Surely we can talk again."

"Yes, we can talk again. But I fear to little purpose. Our viewpoints differ too extensively."

"There must be certain facets of your work that can be safely told. Perhaps not the whole story. . . ."

"I have in mind, Miss Roberts, an alternative suggestion."

"An alternative, Eminence?"

"Yes, how would you like to work for us? We can offer you a most attractive position."

"A position? I'm not looking for a position."

"Please," said the cardinal. "Before you refuse me, allow me to explain. For many years, we have talked of the advisability of writing a formal, authoritative history of Vatican-17, for our own use only. Over the centuries, we have stored the data that would go into such a history—all the happenings, even from the day we first arrived upon this planet, an account of all our work, the hopes, the successes and the failures. It is all there and waiting for retrieval, but somehow we have never gotten around to it. We've had so much to do and, truth to tell, we never have had anyone competent to do it. But now. . . ."

"But now you think that I might write it for you—a thousand years of history. In some detail, I would suppose. How many thousand pages of manuscript? How long would you think that it might take? A lifetime, or two? And you'd pay me well for it?"

"Well, yes, naturally we'd pay you handsomely for it," said the cardinal. "More than you'd make, far more than you'd make, flitting around the galaxy in search of disjointed subjects for your writing. And more than that. Optimum working conditions. All the assistance you might wish. Pleasant surroundings in which to live and work. No pressure for completion."

"That's good of you," she said.

"At least," he said, "you'll accept our hospitality for the moment. Someone can show you the suites available. You can take your pick. No need to go back to Human House. We can pick up your luggage and bring it here."

"I'll have to think on it, Your Eminence."

"Then think on it here. You'll find our suite far more comfortable. . . ."

Good Lord, she thought. All the data here, squirreled away in memory cores, waiting for retrieval!

"You do not answer," said the cardinal.

"Your offer is most kind," she said. "I think I shall accept the hospitality that you offer, since that seems to be your wish. On the other matter, I need some further thought."

"Take all the time you wish," said the cardinal. "We shall not press for an early answer. We'll talk about it later. But let me say we do need your services very badly. The history should be written. But it takes a certain kind of talent to do the writing of it— perhaps a human talent, which we have been unable to acquire. Here on End of Nothing it is difficult to obtain the kind of human talent that we need. The planet is too far and lonely to attract humanity. Go out at night and look up and there are few stars. The galaxy itself is a shimmer in the sky and that is all. But there are certain advantages. There is space, there is newness. A freshness that is not found on many planets. And the mountains. To our humans, the mountains are a constant source of great delight."

"I am sure they are," said Jill.

Chapter Thirteen

"THIS," ECUYER TOLD TENNYSON, "IS OUR REPOSITORY. Here, stored and filed and cross-indexed and ready, close at hand, are the records of the work we've done in the Search Program."

The room was large. There were no windows. Pale ceiling lights marched in converging rows into the distance. Ranks of filing cabinets, floor to ceiling, stretched away farther than one could see.

Ecuyer walked slowly down one row of the cabinets, his hand laid flat against their fronts, sliding along the metal. Tennyson trailed along behind him, lost in this cavern of files. He felt the place closing in on him, pressing close, looming over him with a threat of suffocation.

Ahead of him, Ecuyer halted and pulled out a drawer, fumbling, or pretending to fumble, among the many small crystal cubes that lay within the drawer.

"Ah, here," he said, coming up with one of them. "A cube picked quite at random."

He held it up for Tennyson to see, a gleaming crystal cube four inches on a side. It was, thought Tennyson, quite unspectacular. Ecuyer closed the drawer. "And now," he said, "if you are willing, I should like to show you."

"Show me?"

"Yes, let you experience what is imprinted on the cube—live the experience picked up by the sensitive, the experience that he lived through, what he saw and felt and thought. Put you inside the sensitive. . . ."

He peered intently at Tennyson. "It will not hurt," he said. "You will not be uncomfortable. There'll be no pain, no fright."

"You mean that you want me—that you can connect me some-how to that cube?"

Ecuyer nodded. "Simply done," he said.

"But why?" asked Tennyson. "Why should you want to do this?"

"Because I could talk about our work for the next three days," said Ecuyer, "and not be able to give you an understanding of it such as you can gain from a few minutes on this cube."

"I can see that," said Tennyson. "But why me, a stranger?"

"A stranger, perhaps," said Ecuyer, "but I want you very much to stay here and be a member of the team. We need you, Jason. Can't you understand that?"

"As a matter of fact, I have already decided to stay on," said Tennyson. "I sat on a bench in a beautiful garden this morning and found that I already had made my decision without being aware I had."

"Well, now, that's fine," said Ecuyer. "That's splendid. But why did you wait? Why didn't you tell me immediately?"

"Because you still were sneaking up on me," said Tennyson. "You do it so well that it was fun to watch."

"I'm properly rebuked," said Ecuyer, "and I don't seem to mind at all. I can't tell you how happy it makes me. And, now, how about the cube?"

"I'm a bit nervous about it, but if you think I should, I will."

"I think you should," Ecuyer told him. "It's important to me and I think to you that you know exactly what we are doing."

"So I'll understand this Heaven business better?"

"Well, yes, but not entirely that. I can see you're still a skeptic on what you call the Heaven business."

"Yes, I am. Aren't you?"

"I don't know," said Ecuyer. "I can't be sure. Every fiber in me cries out against it and yet . . ."

"All right," said Tennyson. "Let's get on with the cube."

"Okay," said Ecuyer. "This way."

He led the way out of the stack and into a small room crowded with equipment.

"Sit down in that chair over there," said Ecuyer. "Take it easy. Relax."

A helmet arrangement was suspended over the chair. Tennyson regarded it with some suspicion.

"Go on, sit down," said Ecuyer. "I'll fit the helmet on you and drop the cube into the slot and—"

"All right," said Tennyson. "I suppose I'll have to trust you."

"You can trust me," Ecuyer said. "It won't hurt at all."

Tennyson lowered himself cautiously into the chair, squirmed around to get comfortable. Ecuyer carefully lowered the helmet on his head, fussing to get it adjusted.

"You all right?" he asked.

"All right. I can't see a thing."

"You don't need to see. Breathing all right? No trouble breathing?"

"None at all."

"All right, then. Here we go."

For a moment there was utter darkness, then there was light, a greenish sort of light, and a wetness. Tennyson gasped and then the gasp cut off, for everything was all right, better than all right.

The water was warm and the mud was soft. His gut was full. For the moment there was no danger. Contentment filled him and he allowed himself to sink deeper into the yielding mud. When the mud no longer yielded, he agitated his legs, trying to sink deeper, but this gained him little, although when he ceased the effort, he could sense the mud beginning to flow over him and it was warm and an added safety factor. He settled as deeply, as compactly as he could, the contentment deepening, a lassitude spreading through him. With the mud spreading over him, in no matter how thin a layer, he was shielded from view. The likelihood was that no prowling predator would detect him, snap him up. It is good, he thought smugly to himself. There was no need to move, no necessity to invite attack by moving. He had everything he needed. He had eaten until food no longer had attraction for him. He was warm and safe. He could remain motionless, exert no effort.

And yet there was, he found, an internal nagging that arose

once he was all settled in full enjoyment of contentment. A question that never had come on him before, for up until this instant, there had been no question of any sort at all. Until now he had not been aware there was such a thing as question. He existed, that was all. He had never cared what he might be. The matter of identity had never arisen.

He stirred uneasily, befuddled and upset that the question should arise to so disturb him. And that was not the worst of it. There was something else. It was as if he were not himself, not he who had found the question, the question not internal to him but coming from somewhere outside himself. And there was nothing outside himself—nothing but the warmth of the shallow sea, the softness of the bottom mud and the knowledge that the fearful shadow avid to gulp him down was not present now, could not see him now, that he was safe from the prowling predator that snapped up trilobites.

"My God!" he thought in sudden fear and wonder. "I'm a trilobite!"

With the words, the utter darkness faded and then flickered off, and he was once again sitting in the chair and Ecuyer was standing in front of him, holding the helmet in his hands. Tennyson let out his breath in a gust and stared up at Ecuyer.

"Ecuyer, you said a random cube. That was not a random cube."

Ecuyer grinned at him. "No, I would think not. You recall the sensitive I told you of."

"Yes, the man who was a trilobite. But it was so real!"

"Rest assured, my friend," said Ecuyer. "This was no shadow show. No entertainment stunt. For a while there, you *were* a trilobite."

Chapter Fourteen

When Tennyson returned to his suite, Jill was sitting in front of the fireplace. He hurried across the room to her. "I've been wondering about you. I was about to track you down."

"Hubert is fixing dinner," she said. "I told him I could stay. Is that all right with you?"

He bent to kiss her, then sat down beside her. "That's fine," he said. "How are things going with you?"

She made a face. "Not well. They won't stand still for a story. They offered me a job instead."

"And you accepted?"

"No, I didn't. I'm not sure I will. I hear you are staying on."

"For a time at least. A good place to hunker down."

She gestured at the single rose in the vase standing on the coffee table. "Where did you get that?"

"A gardener gave it to me. I found the garden this morning. I'd like to show it to you."

"They offered me a place to stay," said Jill, "and I moved in this afternoon. Four doors away from you. The robot who moved me told me you were here. You have a drink around?"

"I think there is," he said. "But first let's look at the garden."

"Well, all right," she said.

"You'll like it," he assured her.

When they reached the garden, she asked, "What's all this uproar about the garden? It's just an ordinary garden. What's going on?"

"It's not the garden," he told her. "I imagine Hubert, in the kitchen, had his ears stretched out a foot or so. Do anything in this place and in ten minutes everyone has heard about it. I won't bet they can't hear us in the garden, but at least we have a chance. We have things to talk about."

"It's your Gutshot conditioning," she said. "The cloak-and-dagger business."

He shrugged. "Maybe. Maybe you're right."

"You jumped at the chance, apparently, to stay here. So there can't be too much wrong."

"Maybe nothing wrong," he said. "But strange. Damn strange. There's a woman here—she's the one Ecuyer came to get me to treat. She claims she has found Heaven."

"Heaven?"

"That's right. Heaven. You see, they have this program going on. People going out in their minds to other places, bringing back the data to be fed into the Pope. Although I have a feeling it may be for other reasons than the feeding of the Pope. From something Ecuyer said the other night, it sounds as if there may be some differences of opinion between the Search Program and Vatican."

"Heaven?" she asked. "You mean the honest-to-God Bible Heaven with the golden stairs and the trumpets blaring and the angels flying?"

"Something like that."

"But, Jason, that's impossible."

"Perhaps, but Mary thinks she's found it. Ecuyer half believes in it."

"Ecuyer's a fool."

"No, not a fool," he said. "Jill, tell me. Did they use muscle on you?"

"Muscle?"

"Yes, muscle. Ecuyer hinted rather broadly I might not be allowed to leave the planet."

"No. No one mentioned that. I talked with a cardinal. Purple robes and scarlet skullcap. A single candle burning. Now, wait a minute. Is that why you're staying? Because they won't let you leave?"

"No, not that. They might even let us go. But the threat is there. This place is run by Vatican and what Vatican says is law. But I'm staying because I want to—for the moment. I have no place else to go. Besides, it's comfortable. And I might as well confess it—I'm considerably intrigued."

"So am I," said Jill. "The cardinal wouldn't listen to my writing articles or a book about this place. He said nothing about not allowing me to leave. As a matter of fact, I thought that he would throw me out. Then he offered me a job."

"The iron fist in the velvet glove."

"That could be it. He's a pleasant-enough robot—I almost said a pleasant-enough old man. Pleasant enough, but stubborn. I argued with him and he didn't budge an inch."

"This job?"

"They want a history of Vatican written. The cardinal claims they have no one who can do it; hinted that a robot could not be trained to do it. Would you believe it—they have a complete record of everything that's happened here, all that's been done here, since the first ship arrived. All stored and waiting for retrieval. I said no, of course. Maybe, come to think of it, I didn't say a flat-out no. Actually, I think I said I'd have to think about it. I probably gave the impression I was going to say no."

"And are you?"

"Jason, I honestly don't know. Think of it! The story is all there. Waiting for someone to dig it out. It's been there all these years and not been touched by anyone."

"But what good will it do you if you can't get it out?"

"That's right. No good at all. Jason, do I look like a dirty sneak?"

"Well, yes, now that I think of it."

"I'd never be able to live with myself," said Jill, "if I didn't have a shot at it."

"Jill, it doesn't track. First they refuse to let you write about this place, then they hand the story to you on a silver platter. Unless, of course, they do badly want the history written and are convinced they can keep you here."

"If so," she said, "they must be awfully sure of themselves."

"That's what Ecuyer said the other night. That they are sure of themselves."

"Jason, we may have been a pair of fools to come here. If Vatican wants nothing to leak out, the one sure way to do it would be to make sure that no one, once they got here, could leave."

"But there are all the pilgrims. The pilgrims come and go."

"The cardinal half-explained that to me. The pilgrims, it seems, don't count. They come from scattered planets, only a few from each one. Apparently they are tied up with screwball cults that have little standing. No one would pay attention to what any cult member said, even to the cult, perhaps, if it was said collectively. Whatever word the pilgrims carry back would be put down as religious ravings."

"Vatican has a lot to hide," Tennyson said thoughtfully. "There is Ecuyer's Search Program, which the pilgrims might not know about, might have no inkling of. Maybe it's the Search Program, not Vatican itself, that is important. The searchers are milking knowledge from the universe, from all of space and time—and maybe other places outside of space and time. If there's any such place."

"Heaven could be. If there's a place like Heaven."

"The point is that no one else has anything like it. The Search people have miles of files crammed with the information they've pilfered. It's all there. What are they going to do with it?"

"Maybe they really are feeding it to the Pope."

"Some Pope," Tennyson remarked. "No, I can't think that's entirely it. Ecuyer said something else. I'm trying to remember exactly what. I think it was that Project Pope had become, over the years, no more than an excuse for keeping on with the Search Program. I think that was it. He suggested that I not mention it to Vatican. Gave the impression that some of the old Vatican crowd might be stuffy."

"Vatican has its worries," said Jill. "The cardinal let some of them out. Sort of talking the worries out to me, although I doubt he thought of it that way. He, and possibly some of the other cardinals, think someone is stealing from Vatican. 'Nibbling away' was the way he put it. What seemed to worry him the most was no one knows who or what it is that is doing the nibbling."

Chapter Fifteen

ENOCH CARDINAL THEODOSIUS HUNTED UP HIS BOSOM PAL, Cecil Cardinal Roberts.

"Eminence," he said, "it seems to me that you and I should have a talk."

"You are upset," said Roberts. "What is going on?"

"These two new arrivals. The human man and woman."

"What do you know about them?"

"Nothing about the man. Ecuyer has installed him as Vatican physician. I understand he came here fleeing justice."

"Have you spoken to Ecuyer of it?"

"No, Your Eminence. Of late, Ecuyer has become impossible to talk with."

"Yes, I know," said Roberts. "One gains the impression that he believes the Search Program has become our paramount concern. If you ask me, the man has gotten bigger than his britches."

Theodosius sighed. "Much as we may admire the human race," he said, "there are some of them one finds very hard to live with."

"And the woman, Eminence?"

"I talked with her this morning. She is a writer. Imagine that, a writer! She was the one who wrote us all the letters. I told you about them?"

"Yes, I believe you did."

"She wants to write about us."

"Write about us?"

"Yes, it was all in the letters. You read them, did you not?"

"Of course I did. And put them quite out of mind. It's impossible, of course. The impudence of it."

"Exactly," Theodosius said.

"You told her it was unthinkable."

"Yes, but she refused to accept the refusal. She is a most persistent human. Finally I offered her a job."

"You'll pardon me, Your Eminence, but there is no job. . . ."

"Yes, there is," said Theodosius. "All these years we have been talking about writing a history of Vatican. We have said how fine it would be to get it down on paper so that all might read and wonder. We have even talked about developing a new species of robot to do the work. We robots, it seems, are not cut out for writing chores. And it would be a vast amount of trouble to develop another strain capable of so limited an ability as writing. But here is one, come to us of her own free will, who can do the writing for us."

"And, pray, what was her reaction?"

"I gained the impression she was not enchanted with the offer. But that's not entirely what I came to talk about."

"I thought you said that was what you wished to talk about—the new human man and woman."

"Well, yes, of course. But not of them alone. There is another factor. There are, in recent years, three disturbing human factors that have come upon us."

"Three?"

"Decker is the third. He is the third unknown. What do we really know about him?"

"Why, I guess," said Roberts, "we know very little. We do not know how he got here. He did not come on *Wayfarer*, and I know of no other way that a human could get here. Perhaps you, Your Eminence, know more of him than I do. You have talked with him."

"Some years ago," said Theodosius. "Shortly after he showed up. I donned the habit of a monk and went calling on him, in the pretense of extending welcome. A meddlesome, inquisitive, foot-loose little cleric. I thought that perhaps he would talk to such a monk whereas he might be hesitant of talking with a cardinal. I learned precisely nothing. He told me not a thing. Pleasant enough, but a distant man. And now these two—the woman and the doctor. Will you tell me, Eminence, why we must have a human doctor? We could, in a short time, train one of our robots to be physician to the humans. Fully as knowledgeable, as efficient, as capable, as any human doctor. Perhaps even more so, for we have access to certain new medical knowledge that might be adaptable to humans."

"Yes," said Roberts. "I know. We have talked about it often. Periodically we must import an outsider to be physician to the humans. It's not desirable. No outsider is desirable. The old doctor who died, as all humans must, was quite acceptable, although, if you remember, we had doubts concerning him at first. The one who replaced him was impossible. The humans in the town and those in Vatican—except for the Listeners, of whom we do import a few—are old-time residents. They are descendants of people who have been here for centuries. Of them we need have no concern or fear. They are almost one with us. But outsiders have no real ties to us. They are not accustomed to us, nor are we to them."

"And yet," said Theodosius, "our own people, descendants of those who have been here for ages, probably would not accept a robotic doctor. This perturbs me. It points to a cultural gap that still exists between the robot and the human. I would have hoped that after all the years the gap would have been closed. Certainly there is a difference between robot and human, but—"

"I think, Your Eminence," said Roberts, "that in the subconscious human mind, we still may be tainted, that we still smell faintly of machines. They, if charged with it, would piously deny such a thing, and believe their own denial, but it still is there. I am sure of that. On this matter of a robot doctor, it is true, of course, that we could readily supply them one, but I don't think we should. Here on End of Nothing we could have supplied our humans with many luxury services, but we have refrained from doing so because of the fear that it would seem we were taking them over. We must never seem to do that. It would be simpler, naturally, if we could make pets of them, watching closely after them, shielding them from harm, supplying all their needs. But this we must not do. We must not tamper with them. We must let them go their way and preserve their dignity."

"We face a dilemma," said Theodosius. "We battle with ourselves. We are continually haunted by the regard, the respect, almost the worship that we feel for humans. It is a response to them, I am certain, that we can't root out. Surely not such as you and I, who were forged by humans. We stand too close to them. Some of the second- and third-generation robots, created not by humans but by robots, might be able to root out some of this feeling for the humans. We try to comfort ourselves by saying we are no more than an extension of the human race. I suppose we would like to think so—we must, for we say it often, almost as if by rote. But the bitter truth is that we are a human product."

"Your Eminence," said Roberts, speaking kindly, "you are too hard upon yourself, too hard on all of us. Products we may be, but surely our thousand years of effort has raised us above the level of a product. The thing that bothers us, I think, is that our attitude toward humanity smacks too much of worship. But if you think of it correctly, you'll see the fallacy in that. For centuries we have worked to discover a universal principle that would apply to all—not to robots alone, but to every thinking thing, each speck of intelligence. Eminence, we have paid our dues. We have earned the right to be ourselves."

"Then why am I so concerned with three outsider humans? Am I assuming the attitude of a child toward a father image? A disapproving father who may stand ready to correct me."

"All of us—not you alone, but all of us—are bowed down under an inferiority complex," said Roberts. "It is a cross we must bear as best we can. Give us a few more millennia and we will outgrow it."

"What you say is true," said Theodosius. "I find within myself, upon close examination, so much tangled guilt that I can barely stand up under it. There are even times—forgive me, Eminence—there are even times when I feel a guilt in our having brought about His Holiness. There is a possibility, I tell myself, that in doing this, we have committed sacrilege, that in fact His Holiness is no more than another one of us—not holy at all, but simply another machine, another exquisitely sophisticated robot, a cybernetic shadow with which we delude ourselves."

"Your Eminence," Roberts exclaimed in horror, "I hope you have not repeated such a heresy where others than myself might hear you. As an ancient friend, I can understand the guilt, but . . ."

"I have not breathed a word of this before," said Theodosius. "I have kept it bottled up. Only to such as you, old friend, could I have said a word of it. I would not have said it now were it not for so many happenings. This sighting of Heaven by one of the Listeners—"

"Yes, that is bad," said Roberts. "It has had a greater impact among our brethren than I like. My hope had been that it would blow over soon and be quite forgotten. The Listener, I understand, was very close to death, which would have ended all the foolishness, but this doctor . . ."

Chapter Sixteen

MARY IMPROVED. THE FEVER WENT DOWN AND THE BREATHing difficulty all but disappeared. The blankness left her eyes. She became aware of those around her and was able to sit up.

She became imperious, assumed the attitude of a rather shabby, beat-up old grande dame. She snubbed Tennyson, lorded it over the nursing staff, ignored medical orders with a fine insouciance.

"It's this damned Heaven business," said Ecuyer. "It has set her apart from all the other Listeners, above everyone, in fact. Over the years she has been a top-notch Listener. She has pulled in a lot of data for us. But nothing so obviously important as this. Some of the other findings were important, of course—all data has potential importance—but nothing dramatic. Nothing like finding Heaven. That, on the face of it, is important. I'm afraid the finding of Heaven will ruin the woman as a Listener. To be a good Listener, you must be devoted and sincere and humble. The task of Listening must be approached with humility. The Listener must subordinate himself, or herself, must cancel out personality, must go out with an empty mind or close to an empty mind. It is a pity that Mary's clones—"

"You mentioned clones before," said Tennyson. "You mean that you have created other Marys?"

"That is right," Ecuyer told him. "When we get an extraordinary Listener, we go to cloning. It's only a recent development. I think that, more than likely, the Vatican biological research laboratory has developed more advanced cloning procedures than can be found anywhere in the known galaxy. Foolproof, certain—no aberrations whatsoever. Good Listeners are hard to find. You have no idea how long we search to find a decent one. A decent one, mind you; Mary is superb. We can't lose such a Listener; we must duplicate. We must have more like Mary. We have three clones of her, but they are little more than children. They are still growing up. Even when they are grown, there is no guarantee that any one of them can find her way to Heaven, although we could hope they'd have a better chance than another Listener unrelated to Mary. Superb Listeners, sure, but we can't be sure of Heaven."

"Then Mary might be your only hope."

"That's the truth of it," said Eucyer. "And she knows it. That's what makes her so suddenly important."

"Is there anything that can be done about it? Anything to snap her out of it?"

"Leave her alone," said Ecuyer. "Pay her no attention. The more she gets, the worse she'll be."

Jill accepted the job of writing the Vatican history.

"What the hell," she said to Tennyson, walking in the garden. "It'll be five weeks or more before the ship from Gutshot comes again. Five weeks before I can even think of leaving. I'd go crazy just sitting here. Nothing to do. Nothing to see."

"You could look at the mountains. They keep changing all the time. They change as the light changes. They're never quite the same. I never tire of watching them."

"You watch them," she said. "I'm no mountain freak."

"What if you get hooked on the Vatican history? What if it proves so fascinating you can't tear yourself away from it—if Vatican will allow you to tear yourself away. There might come a time you knew so much, they couldn't let you go."

"I'll take my chances," she told him. "This girl has found herself in tight spots before and always has been able to wiggle out of them. And, God, the information that's there. When they said they kept a detailed record, they really meant detailed."

She threw herself into the job. There were days on end when Tennyson would not see her. Then she'd show up for dinner and a talk.

"I can't tell you," she said. "There is so much to tell. It all is there. Everything they planned or did, everything they thought."

"You're getting sucked into it," he warned her. "You'll never leave. You'll become a research person, so involved in tracking down and pinning down that a lifetime's not enough."

"Somewhere inside of me," she said, "there still remains Jill Roberts, the demon free-lance writer, the galaxy trotter who follows stories to worlds' ends. When the time comes—but let that go. Forget about me. How about you, Jason?"

"I'm getting settled in."

"And happy?"

"Happy? I don't know. What is happiness? Contentment, yes. Contentment for the moment. Medical chores that I enjoy, but not too many of them. I never was, I guess, one of your dedicated doctors intent upon setting his mark high on the medical roll of honor, never devastated with the thirst to do more than passing well for his fellow humans. There is just enough of it here to make me feel professionally competent and that, again for the moment, is everything I want. I get along with Ecuyer and all the rest of them."

"How about your Heaven lady?"

"The Heaven lady? Damned if I know. Physically, she is well enough. . . ."

"But?"

"She's taken a strange turn. She preens herself. She has become the Great Lady. The rest of us are dirt beneath her feet. Her mental processes are all screwed up."

"But you have to understand her, realize what Heaven meant to her. Whether she found Heaven or not, it's still important to her. Maybe the first time in her life that something important really happened to her."

"Oh, she thinks she found Heaven well enough. She is convinced of it."

"So is half of Vatican."

"Half of Vatican? I would have thought all of Vatican."

"Jason, I'm not sure. People don't tell me, but I hear some talk. Hard to understand. Not all of them are entirely happy with Heaven being found."

"Why should that be? Heaven! Jesus, I'd think they'd be thrilled out of their skulls."

"Vatican isn't what it sounds like. Not what we think it is. Because of the terminology—Vatican, Pope, cardinals, all the rest of it—the easy assumption is that it's basically Christian. Well, it's not all Christian. There is much else to it. Just what that much else is I don't know, but you gain the impression that there are an awful lot of things. At one time, it may have been basically Christian; that's all the poor things had when they came out from Earth. But the robots have found so much else, so many hints of so much else, that it's no longer entirely Christian. And there is another factor. . . ."

She hesitated for a moment. Tennyson waited, saying nothing. Then she went on.

"There are two groups of robots in Vatican, not too well defined. There is the old group, the ones who came from Earth. They are still inclined to be closely identified with humans. To them the humans and the robots are tied together. This is not so true of the younger robots, the ones who were created here, built here, forged here, however you may say it, by robots, not by humans. You can sense in them an underlying resentment, maybe not of humans, but of the attitude the older robots hold toward humans. These youngsters want to cut the ties with humanity. Oh, they still subscribe to the debt that robots owe to humans, but they want to cut away; they want to strengthen their own identities. Mary's Heaven, I think, is under some suspicion because it's human-based. Mary is a human and she found a Christian concept—"

"That doesn't follow," said Tennyson. "Not all humans are Christians. I think only a small percentage of them are. I'm not

sure I'm Christian, nor, I think, are you. Perhaps at one time our
ancestors were—although they could as well have been Jewish or
Moslem or—"

"But many of us have a Christian heritage, whether we're actually Christians or not. It doesn't make any difference whether we
are or not. In many of us, the old way of Christian thinking still
hangs on. Look, we still use Christian swear words—hell and
Christ and God and Jesus. Those words roll easily and naturally
off our tongues."

Tennyson nodded soberly. "Yes, I can see how the robots
might think we were, in our hearts, still Christian. Not that it's a
bad thing being Christian."

"Of course not, Jason. But when mankind began leaving Earth,
they lost a lot, or shed a lot, along the way. A lot of us don't know
what we really are."

They sat silently for a time and then she said, her voice soft and
low, "Jason, you don't notice my face any longer—the stigma, that
horrible angry scar. I can tell you don't. I can tell you really don't.
You're the first man in my experience who has ever gotten so he
didn't notice it."

"My dear," he said, "why should I?"

"Because it disfigures me. Because it makes me ugly."

"There is enough beauty in you," he told her, "both inside and
outside you, that disfigurement doesn't matter. It takes nothing
from you. And you're right—I don't see it any longer."

She leaned toward him and he caught her in his arms.

"Hold me," she said. "Hold me. I need it so much, Jason."

One evening only. Most other evenings he did not see her. She
worked long hours digging out the history—extracting it from the
records, pulling it together, trying to understand what she was
finding, wondering at the fanatical devotion that through the years
had driven the robots on their dedicated quest. Not religion, she
told herself at times, not entirely religion, then again she would
become convinced that it was religion. Although as she worked,
the nagging question came in her mind and would not go away:
What is religion?

Cardinal Theodosius came at times to visit her at her work,

hunched on a stool beside her, muffled and overwhelmed in his purple vestments, looking very much like a wrapped-up mummy.

"Do you need more help?" he'd ask her. "If so, we could find more aides for you."

"You've been most kind to me, Your Eminence," she'd say. "I have all the willing help I need."

And she had. The two robots working with her seemed as interested as she. The three of them, grouped about the great desk where she worked, put their heads together in an attempt to puzzle out the occasional obscurity in the record, to debate fine points of theology and meaning, trying to make come clear and understandable the faith and thought that had been put down centuries before.

On one of his visits the cardinal said, without preamble, "You are becoming one of us, Miss Roberts."

"Well, hardly, Your Eminence," said Jill Roberts.

"I did not mean what you appparently thought I meant," said the cardinal. "I was thinking of your viewponit, of your evident enthusiasm and devotion to fact."

"If you're thinking of truth, Eminence, I've always been devoted to the truth."

"It is not the matter of truth so much," the robot said, "as it is of understanding. I do believe you may be beginning to understand our purpose here."

Jill pushed away the papers she had been working on. "No, Eminence, I do not understand. Perhaps you can enlighten me. There are great areas of understanding that are lacking. The principal lack is an explanation of what made you come out here to End of Nothing. What drove you out of Earth? The supposition is that you chafed under the rule that no robot could become a communicant of a church, that you were denied religion. That is what any robot in Vatican will tell you, speaking as if this is an article of faith. But here I find no clear-cut evidence—"

"What came before the fact of our coming here," said the cardinal, "is not in the record. There was no need to put it in. All of us knew why we came here. It was a part of us, it was understood. There was no reason to record it, for it was well known."

She said no more; she was hesitant to argue with a cardinal, even a robot cardinal.

He seemed not to notice she did not pursue the question; possibly he was confident he had explained to her satisfaction. Nor did he push the conversation further. He sat hunched upon his stool for a few minutes longer, then rose and left.

Tennyson's days were filled. He prowled Vatican, observing, learning, talking with the robots he met. He visited with the Listeners and got to know some of them well. He established a singular rapport with James Henry, the man who had been a trilobite.

"So you scanned the trilobite cube," Henry said to him. "Tell me how it struck you."

"It left me," said Tennyson, "funny in the gizzard."

"It left me the same," said Henry. "I've done no Listening since. Frankly, I'm afraid to. I tell myself that back to the trilobite is as far as I should go. The trilobite must be close to the edge of sentience. Go back another step and a man is apt to wind up a lump of mindless protoplasm, knowing nothing but the urge toward food, the flight from danger. That was almost the case with the trilobite. But it was my own mind intruding that made sense of the trilobite. It just could be that if I went back far enough, I could get stuck forever in a mass of living jelly. That would be a hell of a way for a man to end his days."

"You could try for something else."

"You don't understand. Sure I could try for something else. A lot of the Listeners aim for specific areas. Sometimes they make it; a lot of times they don't. You can't quite be sure. Listening is a tricky business. It's not entirely under control. Take Mary, for instance. I suppose she will try for Heaven again, and with a Listener like Mary, she'll probably find her way. But even she can't be sure. You can never be sure. I never really tried to go back along the germ-plasma line. I just happened to."

"Then why are you reluctant to do any more Listening? You might not—"

"Dr. Tennyson," said Henry, "as I told you, I don't know why I started on that route in the first place or why I kept on going back. But I do know this—after the first few times, it was as if I were sliding down a well-greased chute. The chute, I'm afraid, is still there and waiting for me. I didn't mind to start with. It was, in fact, a lot of fun. Very interesting. I was several kinds of primitive men and that was to the good. Scared a lot of the time, of course, doing a lot of running for my life. I tell you, mister, those old ancestors of ours didn't cut too grand a figure in the early days. We were not, you might say, high on the totem pole. We were just one hunk of meat among many other hunks of meat. The carnivores didn't give a damn if it was us they ate or something else. Just protein and fat, that was all we were. Half the time I would be running scared. The rest of the time I scrounged for food—carrion left by the big cats and other predators, rodents I could knock over, fruit, roots, insects. It sickens me at times, remembering the kind of food I ate, gulping it down and happy to have it. It didn't bother me at the time. But there are times still when I dream of turning over a rotting log and scooping up a handful of white grubs that are hiding under it. They wriggle and try to get away, but I don't let them. I hold them tight and pop them in my mouth. They feel good going down. They have a sort of sweetish taste. And I wake up and I'm sweating all over and I have a gone feeling in the gut. But aside from that, it wasn't bad. Even when I was running for my life, it wasn't bad. Scared, sure, but there is a lot of exhilaration in being scared, a lot of satisfaction when you get away, thumbing your nose at the big cat that had tried to get you and saying yah, yah, yah at him. Mocking him. Feeling feisty as hell yourself. Nothing to do but fill your gut and find a place in the sun, where it's warm, to sleep. Horny as a hoptoad, chasing down a female.

"I'll tell you the best thing that I ever was. It wasn't any man, no old human ancestor, or even close to human. I'm not sure some of the old man-things I was were human. This best thing was a sort of lizard. I don't know what it was, nor does anyone else. Ecuyer had a hell's own time trying to figure out what it was. He even sent for some books that he thought might tell him what it was, but they didn't. What it was never bothered me, but it did him. I guess it must have been some sort of missing link, a critter that never left a skeleton for paleontologists to dig up and ponder over. I figure, and so does Ecuyer, that it lived back in the Triassic. I said a lizard, but it probably wasn't any lizard. It wasn't big, but it was fast—it was one of the fastest things that lived at that time. And mean. Christ, was it mean! It hated everything, it fought with everything, it would eat anything that moved. It harried the hell out of everything in sight. I never knew until then how good it made a man feel to be really mean. Bone-chilling mean. A real, low-down bastard. The time I spent as a trilobite was short, but I lived as this lizard for a long time. I don't know how long, for there was no sense of time. I just lived in the middle of forever. Maybe I stayed with it so long because I was enjoying myself so much. Why don't you ask Ecuyer to dig out that lizard cube for you? You'd enjoy it."

"Perhaps someday I will," said Tennyson.

He did not view the lizard cube. There were too many others. Ecuyer had no objection to his seeing them. He gave the robot custodian of the Listening files instructions to show Tennyson any that he wished, suggested a long list that he should see.

It was puzzling, Tennyson told himself. Here he was, a stranger, and still the files were being opened to him. As if, in all fact, he was a member of the project. And in the Vatican library, the historical record had been made available to Jill. None of it squared with what the cardinal had told Jill when she had her interview with him—that Vatican was adamant in its refusal to allow any public exposure. The answer must be, he told himself, that Vatican was confident it could guard against public exposure by refusing to allow anyone with knowledge of its operations to leave the planet.

Or it might be that by revealing its operations to Jill and him, both of them would be won over to the cause. Vatican was made up of a band of dedicated fanatics isolated from the nearby galaxy —the only part of the galaxy that counted, the only part of it that was close enough to be tempted to move in—and out of this dedication and isolation the fact of Vatican and its purpose would loom larger in their eyes than it really was. Thus Vatican would fall victim to its egocentrism, and the cause would seem so grand, so sacred and so clearly reasonable that no one, adequately informed, could do anything but align himself with it. All that needed to be done was to explain and everyone would fall in line.

Tennyson shook his head over the puzzle. The line taken by Vatican was illogical. They could, if they had wished, have sent both him and Jill packing when *Wayfarer* lifted off to return to Gutshot. Certainly both of them would have known something of Vatican, but very little of what was actually going on. Jill could write her article detailing how she had been thrown off the planet. But in the midst of all the causes, all the crusades, all the quarrels, all the problems of the galaxy—such an article would have made no more impression than the slightest ripple occasioned by a thrown stone in a storm-tossed ocean.

The simplest answer, and the one that he was most reluctant to accept, was that both of them were needed here. Certainly there was need of a doctor to care for the human population; it might be true that Vatican felt a real need for the writing of its history. And it was true, as well, that it was difficult for such an out-of-the-way place to attract outside professionals, so difficult that when a couple of them dropped unannounced onto the planet, Vatican would latch onto them. But, for some reason that he was not able to understand, Tennyson was reluctant to accept such a thesis. He could not, for one thing, accept the thought that Jill and he could be so important to them. Unless, and this he kept coming back to, Vatican had no intention of allowing them to leave.

One of the cubes he viewed was highly disturbing. Even inside the mind of one of its inhabitants, which he assumed was where he was, it was a sort of place that made no human sense, was entirely incomprehensible. What he saw, although he realized later that it was not really seeing, was a world of diagrams and equations, or what he took to be diagrams and equations, although he saw no conventional signs or symbols even vaguely comparable to human ones. It was as if he existed somewhere inside a huge three-dimensional blackboard, with the signs and symbols, the diagrams and equations grouped about him and, on all sides, receding far into the distance. And it seemed at times, although how he sensed this he did not know, that he himself, or the entity whose mind he shared, was itself an equation.

He sought vainly for an answer, for an explanation, feebly probing the mind of his host, but getting no reaction. The creature, he thought, more than likely didn't know he was there. It itself needed no answer or explanation; it understood what it was seeing. Perhaps interpreting what it was seeing, sharing in the experience of its interactions with all the other diagrams and equations. But if so, all this escaped Tennyson. He was lost in a sea of unknowing.

He did not give up; he stayed in there and fought for some sort of understanding, trying to seize just one thing, one small bit of relevance that he could tuck away as a start toward an understanding. That one bit of relevance never came. When the cube came to an end and he found himself back in the human world, he knew as little as he did when popped into that other mind.

He sat, stricken, in the chair.

"That was quite something, was it not, sir?" asked the custodian, chirping blithely.

Tennyson rubbed his hand across his face, trying to clear away the fog.

"Yes," he said. "What was it?"

"Sir, we do not know."

"What good, then," he asked, "of finding it, of seeing it?"

"Vatican may know," said the custodian. "Vatican has ways of knowing."

"Well, I sincerely hope so," said Tennyson, rising from the chair. "That's all I can stand today. How about tomorrow?"

"Certainly, sir. Tomorrow. Any time you wish."

Tomorrow turned out to be the autumn land.

It was really nothing; it was just a place. This time, he was sure, he did not exist inside an intelligence. He was simply there. Thinking back on it, he could not be sure he had been anyplace at all, although certainly he had had a sense of being in an actual place. He could swear that he had heard the crackle and rustle of fallen autumn leaves beneath his feet, that he had breathed a sharp, crisp, winelike air redolent of leaf bonfires, of ripened apples hanging on a laden bough, the faint scent of late-blooming flowers and a touch of frost on withering vegetation. He had heard, or thought he heard, the rustle of a field-dried patch of corn, the patter of hickory nuts falling from a tree, the sudden, far-off whir of partridge wings, the soft, liquid singing of a placid brook carrying on its surface a freight of fallen autumn leaves. And there had been color—he was sure of that—the coin-golden color of a walnut tree, the purple of an ash, the shouting sun-bright yellow of an aspen, the bright-blood of a sugar maple, and rich red and brown of oak. And over and above it all that bittersweet feel of autumn, the glory of the dying year when work was done and a quiet season of rest had been proclaimed.

The sense of it, the feel of it, almost the surety, yet not quite the surety of it, had all been there. He had felt at ease with it, had entered wholeheartedly into it. He had tramped the hills and gone along the winding brook, he had stood and stared across the brown and gold of an autumn-haunted marsh, he had heard the shouting of the gold and red and yellow of the painted trees against the sky and he had felt a strange abiding peace within him. The peace that comes at the long end of summer, the peace and quiet before the chill winter of the soul comes howling down. The little time of respite, the time for resting and for thought, the time for binding up the ancient wounds and forgetting them and all the vagaries of life that had inflicted them.

Later, thinking on it, he told himself that this had been Heaven, his own personal Heaven. Not the high shining towers, the great broad golden staircase, the winding of celestial trumpets that was Mary's Heaven—this was the real Heaven, this, the quiet autumn afternoon that fell upon the land after the blazing summer sun and the long and dusty roads.

He went away, reflective, after only a courteous exchange with the blithe custodian. Walking back to his suite, he had tried to catch it all again, to see it and experience it all again, only to become aware of its insubstantiality, the ephemeral quality of this autumn land, somewhere deep in space.

He told Jill that evening, "It was as if I'd gone back to my

home planet, the days of boyhood and early manhood before I left
to enter medical school. My home was an Earthlike planet, an as-
tonishingly Earthlike planet. I can't really judge, for I've never
been on Earth, but I was told that my home planet was Earthlike.
British settled. It was called Paddington—a planet named for a
town, if 'ton' means 'town' and I think it does. The inhabitants
never saw anything wrong with that. The British have no sense of
humor. I judge we were very English, very British, whichever is
the right term. There was a lot of talk of Old Earth, Old Earth
being England, although that was strange, for in my later reading I
became convinced the planet tallied more with North America. In
my boyhood I was obsessed with England, or with the legend of
England. I read a lot of English history. The library in our town
had a large section—"

"I've been meaning to tell you," said Jill, "but it always slips
my mind. Vatican library has a lot of Old Earth books—I mean
books brought from Old Earth. Books, not tapes. Pages between
covers. Anyone is welcome to come in and browse. I think, too,
you can manage a loan if you find something that you want."

"One of these days," said Tennyson, "I'll come in and browse.
I was telling you about Paddington. The land, I was told, was almost a duplicate of Old Earth. The people there were always saying how lucky they had been to find it. There are livable planets,
sure, but not many of them that are like Old Earth. Many of the
trees and plants were much like those found on Earth—but, mind
you, the kind that were found in North America rather than in
England, although North America and England do have some
trees and plants in common. And the seasons were the same as
they were on Earth. In my hometown, we had a glorious autumn—
Indian-summer days, trees aflame with color, the distances smoky
with an autumn haze. I'd almost forgotten it, but today I saw it all
again. Or I think I saw it. I smelled the autumn and heard it and
walked in it again. . . ."

"Jason, you're all upset. Try to forget. Let's go to bed."

He questioned Ecuyer. "This world of equations," he said. "It
makes no sense. Was your Listener able to go back again?"

"Several times," said Ecuyer.

"And?"

"It still made no sense. No sense at all."

"Does this sort of thing happen often?"

"Well, not places with equations. You seldom repeat a specific sighting. In a universe where anything, anything at all, statistically will happen at least once—where everything possible will happen at least once—there's not much chance of repetition. It does happen, but not often. But, yes, these kinds of things do happen, the inexplicable situations that have neither head nor tail to them."

"Then what's the use? What profit is there in it?"

"Perhaps profit for Vatican."

"You mean you just hand this stuff over to Vatican?"

"Certainly. That's why we do it. For Vatican. They have the right, the chance, to review everything. They review it and evaluate it and then send back the cubes to us for storage. Sometimes they may follow up the leads, sometimes not. They have ways of doing things."

"But to follow up on this equation place, someone would have to go there. Actually go there physically, in person. Viewing it from one's own viewpoint, not seeing it through the eyes of an inhabitant. I'm convinced of that."

"Well, there are times that Vatican can go to places that we find."

"You mean actually go there? Travel to those places?"

"That is correct," said Ecuyer. "I thought you understood that."

"No, I hadn't," said Tennyson. "No one ever told me. So it's not always just a matter of peeking through a keyhole?"

"Sometimes it's more than that. Sometimes not. Sometimes we have to be content with our keyhole peek."

"Then why doesn't Vatican go out and pin down the Heaven sighting? I would think—"

"Perhaps they can't," said Ecuyer. "They may not know where it is. They may have no coordinates."

"I don't understand. Can the Listeners at times pick up coordinates?"

"No, they can't. But there are other ways to go about it. Vatican people, in things like this, can be very tricky. One of the simpler ways is to pick up star patterns."

"There are no star patterns in the Heaven cube? I suppose there wouldn't be if it were really Heaven. Heaven probably would have nothing to do with either time or space. But if Vatican did locate it, what would they do? Send someone out to Heaven?"

"I really do not know," said Ecuyer. "I cannot speak for Vatican."

It was a dead end, Tennyson thought. The Heaven sighting was so tied with gut philosophy, the touchiness of theology, the awesome wonder of it that everyone in authority would be scared to death. He remembered what Jill had said about the deep rift of opinion it had brought about among the robots of Vatican.

"Heaven," said Tennyson, "would presume an afterlife, a life after death. Can you tell me—have the Listeners found any clues that would point to such an afterlife, even the outside possibility of an afterlife?"

"Jason, I don't know. I honestly can't be sure. There's no way—"

"What do you mean, you can't be sure?"

"Look, there are so many kinds of life. The universe, it seems, seethes with life, both biological and nonbiological, and the nonbiological, in turn, may be divided into several classifications. We can't be sure."

"Well, yes, of course," said Tennyson. "There are the robots."

"Dammit, I'm not talking about the robots. They are nonbiological, certainly. Manufactured nonbiological. But there is natural life, or what seems to be life, that is nonbiological as well. There is a cloud of dust and gas out in the Orion region, or what on Earth would be designated as the Orion region. A small speck of dust and gas. From here even the largest telescope would fail to pick it up. A welter of magnetic fields, high gas density, massive ionization, heavy drifts of cosmic dust. And there's something alive in there. Perhaps the gas and dust itself. Or maybe something else. But whatever it is, it's alive. You can feel the pulse of life, the rhythm of living—and it talks. Maybe *talks* is not the right word. Communicates would be the better term. It can be heard, or sensed, but it can't be understoood. There is no way to know what it is saying. The life forms within it may be talking back and forth or all of them may be talking to themselves. . . ."

"But what has this got to do with afterlife?"

"Did I say it had something to do with afterlife?"

Tennyson said, "No, I guess you didn't."

At times, Tennyson prowled the countryside, following faint trails, trudging along narrow, green valleys, climbing steep hill-sides, with lunch and a bottle of wine in his knapsack, a canteen over his shoulder. Always the mountains were in view, looming over him, blue and purple, majestic and always fascinating, with shadows drifting along their spurs, the sunlight glinting off the icy peaks. He spent long hours sitting atop the rugged hills, staring at the mountains, never seeing quite enough of them, the mystery and the wonder of them persisting no matter how long he might look at them.

Then, turning back toward Vatican, he'd finally find one of the few roads, little more than a broader trail, to lead him home. He'd trudge along it happily, his feet raising little puffs of dust, the warmth of the sun upon his back, the peace of the mountain on his mind. And a few days later, he would go out again, perhaps in a different direction this time, to prowl up and down the land while the mountains watched.

One afternoon, heading back toward Vatican along one of the narrow roads, he heard something approaching from behind. Looking back, he saw a beat-up surface vehicle, with a man sitting at its wheel. Tennyson was surprised, for this was the first time on any of his hikes that he had seen another person, let alone a car. He stepped well out of the road to give it room to pass, but it did not pass. When the car drew up to him, it stopped and the man said to him, "Are you so dedicated to your walking that you would refuse a lift?"

The man had an honest, open face, with searching blue eyes.

"I would appreciate a lift," said Tennyson.

"I take it," said the man as Tennyson climbed into the seat beside him, "that you are the new doctor over at Vatican. Tennyson, isn't it?"

"That's right. And you?"

"I'm Decker. Thomas Decker, at your service, sir."

"I've been roaming around out here off and on for several weeks," said Tennyson. "You're the first man I've seen in all my rambles."

"And the only one you are likely to see," said Decker. "All the rest of them stick close to home and fireside. They have no curiosity or appreciation for what lies all about them. They look at the mountains every day of their lives and all they see are mountains. You see more than mountains, don't you, Doctor?"

"A great deal more," said Tennyson.

"How about seeing even more? I'm in a mood, if you wish, to conduct a guided tour."

"You have a customer," said Tennyson.

"Well, then, the battery's up," said Decker, "and we have hours of operation. First, let us see the farms."

"The farms?"

"Yes, of course, the farms. You eat bread, do you not? And meat and milk and eggs?"

"Certainly I do."

"Where, then, did you think it all came from, other than from farms?"

"I suppose I never thought about it."

"These robots think of everything," said Decker. "They must feed their humans, so some of them are farmers. Electricity is needed, so they built a dam and set up a power facility. Some solar power as well, but they've not pushed the solar power. However, they have the capability and can expand it any time it's needed. They also have a sawmill, but it runs only part-time, for now there's no great demand for lumber. Some centuries ago, when the building was going on, there was a great need of it." He chuckled. "You can't beat the robots for efficiency. They use a primitive steam engine to operate the sawmill, using slabs and sawdust produced by the mill to drive the engine."

"They're a self-sufficient community," said Tennyson.

"They have to be. Out here they are on their own. There's no such thing as imports, except for small items they may need from time to time. The small items *Wayfarer* hauls in for them. The freight costs a pretty penny. The robots keep pace with the economy's demand by keeping the demands small and simple. If you don't need much, you don't need much cash, and the robots have very little cash. What they gouge out of the pilgrims just about keeps them going. They have a small woods crew that does nothing all the year around but cut logs for the fireplaces that are used by everyone. A steady demand, a steady supply, perfectly balanced. They have it figured out. They have a grist mill to grind their wheat and other grains into flour. Again, a steady demand and a steady supply, with a reserve stashed away against a bad year, although so far, I understand, there has never been a bad year. All primitive as hell, but it works and that's what counts."

They now were driving along a somewhat better road than the one from which Decker had picked up Tennyson, cut into level farming country. Acres of ripening grain stood blowing in the wind.

"Soon they'll be harvesting," said Decker. "Even Vatican people will drop all their sanctified duties and go out into the fields to bring in the crops. Cardinals with their red and purple robes tucked up to guard them against being stained by dust. Brown-clad monks bobbing along, being useful for the only time in the year. They use cradles to cut and gather the grain, swarming about the field like so many ants. They've rigged up a threshing machine that works rather well, and it runs for weeks to get all the threshing done. Another steam engine to operate the thresher. For it they haul in and stack cords of wood well ahead of time."

Interspersed among the grain fields were pastures, lush with grass, roamed by cattle, horses, sheep and goats. Hog pens held thousands of grunting porkers. Hordes of chickens roamed a fenced-in hilly section.

Decker jerked his thumb toward the horizon. "Fields of maize," he said, "to fatten up the hogs. And that small field ahead of us is buckwheat. I told you; they think of everything. Back in the hills, they have an apiary with hundreds of stands of bees. Somewhere around here—yes, we're coming up on it now. See it? Cane. Sorghum cane. Sorghum for the buckwheat cakes you'll be eating later on."

"It takes me back to my home planet," Tennyson said. "Ours was a farming planet. Solidly based on agriculture."

They came on orchards—apples, pears, apricots, peaches and other kinds of fruit.

"A cherry orchard," said Decker, jerking his thumb again. "Cherries ripen early. All the crop's been picked."

"You're right," said Tennyson. "The robots have thought of everything."

Decker grunted. "They've had a long time to think of it. Almost a thousand years—perhaps a little longer, I don't know. Wouldn't have needed any of this if they hadn't needed humans. But they needed humans. Your robot is a silly sort of chap; he has to have his humans. I don't know when the first humans were brought in. My impression is a century, or less, after the robots got their start."

The sun was close to setting when they turned back.

"I'm glad you showed it to me," said Tennyson. "I had no idea."

"How you getting along at Vatican?" asked Decker.

"Well enough. I've scarcely gotten settled in. What I see I like."

"What do you know about this Heaven flap?"

"I hear something occasionally. I'm not sure I know what it's all about. There is a woman who thinks that she found Heaven."

"Did she?"

"I honestly don't know. I'm inclined to doubt it."

Decker wagged his head. "There are always flaps of one kind or another. If not Heaven, then it's something else."

Out of the corner of his eye, Tennyson caught the glitter over Decker's right shoulder. He looked away and then looked back and the glitter was still there, like a haze of suspended diamond dust. He put up a fist to rub his eyes, and as he did, the glitter went away.

"Get something in your eye?" asked Decker.

"It's nothing," said Tennyson. "Just some dust. I have it out."

"Want me to take a look at it? Make sure?"

"No, thank you. It's all right."

Decker headed the car up a winding road that climbed the ridge on which Vatican crouched against the backdrop of the mountains, now purple with approaching dusk.

"You want to be dropped at the clinic?" Decker asked. "Or is there some other place that would be more convenient?"

"The clinic's fine," said Tennyson. "And I must thank you for the tour. It's been enjoyable."

"I go rock hunting every now and then," said Decker. "Out for several days. Back into the mountains. If you could find that kind of time, how about joining me on one of the trips?"

"I'd like to do that, Decker."

"Call me Tom."

"All right, Tom. I'm Jason. There might be periods when I could go. I'd have to pick my time."

"The trip could be adjusted to your schedule. I think that you might like it."

"I'm sure I would."

"Then let's plan on it."

When Decker dropped him at the clinic, Tennyson stood on the roadway, watching the clattering vehicle until it went around a bend in the road and out of sight. Then he turned about and headed for his suite, but on an impulse turned aside and went down the path that led to the garden he had found that first day he'd come to Vatican.

The garden lay in a pool of twilight, a place of softness and strange sweet-flower perfume. It was, he thought, a dimly lighted stage posed against the massive, deep-purple curtains of the towering mountains. And as he looked, he knew instinctively why he had come—here was the place to say farewell to a perfect day. Except that until this moment, he had not realized it had been a perfect day. Had it been Decker, he wondered, who had made it a perfect day, but knowing as he thought of it that it had not been Decker. The man was a new friend, someone who was not tied in with Vatican and, for that reason, somewhat different from the others he had met here. But there had been something else, he knew, although he could not put a finger on it.

A robot came trundling down the brick-paved walk.

"Good evening, sir," it said.

"A good evening to you," said Tennyson, then, "I'm sorry. I failed to recognize you immediately. You are the gardener. How are the roses doing?"

"They are doing well," said the gardener. "Most of them, for the moment, past the best of their bloom, although there'll be more later. I have a group of yellows that are budding now. In a few days, they'll be at their best. You must come by and see them."

"That I shall do," said Tennyson.

The robot made as if to pass him, heading for the gate, then turned to face him squarely.

"Sir, have you heard the news?"

"I'm not sure," said Tennyson. "Of what news are you speaking?"

"Why, sir, the move that is being made to canonize the Listener Mary."

"To canonize—you mean to proclaim her a saint?"

"Exactly, sir. It is the feeling of Vatican—"

"But people are not canonized until they're dead—ordinarily a long time after they are dead."

"I don't know about that, sir. But as one who has found Heaven . . ."

"Now, wait a minute, gardener. Where did you hear this? Who is talking about it?"

"Why, all the Vatican commonality. She would be our first saint. Everyone is convinced it would be an excellent idea. Our first saint; we've never had another, and it is said it is time we had one and—"

"How about the cardinals? What does His Holiness think?"

"Sir, I do not know. I'm not privy to such things. But the talk is everywhere. I thought you'd like to know."

He raised a hand, which still grasped a pair of shears, in solemn salute and went on down the walk, passing through the gate, leaving Tennyson standing alone upon the walk.

A vagrant wind, blowing off the face of the mountains, brought a wave of perfumed lushness.

"For the love of God," said Tennyson, speaking to himself, aloud, "there'll be no living with her now."

Chapter Seventeen

LATE AT NIGHT A SINGLE LIGHT BURNED ABOVE JILL'S DESK. Her two aides were gone—one to perform certain pious duties, the other to fetch her sandwiches and a glass of milk.

She pushed away the pile of notes she had been working on and leaned back in the chair, stretching her arms above her head. Then she folded them across her breasts, hugging herself tightly.

Far places, she thought—strange, impossible places outside of time and space. Where could that be? What lay outside the boundaries of space and the restrictions of time? Once again she drove her mind to understand, but there was no way, nothing on which to base such an understanding, and the records gave no hint. But they did make clear—these records—that, at times, the robots ventured out into that impossible area that lay beyond the space-time continuum, traveling in ships of their own devising. Ships driven by the energy of thought, the power of mind? She could not be certain, but that was the hint that lay within the records.

Good Lord, she thought, what had she gotten herself into? Why did I ever allow myself to be so sucked in? But one thing was clear—now that she had gone this far, she should not quit, she could not turn about and walk away. She could not shut the book and leave it. She simply had to know, and there was so much to learn. Jason had warned her what could happen and she should have listened to him. You'll get sucked in, he'd said; you won't be able to pull yourself away.

The aides had protested at her methods of research, her skipping through the records. This was not the way to do it, one of them had told her—you start at the beginning and go on to the end; you do not skip about. But she had to skip about, she'd told him; she must get an overview, she has to catch the pattern. Otherwise, how could she relate what has happened with what is about to happen? Once we know that, she had told him, we'll go back to the beginning and proceed from there.

The otherwhere, she thought, and the otherwhen. But that was not right. These places were neither where nor when. They were in some far distant country of the mind, but not her mind—the mind or minds of something else, of someone else. Could that far distant world, she thought, be in the esoteric dimensions of magnetic flux where lived those entities that were not biological, although they held not only life, but intelligences for which there were no explanations? No, it could not be, she thought, for outrageous as it all might be, these entities still existed within the common and familiar areas of both time and space, although perhaps one twisted beyond all human recognition. Within time and space, she told herself, the physical laws of the known universe still must operate—there must be energy and matter, cause and effect, being and not being—although within those parameters, there must be room for a consciousness and an intellect and a thinking that could quite conceivably be in advance of biological thinking. That she could buy—it came hard to say, yes, that could be so, but it still was acceptable, it still lay within the bounds of human reason.

What she could not accept was that implied area beyond the borders of either space or time, that implication of a never-never land that could exist with no need of either time or space and, presumably, without the steadying hand of the physical laws that went with them. It was one, she thought, with the energy of thought, with the thrust of mind—and "energy" might not be the right word, for energy was a familiar component and as such could be ruled out of this other place. It all was one with the robots using the power of thought to operate the ships with which they ventured not only across the known universe, but into the areas beyond.

As far as the rest of the history of Vatican was concerned, it was straightforward narrative—the initial landing of the ships from Earth, the early pioneering days, the construction of Vatican it-

self, the construction, continuing even to this day, of an electronic
pope, the bringing in of humans, the setting up of the Search Program, the development of new capabilities in the newly manufactured robots.

The entire project had been well thought out by the robots from
the very start. Before they had ever left the Earth, they had known
what they were looking for—an out-of-the-way planet where casual visitors were not likely to blunder in on them, where they
would be left alone to carry out their work. But they must find, as
well, a planet where it would be possible for humans to live. The
robots could have lived on almost any sort of planet, and had it
not been for the human factor, the search for their base of operations would have been much simpler. But never for a moment had
the robots considered embarking on their project without human
help. Whether at that time they had evolved the principle of the
Search Program, which was based solidly on humans, was not
completely apparent from the record, although Jill was inclined to
believe that they had. The old bond with humanity still existed;
the ancient partnership still held.

Just how many ships the robots had used to transport themselves and their equipment to End of Nothing, or how they had
originally acquired the ships, also was not written out in black and
white. The best estimate she could arrive at was that there had
been no more than three. Several trips to and from Earth had
been made, the later trips to bring in materials that could not be
accommodated on the first flight, with the last trip bringing in the
humans whose descendants still lived upon the planet. Eventually
the ships had been broken up for the metal and other materials
that could be salvaged. Once again, it was not clear when this had
been done, but it made sense, Jill told herself, that it had not been
until the thought-driven ships (if they really were thought-driven)
had been built.

The robots had done much more, at first glance, than it would
have seemed could have been done in a thousand years—that is,
until one considered that robots need take off no time to rest or
sleep. They could work around the clock, if need be, for weeks
and months, perhaps for years, on end. They were never tired or

sleepy. They were never ill. They felt no need of recreation or of entertainment, and she found herself wondering, bemusedly, what a robot might do for recreation or for entertainment. They did not have to take time out to eat; they never paused for breath.

And the remodeling of robots, the designing of new robots (a new generation or generations of robots) was simpler, too, when one thought about it, than would be the mutation and evolution of biologic forms. The genetic shufflings that must take place to bring about appreciable modifications in biological systems would require an enormous amount of time. Natural biological evolution required the death and birth of many generations to pass the gene mutations on and to allow the long, slow process of adaptation. But in a robot society all that would be required to bring about desired changes and new capability would be the redesigning of new forms and mechanisms and the engineering that it would take to translate the blueprints into being.

Behind her a footstep sounded, and at the sound she turned around. It was Asa with her sandwiches and the glass of milk.

He put them down, carefully, in front of her and stepped softly to one side.

"And now," he asked, "what would you have me do?"

"For the moment," she said, "nothing at all. Take a rest. Sit down and talk with me."

"I need no rest," he said. "I have no need to sit."

"It's not against your rules, is it?"

"Well, not against the rules."

"Even cardinals sit," she said. "When His Eminence, Theodosius, comes to visit me, he often sits and talks."

"If you wish," said Asa, perching himself upon the stool the cardinal used on his visits.

She picked up a sandwich and took a bite. It was roast beef and tasted good. She picked up the glass of milk.

"Asa," she said, "tell me about yourself. Were you forged on Earth?"

"Not on Earth, milady."

"Then here?"

"Yes, here. I am a third-generation robot."

"I see. And how many generations might there be?"

"There is no way of telling. It depends on how you count. Some say five, others seven."

"That many?"

"That many. There may be even more."

"Have you ever been to some of the places the Listeners have found?"

"Twice, milady. I have made two trips."

"Ever outside of time and space?"

"On one of them," he said. "One of the two, I was outside of time and space."

"Could you tell me what it was like?"

"No, I cannot. There is no way to tell. It's another place. Not like here at all."

Chapter Eighteen

ONCE AGAIN TENNYSON WAS IN THE PLACE OF EQUATIONS and of diagrams, and this time some of them could be vaguely recognized.

One, he was convinced, was Ecuyer. The diagram somehow had the look of Ecuyer and the equations that were associated with it, in some manner which he could not comprehend, spelled out Ecuyer. Maybe the color, he thought, for Ecuyer's diagram and equations were gray and rose, but why gray and rose should be Ecuyer, he could not imagine. Certainly, he thought, color should have little to do with it—rather it would be the shape of the diagrams and the components of the equations that should determine what they were. Tennyson fought mentally, sweating and gasping, clawing at his intellect, to factor out the equations, but that was impossible because he did not know the conventions and the signs.

Deliberately he backed away from Ecuyer, or what he thought must be Ecuyer. Deliberately, but fighting every step that backed him away. View it all from another angle, he told himself, achieve a perspective from a distance, look away for a while to wipe it from your mind in the hope that when looking back at it again something—either something in the diagram or the equations—will jump out at you.

For he must know, he told himself; it was vital that he know if this was Ecuyer.

The place was hazy and there was a quaver in the air. If only something, just one thing, would be still, he thought—if he could get one good look at something. The trouble was that while it never actually changed, it always seemed on the verge of change. That was it—uncertainty.

Having looked away, he now looked back, swiveling his head quickly in the hope he might catch the diagrams and equations by surprise.

Ecuyer was gone. The gray and rose were gone. In its place was a purple and gold; another diagram and a new set of equations.

Seeing them, he froze. His terror rose to choke him and he screamed.

"Mary! Mary! Mary!"

He struggled to climb out of wherever he was, although there was nothing he could climb and someone had seized him to prevent his climbing.

"No! No! No!" he shouted, and someone was whispering to him.

"There, there, there," the someone said, and soft hands were upon him and when he opened his eyes he found himself in darkness—which was strange, for he had not known his eyes were closed.

The voice said, "No, Hubert, it's all right. He was having a nightmare."

"Jill?" Tennyson asked weakly.

"Yes. It's all right now. I'm with you. You're back again."

He was in bed, he saw, with Jill bending over him and Hubert hovering in the lighted doorway.

"I worked late," said Jill, "and I thought you might be asleep, but I knocked anyway and Hubert let me in. I wanted to see you. I had so much to tell you."

"I was in the equation world," he told her. "I was dreaming it again. Ecuyer was there and he was gray and rose and when I looked away for a moment . . ."

"You were screaming at Mary. Was Mary there? The Heaven Mary?"

He nodded, struggling to sit up, still befuddled with the dream. "She was purple and gold," he said. "And it was horrible."

Chapter Nineteen

IT WAS THE FIRST TIME HE'D RETURNED SINCE HE'D FINALLY walked away from the boat ten—no, it must have been twelve—years ago, and it still was there, where he'd remembered it, lying in a small, grassy valley between two ranges of steep hills. Brambles had grown up around it, but not so thickly or so high as to obscure it. Apparently nothing else had found it, for it lay exactly as he remembered it, and he wondered how he could have found it so easily, walking straight through the tangled foothills to the place he knew it was.

—Whisperer, are you here? he asked.

Knowing that he was, but he had to ask.

—Yes, Decker. Of course I'm here. So is the Old One of the Woods. He's been following us for days.

—What does he want?

—He's curious, is all. You puzzle him. All humans puzzle him. And you puzzle me. Why back to your beginning?

—It's not my beginning, said Decker. I began very far from here.

—Your beginning on this planet, then.

—Yes, my beginning on this planet. You know, of course, what lies down there.

—You told me. A lifeboat. A vehicle that carried you safely through space until it found a place where you could survive. But you never told me more. Decker, you are a close-mouthed man. Not even your best friend. . . .

—Is that what you are?

—If I am not, name one who is.

—I would suppose you're right, said Decker. When the boat aroused me from suspended animation, I had no idea where I was. At first, it seemed an absolutely primitive planet, untouched by any sort of intellectual culture. I explored. I kept no track of time, but I must have roamed for weeks, maybe for months, and there was nothing but the wilderness, although in many ways a pleasant wilderness. Then, after days of wandering away from the boat, going farther than I had ever gone before, I stood on a mountain spur and saw Vatican, shining in the distance. I knew then I was not alone, that there were intelligent beings here, although at the time I had no idea what they were.

—But you did not go rushing in to announce yourself.

—Whisperer, how could you know that?

—Because I know you, Decker. I know you for the kind of man you are, reserved, stand-offish, pathologically disinclined to show any kind of weakness. Always on your own. A loner.

—You know me far too well, said Decker. You are a sneaky bastard.

—So are you, said Whisperer. But with dignity. Always with dignity. Why is dignity so important to you, Decker?

—Damned if I know, said Decker. I suppose it always has been.

The Old One of the Woods was still on the slope above them, hunkered in a patch of woods at the edge of a boulder field, staring down upon them. Decker sensed him now, sensed him very strongly. There were long stretches of time when he had no sense of the lurker, but now and then he did. He had become aware of this one well before Whisperer had announced they were being followed.

—The Old One's still up there, he said.

—Pay no attention, Whisperer told him. It only wants to watch us. It thinks we do not know it is here. It is getting satisfaction out of watching us and us not knowing that it is.

Standing on the slope, Decker went back in time to that day when he first had sighted End of Nothing and Vatican, realizing when he saw them that he was not marooned on a desert planet.

He had come back to the boat and had put together a load of necessities—tools and cooking utensils and other simple things— then had headed out for End of Nothing, pausing only for a quick look back at the boat where it lay in the grassy valley.

Arriving at End of Nothing, he had selected a site at the edge of the settlement and, without leave or hindrance, had built the cabin. He had cut down trees of a proper size, sawed them to a proper length, notched them and rolled them into place. He had quarried stone to construct the hearth and fireplace, had gone down into the small business section of the town to buy windows. He had chinked the logs with moss and clay. He had cut a supply of firewood and stacked it. He had spaded and worked up a garden patch, then gone once again into town to buy seeds to put into the soil. He had lived mostly off the land, hunting for the pot, seeking out wild plants as greens and vegetables, fishing a nearby stream until his garden had started to produce food.

There had been visitors, at first a lot of visitors, all of them with questions trembling on their lips. Among them had been a little brown-robed monk from Vatican, as pleasant a robot as he had ever met, although to Decker it had seemed that he might have been more than a simple monk. His visitors had provided him with a deal of useful information about End of Nothing and an even greater supply of advice. The information he had gratefully stored away, the advice he had generally ignored. And then, having given him the information and advice, his visitors (all of them) had begun their gentle prying into his history and affairs. He did not forthrightly refuse them what they sought; he simply evaded the questioning as gently as he could and they had gone away perplexed. A few of them had come back to visit him again but, getting no more on the second trip—or the third or fourth— than they had gotten on the first, they had not come again, and finally everyone left him very much alone.

Which, he told himself, was fine with him. It was the way he liked it. He felt regret at times that he had dealt with his neighbors as he had, but each time he thought this he became more and more convinced it was the only way he could have handled the situation. Better to be a man of mystery than what he might have been had he told his story. As it stood, he had given them something they could speculate upon, perhaps to their vast enjoyment, all these years.

Why back to your beginning? Whisperer had asked him. Why back to your beginning on this planet? And why, indeed? he now asked himself. A hunch, he thought. A hunch that more than likely had very little basis. And even had it a solid basis, what would he, or could he, do about it? Decker, he told himself, you're crazy—downright stark, staring crazy.

—Decker, that Tennyson I liked, Whisperer said. I liked him quite a lot.

—Yes, he was likable.

—He saw me, said Whisperer. I am sure he saw me. There are very few who see me. It takes an ability to see me.

—He saw you? How can you be sure? Why didn't you mention it before?

—I did not mention it because until now I could not be sure. But having thought of it for days, I now am sure. He saw me and he could not believe it, he could not believe what he had seen. He rubbed his eyes, thinking there was something wrong with them. You remember, don't you? You asked if he had something in his eye and he said only dust. Then you asked again. You asked if you could wipe out his eye, but he said he was all right.

—Yes, now that you mention it, I do recall the incident.

—And I, said Whisperer, I, as well, saw something, but only fleetingly. I don't know what I saw.

—You did not speak to him? You did not try to speak?

—No, I did not try to speak. But there is a strangeness in the man. I am sure of that.

—Oh, well, said Decker, we'll see him again, I'm sure. You may have another chance to plumb the strangeness you think you saw in him.

The Old One of the Woods had moved. He no longer was hiding in the clumps of trees below the boulder field. Decker no longer had any sense of him.

—Let's go down, he said to Whisperer, and see how the boat is getting on.

Chapter Twenty

JILL HAD LEFT JUST HALF AN HOUR BEFORE, RETURNING TO the library, when Ecuyer showed up. Tennyson was dawdling over a cup of coffee. Hubert, after letting Ecuyer in, went back to the kitchen and started making a clatter. Hubert didn't like people who lingered at the table.

"You're up and about early," Tennyson said to Ecuyer. "Sit down and have a cup of coffee."

"I believe I shall," said Ecuyer, "although neither of us has too long."

"I have all the time there is," said Tennyson. "I'm not due at the clinic until—"

"This morning you haven't all the time there is. The two of us have been summoned."

Tennyson stared at him, saying nothing.

"Summoned," explained Ecuyer, "to an audience with His Holiness."

"Oh?"

"Is that all you can say?"

"What did you expect me to do? Fall over dead? Be seized by a fit of trembling? Sink down upon my knees?"

"You could at least show some respect. It is a signal honor to be summoned by the Pope."

"Sorry," said Tennyson. "I would suppose it is. What is it all about?"

"I'm not sure. Perhaps the Heaven incident. Theodosius and Roberts will be with us."

"The cardinals?"

"Yes, the cardinals."

"I can understand why the Pope might want to see you. If it's about the Heaven incident, you're in it to your knees. But I—"

"Mary is your patient. He might have some medical questions about her. I'm not even sure it's about Heaven. It might be just to meet you. Ordinarily a new Vatican staff member will have an audience with the Pope. Certainly he would want to meet the new Vatican physician. I suspect he would have arranged it long before this, but it has been a busy time."

"I have an impression it is always busy here," said Tennyson.

"Well, yes. But sometimes more than others."

They sat drinking their coffee. Hubert kept up his clatter in the kitchen.

"Hubert," said Ecuyer, raising his voice.

"Yes, sir?"

"Cut it out," said Ecuyer. "We have a right to sit here and drink our coffee."

"Why, certainly," said Hubert. The clatter subsided.

"He's spoiled," said Ecuyer. "I spoiled him myself. I don't know what to do with him."

"There's something I have been meaning to ask you."

"Go ahead. Don't take too long."

"I saw this cube—the one with all the equations and diagrams. I think I told you. Have you seen it too?"

"Well, yes, I guess I did. A long time ago. It was taped some years ago. Rather a long time ago."

"You told me the Listener went back several times and could make nothing of it."

"That's right," said Ecuyer. "Are you hung up on it?"

Tennyson nodded. "There is something there. Something that I miss. Something that it seems to me I almost have and then it eludes me. I have a feeling that if I could stretch my mind just a little farther, I could come to grips with it."

"Any idea of what it might be?"

"Not at all. That's the hell of it. I know there is something there, but no idea what it is. I find myself imagining all sorts of things, but I know it's none of them."

"Don't worry about it," counseled Ecuyer. "I can show you things even worse. I had expected you to do more digging into the files than you have done. You are welcome, you know. Anytime you wish, anything you wish."

"There have been other things to do," said Tennyson. "And,

truth to tell, I might be even a little bit afraid of what I'd find. The equation world bothers me. The autumn world still haunts me. I'd like to go back and see the autumn world again, but something keeps me from it."

Ecuyer finished off his coffee.

"Come," he said. "Let us see the Pope."

Chapter Twenty-one

THE POPE WAS A CROSS-HATCHED HUMAN FACE—OR THE SUG-gestion of a face, for to see it clearly required close attention and some imagination—imposed upon a dull metallic plate set into a bare stone wall. It reminded Tennyson of the photo of a sampler from the nineteenth century that he had seen in a book he'd found in a library years ago, and also, in a haphazard sort of way, of the children's game of tic-tac-toe. The face was not entirely and fully apparent at any time, although every now and then he managed to get a fairly comprehensive glimpse of it. No decorative effort was made to soften the bleak starkness of the face, nothing to impart to it any hint of power or glory. And perhaps, he thought, this studied attempt to achieve a dismal plainness made the face all the more impressive.

The small audience room in which they sat was plain as well, with no effort made to conceal the fact that it had been carved out of the granite mass that was the core of the ridge upon which Vatican buildings perched. Just four blank stone walls with a plate set in the center of one of the walls to display the Pope. To reach the room, they had descended a number of stairs, all carved from the solid rock, with galleries running off at the landings of each staircase, burrowing their way deep into the granite. There was no doubt that this computer-Pope was buried deep into the very structure of the hill.

More than likely, Tennyson told himself, there were many other Pope-faces in other audience rooms, some of them undoubtedly

much larger than this one, for there must be times when the entire
Vatican personnel would be gathered into one group for an audience with the Pope. A multi-Pope, he thought, a mechanism so
large and so all-pervading that it could be many places at any
given time, attending to any number of tasks at the self-same time.

The Pope spoke now and his voice was flat, while at the same
time managing to be smooth and cold. An utterly unhuman voice,
and likewise unrobotlike, for while robots did not speak with
human intonation, there yet were times when they imparted some
human warmth to the words they spoke. But this voice was empty
of all emotion; it held no warmth. It was neither a human voice
nor a robot voice, nor yet the harsh voice that one might imagine
a machine to have. It pronounced its words in precise clarity and
the thought behind the words was ruthless and relentless—machine
thought, computer thought, naked electronic thought.

"Dr. Tennyson," said the Pope, "tell me of the Listener, Mary.
What is her mental condition?"

"I can be of little help, Your Holiness," said Tennyson. "I can
tell you of her physical condition; I would not know about her
mind. I am not trained in mental illness."

"Then what good are you?" asked the Pope. "If we had a robot
physician, which has been discussed at times, it would know about
her mind."

"Then," Tennyson said shortly, "build your robot physician."

"You are aware, Holiness," said Cardinal Theodosius, "that the
humans of Vatican would have no trust in a robotic doctor. As
you say, we have discussed it many times. . . ."

"All of this is beside the point," said His Holiness. "You are
using a chance remark of mine to evade my question. How about
you, Ecuyer? Have you some insight into her mind?"

"No insight into her mind," said Ecuyer. "Neither am I trained,
Holiness, to evaluate a human mind. All that I would be able to
do is describe her behavior. Up till now, all the time that she has
been with us, she has been gentle and devoted to her job, but since
she has found Heaven, or thinks she has found Heaven, her personality has changed. She has assumed a haughty importance that
makes it difficult for us to work with her."

"Does that not seem strange to you?" asked the Pope. "To me, it would appear inconsistent. If she really had found Heaven, as she claims, would you not think she might become more devout and humble? The haughtiness you talk of does not appear to be the behavior of one who has acquired evidence of Heaven. As a good Christian, you should know."

"Your Holiness, I am not a good Christian," said Ecuyer. "I'm not sure I'm a good anything at all. Holiness, certainly you know that I am not a Christian. You are baiting me."

"And the Listener, Mary? Is she a Christian?"

"Holiness, I am sure she is. You must understand, however, that Search is not concerned with theological matters."

"That is strange," said the Pope. "I would have thought you would be."

"Holiness, you are being deliberately difficult today," Cardinal Theodosius chimed in, "and your attitude is not worthy of you. You underestimate our friend of the Search Program. Through the years he has performed outstanding services for us."

"Eminence," said Cardinal Roberts, speaking stiffly, "I think you presume too far."

"I think not," Theodosius said stubbornly. "In a deliberative council, such as this, due respect must be paid to every viewpoint raised. The issues must be solemnly and honestly discussed."

"None of you as yet," said the Pope, "has tried to discuss the issue. The finding of Heaven, or the presumed finding of Heaven, is getting out of hand. Are any of you aware that there is a growing sentiment to canonize the Listener Mary, to make a saint of her? We have never created a saint. We have canonized no one. And if we were about to do so, certainly we would want to wait until she was decently dead."

"Your Holiness," said Roberts, "all of us are aware of what you speak. With you, all of us realize the seriousness of it, the danger it could pose. The whole idea is impossible, of course, but at this point in the situation, we cannot step in and oppose it openly. We cannot lose sight of the fact that many—perhaps the most—of the minor members of Vatican, even after all these years, still are caught up in the simplicity and the promise of the Christian faith."

"What promise, Cardinal?" asked the Pope. "Surely no robot, no matter how devout, can ever hope to be translated into Heaven. Nor, if he properly takes care of himself, would ever need to be."

"The fault, perhaps, lies in ourselves," said Theodosius. "Many of our people in the more humble posts—the farm workers, the gardeners, the woodsmen, the laboring brothers, even many of the monks—are very simple souls. With them the basic idea of Christianity, although somewhat faded, nevertheless is a rather powerful force. They don't understand Christianity, of course, but even back on Earth, a thousand years ago, many people who prided themselves on being Christian may have understood it even less. These people of ours do not know all that we have learned; we have not tried to explain any of it to them. We know that life and intelligence can come in many forms—biological, nonbiological, and that strange matrix of intelligence we find in those worlds beyond the space–time universe. We know there is at least a second universe and perhaps a third and fourth, although we cannot be certain. We have a hint, but no more than a hint, that there may be some sort of overriding Principle, more complex than the principle that would apply to a space–time universe alone. So we know that if there is a Heaven (if there could be a Heaven in this sort of multi-universe), it necessarily must be more than a simple Christian Heaven, or a Happy Hunting Ground, or an Island of the Blest, whatever you might choose to call it. It couldn't be so crude and simplistic as a broad golden staircase and winding trumpets and angels blithely flying—"

"That all is true," said Roberts, "but this matter of sharing with our brothers the knowledge that we hold or glimpse has been under continuing review, and in every instance when it has been discussed, we have decided that it would not be advisable to inform the others fully. Can you imagine the kinds of interpretations that would be put upon certain segments of the knowledge? We have created an elite within Vatican; only the elite are aware of the knowledge we have gained. That may be wrong, but I think it is justified by the inherent danger of revealing all the facts. Revealing them, we would have been rent by a thousand heresies. No work would have been done because each robot would be convinced that he alone understood correctly and would have thought it incumbent upon himself to set his erring brothers straight. There would have been bickering and squabbling and animosities that could tear us apart. It was, we agreed in every instance, better that we continue to let the others cling to their residual Christianity, sterile as it might be."

"Bickering!" said the Pope in his cold, terrible voice. "What is this you're doing if not bickering? And worst of all, you've bickered before two humans who would not have been aware of it."

"I, Your Holiness, am aware of a great part of it," said Ecuyer, "and had my suspicions about the rest of it. As for my friend Dr. Tennyson—"

"Yes, Tennyson," demanded the Pope, "what about it?"

"You can rest easy, Holiness," said Tennyson. "If you wonder whether I am thinking of mounting a crusade to inform the other members of Vatican, I can tell you I have no such intentions. I'll just stand by and watch, with some interest, what happens here on out."

"As for the outside universe," said Roberts to the Pope, "there need be no fear that the word will be carried by the two humans who joined us recently. Neither of them will be leaving."

The Pope grumbled, "I don't know. There is this Decker human. He turned up out of nowhere. Have any of you ever learned exactly how he got here?"

"No, Holiness, we have not," said Theodosius.

"If one of them can get in without our knowing it," said the Pope, "another can get out. The humans are a slippery race. We must watch them all the time."

"They are our brothers, Holiness," said Theodosius. "They have always been, and they still are. There is an unspoken pact between robot and human. Through all the years, they have stood side by side."

"They exploited you," said the Pope.

"They gave us all we had," said Theodosius. "Had it not been for humans, there would have been no robots. They fashioned us in their shape—no other race would have done that. No other race has. Other races have made machines, but no robots."

"And still just now," said Tennyson, "you have told me that I can't leave Vatican. That I would not be leaving, neither the woman nor I. Is this the measure of the brotherhood you speak of? Not that I am surprised; I expected it."

"You were fleeing for your life," said Theodosius. "We gave you sanctuary. What more do you expect?"

"But Jill?"

"Jill," said Theodosius, "is quite another matter. I am convinced she does not want to leave."

"For that matter," said Tennyson, "neither have I any great desire to leave. But should I want to, I would like to think I could."

"Dr. Tennyson," said the Pope sternly, "the matter of whether you are to leave or are not to leave is not the subject under discussion. Let us leave it until another time."

"Agreed," said Tennyson. "I'll bring it up again."

"Sure," said Ecuyer, "you'll bring it up again."

"Now," said the Pope, "allow us to get back to a consideration of Heaven."

"It seems to me," said Ecuyer, "that the problem is quite a simple one. Is there a Heaven or is there not? If there's not, all this discussion is entirely pointless. Why don't you go and see? Vatican has the means to go almost anywhere—"

"But there are no coordinates," said Roberts. "The Listener Mary's cube shows no coordinates. We must know where we are going before we start out."

"Mary may make another trip," said Tennyson. "Is it not possible that on the second trip, or on subsequent trips, she may be able to provide coordinates?"

Ecuyer shook his head. "I don't think she will be going on another trip. I don't think she wants to go. I think she is afraid."

Chapter Twenty-two

THE DAY WAS MISTY, WITH LOWERING CLOUDS THAT SLICED off half the height of the mountains and lent to the land a gray-wool quality. The path that Tennyson had been following began to rise, and as he went up the hill, the mist cleared enough for him to make out the cabin that crouched on top of it. He was certain it was Decker's place. He wondered if he would find the man at home or if Decker might be off on one of his rock-hunting trips. Tennyson shrugged. No matter. If Decker was not home, he'd turn about and go back to Vatican. It was a pleasant day to walk and chances were he would have taken a walk in any event before the day was over.

Decker came around the corner of the cabin when Tennyson was halfway up the slope. He was carrying an armful of firewood, but he waved with his free hand and shouted a greeting that was muffled in the heavy air.

He left the door open and when Tennyson stepped through it, Decker came back from the fireplace at the opposite end of the room and held out his hand. "Sorry that I had to leave you on your own," he said, "but I wanted to get rid of that load of wood. It was heavy. Now let's sit down in front of the fire. It's a good day for it."

Tennyson pulled his knapsack off his shoulder, reached into it and hauled out a bottle. He handed it to Decker.

"I found I had an extra one," he said.

Decker held it up to the light.

"You're a lifesaver," he said. "I went through my last one a week ago. Charley sometimes brings me a couple, but not always, not on every trip. He's short himself, I suppose. He steals it, you know."

"Yes, I know," said Tennyson. "If Charley is the *Wayfarer* captain. I never knew his name."

"That's the man," said Decker. "How well did you get to know him?"

"I imagine not at all. We talked off and on. He told me about Apple Blossom."

"His retirement planet. Most everyone has a favorite planet. How about you, Jason?"

Tennyson shook his head. "I have never thought about it."

"Well, go on and sit in front of the fire. Put your feet up on the hearth if you want to. You can't damage anything here. This place is built to use. I'll join you as soon as I can find two clean glasses. No ice, though."

"Who needs ice?" said Tennyson.

Seen from the inside, the cabin was larger than it seemed from the outside. There was only the one room. One corner was fixed up as a kitchen with a small wood stove and shelves attached to the wall. A kettle was simmering on the stove. A bed stood against one wall. Above it was a shelf of books. In the corner next to the fireplace was a flat-topped table and on it stood a group of small carvings. The *Wayfarer* captain, Tennyson vaguely recalled, had told him something about the carvings.

Decker came back with two glasses. He handed one of them to Tennyson and poured. He set the bottle on the hearth within easy reach. Settling back into his chair, he took a long swallow of the liquor.

"God, that's good," he said. "You forget how good it is. Each time you forget."

They sat in silence for a long time, drinking, looking at the fire.

Finally, Decker asked, "How go things at Vatican? Up here on my hill, I hear rumors, but that's all. The whole place, Vatican and village, crawls with rumors. A man never knows what to believe. Generally I wind up believing none of it."

"Probably you are wise," said Tennyson. "I live at Vatican and half of what I hear is hard to believe. Once I get really settled in, I may know better how to evaluate what I hear. I met His Holiness the other day."

"So?"

"What do you mean—so?"

"What was your impression?"

"Disappointment," said Tennyson. "He seemed petty to me. Maybe on big, deep, important questions he can be all solid wisdom. But on the little worries, he is as confused as the rest of us. Maybe more confused. I was surprised that he would concern himself with all the pettiness."

"You talking about the Heaven business?"

"How would you know, Decker?"

"Rumor. I told you there is rumor piled on rumor. Heaven is all the village talks about."

"Much the same is true at Vatican," said Tennyson. "There's a lot of mumbling over the question, which it seems to me is a simple one. Mary either found Heaven or she found someplace else that she thinks is Heaven. I understand Vatican has ways to go and see. But they flap their hands and claim there are no coordinates. Mary maybe could go back and pick up coordinates, but Ecuyer is doubtful she will go; he thinks she is afraid to go."

"And what do you think?"

"My opinion is worthless."

"Nevertheless, what do you think?"

"I think Vatican, the real Vatican, the official Vatican, wants to wash its hands of it. Vatican officials are the ones who are afraid, not Mary. Mary may be afraid as well, of course, but Vatican is afraid right along with her. No one in authority wants to know what it's all about. It appears to me they may be afraid it actually is Heaven."

"Undoubtedly you are right," said Decker. "The cardinals and the other theological hot-shots have spent these thousand years trying to get things figured out. They're clever—you have to give them that. They've pulled in tons of data from all over the universe—whatever the universe may be. Chances are it's not what you and I think it is. They've fed this data into His Holiness and His Holiness, like any sharp computer, has correlated it, probably to a point where they may think they are beginning to see the shape of things, or at least glimpse the shape of things. They may have built up a tentative, but beautiful, theory, perhaps rather delicate in its structure. Mostly it hangs together, mostly the different factors fit, but there are bound to be discrepancies. With certain modifications in the basic theory, the discrepancies may be made to fit. Vatican, more than likely, is just now beginning to believe that another thousand years is all that is needed to nail the whole thing down. And then this silly woman goes to Heaven and Heaven, the authentic Christian Heaven, is the one thing that will knock that beautiful, lovely, half-formed theory all to hell. It is the one piece of evidence, should it prove to be true, that would negate all the rest of it."

"I'm not sure," said Tennyson, "that what you say is the whole of it. Maybe what Vatican fears is a wholehearted reversion of the unofficial Vatican, the under-Vatican, to the Christian faith. That faith undoubtedly still has the capacity for a strong hold on your ordinary robot. You must remember that many robots are Earth-forged and thus closer to humans than the more modern robots that were constructed since the exodus from Earth. Among humans, Christianity still remains a powerful force. Five thousand years after Jesus, it still is a faith sufficiently satisfying to be accepted by huge masses of humanity. While Vatican is not adverse to most of their robots continuing to believe, marginally, in Christianity, it would be a great embarrassment and an impediment to the work that Vatican is doing if there was a strong, perhaps fanatical, resurgence of the faith. Heaven, I am convinced, could do exactly that."

"Certainly you are right," said Decker, "but I still believe that what Vatican fears is any factor that would upset the theory of the universe they seem to be evolving."

"But wouldn't you think," asked Tennyson, "that they would want to know? What are they gaining by sticking their heads in the sand, hoping that by doing nothing, Heaven will go away?"

"Eventually," said Decker, "they will come around to a practical point of view. Whatever else they are, they are not fools. But right now they're recoiling from the shock. Give them a while and they'll get their feet back under them."

He reached for the bottle and held it up in invitation. Tennyson held out his glass. Decker filled both glasses and set the bottle back on the hearth.

"Think of it," said Decker. "A concept built up painfully through the centuries by a rather ordinary life form on an ordinary planet of an ordinary sun, finally culminating in what amounted to an act of faith, continued by that faith, fed by that faith, and now threatening to topple a millennium of concentrated effort by a brainy group of thinkers. Man is not the smartest animal in the galaxy, by no means the most intelligent. Could it be possible, Jason, that man, through sheer intuition, through his yearning and his hope, could have found a truth that—"

"I don't know," said Tennyson. "No one does."

"It is an intriguing thought," said Decker.

"A terrifying thought," said Tennyson.

"If only Vatican were not so single-minded, so hell-bent in their effort to discover the final faith and truth of the universe, do you have any idea of what they could do, what they represent?"

"No, I don't," said Tennyson. "I have no idea what they have."

"They know the answers, I am certain, to questions few others have ever thought to ask. They have dug deeper, I am convinced, into the core of universal knowledge than anyone possibly could guess. They have the clout, the power, the glory that would overshadow this galaxy if they could bring themselves to use it. Thank God, they can't bring themselves to use it. They are so obsessed with this other business, they have no room for power and glory."

Decker set his glass on the hearth, got up and went back to the kitchen area, lifted the lid of a kettle and used a spoon to stir whatever was cooking in it.

In the corner, hovering a few inches above the table on which sat the small group of carven stones, a small puff of diamond dust sparkled in the light from the flickering fireplace flames. Tennyson jerked upright, slopping some of the drink out of his glass. The other day, he remembered, the day that he had first met Decker, he'd seen this glitter of diamond dust poised over Decker's shoulder. He had turned away his head and when he'd turned it back, the glitter had been gone. But the same glitter—he was sure it was the same glitter—this time did not go away. It stayed above the table.

Decker came back to the fire, picked up his glass and settled in his chair.

"How about staying for supper?" he asked. "I have stew, more than enough for the two of us. I'll stir up a pan of cornbread and pop it in the oven. We'll have it warm. I've run out of coffee, but I have tea."

"Tea is fine," said Tennyson.

"I'll crank up Old Betsy and take you home," said Decker. "It'll be a dark night. Walking, you might lose your way. Unless you'd want to stay the night. You could have the bed. I have extra blankets. I could stretch out on the floor."

"I should get back sometime this evening."

"No problem. You pick the time."

"Tom," said Tennyson, "I had the impression you were non-communicative. I'd been told you were stand-offish."

"Charley tell you that?"

"I think so. I talked to no one else about you."

"Everyone else would have told you the same if you had asked."

"But I didn't ask."

"That's the point," said Decker. "Even now you haven't asked. When did I come here? How did I come here? Why did I come here?"

"Well, hell, I haven't told you anything about myself, either," said Tennyson. "Although I wouldn't really mind. What I did or was never seemed important."

"Story is," said Decker, "that you were on the lam. That's what the village says."

"It's true," said Tennyson. "You want to know the details?"

"Not in the least," said Decker. "Here, let me fill your glass."

They sat in silent companionship, drinks in hand, watching the fire.

Decker stirred in his chair. "To appreciate Vatican's view-point," he said, "you have to ask yourself what a robot is. Too often we make the mistake of thinking of him as a mechanical man, and that's not what he is. He is a whole lot more than that and a great deal less. I suspect that a robot often thinks of himself as a slightly different human, and in this, he is as wrong as we are. It's strange that both robot and human should make the same mistake.

"The one question that must first occur to us is to ask ourselves if a robot is capable of love. Of loyalty, yes; of responsibility, yes; of logic, yes. But how about love? Can a robot actually love anyone or anything at all? The robot has no spouse, no children, no kin of any sort, no blood relatives. Love is a biological emotion. It should not be expected of a robot, nor should a robot expect to experience it. Because he has no one to love, a robot has no one to protect or care for—he doesn't even have to worry about himself. With minimal repair and maintenance, he theoretically can live forever. He does not have the specter of old age to worry over. He does not have to amass a fortune to care for himself in his later years. In the way of personal relationships, he actually has nothing at all. Which leaves a big hole in his life, a lot of emptiness."

"Perhaps," said Tennyson, "he would not know about the emptiness. He would not be aware that he is empty."

"That might be true if robots lived entirely by themselves, if they lived apart from biological beings. But they don't; I don't think they can. They're hung up on humans; they must have their humans. And all these years, observing humans, they must realize, at least subconsciously, what they are missing."

"So you think," said Tennyson, "that, lacking the ability and opportunity to love, they turned to religion to fill the emptiness. But that makes no great amount of sense; religion is based on love."

"You forget," said Decker, "that love is not the only factor contributing to religion. There is faith as well. At times a very dogged faith, and a robot is so constituted that he could operate a long way on dogged faith alone. I would think that he could become, with very little effort, a fanatic that would put to shame any human zealot."

"But is what Vatican has a religion?" Tennyson asked. "There are times when I think it's not."

"It probably started out to be," said Decker, "and even now

many of the simple members of Vatican still think religion is their true vocation. But over the years, Vatican's objective has changed. I am sure of that. The Search now is aimed at universal patterns, at what any cardinal probably would define as universal truths. Which, when you come right down to it, would be far more attractive to the robotic mentality than any kind of faith. If, when they reach the end of the road they are following, they find, perhaps with some surprise, that after all they've discovered the true universal theology, they'll feel fairly good about it."

"But if they come up with something else," said Tennyson, "they'll not mind at all."

"That's exactly it," said Decker. "You hit it on the head."

The little puff of diamond dust still hung above the table, hovering like a protective wing over the huddled group of carvings. At times it sparkled, but most of the time it simply hung there, motionless, as if it might be watching.

The question rose to Tennyson's tongue, but he shut it off. Decker must see the little puff of dust himself, must be aware that his guest also was seeing it. If any comment was called for, it was Decker's place to make it. So far no questions had been asked, and that was the way it should be.

Decker said, "Back to the Heaven incident. Have you seen the tape?"

"It's not a tape," said Tennyson. "It's a cube. And, no, I haven't seen it. I've seen others, but not the Heaven cube. I had not wanted to ask. It seemed a sort of private thing."

"You know, of course—in fact, you said that Vatican has a way to go and see."

"That is true," said Tennyson, "but there are no coordinates."

"I have a hunch," said Decker, then he said no more. Tennyson waited.

"Yes?" he finally asked.

"I have a hunch," said Decker, "I know where Heaven is."

Chapter Twenty-three

"I DON'T KNOW WHAT HAPPENED," SAID ECUYER. "I HAVEN'T the slightest idea. But now Mary insists she wants to make a second trip to Heaven."

"If she can," said Tennyson.

"I think she can," said Ecuyer. "She is the best Listener we have. She has the capability to make a second trip. I don't know what kind of capability is necessary to go back unerringly to a place again. But, over the years, some of our Listeners have demonstrated, again and again, they do have the capability. We have tried to determine what that capability may be. If only we knew what it is, we could train our people for it. But enough of that. What bothers me is why Mary should want to do it now. A few days ago she had no intention of it."

"Maybe she wants to do something that will get her renewed attention," said Jill. "You two fellows have more or less been giving her the treatment. You've put yourselves out to make it apparent to her she is not nearly as important as she thought she was."

"It was the only thing we could do," said Ecuyer. "Or, at least, I thought so and Jason concurred with me."

"Right or not," said Jill, "it apparently has worked. And now that she is going, is there any way you can impress upon her the necessity of picking up some coordinates?"

"We can talk to her," said Ecuyer. "Try to impress the necessity upon her. Whether she'll pay attention, I don't know." He said to Jill, "You might talk to her. Woman to woman."

"I don't think so," said Jill. "We have never met. I doubt she'd trust me. It might appear that everyone was ganging up on her."

"Decker," said Tennyson, "seems to think he may know where Heaven is. I talked with him the other day—"

"How would he know?" asked Ecuyer. "How *could* he know?"

"He didn't say and I didn't ask. He has a phobia about his privacy. You do not ask him questions. I think he might have expected me to, but I didn't. And having said what he said, he said no more."

"You should have asked him," said Jill. "He may have wanted you to ask."

"I don't think I should have asked. I may be wrong, but I had the feeling he was setting up some sort of test. He gave me several openings to ask questions on other matters and I asked nothing. I was burning to, of course, but I managed to keep quiet. He's a strange man. Things were going well and I meant to keep them that way."

"I think," said Ecuyer, "that all these years we have written Decker off as a sort of freak. A loner, which he certainly is. A man standing apart and wanting to stand apart. Jason is the first one to get anything like close to him. That could be valuable; we don't want to throw it away. I feel there may be far more to the man than any of us have guessed."

Hubert came in with a new-brewed pot of coffee and refilled their cups, then, saying nothing to them, went back to the kitchen.

"He's still huffy at me," said Ecuyer. "I chewed him out the other day." He told Tennyson, "You have to do it now and then. Keep him in line."

"One thing you have to say about him," said Tennyson. "He makes a splendid cup of coffee."

"One thing I want to know," said Jill. "Is Mary human? Is she still human? How many of the Listeners are human?"

"Why, of course Mary's human," said Ecuyer. "Why should you ask?"

"The Listeners," said Jill, "have had so many—what would you call them—other-worldly, perhaps—so many other-worldly experiences and not only that, but so often they have been or have seemed to be other-worldly creatures—I guess that I've been wondering how, in the face of all this, they have managed to retain their humanity."

"I've often wondered the same thing," said Ecuyer. "But no matter how often I have wondered, I have never dared to talk with any of them about it, to ask them about it. With sensitives most times you have to walk on eggs. All of them are strong personalities. Maybe that's what saves them. Maybe a strong personality is a prerequisite for being a sensitive. But despite their strong personalities and deep strengths of character, many times they are haunted by their experiences. There are those who do refuse to go back to what they've found—willing to go on to something else, but not to what they've touched before. But there's never been a crack-up. No single sensitive has ever become unstuck."

Ecuyer finished off his coffee. "I suppose," he said, "I best had go and talk with Mary. Jason, do you want to come along?"

"I think not," said Tennyson. "I'm not her favorite person."

"Right now, neither am I."

"You've known her for a long time. That should help."

"Maybe it will," said Ecuyer. "Well, I'll be seeing you."

After he was gone, Jill and Tennyson sat for a time in silence, then Jill said, "It seems to me, Jason, we may be coming on something. I have that feeling in my bones."

Tennyson nodded. "If Mary goes back to Heaven and if she does find something, if she finds more than she found before . . ."

"I don't think I rightly understand what's going on," said Jill. "Vatican is divided in a funny sort of way. What's dividing it? Oh, I understand some of it, but not all. The worst is that I don't know what Vatican is. Is it a religion or a research think-tank? What does Vatican expect to find?"

"I would doubt," said Tennyson, "that Vatican itself knows what it expects to find."

"I've been thinking about the cardinal—I think it was Roberts, wasn't it?—who said we will not be allowed to leave."

"That's what he said," Tennyson told her. "Saying it almost in passing. I don't know how hard the decision is."

"At the moment," said Jill, "the decision, for me, is an academic one. I can't leave right now. I'm just beginning to dig out the history of Vatican. When I write my book—"

"Your book? I thought it was Vatican's book."

"My book," she insisted. "It will sell billions of copies. I'll wade in money up to my navel. I'll never have to work again. I can buy anything I want."

"If you can leave End of Nothing."

"Look, friend, Jill goes where she wants to go, when she wants to go. There never was a place she couldn't leave, never a spot so tight she couldn't wiggle out of it."

"Well, bully for you," said Tennyson. "When you go, will you take me along?"

"If you want to go," she said.

Chapter Twenty-four

IT WAS AS IT HAD BEEN BEFORE—THE BROAD AND SINGING road of light that reached deep into the distance, arrowing straight into the burst of glory that lay far and far and far. She was well above the road in a void that ached with emptiness; she was moving through the void toward the singing road, but not fast enough. She strained every nerve and fiber to speed her to that road of glory.

This time, she told herself, I will look the better. I will impress upon myself certain landmarks and certain signs and I will know where I am so I can tell them where I was, so I can offer proof of Heaven. For they did not believe me—and this time they must all believe. There must be no doubt or quibble. Coordinates, Ecuyer said, and what are coordinates? How do I find the coordinates that will convince them? For there might be none except those of faith, and in these they must believe. This time I must bring to them the faith that will force unquestioning belief, so that they may know I am the one who found Heaven for them.

I know what they want, she told herself. They want me to bring back a roadmap so they can crank up their ridiculous machines and follow me to Heaven. The fools, she thought, at once enraged and sad at their foolishness—the fools believe they can go physically to Heaven, not knowing that for mortals Heaven is—what had that moron of a doctor called it?—a state of mind. And he was wrong, she thought, he with his professionally kind face, his mincing devotion to his science. For Heaven is not a state of mind; it is a state of grace. And I alone, of all of them, am the only one who has attained the state of grace required to seek out Heaven.

The state of grace so laboriously attained, and yet, perhaps, not laboriously, for there had been no labor in it, no labor, but a striving—a striving toward that deep sense of holiness, the selfless submission of one's self to a sweet authority. And at times, with all the striving, managing to touch the hem of holiness, but never grasping it; at times stripping away all thought of self, and then a stray, feebly wriggling, impossible-to-suppress thought of self creeping back again to cuddle against the emptiness to which it had been condemned. She never had attained her goal, she reminded herself—but enough, it seemed, to tread this road of glory that now lay just before her.

She came out of the void and her feet seemed to touch the road, although it did not feel like any road she had walked before. It was smooth and shining and it stretched straight before her, with the burst of glory far away. Perhaps, she thought, too far for her to walk. And what would she do, what could she do, if out of sheer exhaustion, out of lack of strength, she should collapse upon the road before she came in sight of the shining, lofty towers?

But there seemed to be no problem, for she did not have to walk. Somehow or other, she was being wafted down the road with never a step to take. The music and the singing welled all around her and she wondered for a moment if it was the singing, the strength of sonorous song, that carried her along.

She seemed to hang in a strange lassitude, with a mist closing all around her so that she saw only the road and the gloryburst at the end of it, although the lassitude was tinged with a consuming joy and she moved along the road through no effort of her own, as if a gentle tide had caught her and was carrying her toward a far-off shore. The music became more glorious and the light seemed to grow the brighter. She closed her eyes against the brightness of the light and a holiness (a holiness?) caught her up and held her.

Then, without warning, the music went away and a silence fell and she came down upon her feet, no longer carried, no longer held, with her soles pressing hard against the road. Startled, she

opened her eyes. Much of the brightness, she saw, had gone from
the light. There now was a glow rather than a brightness, and in
the glow the mighty towers stood up against the high, blue sky.
The towers, and there were many of them, rose white against the
blue. Pure white against pure blue and from far away, from
among the towers, came the hint of music that had the sound of
falling water, with each falling drop striking a distinctive note that
blended with the others.

She looked for the angels, but there were no angels flying. Perhaps, she thought, they were flying so far away, so high, that no
mortal eye could see them.

Beginning just a short distance from where she stood was the
staircase, wide and steep, and of the purest gold, climbing toward
the towers, narrowed by distance as it climbed so that at the very
top, it seemed a thin pencilstreak of gold.

It was far to climb, she told herself, yet she must—step by step,
until she reached the towers. There at the top there would be
trumpeters to greet her with a celestial flourish.

As she prepared to take the first step of the climb, the mists that
before had closed her in began to clear away and, beyond the
road, the ground spread out before her and she saw the rabble
that camped there on either side of the road. There were tents and
huts and ramshackle buildings, with here and there great temples
rising above the squalor, and crowded among all these, the rabble
—a great concourse of beings such as she had never seen before.
For some reason that she could not understand, she could not see
them clearly, but she got the impression of horrendous shapes and
hues, of a surge of terrifying life entangled in a loathsome mass.

She fled in senseless terror up the great staircase, running with a
desperation that left her weak and gulping. Finally stumbling, she
fell and lay huddled on the stairs, clutching at the smooth stone in
the fear that she might go sliding back into that pit of horrors.

Gradually she regained the even rhythm of her breath and the
trembling of her body quieted. She lifted herself cautiously to look
back down the stairs. The mists had closed in again; the rabble at
the foot of the stairway again was blotted out.

Pulling herself erect, Mary started up the stairs again. Now the music was somewhat louder, although it still seemed far away. The towers gleamed white against the blue and a peace came down upon her, wiping out the terror that had engulfed her when she had seen the rabble.

The towers seemed as far away as ever. All the climbing she had done, all the running up the stairs, seemingly had gotten her no closer to the towers. And now, far up the stairs, she saw a dot that wavered in the golden light. For a moment she stopped her climb to watch, trying to make out what it might be. At first she thought it no more than bad eyesight. But the dot remained, dancing in the light reflected from the golden stairs.

Someone is coming to meet me, she thought. Someone is walking down the golden stairs to welcome me to Heaven!

She began to hurry—hurrying to meet that one who came to welcome her. The dot grew larger and ceased its wavering and she saw that it was man-shaped, that it walked upon two legs. But there was no sign of wings. And that was faintly disappointing, although she reminded herself that not everyone in Heaven necessarily would have wings. When she thought about that, she was astonished to realize how little she actually knew of the residents of Heaven. She had always thought of Heaven in terms of angels, and this manlike creature coming down the stairs was surely not an angel.

Nor, as he came closer and she saw him more clearly, could she be sure he was a man. Manlike, yes, but not entirely human and not heavenly. For one thing, he was black.

Disturbed, she slowed her climb and finally stopped, standing on the stairs and staring up at the one who was descending toward her. His ears were high and pointed and his face was narrow, like a fox's. The lips were thin and the mouth was wide. His eyes were slanted and they were yellow, like a cat's eyes, with no white showing in them. He was so black that he shone like a polished shoe.

What his body might be like or what he wore, she never even noticed. She was so fascinated, so hypnotized, so repelled by the face that she noticed nothing else.

He stood two steps above her. He raised a hand and shook a

finger at her, as a parent or a teacher might shake a finger in rebuke. His voice thundered.

"Naughty!" he shouted at her. "Naughty! Naughty! Naughty!"

She turned about and fled, running down the stairs, with that single word hammering in her brain. She tripped and fell and rolled. She tried to stop herself, to recover her balance, but there was no way to recover from the fall. She kept rolling, bouncing on the steps, end-over-end and spinning.

And then she was no longer falling and she sat up dazedly. She had reached the bottom and was sitting on the road that came up to the stairs. The mist had cleared and she saw the rabble, packed tight on either side of the road, but not encroaching on it, as if there might be an invisible fence that held them off. They were jam-packed on either side of the road and they were laughing at her, hooting at her, jeering at her, making obscene gestures at her.

She scrambled to her feet and turned to face the stairs. The one who had come to meet her was standing on the bottom step. He still was shaking a finger at her and shouting.

"Naughty! Naughty! Naughty!"

Chapter Twenty-five

JILL HAD GONE TO THE LIBRARY; HUBERT HAD LEFT AN HOUR or so before, off on some errand of his own. Tennyson sat in front of the fireplace, fascinated by the flame. In just a little while he was due at the clinic, although more than likely there'd not be much to do there. Vatican and End of Nothing humans seemed to be an unnaturally healthy lot. Except for Mary, he had tended no serious illnesses since he had been there. Minor complaints—a few common colds, an ulcerated tooth, a couple of backaches, occasional upset stomachs, one sprained ankle and that had been all.

And now Mary was off to Heaven for the second time. He wondered idly what possibly could have happened to make her decide to try it once again. The last word he had had was that she had been unalterably opposed to returning there. And what, he wondered, would she find there—a renewed conviction that she really had found Heaven, or would she return with doubt? It could not be Heaven, he told himself; the whole idea was ridiculous, akin to the psychotically induced visions and revelations that filled the history of Earth's medieval age.

He slumped lower on the couch, staring at the fire. In just a short time, he reminded himself sharply, he'd have to get out of here and walk down to the clinic. There might be people waiting.

He felt an uneasiness, thinking it. And why, he wondered, should he be uneasy thinking of the people who might be waiting at the clinic? He hauled himself to a normal sitting position and craned his neck to look around the room. There was no one there and that was not strange, for he had known that there was no one there. He was alone and yet, quite suddenly, he was positive that he was not alone.

He rose to his feet and whirled around, his back to the fire so that he could examine the other side of the room, seeking out the shape that was lurking there. There was no one, nothing, lurking. He was sure of that. Still the uneasiness refused to go away. There was no reassurance in the emptiness of the room. There was, he was certain, something there, someone or something in the room with him.

He forced himself to speak, croaking rather than actually speaking. "Who is there?"

As if in answer to the question, he saw it in one corner, next to the spindly gilded chair that stood beside the table with the marble top—the faint glint of drifting diamond dust.

"So it's you," he said, and as he spoke the glitter disappeared and there was nothing beside the gilded chair. Yet he still felt its presence. The glitter was gone, but the thing that glittered had not gone away.

Questions surged inside him, howling to get out. Who are you? What are you? Why are you here? But he did not voice them. He stood quite frozen, not moving from where he stood, still staring at the corner where he had seen the glitter.

Something spoke inside of him.

—I am here, it said. I am here inside of you. I am in your mind. Do you wish that I should leave?

It was a gentle voice (if it was a voice). Gentle and gentlemanly. He could not move a muscle. Terror—and yet it wasn't terror—held him in its grip. He struggled to speak, struggled to think, and yet there was no word or thought. His mind was frozen with his body.

—Do you wish that I should leave?

Words came to Tennyson.

—No, he said, not speaking aloud, but only in his mind. No, don't leave, but please explain yourself. You belong to Decker. Do you bring me word from Decker?

—I do not belong to Decker. I belong to no one. I am a free agent and I am Decker's friend. That is all I am. I can talk with him, but I cannot be a part of him.

—You can be a part of me. Why can you be a part of me and not a part of Decker?

—I am Whisperer. That is what Decker calls me. It serves as well as any name.

—You did not answer my question, Whisperer. Why can you be a part of me and not a part of Decker?

—I am Decker's friend. He is the only friend I have. I tested him long and hard to be sure he was a friend. I have tried with others and they might have been friends as well, but they did not hear me, did not recognize me. They did not know I was there.

—And now?

—I tried with Decker, but there was no getting inside of him. Talk with him, yes, but no getting in his mind. On that first day, I felt you might be the one.

—And now you'll desert Decker? Whisperer, you can't do that to him. I will not do that to him. I will not steal his friend.

—I will not desert him. But can I be with you?

—You mean you'll not insist?

—No, not insist. You say go, I go. You say stay away, I'll stay away. But, please!

This, thought Tennyson, this is all insane. It is not happening. I must be imagining it. There is no such thing.

The door burst open and Ecuyer stood within it.

"Jason," he shouted, "you must come with me. You must come immediately."

"Why, of course," said Tennyson. "What is the trouble?"

"Mary is back from Heaven," said Ecuyer, "and she's a basket case."

Chapter Twenty-six

AGAIN, DECKER RELIVED THE MOMENT. FOR YEARS HE HAD not thought of it, but now, ever since he had gone back to the boat, he had thought of it often, running the filmstrip of memory through again, with the old and faded recollection becoming the sharper with each rerunning.

He reached out and touched the metal box that stood upon the desk, the box he'd brought back from the lifeboat. It would all be there, he thought, in the records that the ship had made. But he flinched away from opening it and getting at the records. Perhaps, he told himself, he should have left them in the boat, where they had rested for twelve years, virtually forgotten.

Why was it, he wondered, that he hesitated to listen to the records? Was it that he feared the terror would be there? Could the ship have recorded the terror? Could it still lie there, as fresh and raw as it had been that day so many years before? He crinkled up his face in an effort at concentration. He had known that ship, had sailed it for years, had known every twist and turn of it, had loved it, been proud of it, talked to it in the lonely hours in the depths of space. At times, or so it seemed, the ship had talked back to him.

There was about it only one thing of which he had not been certain, and that was the true capabilities of the recordings that it made. That they had been detailed and clear, that they had missed nothing of significance, of that he was very certain. They recorded locations and distances, pegged coordinates within a small fraction of their value, pinpointed temperatures, pressures, chemical components, gravitational values, sniffed out life if life was present, sought out nonapparent dangers. But emotions—could they peg emotions? Could they have put on record that overwhelming terror that had driven his tough and seasoned crew in a mad frenzy for the lifeboats?

He sat at the desk, his fingers still touching the metal of the box, and closed his eyes the better to remember, seeking out, for the tenth time or more in the last few days, that one elusive thing that had escaped his memory.

They had been heading toward the deeper recesses of the Coonskin system when the warp had seized them. Strange thing, he thought—he'd always considered it to be a warp, that storied, unexplained rift in the space–time continuum that was little more than legend, a rift that had hurled the ship into another time and/or space. There were rich, tall tales told of such happenings in every bar of every frontier planet, but the fact of their telling by the ones who told them, swearing solemnly and often to the veracity of the tales, did little to confirm the existence of the warps, or even the most remote possibility of them.

But warp or not, something violent had happened to the ship. Seemingly, as was always the case in FTL flight, the ship had been hanging in black nothingness, with no semblance of motion, when it had staggered, lurching and careening through whatever limbo of foreverness in which it had been situated. Decker remembered that he had been standing alone before one of the forward vision ports, staring out into the featureless emptiness outside the ship, fascinated, as he always had been, by the utter lack of any aspect that might be used to characterize it. It was black and it was empty and that was all it was. The blackness, however, failed in being actually black; it was black because there was nothing there, and empty not with any sense of deprivation, but by the fact also of there being nothing there, not an emptiness achieved by taking away what had been there, but empty because there never had been anything—and, more than likely, never would be anything. Many times he had wondered what it was that attracted him to this desolate and barren blankness and never, in all his wondering, had he ever arrived at any hint of its attraction for him.

Under his feet, the deck had heaved and thrown him sprawling. He had hit the deck and skidded, his direction changing as the ship yawed and tumbled. He had sought to stabilize himself, had clutched at stationary objects, missing some, his fingers sliding off those few that he could grasp. He had banged against something solid and bounced off it. And, suddenly, he had hit his head a glancing blow on some hard and solid object and the world was filled with shooting stars.

He may have been knocked out for a time, of that he never had been sure. He had thought back on it many times and never could be sure.

The next thing he recalled was trying to pull himself erect, trying to climb one of the pilot chairs set before the navigation panels. His head buzzed and there was far-off screaming—the full-throated screams of frightened men, the raw, uninhibited howling of men so terrorized that they had lost control.

The damn fools, he had thought—what is the matter with them? But even as he wondered it, he knew what was the matter with them. The terror struck him straight between the eyes. It filled the ship to a point of suffocation and it hammered at him as if it were physical rather than emotional. Somewhere, the words booming but muffled by the terror, a great voice was shouting, but he could not make out the words.

The ship no longer bucked and heaved. He clung to the chair to keep himself from falling. When he tried to stand, his legs buckled under him. He glanced at the vision ports and saw that the black emptiness was gone; the ship was back in normal space.

The terror came in waves, buffeting him, striking him as an opponent might strike him with knotted fists. His stomach churned. Still clinging to the chair, he bent over, retching, trying to vomit but unable to.

Sheer terror. Nothing visible to indicate where the terror might be coming from; nothing to show why it should be visited upon him. Pure essence of terror without reason and all the time that background, booming voice shouting at him—at him personally, not at someone else or others, but centered on him personally. Intermingled with the booming voice, between the cracks of the

booming voice, he could still hear the far and increasingly farther
off howling of the crew, fleeing the terror, leaving him behind. He
heard a thud and then another thud and knew that the thuds were
the sounds of lifeboats launching.

By now he was on his feet and his legs seemed more sturdy
under him. He put a hand to his head and felt the hank of sopping
hair pasted against his skull. His hand came back red and drip-
ping. He pushed away from the chair, aiming himself at the
nearest vision port. Reeling across the deck, he reached the hull
and clutched at it with his fingers, his face almost touching the
hard crystal of the port.

Beneath the ship lay a planetary surface and it was far too
close. Roads, thin from the distance that he viewed them, converged like the spokes of a wheel upon a central hub that lay just
ahead of him. The ship, he knew, was in a tight orbit and closing
fast. It was only a few minutes, more than likely, from crashing.
Had it not been for the waves of terror that still came crashing in
upon him, he would have heard, he knew, the thin, shrill whistle
of the craft cutting into atmosphere.

His body was trying to shrivel, to sink in upon itself, drawing in
and withering as a fallen apple, lying in the grass, would wither
through a winter. He clutched tighter at the metal hull, although
there was nothing he could clutch, but nevertheless he continued,
insanely trying to sink his fingers into the very metal. Staring down
and ahead, he saw more clearly now the hub upon which the
roads converged. The hub was a height, a pyramid, an upthrust of
rock that soared above the flatness of the surrounding countryside.
The roads, he saw, did not terminate at the base of the great rock
upthrust, but climbed the slope, arrowing upward toward the center of the hub.

For an instant only he saw the center of the hub, a sudden upheaval of spearlike structures that seemed to be reaching up as if
to grasp him and impale him. And as he saw the center of the hub,
he knew instinctively the source of the terror that was beating in
upon him. With a cry wrenched from his throat, he reeled back
from the port and for an instant stood cringing, undecided. Then
years of training spoke to him subconsciously and he wheeled

about to rush to the instrument panel. His hand reached out to seize the flight recorder. He jerked it free and, tucking it underneath his arm, turned and ran.

He had heard only two thuds, he remembered, and if that was correct, there was still a lifeboat left. Sweat broke out and ran down his body at the thought that he might have missed a thud and all the boats were gone.

His memory had not played him false. There had been only two thuds. The third boat was still in place.

Chapter Twenty-seven

MARY STRUGGLED TO SIT UP.

"They threw me out," she cried. "They threw me out of Heaven!"

The struggle ceased and she fell back onto the pillow. Fine-spun, foamy spittle clung and bubbled at the corners of her mouth. Her eyes stared wildly, with the look of seeing nothing.

The nurse handed Tennyson the syringe, and he jabbed the needle into Mary's arm, pushed the plunger slowly home. He handed the syringe back to the nurse.

Mary lifted a hand and clawed feebly at the air. She mumbled and after a time words came from the mumble. "Big and black. He shook a finger at me."

Her head sank back more tightly on the pillow. The lids came down across the manic eyes. She tried to lift a hand, fingers flexed for clawing, but then the hand fell down onto the sheet and the fingers lost their hooklike attitude.

Tennyson looked across the bed at Ecuyer. "Tell me what happened. Exactly how it happened."

"She came out of the experience," said Ecuyer. "I know that's an awkward way to say it, but the only way that fits—she came out of the experience raving. I think raving with fright. . . ."

138 Clifford D. Simak

"Does this happen sometimes? Does it happen to other Listeners?"

"At times," said Ecuyer. "Not often. Very seldom, in fact. Sometimes they do come back upset from a particularly bad scene, but ordinarily it's only surface fright, superficial fright. They realize the experience no longer obtains, that they are safely home and there's nothing now to harm them—there never was anything to harm them. In particularly bad instances, an experience may leave a mark upon them. They may dream about it. But the effect is transitory; in a short time it goes away. I have never seen anything as bad as this. Mary's reaction is the worst I have ever seen."

"She'll be all right now," said Tennyson. "The sedation is fairly heavy. She won't come out of it for several hours, and when she does, she should be fairly woozy. Her sensory centers will be dulled. Even if she remembers, the impact of her memory should not be violent. After that, we'll see."

"She still thinks that she found Heaven," said Ecuyer. "Even thrown out, she still thinks it's Heaven. That's what hit her so hard. You can imagine the emotional repercussions. To find Heaven and then be thrown out."

"Did she say more? I mean earlier. More than she said just now."

Ecuyer shook his head. "A few details, is all. There was this man—black and huge. He threw her down the stairs. Down the Golden Stairs. She rolled all the way to the bottom. She is convinced she is black and blue from bruises."

"There's not a mark upon her."

"Of course not, but she thinks there is. This experience, Jason, was very real to her. Vivid in its cruelty and rejection."

"You haven't looked at the crystal yet."

"Not yet. To tell you the truth, I'm reluctant to. Even knowing what it is. . . ."

"I understand," said Tennyson.

"What worries me, what really worries me, is that Heaven, or the things in Heaven, or whatever may be out there, has detected our spying. That they can trace Mary back to us. We should have—"

"I think you're letting your fears run away with you. I don't see how they can trace her back. I can't imagine how they could have detected her. She wasn't really there, not in her corporeal being."

"God, I don't know," said Ecuyer. "I don't know anything anymore. We never should have let her go; we should have recognized the danger."

"I can't think there is any possibility she was detected, that the project was detected."

"This black man—this devil of hers—chased her down the stairs."

"All right," said Tennyson. "All right, maybe he did. Although I don't think he had anything to chase. Mary wasn't there. But even if, through the wildest of possibilities, she was and he chased her, you can't blame yourself. There was no way to know, no way that you could know."

"Almost never is there any direct reaction to any of our Listeners in those other worlds," said Ecuyer. "Ordinarily our people are no more than observers. When they are more than observers, they become involved by becoming one of the residents of these other worlds—by forming some link with one of them or by somehow programming their minds so they become one of them or— Jason, I just don't know. I have never known. I don't know what our Listeners do when they arrive someplace or how they go about handling the situation. I can't figure it out, and they're no help; they can't tell me how they do it. What happened to Mary has never happened before. When our people get really involved, when they enter into the physical aspects of some other place, they become involved as something other than themselves. But Mary got involved as Mary. She was in Heaven, so far as she was concerned, she herself actually was in Heaven and she met this man and he chased her down the stairs. . . ."

"That's what she says."

"I'll tell you something," said Ecuyer. "I'll bet you that it happened that way. I'm convinced that the crystal will show—"

"Of course it will," said Tennyson. "If that's what she thinks

happened, that is what will be on the record. It's not what happened, but what she thinks happened, that will show up in the
crystal. But even if the record is accurate as to what really happened, even if this creature she thinks chased her down the stairs
did exactly that, how can you be so sure he or his fellows could
trace her back to us?"

"I don't think I'm sure," said Ecuyer. "But I do think the possibility is there. The possibility is that she—how do you say it?—that
she has given us away. Our Listeners never can be certain what
they'll find out there. The man who chased her may not be the
kind of being that she thinks she saw. He may have been something that was incomprehensible, so Mary's human mind translated him into human terms, into the sort of creature, horrible as
he may have appeared to her, that she could understand, that
would be bearable and that she could accept. Mary is an experienced observer, one of our most valuable. I'm certain she would
know what she saw and certain as well that if she ran into some
life form too horrible to look upon she'd instinctively protect herself by translation."

"I don't understand your fear," said Tennyson. "Vatican robots
go out in thought-ships, or whatever you call them, to some of the
worlds that your people seek out."

"That is true," said Ecuyer, "but there is a difference. The robots don't go blind. They know what they are getting into. Their
shots are picked very carefully."

Mary was resting comfortably, the sedation having taken hold.

"She'll be all right now," said Tennyson. "The worst is over.
She'll remember some of the event when she wakes, but the sharp
edges of the experience will be dulled. All she needs is rest for the
moment. Later it might be well if she could switch over to something else. Would that be possible? We can't take the chance of
letting her go back to Heaven. If we can't be sure that she won't
go back, it would be best to take her off the program entirely. In
such a case, however, she'd brood over it. It would be preferable
if she could go on to something else. New experiences would serve
to blur this one. It's unlikely she'd run into anything as traumatic
as Heaven."

"I don't know," said Ecuyer. "When she is rational, we'll have to talk with her and try to think it through."

"I have patients waiting for me," said Tennyson. "I'll drop in later on."

There were only a couple of patients. When he was finished with them, Tennyson did not immediately go back to Mary. She'd still be deep in sedation and the nurse would have sent word if anything was wrong.

It was early afternoon and the day was fine. The mountains stood up a deeper blue against a pale-blue sky. Looking at the mountains, Tennyson knew where he wanted to be, where he needed to be—a place where he could sit alone for a time and think. In the last few days, even in the last few hours, too many things had happened and they needed sorting out. Near at hand was a place made to order for exactly that.

The garden was deserted. Usually a few monks could be found pacing silently along the paths, but none were in evidence. Tennyson headed for the bench that stood near the roses. Only one rose was in bloom—a pale-yellow bloom that was past its prime, the petals already beginning to come loose to be scattered by the wind.

Sitting on the bench, he looked toward the mountains. Strange, he thought, that they should exert so powerful an attraction for him. Someday he'd have to take Decker up on his offer and, with this new friend of his, make an expedition into them. Although more than likely, he told himself, a few days' trip such as Decker had suggested would not carry them far into the mountains, perhaps no farther than the nearer foothills.

Soon, he thought, he'd have to see Decker and talk with him about Whisperer. Whisperer, he thought, what a silly name! And what, for the love of God, was Whisperer? Something that could get inside one's mind? That could become one with him? *I am inside of you and can become a part of you.* Was that, Tennyson wondered, what Whisperer had said? Or was it no more than imagination?

He tried to brush the entire matter away; it was a disconcerting business to even think about. He'd know more about it when he talked with Decker, and there was no gain by puzzling at it now. Surely by this time Decker had learned considerable about Whisperer.

A foot crunched on the walk and Tennyson looked up. The gardener was standing beside him.

"So it's you again," said Tennyson.

"Who else should it be?" asked the gardener. "Who else has more right to be here? This is where I belong. This place is mine or as close to mine as any place can be."

"I wasn't questioning your right to be here," said Tennyson. "It seems, however, that each time I come here I run into you."

"The place is small," said the gardener, but did not go on to explain what he meant.

"When will the roses bloom again?" asked Tennyson. "Now only one is left."

"But beautiful. Do you not think that it is beautiful?"

"Yes, beautiful," said Tennyson.

"I hear, with much regret, that Mary is ill again."

"Yes, quite ill."

"It has come to my ears she went to Heaven once again."

"I do not know about that," said Tennyson, lying like a trooper. "I only know she's ill."

It was, he told himself, none of the gardener's damn business.

Chapter Twenty-eight

THE ROBOTS, WHEN THEY CAME FROM EARTH, HAD BROUGHT mice with them. Perhaps not intentionally, but the mice were there.

Working late at night, Jill had met the first of them. There were others that she glimpsed from time to time, but the first one had become a friend. It came to visit her in the quiet and lonely hours, peering at her from behind a pile of tapes or a stack of crystals, its soft, round ears spread wide to catch the slightest sound, its pink nose busily wriggling to catch the slightest scent. Then, sure that all was well, that no one but she was there, it came out, still moving cautiously, not too sure of its welcome, to share a midnight snack with her, picking up a crumb of bread or cheese in its tiny forepaws, sitting erect upon its haunches, with its fat white paunch thrust forward. Watching her, always watching her with its bright, small marble eyes, it nibbled at the crumb.

She talked to it, speaking softly, for any other tone would have frightened it. Little refugee, she called it, little refugee from Earth. At times, when it was not too busy with its crumb, it would squeak at her, a companionable, conversational squeak that said it liked her, too.

At first she had quailed at the thought of the havoc mice could wreak in a library, then realized that this was not a library in the sense that she thought of one. The precious Old Earth books that were here were housed in glass cupboards, as were any written records. The tapes and crystals were locked in steel cabinets. Even the paper supply was stored in metal bins. There was little in the place that a mouse could get at.

There were not many mice, perhaps no more than a dozen, and with the exception of her friend, who came regularly for his handout, they appeared only now and then. Once her scrounging friend had finished with his lunch, he disappeared as well. This puzzled her. There was no preliminary scampering about prior to his disappearance, no zigzag explorations. He finished his crumbs of bread and cheese, then left, and never once had she been able to see where he had gone. At first this did not bother her. It was of small concern to her where or how he might have gone. But as time went on, for no logical reason that she could determine, she found herself wondering where he went when he finished eating and what route he took to get there. At times she became angry at herself for wasting time in thinking of such a matter. After all, what difference did it make? Even should she find out, what would she gain?

She put it away as an inconsequential item, but from time to time she still would think of it. Then one night, quite by accident, she saw where the mouse went. It ran straight across the floor between her desk and a paneled wall and disappeared into the wall. It went in a straight line, scampering, with its rigid tail held high, as if it might be following a well-beaten path (although there was no path, not even a mouse path), going fast and never slackening speed, and when it reached the wall, it did not stop but went through it.

Puzzled, she rose from her desk and, without moving her eyes from that place in the wall where the mouse had disappeared, walked across the floor until she reached it. Dropping to her knees, she ran her hand across the wall. There was no mouse hole. The paneling ran down flush to the floor—or did it? She ran her fingers along the juncture between the paneling and the floor, and as she slid them along it, one finger found a little space—a space of no more than an inch, but possibly big enough for a mouse to squeeze through if it knew exactly where it was and could flatten itself enough.

"The little devil," she said, speaking aloud.

The crack ran for only a couple of inches, then on either side the paneling came down to the floor again. Perhaps the floorboard had sagged, she told herself, to create the opening. She ran two fingers into the gap and curled them against the opposite side of the paneling. Strange, she thought—there was a strangeness here that she could not understand. She had thought a floorboard might have sagged, but when she ran a palm along the floor, she could not detect such a defect.

She inserted her fingers into the crack again, curled their ends against the paneling and pulled. With some creaking and scraping, a door came open. Behind it was a cubbyhole, a closet. From a hook in the wall hung a faded crimson robe, a cardinal's robe. To one side of the robe stood a pair of sandals. In one corner stood a wastebasket. That was all—the robe, the sandals and the basket. The entire area smelled of mouse droppings.

She stepped inside the closet, lifted out the basket, then shut the door.

Back at her desk, she explored the basket. Crumpled-up paper almost filled it; at the bottom was a huge mouse nest of chewed-up paper, a nest that probably had been used by generations of mice, with an occasional new occupant adding to its dimensions.

Rescuing the undamaged or relatively undamaged papers, she laid them out in a pile on the desktop. When she had finished, with only the mouse nest remaining in the basket, she started going through the papers, starting with the one on top and working downward.

It was disappointing trivia. Several papers bore scribbled mathematical calculations that did not appear exciting; another was a list of tasks to be done, with most of them crossed out, probably signifying that they had been done; a number of the sheets were filled with jotted notes, now cryptic, but probably at one time carrying some meaning for the one who had written them; one sheet was the beginning of a letter, undated, and continuing for only a line or two—*Your Eminence, I have been thinking for the last several days on the matter we discussed at some length in the garden and have finally arrived at my decision* . . . and then came to an end, crumpled and thrown away; another sheet was headed *Notes for the consideration of His Holiness,* but the rest of the sheet was blank; an enigmatic list: *600 bu. wheat, 30 cords of good hard wood suitable for long burning and for holding fire, 150 lbs. of the best potatoes, 7 tons of honey*—and then came to an end. There were other sheets and scraps of paper, perhaps intriguing if one had the time to puzzle out their purposes and the circumstances under which they had been written—the greater number of them probably of no importance whatsoever.

Despite their trivia, Jill piled them all neatly, putting each one down against the hard surface of the desk and running the palm of her hand over it to partially iron out the wrinkles that had come from being crumpled. Someday, she told herself, she would find the time to go over them more carefully. Just possibly she might find a valuable clue here that would make for a better understanding of Vatican.

Thinking this, she stopped as if thunderstruck, staring at the pile of paper, realizing for the first time the depth of her commitment to this task she had undertaken—a commitment that could bring her to stack up obviously worthless sheets of scratch paper in the premise that someday she would study them, wringing from them some minor footnote that might point up some piddling fact or insight. This was not, she told herself, the way that she had planned, this was not the approach she had first taken to the job. Then she had regarded it as no more than a stop-gap measure, a chore that would give her an excuse for staying on while she worked on her original purpose for coming to Vatican. Jason had warned her, she remembered. You'll get hooked, he'd told her, you'll get so immersed in the research you can't pull yourself away. And now, she knew, the both of them were hooked, he as much as she, although he never had pretended that he would not stay here, for a while at least. She had been the one who had planned to leave if she was not allowed to do the reporting job she had come to do. If the chance came to get away from End of Nothing now, she asked herself, trying to be honest, would she take it? Thinking it, she found she had no answer.

She continued going through the pile of papers. Near the bottom of the pile she came upon a sheaf of several sheets clipped together, written in an atrocious longhand that she had some difficulty making out:

I, Enoch, cardinal, write this unofficial memo to myself, well knowing that it cannot be made a part of the official record, since the incident I write of was not placed in the official record, purposely not placed in the official record. I write this memo as a warning to myself, principally to myself, although as well to others to whom sometime I may pass it on, although at the present moment I have no intention of sharing it with anyone at all. I do not write it through any fear of forgetfulness (for I am not forgetful; over many centuries, I have not been forgetful), but because I wish to get down in words my feelings on the matter, my emotions (so far as I have emotions) and my fear (especially my fear and apprehension) before time has had the chance to dull or temper these impressions.

I call it an incident, for that is all it was, a rather fleeting incident, but an incident alarming in its implications. For long we have felt secure upon this isolated world of ours, located at the extreme rim of the galaxy in a region where there are few stars and our star so unspectacular that it will not attract attention. But now, since the incident, I am not so certain of our security. No others of my fellows has expressed, at least to me, any of the apprehension that I feel and I, in turn, have been careful not to show or otherwise communicate the apprehension that I feel.

For this reason—that I am reluctant to give expression to what I feel (for what reason I cannot imagine) and in the fear that in the long run I may subconsciously smother my fear (which I regard as a valuable fear)—I write this memo to myself as a reminder, in the days to come, that I did entertain this fear and am convinced that it is a real and logical fear and must be taken into consideration in our future planning.

Yesterday, we were VISITED. The visitors were unlike anything our human Listeners ever have encountered. Many of us, I am certain, never saw the beings at all, thinking that there was no more than the bubbles that they saw. I, who caught several glimpses of the riders of the bubbles, know that the bubbles were no more than transportation conveyances. In one of those instances in which I glimpsed the riders, I was for a moment face to face with the creature that peered out from inside the bubble. The face, I am sure it was a face, but not a robot face, nor yet a human face, was little more than a blob of drifting smoke, although I know that it was not smoke, but a face that looked like a swirl of smoke. It was a mobile face, like a rubber face pulled out of shape, capable of many shapes. Never shall I forget the expression that I saw upon it as it peered down at me from a distance of no more than thirty feet. There was upon it a smirk of amused contempt, as if it were a god looking down upon a pig sty. Seeing that look of immense disdain, I shriveled all inside. I became a small and crawling thing, mewling in pity for myself and for my kind, groveling in the filth of my debased society and all I'd done and been for naught.

There were perhaps a dozen of the bubbles, although no one seemed to have had the sense to count them. They came quickly and left quickly; they did not stay for long, perhaps for no longer than ten minutes, although it may have been even less than that. They appeared and disappeared; suddenly they were there, bursting out of nothing, and then as suddenly they disappeared, going into nothing.

They came and looked us over very briefly, wasting little time on us. Probably they had no need to stay any longer; more than likely they saw far more than any of us can imagine that they saw even in so brief a time. They gazed down upon us with amused contempt, knowing who we were and what we were doing here and more than likely scratching us out as something that was beneath their notice.

They may pose no danger to us, but now we know (or at least I know) that they are aware of us (even if they scratched us out, they are still aware of us) and I feel safe no longer. For they do know of us and even if they do nothing to or about us, the very fact they know of us constitutes a danger. If they could find us on a casual survey and look us over (even deciding we were not worth their time), then there may be others (almost certainly there are others) who can, for reasons quite unknown, seek us out.

We have sought security in remoteness and by subterfuge. We have tolerated and even encouraged pilgrims—not so much because we need the money that they bring, but in the thought that if we are noticed, the pilgrims may make it appear we are no more than another shabby cult and not worthy of any further notice. But we may have calculated wrongly and if so . . .

The writing came to an end. Jill tried to smooth out the crumpled pages. Carefully she folded them and put them in a pocket. Never before had she walked out of the library with any material, but this time she intended to do just that.

Enoch Cardinal Theodosius, she thought, that stodgy old robot —how could he have written this? A sharper mind, a more imaginative mind than she had guessed lay inside that metal skull.

Chapter Twenty-nine

DECKER WAS HOEING IN HIS GARDEN. THE PLOT, TENNYSON noted, was clean and neat. The vegetables marched in sturdy rows. There were no weeds. Decker wielded the hoe with unhurried strokes.

Tennyson walked to the edge of the garden and waited. Decker, finally seeing him, hoisted the hoe and put it on his shoulder, walking down the row.

"Let's get out of the sun," he said to Tennyson. "It's hot out in the garden."

He led the way to a shaded area where two rough wooden chairs flanked a low wooden table with a pail sitting on it.

Decker reached for the pail. "It's only water," he said. "It's probably warm, but at least it's wet."

He held it out to Tennyson, who shook his head. "You go first. You've been out there laboring."

Decker nodded, lifted the pail and drank from it, then handed it to Tennyson. The water was tepid, but as Decker had said, it was wet. He put the pail back on the table and sat down in the chair across the table from Decker.

"I keep a pail of water out here while I work," said Decker. "It's too far to walk back to the house to get a drink when I need one."

"Am I interfering with your work?" asked Tennyson. "If you have a second hoe, I'm not bad at hoeing."

"No interference. In fact, you gave me a good excuse to stop. I'm just polishing the garden. It really does not need a hoeing."

"There's something I have to say to you," said Tennyson. "I don't know if you and I are friends. I rather think we are, but it would depend on one's definition of a friend."

"Let's proceed on the assumption that we are friends," said Decker, "until we find out otherwise."

"It's about Whisperer."

"So he came to you."

"That's right. How did you know?"

"I was fairly sure he would. He was entranced by you. He told me so. I knew he'd hunt you up."

"He did more than hunt me up. He became—how the hell can I say this? He got into my mind; he became a part of me. Or at least he said he was a part of me. I can't be sure of that. He didn't stay too long."

"You threw him out?"

"No. He offered to leave if I wanted him to go. He was a gentleman about it."

"What happened?"

"About that time, Ecuyer came tearing in. Mary had got back from Heaven and was pretty well shook up."

"What happened to Mary?"

"We haven't the full story as yet. She was scared out of her skull. She's still not quite coherent."

"It would seem, then, that it wasn't Heaven."

Tennyson shook his head, perplexed. "We don't know. We can't make sense out of any of it. But about Whisperer. I told him he belonged to you; that I'd not lift a hand to steal him."

"I don't know if he belongs to me. I don't think he does. We are friends, that's all. It is quite a story. For years he pestered me. Played a game with me. It was the damnedest thing. He'd trail me and ambush me when I was in the wilderness. Challenging me. He wanted me to hunt him. He talked but not with a voice. Just words inside my mind. Probably you know how it is."

"Yes, he talked with me."

"I figured he was some big bloodthirsty beast. A ravening man-hunter with a twisted sense of humor. A couple of times, I got a bead on him, or what I thought was him. I had him in the sights, fair and square, but I didn't pull the trigger. I don't know why I didn't. I suspect that by that time, I'd gotten to like the bastard. There were times when, if I could have seen him, I would have clobbered him. Just to get shut of him, you understand, to get him off my back. But when it came right down to it, I couldn't pulled the trigger. He claimed later on that he was only testing me to make sure he could trust me as a friend. Not pulling the trigger must have convinced him, for he finally showed himself and there, instead of a ravening beast, was this little puff of shining dust."

"Since then he has lived with you."

"He's in and out. Off and on. You saw the carvings on the table?"

"Yes, I saw them."

"Whisperer carves them. I don't know how. I have a feeling that he can manipulate molecules—break them down, remove them from those areas he wants to carve away. I'm not sure of that. It's just a possible explanation that I came up with, out of thin air. He helps me hunt gems. Again, how he does it, I don't know. But he sniffs them out somehow. He locates them, tells me where to find them. Once we have them, he picks the ones he wants to carve."

"But you talk with him. You could have asked him. He could have told you."

"I don't think so, Jason. Our conversations are not on that high a level. At times I've felt funny with him, sensed a strangeness. Now, from what you've told me, I think I know what it was. He was trying to get inside my mind—trying, but unable to make it."

"You're probably right," said Tennyson. "He told me he had tried with you."

"But he can get into your mind."

"Tom, I can't be sure. He told me he had sneaked into my mind. I can't swear to it. All I have is his word for it. If he was, it was not for long. It was only a minute or two before Ecuyer arrived. I'm not sure I like this business of Whisperer. I'm not sure I want him messing around inside my head. Myself is enough; I'm not sure there's room for anyone else."

"I doubt you have anything to fear," said Decker. "He's a gentle soul. All that's wrong with him is loneliness. I helped him some with that. He thirsts for friends. I am, or was, the only one he has. Strange I feel a friendship for him. That seems impossible, that a man could feel friendship for a pinch of dust. I can sense the alien in him, but it doesn't put me off. I don't know who he is—"

"I wanted to ask you that. I thought that by now . . ."

"I've never asked him. I thought it was none of my business. And he's never told me. I thought at one time that perhaps he would, but he never has. Maybe it's too complicated to tell. I've done some speculating, of course, but I doubt I've ever gotten close."

"So you have no objection if I let him into my mind? If I tell him to stay out, I'm sure he will stay out."

"No objection," said Decker. "I think you should let him in, if you have no objection, if you're not too queasy about it. Maybe he'll tell you things when he's inside your mind that both of us should know. He's been on this planet for a long time. He must have been here even before Vatican. Maybe he can shed some light on Vatican. I know he's interested; he's forever poking around over there. I have the impression, though, that he doesn't find out much."

He got out of his chair. "Would you have a drink with me if I can find a jug?"

"Yes, of course I would."

"You stay here, then. I'll go up to the shack and get it. It's too nice a day to be sitting in a house."

"It is that," said Tennyson.

After Decker left, Tennyson sat quietly in his chair. Before him stretched the garden patch and a small open woods. Far off, the mountains reared into the blueness. Over all lay a sense of peace and quiet. Far off, a bird made half-hearted song, and at times a tiny breeze made a small, whispering rustle in the leaves. Even the sunshine was a quiet sunshine.

Off to the left he could see the gray and white of Vatican, the buildings blending into the background—unobtrusive, almost apologetic for intruding on the world. A quiet institution in a quiet world, thought Tennyson; no bad place to be. Over there, Jill was working in the library. He tried to separate the buildings in order to distinguish the library, but was unable to tell one building from another. At this distance, they made up a single huddle.

Jill worked too hard, he told himself; she was spending too many hours going through the records. The whole business had

become an obsession with her. No longer did she mention leaving
End of Nothing. Sitting there, he called her up in mind again—the
intense face in the lamplight, telling him what she'd found that
day, talking it out with him, trying out ideas on him—and all the
time that ugly scarlet slash across one side of her face, a stigma
that he scarcely ever noticed now, but it was, he thought, a pity
just the same.

So deep was he in his thoughts of Jill that he was startled when
Decker returned to thump down a bottle and two glasses on the
table.

"Drink up," he said. "This is the last of the bottle that you
brought me, but Charley is due in another day or two. He'll bring
me more."

"You don't have to depend on Charley," said Tennyson. "I'll
fetch you a couple or three bottles. Ecuyer has a cache of it. More
than the two of us possibly can use."

Decker grunted. "I said Charley would be showing up in a day
or two and I got no flicker of interest out of you. Does that mean
you're not going to try to arrange a deal to go back with him?"

"It's too soon," said Tennyson. "Gutshot will still remember
me. There might be someone hanging around on the watch for me.
Even if that weren't so, I don't think I want to leave. Not quite
yet, anyhow."

"How about Jill?"

"She'll probably stay on for a while as well. She's all caught up
in her history project."

"Both of you," said Decker, "are learning what I learned. End
of Nothing is a fairly tolerable planet. Good climate. Productive
land. No one pushing other people around. That's the best of it.
There is no pushing around."

"That's why you stayed?"

"That's part of it. The other part of it is that I am a couple of
hundred years out of my time. I'll tell you the whole story someday, when the time comes and you have a lot of leisure to listen.
But the gist of it is that I had to abandon ship. My crew ran off
and left me, but somehow, in panic and by oversight, perhaps,
they left one lifeboat. Not for me, not intentionally for me, I am

sure; they probably just overlooked it in their mad rush to escape. I got into it and went into suspended animation. The ship got me here safe and sound, sniffing out a planet that would support me, but by the time it got me here a couple of centuries had passed. I am an anachronism, a man two centuries out of his world. I can't go back to the galaxy again; I'd be out of my depth. Here it doesn't matter. Most of the humans here are more outdated than I am. And the robots, God knows. In a lot of ways, they haven't advanced an inch beyond the time they came here a millennium ago. In other ways, they may be a million years ahead. They're brain-picking the galaxy, perhaps the universe."

"You have any idea what they really have?"

"No inkling at all. Whatever they have, they keep it bottled up."

"And yet they are afraid. Jill found a memo one of the cardinals wrote. Undated, so there's no telling when it was written. It tells of a bunch of aliens, riding in bubble ships, that came here. On a survey, more than likely. They stayed only a short time, less than an hour. But this cardinal was scared pink with purple spots."

"There's a legend of the visit," Decker said. "It must have happened years ago. The Day the Bubbles Came. It has all the markings of an ancient folktale, but the memo probably means that it has some historic basis."

"Why should the robots be so upset about it? The visiting aliens offered no harm; they didn't hang around."

"You must realize," said Decker, "that the robot never is an adventurer. He always plays the averages. He never takes a chance. He is always cautious. That's the true measure between a robot and a human. Men take chances, plunge ahead, go for broke. A robot never does. It may be a reflection of his inferiority complex. He talks big, acts big at times, but he's never really big. He hunkers down a lot. He jumps at his own shadow. Vatican robots have been fairly successful here; there's not much here to spook them."

Chapter Thirty

JOHN, THE GARDENER, WENT DOWN THE MANY LONG FLIGHTS of stone stairs beneath Vatican and finally came to Pope country. He went along a corridor until he reached a small door. From a compartment in his waist, he took out a key and opened the door that led into a tiny room with only one chair in it. The lock snicked when he pushed the door closed behind him. On the wall facing the chair a metallic plate was set into the solid stone.

The gardener sat in the chair. "Your Holiness," he said. "John is here to make a report."

The cross-hatched face appeared slowly, deliberately on the plate.

"It is good to see you, John," said His Holiness. "What brings you here this time?"

"I am here, Your Holiness," said John, "to tell you some of the facts of life. I hope this time that you pay attention to me. I'm not out there playing the fool for nothing, putting on my act as a silly gardener mumbling to his roses. I am doing your work, your personal work that you can't trust to your stupid cardinals. I'm out there spying for you, listening for you, gathering information for you, starting rumors for you. The least you can do, Your Holiness, is listen."

"I always listen, John."

"Not always," John said grumpily.

"I'll listen this time, John."

"There is a rumor," said John. "No more than a rumor, but a good strong rumor, that the Listener Mary went back to Heaven for the second time and was thrown out."

"I haven't heard that," said the Pope.

"No, of course you haven't. The cardinals wouldn't tell you. They'd pussyfoot around—"

"In time," said His Holiness, "they would have gotten around to telling me."

"In time, yes. After they had stumbled around a lot and talked it over among themselves, viewing it from all angles and trying to figure out how best to break it to you, to tell you so it went down easy."

"They are good and faithful servants. They only do what they do out of their thoughtfulness for me."

"They do what they do," said the gardener, "to twist your direction and your purpose. When Vatican first was established, Your Holiness, its aim was to seek out a true religion. Unlike the humans of Earth, we had the honesty to admit we were hunting for a better faith than the one we had known on Earth. Do you still, Your Holiness, seek a true religion?"

"I believe I do," said the Pope. "Among other things."

"That's the gist of it—among other things. There have been too many other things. Technological systems. Philosophical trends that have little to do with our primary purpose. . . ."

"But philosophy, John, does have much to do with what you call our primary purpose. I take it that you would cancel all else but a mad, frantic search for a faith we felt, at one time, we would find."

"Do you think so no longer, Your Holiness?"

"You're asking me if I still believe in the logic and necessity for the search. The answer is that of course I do. But what seemed simple a thousand years ago appears not so simple now. It is not a matter of faith alone, not only the matter of finding the right deity, if deity is the term we want, but a matter of untangling the many survival and evolutionary systems that have been developed by the people that our Listeners are discovering. It is only by the study of such systems and the thinking of the beings residing in those patterns, I am now convinced, that we can find the answers that will lead us to what you call a true religion."

"Your Holiness, you mock me!"

"I would not mock you, John. We have worked too long together for me ever to do that. But I do think that our viewpoints, through the years, have grown very far apart."

"You have changed more than I have, Your Holiness. I am still the simple robot that came out here from Earth. My viewpoint is closer to our original plan than is yours. I helped plan and fabricate you and we tried to build a greatness and a deep wisdom in you, a love of holiness. You are not—you will pardon me for saying this—but you are not that same pontiff that we fabricated."

The Pope made a noise that sounded like a chuckle. "No, certainly I am not. Would you expect me to be? Did you think that you could cast my pattern and that it would not deviate? That in the light of new fact and new thought, the pattern still would persist as the image of what you and your fellows thought a thousand years ago? You are right; I am no longer pure robot; I have lost much of the humanity that you put into me. I have grown—well, let us say *more alien,* as the centuries have crept along. I have so much alienness fed into me—some of it, in part, pure garbage—that I have become, in some aspects, alien. This could have been expected even by you, John. It was necessary. I had to develop certain alien faculties to handle all the alien concepts that are dumped into me. I have changed. Certainly I have changed. I am no longer the instrument that you robots made. I am amazed that you are not aware of that. I have a backlog of data that is catalogued and waiting to be fitted into whatever matrix that conceivably could make use of it. I can tell you from sad experience that my trillions of little jigsaw pieces often do not fit, even when they appear to be a perfect fit, but have to be taken out and put back on the shelf until another pattern shows up where one or two, or a dozen, or a hundred of them, might appear to be of value. I don't mind telling you that I am crammed with half-finished puzzles, some of which may need only a few more pieces to make them come together, but others, many others, that may never come together, that will never come to anything at all. That's the trouble with you robots. You want answers and I haven't any answers. As I told you, the universe is not so simple as it once appeared. I am a long-range project and you people are expecting short-range results from me. . . ."

"Your Holiness, a thousand years is not short-range."

The Pope made the chuckling noise again. "In my kind of business, it is. If I last a million years—"

"You will last a million years. We will see you do."

"Well, then," said the Pope, "there is some hope that we will attain your goal."

"*My goal.* Your Holiness, you speak as if it isn't yours."

"Oh, it's mine, all right. But the other aspects of our research cannot be ignored. There is no way of knowing in what direction any segment of research will lead—many times in unsuspected directions."

"Your Holiness, you have allowed Vatican to become sidetracked, you have encouraged it to go baying off in all these other directions that you speak of. The cardinals are grabbing for power—"

"I do not deny," said His Holiness, "that some of my cardinals have turned out to be a poor lot, but they're not entirely bad. Administratively, some of them are sound. For example, the pilgrim program has been handled rather neatly."

"I am amazed you're so cynical, Your Holiness, as to mention the pilgrim program. We keep it going only for the revenue it brings. We feed these poor pilgrims a sordid mish-mash of religious concepts that they cannot understand, but that have a pleasant sound, although very little truth and less sincerity. The worst of it is that because they cannot understand the concepts, they believe in them."

"Very little truth, you say. I could ask you what is truth, but I won't, for you'd try to answer and confuse me all the more. I'm not sure but that I agree with you about the pilgrims, but the program does bring in a handsome revenue of which we stand in need and it furnished us an excellent cover as a crackpot cult—in case anyone ever thinks of us, which I doubt they do."

"I deplore that attitude," said the gardener. "In the pilgrim program we are only going through the motions and we should do more than that, we *could* do more than that. We should touch every soul we can."

"That's what I like so much about you, John. Your concern with soul even when you must know you do not have a soul."

"I do not know I have no soul. I rather think I have. It makes sense to say that every intelligence has a soul."

"Whatever a soul may be," said the Pope.

"Yes, whatever a soul may be."

"No one else could say such things to me," said His Holiness, "nor I such things to them. That is why you're so valuable to me, so much a friend, although the way we talk does not seem to indicate we're friends. There was one time I thought of you as a cardinal, but you were of infinitely greater help as a gardener. Would you like to be a cardinal?"

The gardener made an obscene sound.

"I suppose it's just as well," said the Pope. "You are dangerous as a gardener; you'd be even more dangerous as a cardinal. Tell me now and don't stammer to give you time to make up a lie. You were the one, were you not, who set off this business of canonizing Mary?"

"Yes, I was. I do not apologize for it. The people need a saint— the devout robots in Vatican and the humans in the village. Their faith grows weak; it needs some reinforcement. There must be something soon to reaffirm the purpose that we held when we first came here. But if Mary was booted out of Heaven . . ."

"John, do you know that as a fact?"

"No, I don't. I told you it was but a rumor. Mary did go somewhere and was traumatized—how, I am not sure. Ecuyer has dug in his heels and refused to turn the crystal over to Vatican. That prissy little doctor of ours evades my questions. He knows whatever Ecuyer knows. The two of them are buddies."

"I'm not comfortable with the procedure of hauling forth a saint," said the Pope. "It's a throwback to the Christianity of Earth. Not that Christianity was a bad thing—it was not—but it was far from what it pretended to be. I use the past tense, knowing full well Christianity still survives, but speaking in the past because I have no idea how it has developed, if it has developed."

"You can be sure," said John with some bitterness, "that it has changed. Not necessarily developed, but changed."

"Back to the saint idea. Your proposal that Mary be made a saint is somewhat tainted now if the rumor you mention should be

true. We cannot make a saint out of a woman who has been
kicked out of Heaven."

"That's exactly what I am trying to explain to you," said the
gardener. "We need a saint or some other symbol that will serve
to anchor our faith into the foreseeable future. I have watched and
waited for a saint but none showed up—not even a marginal saint.
Mary is the first one, and we must not allow her to slip through
our fingers. Vatican must get hold of the Heaven cube—this last
Heaven cube—and either destroy or suppress it. We must deny
with all our strength and authority that she was booted out of
Heaven—"

"First of all," said the Pope, "you must know that it isn't
Heaven."

"Of course it's not," said John.

"But you are willing to allow the lesser breeds to believe it is."

"Your Holiness, we need a saint. We need a Heaven."

"We talked a while ago about our search for a more honest
religion and now—"

"But, Your Holiness—"

"If it's a saint we need," said His Holiness, "I can suggest a
better candidate than Mary—an intelligent, deeply ambitious robot
so selfless in his love of his people and his hope for their salvation
that he gave up his chance to a high post in Vatican to work as a
humble gardener communing with his roses. . . ."

The gardener made a disrespectful sound.

Chapter Thirty-one

THE OLD ONES OF THE WOODS TALKED AMONG THEMSELVES,
the comfortable, neighborly talk of little consequence—from all
around the planet they talked to one another, filled with respect
for one another, easy with their relationships.

—There was a time, said one of them who dwelled on a verdant
plain that stretched for hundreds of miles on the other side of the

mountain range that towered over Vatican, there was a time when I was much concerned with the metal race that settled on our surface. I feared they would expand, reaching for our soil and trees, for our mineral treasures, wasting our water and our land. I was even more concerned when we learned that the metal race was the creation of an organic folk who designed them as their servants. But after long years of keeping watch, there appears to be no danger.

—They are decent folk, said the Old One who lived in the hills above Decker's cabin, from which point he kept close watch on Vatican. They use our resources, but they use them wisely, taking only as they need, careful to preserve the fertility of the soil.

—In the beginning, said another who dwelled among the high peaks to the west of Vatican, I was disturbed by their extensive use of trees. In the beginning, and even now, they have the need of vast amounts of wood. But they harvest wisely, they are not wasteful and they never overcut. At times they plant young saplings to replace the trees they've taken.

—They are most satisfactory neighbors, said still another one who lived beside an ocean halfway around the planet. If we were fated to have neighbors, we have been lucky in them.

—Yet, said the one living on the plain, a short time ago it became necessary to kill. . . .

—Not the metal ones, said the Old One who lived on Decker's hill, but members of that organic race we have spoken of. There are others of them here, there have been others here ever since the coming of the metal ones. But those who live with us permanently must be a special breed. They have no designs on our planet or ourselves. Rather, they are afraid of us, a situation we do not wish, but an attitude of which it would be difficult to disabuse them. The ones we killed included an outsider newly come to us and a different folk entirely. He had a weapon which he felt certain could put an end to us, although why he should have wanted to put an end to us, I do not understand.

—Obviously, said another one, we could not put up with that.

—No, we could not, said the Decker Old One, although there was much regret at doing what we had to do. Especially we regretted the killing of the others who accompanied the one who sought an end of us. They were not so depraved as he, but they did go along with him.

—It was the only way we could have acted, said the Old One by the ocean. You pursued the proper course.

They ceased their talk for a moment, silent, but showing one another what they saw and sensed—the wide, flat prairie with its far horizons, grass blowing in long swaths before the wind, like waves upon a sea, the soft color here and there of prairie flowers, sisters to the grass; the wide sand beach that ran for miles along the foaming ocean, with birds that were something less and something more than birds running on the sands, not each one alone, but all of them together in formations that fell just short of a formal dance; the deep, hushed solemnity of a shadowed forest, the forest floor clean of undergrowth, the stark, dark trunks of trees forming, in whatever direction one might look, long blue-misty aisles that led into foreverness; a deep tree-and-brush-shrouded ravine, with great outthrusts of naked rock along both of the steep converging hillsides that formed the ravine, a place alive with tiny, skittering, friendly life that ran and squeaked among the outthrust rocks and the fallen rotting tree trunks, with the crystal singing of a hidden brook that dashed and foamed along the rocky bed where the hillsides came together.

—We have been lucky, said the one who crouched above the singing ravine. We have been able, with no great labor on our part, to preserve the planet as it was created. As wardens, we have done little more than watch over it, checking from time to time to see that all is well. There have been no invaders who held intent to misuse the planet or do it harm. Had we faced such a challenge there have been times when I've wondered how well we could have carried out our charge.

—We would have done well, I'm sure, said the One atop the mountain above Vatican. Instinctively, we would have known how to act.

—We did fail in one regard, said the Decker Old One. We let the Dusters get away.

—There was nothing we could have done about it, said the Old

One on the plain. We could not have stopped their leaving. I am not sure it would have been right for us to do so. They were intelligent creatures and should have been accorded free will.

—Which we accorded them, said the One beside the ocean.

—But they originated here and developed here, said an Old One who lived in a distant desert. They were part of the planet and we allowed them to depart. Their leaving subtracted something from the planet. I have often wondered what function they might have carried out if they had stayed.

—Old Ones, said the One within the forest, this is footless speculation. They left long ago. Whether they would, in time, have exercised some influence on the planet, we cannot know. The planet may not have suffered from their leaving. Their influence, if there had been any, might have been adverse. I find myself wondering why this matter was brought into our conversation.

—Because one of them remains, said the Decker Old One. It lives with one of the organic beings that created the metal ones. When the others left, it remained behind. I have puzzled over why it should have remained behind. More than likely it was simply left here when the others went away. They may, as a matter of fact, have left it intentionally. You see, it is a runt. . . .

Chapter Thirty-two

THE GLITTER OF DIAMOND DUST FLOATED IN THE AIR JUST above the spindly, gilded chair that stood beside the table with the marble top.

—So you're back, said Tennyson.

—Please, said Whisperer. Please!

—I am not about, said Tennyson, to cave in to your pleas. But I think it's time for us to talk.

—I'll talk, said Whisperer. I'll talk most willingly. I'll tell you who and what I am, and no other knows who or what I am. I'll answer all your questions.

—All right, then, tell me what you are.

—The Old Ones call me Duster and Decker calls me Whisperer and—

—It's immaterial what you may be called, said Tennyson. Tell me what you are.

—I am an unsubstantial conglomerate of molecules, all the molecules disassociated and yet making up myself. Every molecule of me, perhaps every atom of me, is intelligent. I am a native of this planet, although I can remember no beginning and I anticipate no end. I may, in fact, be immortal, although I've never thought upon it. Although, come to think of it, I am sure I am. There is no killing me. Even were I scattered, so thoroughly scattered that no atom of my being ever found another atom of my being through all eternity, yet I know each atom would be a life within itself, still sentient, still intelligent.

—It would seem to me, said Tennyson, that you are an efficient fellow. You're immortal and intelligent and no one can so much as lay a hand on you. You've got it made.

—But I have not got it made. True, I have intelligence and, as an intelligent being, I have the drive to learn and know, but I lack the tools to learn and know.

—So you seek a tool.

—You put it very crudely.

—You want to use me as a tool. A tool to help you learn and know. What is it that you want to know?

—I need to know of Vatican and of the work that's done here. I need to enter into the worlds the Listeners are finding. For long and long I've tried, and I have learned a little, but so very little. One does not enter into the thought processes of machines. They've not that kind of mind. My probing of them, or my attempts to probe them through the years, has made Vatican suspicious. They know there is someone probing, but they don't know who it is. They try to seek me out but they do not find me. They probably are unaware that I exist.

—You think that I can help you? That I'd be willing to?

—You can help me. Of that there is no question. You can view the cubes. If you only let me in your mind so I can share what you see within the cubes, then the two of us together . . .

—But, Whisperer, why me? There is Ecuyer.

—I have tried with Ecuyer. He is insensitive to me. No more sensitive than the robots; he does not know I am there, does not even see the glitter of me. Decker sees the glitter and I can talk with him, but he cannot view the cubes and his mind is closed to me. That leaves only you, and perhaps one other.

—One other?

—The one that you call Jill.

—You have talked with her?

—No, I have not talked with her. But I think I could; also her mind is not closed to me.

—Let's leave her out of it, said Tennyson. For the moment, leave her out of this. Is that understood?

—It is understood. We'll leave her out of it.

—You want to view the cubes with me. To get inside my mind and view the cubes with me. Is that all you want?

—Perhaps not all. But the most important.

—Now tell me why. Why is it so important that you view the cubes?

—To regain my heritage.

—Now, back up a minute there, said Tennyson. What has your heritage got to do with it?

—I was, so long ago that time grows dim in the thinking of it, only one small part of a cloud of me—a cloud of other Dusters, or if you wish, of other Whisperers. I say a cloud of me, for I do not know if the cloud was one, if I was a minor part of a larger entity, or if the cloud was made up of very many single entities like me. The cloud had a heritage, it had a destiny—perhaps you could say that it had a task. That task was to know the universe.

—You don't say, said Tennyson.

—But I do say. Would I deceive you, running the chance that you should learn of my deceit, thus losing any hope of the cooperation that I seek of you?

—That makes sense. I don't suppose you would. But what happened to the cloud?

—It went away and left me, said Whisperer. Why I do not know. Nor do I know where it went except that I know it went to seek out the universe. In bitter hours I've pondered why it went and left me. But leaving me, it did not take away my heritage. By every means I still seek out the universe.

—Of course you do, said Tennyson.

—You mock me. You lack belief in me?

—Let's put it this way, said Tennyson. I am not overwhelmed by belief in you. All you've told me so far is what you want to do and how you need my help. I ask you now—what is there in it for me? What do I get out of it? Something more, I hope, than the pleasure of your company.

—You are a hard man, Tennyson.

—I am not a fool. I don't propose to let you use me. It seems to me that in this, somewhere, there should be a bargain struck.

—A bargain, said Whisperer. Yes, of course, a bargain.

—So all right. A bargain with the devil.

—Which one of us is that devil that you speak of? If my understanding of the term is correct, I am not a devil. Neither, I think, are you.

—Okay, then, no devil.

—Without your leave, said Whisperer, I dipped briefly in your mind. For which I beg forgiveness.

—You are forgiven. If it was only for an instant.

—I tell you true. It was only for a moment. In your mind I snared two worlds. The autumn world and the equation world. Which would you like to visit? Which one would you prefer to go to? Which would you want to see? Not to see, not to stare at, not to wonder over, but to actually go to.

—You mean that you could take me there? That I could walk those worlds?

—With me, you could walk those worlds. Perhaps understand them, although I'm not sure of that. But you could see them clearly, lay your hands on them.

—And the Heaven world?

—You have not seen the Heaven world.

—No, I've not, said Tennyson.

—Well, then?

—You mean go to one of the worlds and then come back?

—Yes, of course come back. You never go to a place from which you can't return.

—You would take me over—

—No, not take you over. The two of us together.

Impossible, Tennyson told himself. It could not be done. Either he was dreaming again or he faced the sleekest con . . .

—It's possible, said Whisperer. It can be done. It is not a con. You have pondered on the equation world. You have dreamed of it. It will not let you be.

—I could never get a good look at it, said Tennyson. It was always hidden. I knew there was much there that I wasn't seeing.

—Then go with me and see it.

—And understand?

—No, I'm not sure we'll understand. But, together, better than one of us alone.

—You tempt me, Whisperer. Should I take a chance on you?

—No chance, my friend. May I call you friend?

—Not a friend, Whisperer. A partner. Partners also must have trust and faith. And if you fail. . . .

—If I fail?

—Decker would hear of it. You'd lose your only friend.

—The threat is unworthy of you, partner.

—Perhaps it is.

—But you let it stand?

—I let it stand, said Tennyson.

—So let you and I go together to the equation world.

—We'll have to view the cube.

—No need of it. It is fixed within your mind.

—Yes, said Tennyson, but imperfectly. I do not see it all. Some of it is missing.

—It all is there. It needs the digging out. You and I, together, as one person, we can dig it out.

—This togetherness, said Tennyson, is beginning to wear thin on me.

—Think of it as oneness, then. Not two of us, but one. Now think deeply of the equation world. Remember it as best you can. We'll essay to enter it.

Chapter Thirty-three

ENOCH CARDINAL THEODOSIUS WALKED INTO THE LIBRARY and clambered on his stool, looking more like a well-dressed scarecrow than he did a cardinal.

"I hope," he said to Jill, "that you don't mind these visits from a clanking old robot who does not have enough to do to occupy his time."

"Eminence, I love your visits," said Jill. "I look forward to them."

"It is strange," said the cardinal, pulling up his feet to place them on the lower rungs of the stool, shucking up his robe about his middle and crouching forward, hands clasped around himself as if he might have a bellyache. "It is strange that such as we should find so much to talk about. I think that our conversations have good substance to them. Do you not agree?"

"Yes, Your Eminence, I do."

"I have gained great respect for you," he said. "You work hard and enthusiastically. You have a mousetrap mind. There's not much escapes you. Your assistants make good reports of you."

"You mean that my assistants are spies who make reports to you?"

He flapped a hand in distress. "You know that's not my meaning. I have occasion at times to talk with them and your name is mentioned. You have impressed them very much. You think like a robot, so they tell me."

"Oh, I hope that's not the truth."

"What's so bad, milady, about robotic thinking?"

"Nothing, I suppose. But robotic thinking is wrong for me. I should be thinking human."

"Humans are strange folk," said the cardinal. "That is a conclusion I have reached through long years of watching them. You may not be aware of it, but robots are obsessed by humans. They are one of our favorite conversational subjects; we spend long hours in talking of them. I suppose it is possible for a human and a robot to establish strong relationships. There are myths that describe such closenesses. I have never had such a relationship and I feel, somehow, that for the lack of it, I've suffered. I must be frank and say that in my visits here I have detected the beginning of such a relationship to you. I hope you do not mind."

"Why, of course not. I am honored."

"Up until this time," said the cardinal, "I've had but small contact with humans. Ecuyer is the only man with whom I've had contact for any length of time."

"Paul Ecuyer is a good man," said Jill.

"Good. Yes, I suppose he's good. A bit stiff-necked, however. He lives for his Listeners."

"That's his job," said Jill. "He does it well."

"That is true, but there are times when he tends to forget for whom he's doing it. He gets too wrapped up in it. He assumes more than a normal amount of responsibility. His project is a Vatican project. There are times when he acts as if it's his and his alone."

"Your Eminence, what is this all about? Is your nose all out of joint over the Heaven incident?"

The cardinal lifted his head and stared at her. He grumbled at her. "Miss, sometimes you are too smart for your own good."

"Never that," she said. "Stupid sometimes when I am trying to be smart."

"I am concerned," he said, "over this saint business. I'm not sure we need a saint. A saint might cause us more trouble than it would be worth. What are your thoughts on it?"

"I haven't really thought of it. I have heard some talk. That's all."

"Ecuyer is slow in turning over the cube of the Listener Mary's second trip to Heaven. I have a feeling he'd just as soon not turn it over to us. I don't know what happened. I'm not sure anyone knows. There have been some ugly rumors."

"Probably none of them true."

"Yes, that's more than likely. Often rumors have little truth in them. But why hasn't Ecuyer given us the cube?"

"Probably he's been busy. He is a busy man. Does he always turn the cubes over to Vatican immediately?"

"No, I guess he doesn't. He gives them to us when he gets around to it."

"There, that's it," said Jill. "He simply hasn't gotten around to it."

"I don't know," said the cardinal. "Ecuyer is a close friend of Tennyson and Tennyson knows Decker."

"Your Eminence, you sound as if the three of them were closing in on you. What have Tennyson and Decker got to do with it? You have nothing to fear from either of them. Ecuyer and Tennyson are Vatican men. Decker never interferes in anything at all."

"You could help me with this."

"I'm not sure I could," she said. "What makes you think that I could help you out?"

"You must know about it. You sleep with Tennyson."

"Shame on you, Your Eminence," she said. "I never knew that robots paid attention to such things."

"Oh, we don't," said the cardinal. "Not in the way you mean. But Tennyson must have talked with you about it."

"It's not Mary being made a saint," she told him, "that is bothering you. It's Heaven, isn't it? If it worries you so much, why don't you go and find out what it is?"

"We have no coordinates. We don't know where to look."

"I think you are afraid," she said. "Your Eminence, even if you had the coordinates, I think you'd be afraid to go. You are afraid of what you'd find."

"My fear is not that," he told her. "My fear is of something greater. It is the present state of Vatican. For many centuries this place ran smoothly. There have been ups and downs, there have been differences of opinion, but never for a moment, until now, have I ever doubted that this institution would stand, solid as the rock in which it's rooted. But now there's an undercurrent of— what shall I call it?—perhaps an undercurrent of rebellion that would not hesitate to strike at our structure and the underlying principles on which it is founded. From where it comes I do not know, but I do know that there must be somewhere a very active mischief maker who is bringing it about, who is triggering it and fueling it to keep it going. For a long time, I have been aware that there was someone or something nibbling at our stores of knowledge. Not getting very far, but still nibbling, like a lone mouse, all by itself, nibbling at a ton of cheese. Whether the two of them, the nibbling mouse and the mischief maker, are one and the same, or otherwise connected, I do not know. Nothing must happen to Vatican, nothing must be allowed to interfere with it. We have too much at stake."

"Your Eminence," said Jill, "I think you are unduly worried. You have built too well. Vatican is too strong. There is nothing that could bring it down."

"Not Vatican itself," said the cardinal, "but its purpose. We came here, so long ago, as you must know from your study of our history, to seek a better and a truer faith. There are those who feel that we have abandoned that purpose, that we have gone haring off in pursuit of technological and philosophical knowledge that has nothing to do with our search for faith. In this I am convinced that they are wrong. Faith, I believe, is tied to knowledge, tied, perhaps, to one specific knowledge, but that to reach that knowledge, to arrive at that one answer, we must arrive at many answers. We may run down false trails at times, but perhaps these are trails that we must follow to be certain that they lead nowhere, or that they lead in the wrong direction."

"Your views have changed, then," said Jill. "In the early years the emphasis was on faith and not on knowledge."

"Yes, superficially you are right. But at first we did not realize that faith must be based on knowledge, not on blind belief, not on the repetitious mumbling of untruths, over and over again, in a desperate attempt to make them turn into truths. We cannot accept untruths; we must *know*."

He paused and stared at her with his direct, unblinking, upsetting robot stare. He raised an arm and waved it. Instinctively, Jill knew that he was waving at the universe, at all of space and time outside the room in which they sat.

"Somewhere out there," he said, "there is someone or something or somewhat that knows all the answers. Among all those answers we can winnow out the one we seek. Or it may be that we'll need all the answers, every one of them, to point to the one, still unfound, that we seek. Our job is to find that answer—all those answers or that one specific answer, whichever it may be. We cannot retreat into self-delusion for the comfort and the glory it may give us. We must keep on the search that we have started. No matter how long it may take or where it may lead us, we must bend to our task."

"And Heaven," she said, "would form a basis, a strong basis for the self-delusion that you fear."

"We can't take the chance," he said.

"You must suspect that it is not Heaven. Not the old Christian Heaven, with the trumpets sounding and the streets of gold and all the angels flying."

"Yes, intellectually I'm fairly sure it's not, but what if it should turn out to be?"

"Then you'd have your answer."

"No, I don't think we would. We might have an answer, but not *the* answer. Satisfied with an answer, however, we would no longer seek *the* answer."

"All right, then, go out and prove it isn't Heaven. Then come back and go on with your work."

"We cannot take the chance," said the cardinal.

"The chance that it could be Heaven?"

"Not that alone. Either way, Vatican would lose. It's what you humans call a no-win situation. If it is not Heaven, then we face the mistaken conviction on the part of many of our people that the Listeners are unreliable. If Mary—don't you see that if Mary should be proved wrong, then the cry would go up that we can no longer be sure about the Listeners, that many of them are wrong, that most of them are wrong. Ecuyer's Search Program is the one great tool we have. It cannot be placed in jeopardy. It has taken us centuries to build it to its present point. Were it disrupted, should overwhelming doubt be cast upon it, it would take centuries to reestablish, if indeed it could be reestablished."

Jill said, shock in her voice, "You can't allow that to come about."

Said the cardinal, "God forbid it should."

Chapter Thirty-four

WHEN HE HAD BEEN THERE BEFORE, THE EQUATION WORLD had been quavery, as if he were seeing it through the shimmer of brilliant sunlight off a smooth and glittering lake, but now there was no shimmer and there was solid ground, or at least a solid surface, underneath his feet. The equation diagrams stood out in orderly array, spread out across the plane, smooth surface upon which he stood. There was a horizon, far off, rising much higher than any horizon he had even seen before, with the pea-green carpet of the planetary surface (if it was, in fact, a planet) merging almost imperceptibly with the pale lavender of the shallow bowl of sky.

—Whisperer! said Tennyson.

But there was no Whisperer. Only himself. Although, he told himself, that was not entirely true. Whisperer was there, but not as a separate entity. What stood there upon this alien ground was not him alone, but he and Whisperer, melded into one.

He stood without moving, wondering how he knew this, how he could be so sure of it. And knew, even as he wondered, that it was not he who knew it, not the Tennyson, but the Whisperer who was part of him. Yet, despite this knowing, he was not aware of Whisperer and he wondered if this might not be true, quite in reverse, for Whisperer, who might be aware of himself alone and not at all of Tennyson. There was no answer to his wonderment, no clue from Whisperer that this was the case.

The funny thing about it all, he told himself, was that he seemed actually to be there in this equation world—not merely seeing it, but there in person. He could feel the solidity of the surface underneath his feet and he was breathing—breathing as easily as he would on an Earth-type planet. Frantically, he ran through his brain the odds against finding an environment in a place such as this that would be compatible to an unprotected human—suitable air to breathe, an acceptable atmospheric density and pressure, a gravity factor that was bearable, ambient temperature that would be kind to a human body. He shuddered at the odds that his quick calculation gave him. The odds, furthermore, he knew, might be much higher than he had calculated, for not only were the life factors bearable; they were comfortable.

The equation diagrams were in as many, if not more, colors than they had been when he had seen them in the cube, and later in his dreams. Both the cube and dreams, the dreams more so than the cube, had made them somewhat fuzzy, but here the colors were sharper and more brilliant and not fuzzy in the least. There seemed to him to be many more of them than he had seen in either cube or dream, and the equations and the diagrams were more varied and outrageous. Looking more closely at one group of them, he saw that no two of them were alike, in color, equation or diagram. Each of them stood out as an individual.

Since arriving he had stood rooted in one spot, made numb by being there, but standing in a place where one doubting part of him, perhaps the Tennyson, had never for a moment thought that he could come. But now he moved, one slow step and then another, testing out whether he could move, not certain that he should. But the equations were not moving and someone had to move. That is, someone had to move if anything was to be done, any contact made. It would not be right, he thought, to come here, to stand and stare in disbelief, not moving, and then to go away. To do this would have made the venture no better than the cube or dream.

Slowly, he moved across the surface until he was quite close to one of the equations. He could see that it was about eight feet tall, the top of it somewhat above his head, and twice as long. From where he was standing, since it was broadside to him, he could not estimate its breadth, but by looking at another one standing nearby, he calculated the width to be nine feet or so. They might run in different sizes, he realized, but all of those he saw seemed to be uniform, one with another.

The equation that he had walked up to was a deep-purple background with the equations and diagrams predominantly in orange, although there were touches here and there of red and green and yellow. He tried to puzzle out the equation (a very lengthy and complicated one) that it carried on its surface, but the signs and symbols were unlike any he had ever seen.

The cube from which he had calculated the width was a bright and startling pink, with the equations green, and just beyond it was another that was ash gray specked with copper spots, the equations in a lemon yellow and the diagrams in lavender. It was a fancy one, the fanciest of all those in sight.

There had been no reaction from the cubes when he had walked up to them, and there continued to be none. They all sat there, unchanging.

Now, for the first time, he realized that there wasn't any sound. This was a silent place. In all his life, he realized, he had at all times been accustomed to some level of sound. Even at a time of quiet, there always had been some marginal noise—a board creaking in a house, a soft breeze stirring leaves, tiny insects singing. But here there was nothing, absolutely nothing, no noise of any kind.

He shuffled closer to the equation cube and noted with some interest that his walking made no sound. Hesitantly, he reached out a hand and touched the cube with an index finger, ready to snatch it away at an instant's notice. The cube was soft to the touch, not hard and rigid as he had expected it might be, and neither warm nor cold. It made no indication of reaction to his touch, so he laid his hand upon it. With his palm flat against its surface, it seemed even softer than it had before. He pressed lightly upon it and felt the quiver underneath his palm, as if he had placed his hand upon a plate of jelly.

On the surface of the cube something moved and, startled, he

stepped away. The equations, he saw, were changing and shifting
about, and the diagrams were changing, too. The changing and the
shifting at first was slow, deliberate, but quickly they became
faster. They ran in a fascinating fluid motion, dissolving and running and combining into something else and then the something
else was gone and there was something new. It is talking to me, he
told himself, trying to communicate, attempting to bridge the gap
that lies between the two of us. He watched hypnotically, and
every now and then it seemed that he might be arriving at some
understanding, but then the equations and the diagrams would
change and he'd lose what had seemed, for a moment, to be some
feeble inkling of the meaning that was being written on the blackboard surface of the cube.

Out of the corner of one eye, he glimpsed a movement and
quickly stepped away, but there was no place to go, no place he
could run. The other cubes were closing in on him. Already a tight
ring of them had formed, blocking all possible escape. On the surfaces of all of them the equations and the diagrams were changing
and shifting. It was an unnerving sight; while there still was no
sound, he had the impression that all of them were shouting at
him.

More were arriving all the time and some of them soared off the
ground to perch upon those that had surrounded him and others
came and settled down upon the second tier, as if they were con-
crete blocks and some invisible mason was using them to erect a
wall around him. They were towering over him, and all the time
they were moving in and he was half dizzy with the riotous running of their colors as the equations raced and scintillated to effect
the changes. He had the fleeting impression that they no longer
were trying to communicate, but under some impelling circumstance had come together to solve some weighty and complicated
problem, with the equations building to immense complexity and
the diagrams becoming twisted into inconceivable dimensions.

Then they toppled in upon him, the wall of them that had been
built around him caving in and crashing down upon him. He
screamed in terror, but as they came down upon him, the terror
went away and he was left with a sense of wonder that was so

deep it seemed to engulf all the universe. He was not crushed.
Nothing at all happened to him except that he now stood in the
center of the pile of cubes that had collapsed upon him. He stood
unharmed in the midst of a sea of multicolored jelly and he
feared, for a moment, that he'd either drown or suffocate, for in
this close-packed jelly mass, there could be no air and his nostrils
and his mouth and throat would fill with jelly and it would get
into his lungs—

This did not happen. He felt no discomfort. For a moment he
struggled to swim through the mass of jelly, seeking to rise to the
surface where there would be air to breathe. Then he ceased his
efforts, for somehow he knew he had no need of air and that he
would not drown. The equation cubes were sustaining him, and
within the midst of them, no harm could come to him. They did
not tell him this, but he knew it. He had the impression that he
had absorbed the message by a strange osmosis.

All the time the equations kept running around him and some
of them twined themselves around him and some of them went
through him and others of them went inside of him and stayed
there and, in that moment, he seemed to understand that he had
become an equation among all the rest of them. He felt the equations flowing through him and all around him and some of the diagrams joined together and constructed an intricate house for him
and he crouched inside it, not knowing what he was, but for the
moment quite content with being what he was.

Chapter Thirty-five

A GROUP OF LISTENERS GATHERED FOR THE COFFEE HOUR.
"What is the word on Mary?" asked Ann Guthrie.

"No one seems to know," said James Henry. "At least no one
is talking."

"Doesn't anyone ever go to see her?" asked Ann.

"I did," said Herb Quinn. "I could only go in for a moment. She seemed to be sleeping."

"Or under sedation," said Janet Smith.

"Perhaps," Herb agreed. "The nurse marched me out. Visitors are not welcome."

"I'd feel better," said Ann, "if Old Doc were still around to take care of her. I don't know about this new doctor."

"Tennyson?"

"Yes, Tennyson."

"I think you're wrong," said James Henry. "He seems an all-right guy. I had a talk with him a few weeks ago."

"But you don't know how good a doctor he is."

"No, I've never been to him."

"I had a sore throat a while ago," said Marge Streeter. "I went to him and he cured it for me quickly. He is a pleasant man. Easy to talk with. At times Old Doc was grumpy."

"That's right," said Herb. "Used to give me hell for not taking care of myself."

"I don't like some of the stories that are going around about Mary," said Ann.

"None of us do," said Herb. "Vatican's always full of gossip. I never believe anything I hear."

"Something must have happened," said Janet. "Something rather terrible. All of us have had shocks. It can happen."

"But we come out of it quickly," said Herb. "A day or two."

"Mary's getting old," said Ann. "Maybe she's not up to it anymore. She should ease up. There are clone Marys coming up. They could take over."

"Cloning bothers me," said Marge. "I know it makes a lot of sense and is generally accepted throughout most of the human galaxy. Still, it has a creepy feel to it. Anyone who dabbles in cloning must think they have a license to play God. The whole idea is unnatural."

"Playing God is nothing new," said James. "Throughout all of history, both human history and otherwise, there has been a lot of God playing. The most flagrant example is the race that Ernie ran across. You remember it. Several years back."

"That's the one," said Herb, "that creates worlds and peoples them with creatures out of their own imagination. . . ."

"That's right," said James, "but the worlds are logical. Not a few sticks and a pile of mud and magic mumbled over them. That race's worlds are well engineered. All the factors that should go into the creation of a planet. Nothing phoney about them. All the right pieces put together correctly. And the creatures they put on them logical as well—some terribly screwy biological setups, but they work."

"Yes, I know," said Herb, "and then what happens? Each world becomes a stress world, a living laboratory with the populations subjected to all sorts of tests, faced with all kinds of situations that have to be solved if they want to survive. Intellectual beings used as test animals. Probably a lot of data is obtained and some social problems studied in some depth, but it is rough on the planet populations. And for no purpose."

"Maybe there is a purpose," said Janet. "Mind, I'm not defending the action, but there could be a purpose. Maybe not one that we would find sufficient, but . . ."

"I don't know about that," said Ann. "I'm inclined to doubt it. There must be, there simply *has* to be a set of universal ethics. There must, through all of space and time, be some things that are wrong and others that are right. We can't excuse a vicious race for its vicious acts on the sole ground that the race itself is vicious, that it knows no better."

"That is an argument," said James, "that could go on forever."

"Did Ernie ever pin down the coordinates for that race of planet-making gods?" asked Marge.

"I don't believe he did," said Herb. "He went back several times, made a number of observations. In a perverse sort of way, he worked up some interest in the situation—that and all the various world situations that the race cooked up. But he finally decided he was not getting much of any real interest, so he pulled back and canceled out."

"He was lucky he could cancel," said James. "Sometimes these experiences build up so much fascination that we get pulled back—just as Mary was pulled back to Heaven."

"The one that I keep thinking about," said Marge, "is that old senile computer Betsy blundered into several years ago. Out on one of the globular clusters centered almost exactly above the galactic core. The computer is still in command of a vast array of rather mysterious machinery created for some unknown purpose. Some of the machinery apparently is beginning to break down because of lack of maintenance. What the machines were supposed to do, Betsy hasn't figured out. The entire planet's haywire. At one time there apparently was an intelligent biology there, but whether it built the machines Betsy doesn't know. The biology by now is fairly well wiped out, and what is left of it gone into hiding."

"Betsy is still working on that one," said Ann.

"And likely to be for some time," said Herb. "Vatican has a special interest in the senile computer. They would like to know how and why a computer can fumble its way into senility. No one says so, but Vatican probably has His Holiness in mind."

"The Pope's not old enough," said Marge, "for anyone to suspect him of senility."

"Not yet," said James. "He is still a youngster. But the time could come. Give him a million years or so. I suspect Vatican is quite capable of thinking a million years ahead."

"Vatican won't exist for a million years," said Ann.

"Don't bet on that," said Herb. "Robots are the most stubborn thing there is. They don't cave in. They won't give up. These Vatican robots have too much going for them to even think of it. In a million years they well may have the galaxy in the hollows of their hands."

Chapter Thirty-six

JILL WENT TO THE CLINIC TO VISIT MARY. THE NURSE MET her at the door. "You can stay for only a few minutes," said the nurse. "Don't try to speak with her."

Jill moved a few feet into the room and stopped, looking down upon the frail, pallid woman on the bed, her body so thin and unsubstantial that its shape barely showed beneath the sheet. Her gray hair was spread out on the pillow. Her two clawlike hands lay outside the sheet, clutched together, the fingers interlaced, as if in desperation. Her thin lips were loosely pulled together. The jawbone and the cheekbones stood out in all their starkness, thinly covered by a parchment skin.

There was about her, Jill thought with some alarm, a certain look of skin-and-bones holiness, reminiscent of a drawing she once had seen of a fanatic medieval hermit who had managed to starve himself into acceptable holiness. This, she thought, this poor wreck of a woman, this skeleton—this is the one who is being touted as a saint!

Mary's eyes came open, slowly open, not naturally, but as if she'd forced them. Her head was so positioned on the pillow that the opened eyes looked squarely into Jill's face.

The loose lips moved and a question came out of them, a thin whisper that cut across the silence of the room.

"Who are you?" she asked.

Jill whispered back at her. "I'm Jill. I dropped by to see you."

"No," said Mary, "you are not Jill. I have heard of Jill but I've never seen her. And I've seen you. Somewhere I have seen you."

Jill shook her head slowly, thinking to calm the woman on the bed.

"I recognize you," insisted Mary. "Once, long ago, we talked together, but I can't remember where."

The nurse stalked toward Jill, then halted when Mary spoke again.

"Come close," she said. "Close so I can see you better. My eyes are bad today. Bend down so I can see you."

Jill moved close to the bed, bent down.

On the sheet the two clasped hands came apart and Mary lifted a paper-tissue hand and patted Jill upon the cheek.

"Yes, yes," she said. "I know you."

Then the hand fell back and the lids slid down across the eyes.

The nurse was beside Jill, tugging at her. "You'll have to leave now."

"Get your hands off me," said Jill in sudden anger. "I'm going."

Outside the clinic, she drew in a deep breath, suddenly feeling free. There was death inside that room, she told herself. Death and something else.

The sun was moving down the west, hanging just above the purple mountain wall, and this final hour of sunlight lay like a soft benediction on the land. Now, for the first time since she had come to End of Nothing (how long had it been—a few days, a few weeks, a few months?)—now, for the first time, she saw the land on which she stood not as an alien world, not as a grotesque setting for the great incomprehensibility that was Vatican, but as a place where she lived, as an environment in which she had comfortably settled herself.

Vatican lay against the land, now a part of it, growing out of the land as if it had sprouted roots deep into its soil—not a glaring obtrusion, but something that had grown as naturally as trees, blending into the biota of the planet. To the east and south lay the fields, the gardens and the orchards, an idyllic oasis that moved in close to the mass of squat, spreading buildings that made up Vatican, an ordered interface that linked Vatican to the primal soil. To the west were the mountains, the cloudlike mass of blue that was forever shifting shades, the continual shadow-show that Jason Tennyson had fallen in love with that first moment he had set eyes upon it. When he had drawn her attention to the mountains, she had not been impressed; to her, at that time, a mountain was a mountain and that was all it was. She had been wrong, she told herself. A mountain was a friend, or at least it could be one if you allowed it to be. The feeling for the great blue surge against the sky had stolen on her gradually from days of seeing it, becoming acquainted with it, and now realizing for the first time what it had come to mean to her—a landmark in her life, an ever-watching, surprisingly protective presence, a familiar figure that she could always turn to. It was only, she told herself, that until this moment she had never taken the time to stand and look. She had been wrong and Jason had been right.

Standing there, thinking of Jason and the mountains, it seemed suddenly imperative that she see him. He had not been at the clinic, which might mean he was home, although she could not be sure he was. He had fallen into the habit lately of going on long walks, or he might have gone once again to call on Decker.

She rapped on his door and there was no answer. He might be napping, she told herself, and turned the knob. The door came open when she pushed on it. On End of Nothing, few doors were ever locked. There was little need of locks.

The apartment was empty; it had an empty hollowness. There was no clatter in the kitchen, so Hubert wasn't there. A small blaze burned on the fireplace grate.

"Jason," she called, speaking more softly than she had intended to, the hush of the room imposing an instinctive urge to silence. She saw herself reflected in the large mirror mounted on the wall above the fireplace, a lost figure standing in the emptiness of the vacant room, a pale smudge of face emblazoned by the redness of the disfigured cheek.

"Jason," she called again in a slightly louder voice.

When there was no answer, she walked through the open bedroom door. The bed was made up, the colorful coverlet drawn over it. The bathroom door was open.

She turned back to the living room and there stood Jason, in front of the fireplace, with his back to it, facing out into the room, staring out into the room, but there was a blankness on his face that seemed to say he was seeing nothing. Where had he come from? she wondered. How could she have missed him? She had not heard the door open or close and, as a matter of fact, there had been too little time since she had left the room for him to come through the door and walk across the room to the fireplace.

"Jason," she said sharply, "what's the matter with you?"

He swung his head toward her at the sound of her voice, but he registered no recognition at the sight of her.

She moved quickly to him, stood facing him, reached out with both her hands and grasped him by the shoulders. She shook him. "Jason, what's going on?"

His eyes, which had seemed glazed over, brightened slightly.

"Jill," he said in a halting, doubtful voice, as if he was not able to accept the fact that she was there. "Jill," he said again, reaching out to grasp her by the arms. "Jill, I've been away."

"I know you have," she said. "Where have you been?"

"Another place," he said.

"Jason, snap out of it. What other place?"

"I went to the equation world."

"That place you dream about? That you have nightmares over?"

"Yes, but this time it was not a dream. I was there. I walked its surface. I and Whisperer . . ."

"Whisperer? That little puff of diamond dust you told me about?"

"We went as one," he said. "We went together."

"Come on, sit down," she said. "Is there something that you want? I'll get you a drink."

"No, nothing. Just stay with me."

He lifted a hand off her arm and ran it across her cheek in a caress—the cheek that carried the ugly, angry scar. He had grown into the habit of doing that—as if he might unconsciously be trying to express his love of her despite her disfigurement. At first she had flinched away from the gesture. Other than that caress, he had never, since shortly after they had met, made any move or said a word to indicate that he was aware of it. That, she knew, was one of the many reasons that she loved him. No other man, no other person, had ever been able to be, or seem to be, so unaware of that terrible scar. Now she no longer flinched away from the caress. She had come, instead, to value it, as if it might be some form of benediction.

His hand passed across her cheek. She was facing the mirror above the fireplace and she could see how the hand came out to stroke the cheek and, in that very motion, she saw the sign of love.

His hand dropped away and she gasped in disbelief. It was her imagination, she told herself, it was a moment of latent wish-fulfillment. She wasn't really seeing what she thought she saw. In another second or two the imaginative process would pass away and she'd return to normal.

She stood rigid as the seconds passed away. She closed her eyes and opened them and the wish-fulfillment was still working.

"Jason!" she said, speaking low, trying to control her voice, but unable to keep it from shaking.

"Jason!" she said again, the word cracking with emotion.

Her cheek remained unblemished. The stigma was no longer there.

Chapter Thirty-seven

DECKER HALTED WELL BEFORE SUNSET, HAVING FOUND A spot where he could camp for the night. A spring gushed from a hillside, giving origin to a small stream that went trickling down a valley. A grove of low, dense mountain shrubs grew to the north of the spring, promising protection against night winds swooping from the peaks that loomed ahead. There was a dead tree fallen just downstream of the site, propped up against a nest of boulders, providing an easy supply of dry wood.

Decker set to work methodically. He hauled in wood from the dead tree and got a cooking fire started, then chopped and stored wood against the night. He set up a small tent that would serve to shelter him if rain came and unrolled his sleeping bag. He brought a pail of water from the spring and hung a kettle to boil for coffee, then unwrapped two fish he'd caught earlier in the day and prepared for the pan on the spot, wrapping them in leaves against the time when he would need them. These he put into a pan and settled down to cooking supper. First, however, he made sure the rifle was propped against a boulder within easy reach. In all the time he'd spent on his trips into the mountains, he had seldom needed it, but natural caution told him he could not rule out the possibility of sometime needing it.

Whisperer as yet had not caught up with him and, thinking this, he knew the thought was illogical. Whisperer had not known that he was planning on the trip—in fact, he had not really planned it; he'd simply up and left. It had not been an impulsive action; there had been no sense of urgency to get going, no sudden need to

leave and go into the mountains. The trip had come quite naturally, as a matter of course. The garden was all hoed and the
woodpile was well up and there had been nothing else to do.
Without much surprise, he had found himself preparing for the
trip. He had not thought of it as something special; it had been
just another trip, in the course of which he would pick up some
gemstones if he should be lucky. He had thought momentarily of
driving down to Vatican to see if Tennyson might want to go with
him, but had told himself it might be a bad time for Tennyson. As
Vatican physician, Jason probably would have to stick around to
keep an eye on Mary. Some other time, he had told himself.

It was not that he wanted to be alone; he liked the man. Tennyson was the first man he had met in years that he really liked.
He was, Decker thought, a man very like himself. Tennyson never
talked too much and never about the wrong things. He asked few
questions and those he asked were sensible. He had the knack of
approaching an awkward situation with diplomatic ease. What
he'd had to say about Whisperer could have been a sticky matter,
but he'd come to it directly and with a frankness that was refreshing in itself and it had not been awkward in the least for either one
of them.

As he squatted by the fire, tending the frying fish, he found
himself wishing that Whisperer were with him. If Whisperer had
known that he was going into the mountains, he'd probably have
come along. Whisperer liked the trips they took. There always was
a lot for them to talk about, and Whisperer derived as much fun
as he did out of searching the streambed gravels for the gems they
often came upon. Whisperer, he recalled, invariably was a good
sport in this regard. He never bragged unduly about the gems he
found that Decker had passed by, unseeing.

He had realized when Tennyson first told him what had occurred with Whisperer that he might see less of him. Sometimes
that might have been a plus, for no question about it, there were
occasions when Whisperer could be something of a pest. But he
had been certain that the old friendship would not be broken—he
and Whisperer had been together too long for that to happen.
Thinking of it now, he was certain that it had not happened, that

Whisperer's present absence was not due to any lessening of their association. With Tennyson, Whisperer probably would pick up some new interests, and he might now be off somewhere running one of them to earth. But in a short while he'd be back. Decker was sure of that. Before this trip was over, chances were that Whisperer would come sniffing down his trail to join him.

The coffee kettle threatened to boil over, and he reached out a hand to grasp the forked stick that held it, intending to move it away from the heat of the fire. The kettle exploded in his face. It went flying through the air, crumpled by an unseen force. Boiling coffee sprayed his face and chest.

In an automatic reflex action, Decker dived for the rifle propped against the boulder and as his fingers grasped it, the sickening, snarling crack of another rifle sounded from the hillside above him.

Rifle in hand, Decker rolled behind the boulder, raised himself cautiously to peer above it. The shot had come from the direction of a rocky outcrop halfway up the hill, but there seemed to be nothing there.

"The bastard shot too soon," Decker said aloud. "He could have crawled a little closer and had a better chance. He was too anxious."

The crumpled kettle lay a good ten feet or more beyond the campfire. The fish in the pan, he saw, were smoking, crisping. If he was tied up here too long, they'd be ruined. Dammit! he thought—he had been looking forward to those fish. He could almost taste them.

Now who would be shooting at him? Who would want to kill him? He was certain he had been the target of the rifleman. Not the coffee pot. The shot had been to kill, not to frighten.

He watched, flicking his gaze along the hillside, intent on catching any movement, any sign of movement. This could not have happened, he told himself, if Whisperer had been with him. Hours ago, Whisperer would have spotted the one who had been stalking them. It would have to be someone, he told himself, who would have known that Whisperer was not with him—but that was wrong, he thought, it had to be wrong, for no one in End of Nothing knew of Whisperer. He had never told anyone and so far as he knew no one could see Whisperer; therefore no one could be aware of him. Tennyson was the only one who knew—and probably Jill, for there were no secrets between the two of them. Could Tennyson have told Ecuyer? he wondered. It seemed unlikely. Tennyson and Ecuyer were friends but Tennyson, he felt certain, would not tell Ecuyer of Whisperer.

All this, he reminded himself, was footless speculation. Undeterred by Whisperer, for no one knew of Whisperer, anyone could have come hunting him. It was just his tough luck that, without Whisperer, he had been caught flat-footed. It couldn't be Tennyson up there on the hillside. Tennyson had no reason. Even if he had, this was not his style.

There were some rifles—a few rifles—in End of Nothing. Some hunters occasionally went into the woods in search of meat. Mostly small caliber, however. From the sound of it, the one up there on the hill was a heavy caliber.

He ran down the names of people who might want to kill him. He could scarcely think of any, having to stretch his imagination to make up a list. Having come up with one, he rejected each of the names. The few that he could think of could not possibly have that strong a motive. A few, at times, might have been offended by something he had said or done, but certainly not so touched to the quick as to come hunting him. The whole idea of someone out gunning for him was ridiculous. And yet there was someone out there, hiding on the hillside with killing in his heart, waiting for him to move and betray his position so the watcher could send a bullet through him.

Something hard and going fast hit the boulder's edge, four feet or so from Decker. Chips of granite flew and a few of them struck his cheek and neck with stinging force. The report of the shot reverberated in the hills. The bullet, up-ended in its flight, went howling off in a ricochet, tumbling end for end.

Up there, Decker told himself, up there by the stone outcropping—a tiny spot that had momentarily glittered in the rays of the setting sun. Decker tried to make out what it was but was unable to. He slid the barrel of his rifle along the boulder until it was pointed approximately at the spot.

Nothing happened. Nothing stirred. There was no sound. The killer waited. Then Decker saw the beginning of a shape and traced it out—a shoulder, a hint of torso, the suggestion of a head.

He crouched close against the rifle, cuddling it hard against him, lining up the sights. The shoulder, and there was the head, half in shadow, not sharply outlined, but it had to be a head. He took it in his sights, froze them on it, drew in a breath and held it, began the trigger squeeze . . .

Chapter Thirty-eight

TENNYSON WOKE JUST BEFORE DAWN. JILL LAY BESIDE HIM, asleep, breathing softly, regularly. He propped his pillow against the headboard and slid his body up to lean against it. The dark was quiet. Faint predawn light filtered through the windows of the living room; the blinds were drawn and no light could seep into the bedroom. In the kitchen the refrigerator was humming to itself.

He glanced down at Jill to see if the cheek was still clear and unblemished, but she was turned so that it was against the pillow. Even had it not been, he told himself, in the faintness of the light reflected from the living room he probably would not have been able to be sure.

Thinking of it now, even hours after it had happened, he still felt the stir of disbelief. Yet there had been evidence, hours of evidence, that the angry red scar was no longer there. Surely, if for whatever reason, it had been only a temporary effect, it should have started to return within those hours.

He raised his right hand in front of him, close to his face, and stared at it. It was shadowed in the darkness; all he could see was the shape of it. The hand was in no way different. It did not glow in the dark; it was as it had always been.

And yet the touch of it. . . .

He shivered in a sudden coldness, although the night was warm. He tried to remember back, digging back through the folds of otherwhere, to the equation world. The equations had spun around him in a dizzy swirl, they had gone knifing through him; some of them, he was sure, had lodged inside of him and stayed. There had been a time toward the end of what he could remember when it had seemed that he, himself, had shrunk to an equation— shrunk, he thought, or grown? He tried to remember what sort of equation he had been—if, in fact, he had ever known. Certainly not one of those fat, monstrous equations, frightening in their very complexity, that he had glimpsed while he lay buried in the quivering jelly sea. Perhaps he had been a very simple equation, a simple statement of himself. When the diagrams had built the house for him, he recalled, he had quickly scuttled under it and had crouched, not knowing what he was, but quite content with what he was. A simple thought, a simple reasoning that might have gone along with a very simple equation. Had the diagrams built the shelter, he wondered, to protect him against the ravening equations that flashed and whirled outside it, spinning all around it?

Then, suddenly, with no warning, he had been free of the equation world, to find himself standing in the living room with his back turned to the fire. Free—but not entirely free, for he had brought back something from the equation world, some quality, some ability that he had not had before. There had been one evidence of that new ability; would there now be more? What am I, he asked himself, what am I, the continuing question that he had asked when he had huddled in the house the diagrams had built.

Human, he wondered, am I human still? How many alien concepts can be grafted onto human stock and it still stay human?

Had the folk of the equation world, he asked himself, known or sensed that he was a physician, a healer? Had they confined their rebuilding of him—if it had been rebuilding—to the sole purpose of designing him into a better healer? Or had they tinkered with other facets of his life as well?

Thinking of it, he was frightened, and the more he thought

about it, the more frightened he became. He had meddled into something that he had no right to meddle with and he had not come out unscathed. He had been changed and he desired no change. Change was uncomfortable under any circumstance; a change in one's self was terrifying.

Yet why should he feel such terror? The change, whatever it might be, how limited or extensive, whatever it might come to in the future, had made it possible for him to give to Jill—unwittingly, and yet he'd given it—a gift that no other human could have given her.

And that was it. There was no point in being frightened or being terrified. In the end, so far as he was concerned, it all came down to Jill. If in all the future there was nothing else—if, in fact, in future time he should suffer for it—there would be no regret. Any future price that might be exacted from him would be worth what he had done. He had been paid in full in that moment he had laid his hand upon her cheek.

Thinking this, he felt a calmness in him. He stayed propped up in bed, not sliding back down again, staring into the gray edge of the early dawn. In his thoughts he went back again to the equation world, trying to puzzle how he had managed to go there in person, although he knew without question that it had not been he who had been able to go there but Whisperer who had been able to take him there. To understand how Whisperer had done it, he'd have to know a great deal more about Whisperer than he knew.

Turning his head slowly, he scanned the room, looking for some evidence of Whisperer—a glitter in a corner, a sparkle in the air. He saw no glitter or sparkle. He searched inside himself for Whisperer, for Whisperer might still be with him. But there was no hint of him, although that was not good evidence, for in the equation world, he'd not been aware of Whisperer.

He jerked himself more fully awake, for there was a tapping. It stopped for a moment and then started up again. It seemed to have no direction, it could come from almost anywhere. Listening closely, he identified it. There was someone at the door. He swung himself easily out of bed, sitting on the edge, his feet seeking blindly for the slippers that did not seem to be there.

Jill stirred in the bed, making an inquiring sound. "It's all right," he told her. "You stay here. There's someone at the door."

He failed to find the slippers and stood up without them, making his way around the bed and into the living room. He closed the bedroom door behind him. The tapping on the door had stopped for a time, but now it began again, a discreet tapping, not insistent.

Without turning on lights, Tennyson made his way across the living room, skirting chairs and tables. When he opened the door, for a moment he did not recognize the man who stood outside it, then saw that it was Ecuyer.

"Jason, I am sorry. This ungodly hour . . ."

"It's all right," said Tennyson. "I was just lying there and thinking. Ready to get up."

"Could you spare a drink? Some brandy if you have it."

"Certainly," said Tennyson. "Sit down in front of the fire. I'll put on another log."

He closed the door and had a closer look at Ecuyer. The man was dressed in slacks and jacket.

"Up early?" he asked. "Or didn't you go to bed at all?"

"Never went to bed," said Ecuyer, reaching the couch before the fire and collapsing onto it.

Tennyson found the brandy and brought Ecuyer a snifter with a generous helping.

"You look all tired out," he told him.

"I am tired out," said Ecuyer. "Something horrible has happened. Something that's never happened before. Or I don't think it has."

Tennyson put another log on the fire and walked back to the couch, sitting down beside Ecuyer and hoisting his bare feet up on the coffee table. He wiggled his toes. The heat from the fire felt good on them.

Ecuyer took another deep drink of the brandy. "You won't join me?"

Tennyson shook his head. "Too early in the day."

"Ah, well," said Ecuyer, "since I never went to bed . . ." He drank more of the brandy.

"There's something you came here to tell me," said Tennyson, "and you're taking a long time getting to it. If you have changed your mind . . ."

"No, I'm just putting it off. It's something you have to know. It's a bit painful."

Tennyson said nothing. Ecuyer continued working on the brandy.

"It was like this," Ecuyer finally said. "I've been putting off having a look at the second Heaven cube. You know I have. You've been bugging me about it. Jason, did you ever get around to viewing the first Heaven cube?"

"No. Somehow I felt a strange reluctance. Maybe slightly afraid of it. Uncomfortable at the thought of it. I know I should have. I might have found something that would have helped me to treat Mary."

"I felt the same reluctance with the second cube," said Ecuyer. "I kept putting it off, finding reasons to put it off. Maybe I was afraid of what I might experience. I don't know. I tried to analyze my feelings and came up zilch. Then last evening I decided— forced myself to decide—I'd fooled around long enough."

"So you finally viewed it."

"No, Jason, I didn't."

"Why the hell not? Shy off at the last moment?"

"Not that. It wasn't there."

"What do you mean, it wasn't there?"

"Just that. It isn't there. It isn't where we put it. We, old Ezra and me. You know Ezra. He's the custodian."

"Yes, I know him."

"He followed procedure. He always follows procedure. He never misses a lick. He always does what he's supposed to do. I've worked with him for years; I'd trust him with my life."

Tennyson waited and in a few moments Ecuyer resumed. "When a new cube comes in, I deliver it to Ezra and he puts it in a safe. After I have viewed it, it may go to Vatican, and when it comes back from them, it is filed in one of the cabinets. Often a cube does not go to Vatican immediately, or may not go at all if we judge it would have no particular interest, in which case it also

is filed in a cabinet. Ezra has a system all his own. I don't know
what it is; maybe no more than his memory. We have thousands
of cubes; ask him for one and he can lay his hands on it instantly.
He never falters. He goes straight to it. So far as I know, there is
no actual filing system as such, but somehow or other Ezra can
find anything you ask for. There's a measure of security, of
course, in such an arrangement."

Tennyson nodded. "Ezra is the only one who knows."

"That's right. There are a few cubes, a few special ones, I can
come up with without help from Ezra, but not many."

"But until you view a new cube, it stays in a safe. The Heaven
cube wasn't in the safe—is that what you're telling me?"

"Jason, that's what I am telling you. Ezra opened the safe and
it wasn't there. There were three other cubes, but not the Heaven
cube. Three that I hadn't got around to viewing—"

"One of them labeled wrong?"

"No. To be certain, I viewed the three of them. None of them
the Heaven cube. Stuff that came in just recently."

"Paul, who else could open that safe?"

"No one. Not me, not anyone but Ezra."

"All right. So Ezra . . ."

"Impossible," said Ecuyer. "That repository is Ezra's life. His
whole existence centers on the Search Program. Without it, he'd
be nothing. He'd be empty. I'd trust him further than I would trust
myself. He's tied even more closely to the program than I am.
He's been with it longer. He was assigned to it when it first
started, centuries ago."

"But if someone in Vatican . . ."

"Not a chance. Not even the Pope. Ezra's loyalty belongs to
Search, not to Vatican."

"Then someone must have learned the combination. Would
that be possible?"

"I suppose so. An outside chance. An extremely outside
chance."

"The cube couldn't have been mislaid?"

"No. Ezra put it in the safe. I stood by and watched him put it
in and lock the door."

"Paul, what do you think?"

"God, Jason, I don't know. Someone stole the cube."

"Because they didn't want it viewed?"

"I would suppose so. There's this theological faction in Vatican. The ones who advocate canonizing Mary—"

"The ones who'd like to get rid of Search. Who'd like to discredit you."

"I can't be sure of that," said Ecuyer, "but I assume they would —if they had a chance, that is."

The two men sat in silence for a moment. The new log Tennyson had thrown on the fire was blazing now, crackling as it burned. Dawn light had flooded the room.

"That's not all of it," said Ecuyer. "I haven't told you all of it."

"What else is there to tell?"

"The first cube, the first Heaven cube, is gone as well. It also has disappeared."

Chapter Thirty-nine

THE WHISPER WENT INTO VATICAN, ACROSS ALL OF END OF Nothing.

Mary has performed a miracle. She has cured Jill of the stigma. She put her hand on Jill's cheek and the stigma went away. . . .

The nurse said she'd seen it happen. Mary had asked Jill to bend over so she could reach out and touch her. As soon as Mary touched her cheek, the ugly blemish had been no more. Her cheek no longer bore the mark.

A miracle! *A miracle!!* A MIRACLE!!!

There could be no question of it. The few who caught a glimpse of Jill cried out the miracle, bore fervent testimony that the shameful mark was gone.

After a few people had cried out the miracle, Jill fled.

A worried band of cardinals carried the word to His Holiness, and His Holiness, not entirely happy with all their foolishness,

clucked and made other derogatory noises, counseling the cardinals to assume a more skeptical attitude until more evidence was
in. When one cardinal suggested that an ecclesiastical judiciary inquiry aimed at determining the advisability of beatification be convened, the Pope said it was much too early for such steps. His
Holiness, somewhat upset, was essentially noncommittal, keeping
his options open.

A general holiday, automatically, almost instinctively, was declared. Workers on the farms, the gardens, and the orchards
dropped their tools and joined in a haphazard processional, heading for Vatican. Woodcutters came scurrying in from the forests.
Many monks and other Vatican workers streamed out to join the
happy throng. Vatican guards had their work cut out to prevent
the mob from an indiscriminate invasion of Vatican. In the vast
basilica, humans and robots fought for kneeling room to pray. At
first the bells were silent, but, finally, in an attempt to placate the
crowd, which had been shrieking against Vatican's apparent
indifference to the self-evident miracle, pealed out and all the
world was happy.

Knots of people gathered around the clinic, chanting for Mary,
invading the little garden, trampling the shrubbery and the flowers.
Guards held back the assemblage that continued to grow larger by
the minute.

Mary, wakening, heard the chanting—"Mary! Mary! Mary!"—
and managed to sit up in bed, amazed that many voices should be
calling out her name. The nurse was not in the room; she had
stepped into another room where, leaning out the window, she
could see to better advantage what was going on.

Mary, summoning all her strength, slid out of bed, holding onto
a chair to pull herself erect. She tottered to the door and, leaning
against the wall for support, made her way down the corridor to
where the great front door stood open to let in fresh air and
coolness.

The crowd caught sight of her as she came out the door, clinging to it with one hand to keep from falling. A hush fell on all
those who were gathered there, all eyes turned to take in the

frailty and unquestioned holiness of the woman who stood there in the door.

She raised her hand to them, fist clenched, one finger extended, shaking that one finger in their collective faces. Her voice was thin and reedy, a quavering screech, and it carried far in the awe-struck silence.

"Naughty!" she shrilled at them. "Naughty! Naughty! Naughty!"

Chapter Forty

"IT DOESN'T LOOK AS IF ANYONE'S AT HOME," TENNYSON TOLD Ecuyer.

"How can you tell?"

"No smoke from the chimney."

"That doesn't prove a thing."

"Perhaps not. But Decker always has a fire. Sometimes, perhaps, not a large fire, but something burning so he only has to put on some wood to start it up. I've never seen the shack when there wasn't some smoke coming from the chimney."

"Well, we'll soon know," said Ecuyer.

They continued climbing the hill. Decker's beat-up vehicle was parked to one side of the shack. A neatly stacked rank of firewood stood between two trees, the trees serving as a crib for the wood. Off to one side was the garden, with its straight green rows of vegetables and one corner of it a riot of blooming flowers.

"It's not a bad place," said Ecuyer. "I have never been here."

"You've never met Tom?"

"No. He's not an easy man to meet. He makes himself somewhat unavailable. Do you think he'll talk with us?"

"Sure, he'll talk with us. He's not a savage or a boor; he's a civilized, educated man."

"Exactly what did he say about knowing where Heaven is?"

"He only said it once, that he thought he might know where

Heaven was. He made no further mention of it and I never pushed him. I was afraid to, afraid he might shy off. I let him take his time."

"Maybe he will tell us now. If we explain to him how important it is. With the cubes gone, there is no chance at all of coming up with the coordinates we need. Maybe even with the cubes, there was not too great a chance, but now there is none at all. And now I agree with you. We damn well need those coordinates. Someone has to go to Heaven."

"I keep hoping," said Tennyson, "that Tom may really know. I can't be sure any longer. At one time I was fairly sure he knew, but now that we're down to the crunch, I'm not quite as sure as I was to start with. He did tell me his ship ran into trouble and he got away in a lifeboat. That's how he got here. The boat brought him here."

They came up to the shack and Tennyson knocked on the door. There was no answer. He knocked again. "He might be sleeping in there," he said.

"It's unlikely," said Ecuyer. "He'd hear you. Let's take a look around."

They took a look around. They shouted for Decker and Decker did not answer. They went back to the shack. This time Ecuyer pounded on the door. After they had waited for a time, Ecuyer asked, "Do you think we should go in?"

"Yes, let's do that. I doubt that Decker would mind. The man has nothing to hide."

Ecuyer lifted the latch and the door opened. Inside they stood for a moment to become accustomed to the dimness.

The place was neat. Everything was picked up and put away.

Tennyson looked around. "His rifle is gone," he said. "It hung over there on the wall beside the fireplace. His knapsack and sleeping bag were stored on the shelf above the table. They're gone, too. More than likely he is on one of his rock-hunting trips."

"How long?"

"I don't know. Probably the time would vary. He asked me to come along on one of the trips. When you can spare a few days, he said—as if we'd be gone only a few days. I would think he'd be back soon."

"Jason, it is important that we know as soon as we can. We can't allow the theological faction to get too much of a jump on us. If we could leak the word there was a good possibility of going out to have a look at Heaven, they'd back off."

"You're really afraid of them, aren't you, Paul?"

"If they get well entrenched, they'll eliminate the Search Program. That's what they've wanted to do all along. Either eliminate us or dictate the kind of work we do or, worse yet, control the interpretation of what we find. I'm not worried about myself, you understand. They'd do me no harm. I could stay on and be taken care of. They might even let me piddle around with the program a little, enough so I could tell myself I was doing something. But the program, as such, would be eviscerated. And I can't let that happen. It's the soul of Vatican, I tell you. Sure, let them mess around with their theological doings if they want to, but the real work stems from the Search Program."

"You must have some support in Vatican."

"Some, I think. I don't know how much. Some of the cardinals. A few others I can be sure of."

"His Holiness?"

"No one can ever depend on the Pope. He is a cold, mechanistic mind. You never know what he is thinking. He is so clogged with all the material that our Listeners have fed into him that, despite his great capability, he can't have much time to consider present policies. Besides, I would guess that sometimes he gets confused. His job, after all, is not to guide Vatican at the moment. His is the long-range job of what Vatican should be in the far future."

"It would seem to me," said Tennyson, "that Vatican can't get along without the Listeners. I've heard all sorts of hints as to what it's gained from your observations. The thought-ships, for one thing. What else do they have?"

"I'm not sure I know everything they have. But they have a lot. You know about their cloning. But it's more than cloning. They don't need a cell as a starter. They can start from scratch, build a

DNA pattern and go on from there. Artificial life. Engineered life, of any kind at all. And time travel. Hell, they have something better than time travel. They employ neutrinos—although they're not actually sure what they are using are neutrinos, they may be something else. But with their aid, using them, whatever they may be, they are on the verge of being able to travel a number of directions in time—not only past and future, but other directions as well. You're surprised to learn there are other directions. Well, so was I. I'm not sure I understand it. They can hunt down past and future, or will be able to as soon as they have the technology well developed, and they also will be able to go to conditions other than past or future. Maybe alternate worlds and universes. I don't know. It's all too deep for me. But whatever they have, it is the key to time travel, dimensional travel, probably other things. These two examples give you some idea of what they have."

"Having all of this, they would give it up?"

"Not all of them. Not willingly. The theological party is a different matter. Some of them honestly feel Vatican has lost sight of, or betrayed, its original purpose. The others, which are the most of them, are scared. The universe has proved bigger than they thought. It has in it many more and stranger conditions and situations than they had ever dreamed. They are overwhelmed by the sheer magnitude of what the Listeners are finding. The universe is so vast, the possibilities so mind-boggling, that they're beginning to feel naked. They're looking for a place to hide."

"We could run a bluff," suggested Tennyson. "Float a rumor that we have found a way to get to Heaven. They don't want anyone going to Heaven. If someone went there and found it wasn't Heaven, that would jerk the rug out from under them. Such a rumor would at least slow them up for a while, give us time."

Ecuyer said, "No, we can't do that. If we ran a bluff and they called us, that would strengthen them, would make them more sure of themselves than ever. If, and when, we make our move, we must be fairly confident we can follow through."

"Yes," said Tennyson. "Yes, I suppose you're right."

"Jason, when Decker told you he was sure, or fairly sure, that he knew where Heaven is, did you get the feeling that he might have some documentation, that he wasn't only speaking from memory?"

"You mean like a log book?"

"Yes, that's the sort of thing I was thinking of. Ships carry flight recorders, don't they? He ran into trouble out in space. Could he have taken the flight recorder before he got into the lifeboat?"

"To tell you the truth," said Tennyson, "I did get that impression. I thought that he might have documentation more solid than memory alone. But he never said so. He gave me no reason to think so. I don't know why I did. I did have the impression at the time, but now I'm not sure at all."

"Do you think we might . . ." Ecuyer did not finish his sentence and Tennyson hesitated before he answered.

Finally he said, "It would go against my grain. Decker's my friend and he trusted me."

"But, Jason, we have to know! I have to know!"

"All right, then," said Tennyson. "You're probably right. Let's get to work. But neat, Paul. Everything goes back exactly where it was."

They got to work. Tennyson noted that the gem carvings Whisperer had done were no longer on the table in the corner; later he found them packed in a small box on one of the shelves. Decker apparently had put them away before he left.

They found nothing they had been looking for.

"Maybe he has it stashed away somewhere outside the cabin," said Ecuyer.

"If he has anything, that is," said Tennyson. "If he has it and has it hidden somewhere, we're not going to find it."

He thought to himself that Whisperer might know.

"There's one other possibility," he said.

"What is that?"

Tennyson shrugged. "I guess not. Forget it."

He had not mentioned Whisperer to Ecuyer and he had no intention of doing so. Thank the Lord, he had caught himself in time.

There was, or had been, another possibility so far as Whisperer was concerned, and that, he told himself, now was gone as well. In the back of his mind it had occurred to him that if Whisperer could take him to the equation world, he could take him to Heaven, too. But that was now impossible. Whisperer would have nothing to work with because he, Tennyson, had viewed neither of the Heaven cubes.

Jill was the only one other than himself and Decker who knew of Whisperer and that, he told himself, was the way that it would stay.

So it finally came down to Decker; Decker was their only hope. When Decker came back from his trip, he might be able to help them. If he couldn't, if what he knew was not definitive enough, then Vatican's last chance was gone. The Search Program would be abolished, or, at best, restricted, and Vatican would become what it had first intended itself to be—a blind fumbling after the will-o'-the-wisp of spirituality.

Whisperer, he thought, probably was with Decker, and so he would have to wait for their return before he could know what hope might still remain.

They left the shack and closed the door behind them, making sure the latch was firmly in place. On top of the hill, they stood together and looked out over Vatican. In the harsh light of forenoon, the buildings stood out white and stark against the background of woodland and the foothills of the lofty mountains.

As they stood there, looking at the clumped buildings in the distance, a faint tolling sound came to them.

"It's bells," said Ecuyer. "Why are they ringing bells? This is not the time of day to ring them. Only at certain times of day. And there are too many. . . ."

A shift in the wind carried the full-toned sound to them, the full-tongued pealing of great bells.

"Those are the big basilica bells," Ecuyer exclaimed. "What the hell is going on?"

Hurriedly the two of them went down the hill.

Chapter Forty-one

SHE HAD NEVER BEEN SO HUMILIATED IN ALL HER LIFE, JILL told herself—nor so angry. What was the matter with these people? Whatever had possessed that silly nurse to say what she had said?

Jill slammed the door behind her and stalked across the room. She sat down on the couch in front of the fireplace, but found she couldn't stay there. She rose and began to pace the room.

The miracle was not Mary's miracle despite that lying nurse. If anyone's, it was Jason's—and it was no miracle. If it only could be learned, there must be a perfectly reasonable explanation to account for it. The hell of it, she thought, was that she could not explain what had happened. If it was for anyone to tell, it would be Jason, and she was sure he would say nothing. She could not even attempt to refute what the fools were yelling out there in the street.

She stopped pacing and went back to the couch, staring at the small flicker of flames that ran along the almost-consumed logs in the fireplace. After a time, she thought, she would have to go out there and face the world, although every instinct in her cried out against it. All she wanted to do was huddle here, to lick the wounds of public humiliation. But she knew that in time she would go out and face it down. Vatican couldn't beat her; nothing had ever beaten her. Jill Roberts, in her day, had faced down worse things than this. Nothing had ever beaten her, and the stinking robots and the witless humans out there could not stand against her.

And another thing—they'd not drive her from Vatican; they could never do that. She had her heels dug in and she had no thought of leaving. Which was, she reminded herself, a far different attitude from the one she'd held when she first had come here. Then she had felt disgust and disappointment, had been enraged by the clever little game the cardinals had played—trying to discourage her from coming by not answering her letters and when, despite their attitude, she had arrived, refusing to cooperate. Since then her perspective and priorities had changed. It had taken some time to recognize the importance of Vatican—not only to the robots, but to the humans, and not only the humans here at End of Nothing, but to all humans everywhere. There was a greatness here, a very human greatness of conception and of thought, that she could not turn her back upon. In a way she had become a part of it and she meant to remain so, along with Jason, who had become as much a part of it as she. In any case, she told herself, she would not leave even if she wanted to, for Jason was happy here and had found in this strange community the kind of life that fitted him. She could not part from him; she could not bring herself to part from him. Especially she could not leave him after what had happened the night before—his fingers reaching out and wiping away the shame upon her cheek. For it had been a shame, she now admitted to herself, much as she might have tried to pretend that it was not, treating it with a nonfeminine bluntness, flaunting it because she could not hide it, bluffing it out before the entire world.

But it was not just Jason who bound her here. Another was the old cardinal Enoch, who came to see her every day, hunching upon the stool beside her desk and talking the hours away, talking as if she were another robot or he another human. In many ways he seemed to be a doddering old idiot, but never, she told herself, an idiot—it was just his way. And kind. She had never thought a robot would be kind, but Enoch had been kind and more considerate than there was any need to be. To start with, she had called him Eminence with meticulous attention to Vatican protocol, but of late she often forgot and chattered away at him as if they were two silly schoolgirls. He did not mind at all; maybe it was refreshing for him to talk with someone who could forget for long stretches of time that he held a high post in Vatican.

Jason had told her of the equation world and now, once again, she found herself wondering what it really had been like. He had described it to her, as best he could, trying to tell her in detail what he had seen and experienced. But it was the kind of place and the sort of happening that was quite beyond all telling, an experience so vast the human mind must fall short of taking in all of it, impossible to put into words that would make another human see it. "I cannot tell you, Jill," he'd said. "I can't tell you all of it; I cannot find the words, for there were certain things about it for which there are no words."

The yelling and the yammering continued in the street. Were they hunting her? she wondered. Must they feel compelled to look again upon the evidence of the great miracle that had not come to pass? The fools, she thought, the fools!

"There are certain things about it for which there are no words." A culture so ancient, so self-sufficient that it operated on a system of logic that was so far advanced over human knowledge and capability as the fusion of atoms was advanced beyond the chipping of stones into primitive tools. A group of cubes sitting on a great green plain manipulating symbols and diagrams—playing a complicated game or solving problems? Or were the symbols and diagrams the visual manifestations of alien thought, perhaps a band of philosophers sitting around in an informal seminar arguing hair-splitting hypotheses, a mere passing of idle time or the long, slow process of formulating new universal truths? Could the equation folk, in time long past, have penetrated to the edge of space and the end of time and now, retreated back to the place where they first had set out, wherever that might be, now be engaged in trying to pull together and evaluate all that they had seen and sensed?

What astonishment, she thought, must they have felt to be so rudely visited by Jason, a life form similar to others they may have seen in earlier times and now forgotten, or a life form they had missed entirely and had never seen. No wonder they had acted as they had—no wonder they had gone wild with flashing, running symbols and racketing diagrams, no wonder they had built a house of diagrams to hide Jason from their sight. Yet they had given him a gift as one might give a gift to a stranger who came visiting.

She settled back, trying to calm herself, to pull herself together. It was then she saw the flicker in one corner of the shadowed room. I'm seeing things, she told herself—now I'm seeing things.

It was no longer, she saw, a flicker, but a hazy globe of shining dust, a tiny globe of sparkles.

—Whisperer? she asked, speaking to the flicker instinctively as Jason told her he had spoken to him.

—You can see me, Jill?

—I see you, Whisperer.

—And you can hear me?

—Yes, I hear you.

She was numb with wonder, thinking: It is impossible; Jason never even hinted he might come to me or, even if he did, that I could see and talk with him.

—Jason said leave you out of it, said Whisperer. I told him I could talk with you and he said, no, to leave you alone. But, Jill, I cannot leave you out of it. I must come to you.

—It's all right, she said.

—You may see differently than Jason. You may see the better.

—See what the better?

—The equation people.

—No, said Jill. Oh, no!

—Why not? Would you be frightened?

—Yes, I would be frightened. These are terrifying creatures.

—You owe them your face.

—Yes, I owe them that.

—Jason brought back a gift with him. They'll make you a gift as well. They have much to give.

—Why should they give us anything?

—I do not know, said Whisperer. With Jason I dig very deep, but not deep enough.

—Jason did not tell me that.

—Jason could not share it all with me. He could not grasp the wonders that I found. Nor could I grasp all he found. We are very different minds.

—And I? I'll understand no more.

—But differently, perhaps. Jason could see what you could not, and you see what Jason could not.

—Whisperer, I could not go to the equation world. I did not see the cube.

—I've been there, said Whisperer. That is quite enough. It is imprinted on me. I can find the way.

—Whisperer, I don't know. Whisperer, I can't!

—No need to fear. Jason and I came back. There was no danger to us.

—How do you know there was no danger? The two of you might only have been lucky.

—It is important, Jill.

—I'll have to think about it.

—Jason said leave you out of this. He said not to bother you. And I have bothered you.

—I told you it was all right.

—I will urge no further. If you say no, it's no.

I can't, Jill told herself. I'd be petrified. And there is no need of it. Jason has been there. There is no need for me to go. And yet . . .

—I've never in my life, she told Whisperer, backed away from anything. Not from End of Nothing. Not from anything. If there was something that I should see, I always went and saw it.

That was the truth, she thought. She had always gone—the good reporter, shaking in her shoes, perhaps, scared of what she'd find or how it would turn out. But she'd gone. She'd gritted her teeth and gone. There had been times when it had been very hairy, but always she'd come back, with her notebook filled with jotted words, with rolls of exposed film, with her nerves rasped raw and her mind seething with ideas.

—All right, she said, I'll go. You can take me, Whisperer? Even if I've seen no cube?

—First I must join your mind. We must be as one.

She hesitated, rebelling against another entering her mind— especially another that she did not know, another that was so unlike any creature she had ever seen before.

Yet this strange creature, this Whisperer, had been in Jason's mind. "I did not know that he was there," Jason had said. "Yet I was sure he was. At times I could feel him, faintly, but actually never was aware of him. There was, I think, that extra dimension

of myself, but I was scarcely aware of it. Just a greater power, a
deeper sense of knowing."

—All right, she told Whisperer.

And she was in the equation world. There was no getting ready,
no preliminaries, no drawing a deep breath.

There, as Jason had described it, was the flat green carpetlike
expanse of surface melding imperceptibly with the soft lavender of
sky. On the green carpet of the surface sat the cubes of the equation world, brilliant in their color and with the semblance of life
afforded them by the quiver and the flicker of the changing diagrams and the smooth, even flowing of equations.

Hell, she thought, I should have brought my cameras. She could
have slung them around her neck and taken them, for they would
have come along. Her clothes had come along with her, she was
not standing naked—and if the clothes could travel with her, the
cameras could as well.

How stupid it had been to forget the cameras!

"Whisperer," she said aloud, thinking to ask him if he knew by
what means they had traveled there. But he did not answer and
within her mind there was no sign of him. That, she told herself,
was no more than she should have expected. Jason had told her
how it had been with him. He also had called out to Whisperer
and the pinch of diamond dust had been nowhere to be seen because he had not come separately, but had come with Jason and
was somewhere inside of him, presumably the scattered atoms of
him mixed with the atoms of Jason's human mind, and this, of
course, was what had happened with her as well.

—Whisperer, she said. Damn you, answer me. Give me some
sign that you are with me.

Whisperer did not answer.

Was it possible, she asked herself, that the little twerp had
thrown her into this place while he had stayed behind? She
thought about this and it appeared unlikely. Whisperer was an
eager beaver, hell-bent on an exploration of the universe. To explore it, apparently, he had to have a guide to show him where to
go. Although once he had been shown the way, he would know

the way and could go there by himself, or take someone else·
along, as he had taken her.

—All right, she said, go on hiding. Go on playing these silly
games of yours. I can get along without you.

Why had she ever come? she wondered. Because she was a
dedicated reporter who could not allow anything to happen if she
wasn't in on it? Because she wanted to stand upon the ground on
which Jason had stood, to find here a new strand that would tie
her the closer to him? God knows, she thought, there is no need of
that. Or had she swallowed Whisperer's pitch—that she might see
things that Jason had not seen, thereby gaining a greater understanding of the equation world?

She shook her head. None of it made sense, but she was here
and if she was going to interview these people (people?), she had
better be about it. Interview them? she asked herself—that was
plain ridiculous. There was no way she and they could communicate. She'd jabber at them with her mouth and they would
jabber back with their equations and neither of them would have
the slightest idea of what the other might be saying.

Nevertheless, she walked toward the cube that was nearest her,
a rose-red creature bearing on its surface a squiggle of damson-
plum equations and an outrageously twisted diagram that glowed
in sulphur yellow.

"I am Jill Roberts," she said, speaking loudly. "I have come to
talk with you."

Her words shattered the silence that hung like a gentle veil
draped about this world, and the rose-red cube appeared to cringe,
its color fading to a washed-out pink. Slowly, it began to edge
away from her, as if it wanted to turn about and run but knew it
would not be polite to turn about and run.

She thought: What a silly thing to do. I knew this was a quiet
world; Jason had told me how terribly quiet it was, and I come
busting in here and begin hollering out my questions. And what a
silly thing to say, as well. Telling them I am Jill Roberts, and they,
even if they could hear me, would not know what a jill-roberts
was. If I am going to talk with them, she told herself, probably the
only way to do it is to talk to them the way I talk to Whisperer. If

I am going to tell them who I am—no, that won't do at all. I have to tell them *what* I am and not who I am. How can I go about telling them what I am? How can I or any other human, or any other form of life, tell a different form of life what it is?

Maybe, she thought, I should begin by telling them I am an organic being. But would they know what organic meant—even if they could hear and understand, would they know what organic means?

The answer seemed to be that probably they wouldn't. If she was going to talk with them, she'd have to start on a more simple level. She would have to tell them what organic was. Maybe, once she got the idea across they might understand, for it was just possible (not probable, but possible) that they had encountered other organic life. Why was it, she wondered, that she had the idea (although she was not absolutely positive that she had the idea) that they were not organic life, but something else entirely, something very strange?

If she was going to reduce organic life to more basic concepts, how could she go about it? Come right down to it, what the hell was organic life? I wish I knew, she said. I deeply wish I knew. If Jason were here, he could be some help. Being a doctor and all, he'd know what it was. There was, she seemed to remember, something about carbon but what it was about carbon she simply did not know. She tried to remember back, wondering if she had ever known. Damn, *damn,* DAMN, she said, I've made it a point all my life to know so many things, to have a good working knowledge of so many things, and now that it comes right down to it, I don't know the things it is important I should know. As a reporter she had always made it a rule to bone up on any subject that she was going to talk with someone about, to know something about the creature or the human that she would be asking questions of, knowing something about its background and its interests and its work so she could hold the foolish questions down to minimum. But even had she had the time, there would have been no way she could have boned up about the equation people; there was no resource material. Maybe somewhere, but not in the human world.

The maddening thing about it was that she was trying to do it all by herself. Whisperer was here with her and he should be part of the act, not just she alone, but she and Whisperer. The little stinker was just lying doggo, not doing anything, not helping her at all.

The rose-red cube had stopped retreating and now stood at a distance from her, but not a great deal farther than it had been when she first had walked toward it. Other cubes were beginning to move in, gathering behind it, forming a solid phalanx behind it. They are ganging up on me, she thought, the way they ganged up on Jason.

She took a few tentative steps toward the rose-red cube, and as she did, it wiped off its surface all the equations and the ugly twisted diagram and for a moment that side of it that faced her was no more than an unblemished rose-red panel.

She came up close against it, so close that she had to tip her head to see the top of it. The blackboard side of it still remained a rose-red panel and the other cubes that stood behind it and to either side of it remained exactly where they were, with their equations and their diagrams still frozen on their blackboards, not quivering, but stark and frozen there.

Now, slowly, hesitantly, the rose-red cube began to form a new diagram upon its blackboard, drawing it in a brilliant gold, working carefully, as if it might not be sure what it was doing, as if it were feeling its way.

First, high up, it formed a triangle, an upside-down triangle, with its apex pointing downward. Then another, larger triangle with its apex pointing upward, meeting the apex of the smaller triangle. Then, after some deliberation, it formed two parallel, vertical strokes, two sticks attached to the base of the larger triangle.

Jill stared at it, uncomprehending, then sucked in her breath and said aloud, but very softly, "Why, that's me. The upper triangle is the head and the lower triangle is my body dressed in a skirt and those two sticks are legs!"

Then, off to one side of the diagram that was Jill Roberts, a jagged line was formed—a jagged line with five points.

"That's a question mark," she said. "I'm sure it's a question mark. They are asking what I am."

—That is right, said Whisperer, speaking from inside her mind. You have caught their attention. Now let me take over.

Chapter Forty-two

DESPITE THE FLARING CANDLES THE ROOM WAS DARK, THE darkness soaking up the candlelight. The humped shadows of furniture crouched like stalking beasts. The guard stood, spraddle-legged, against the door. Cardinal Theodosius sat in his huge, high-backed chair, seemingly muffled in his robes.

"Dr. Tennyson," he said, "in all the time that you've been here, this is the first time you've done me the honor of dropping in on me."

"I knew how busy you must be, Your Eminence," said Tennyson. "And, heretofore, there was no need."

"There now is need?"

"I think there is."

"You come to me at a time of some difficulty. We have few such times in Vatican. But now we do. Those fools out there."

"That's why I came to see you. Jill . . ."

"I would have expected such action from the humans. You humans are a flighty tribe. Solid folks, but excessively emotional. At times it seems to me that you do not have good sense. With the robots I would not have expected it. We are a stolid people, at times phlegmatic. You would not have thought that robots could work themselves into such a state of hysteria. You were about to speak of Jill?"

"Yes, I was," said Tennyson.

"She is one of the finest humans I have ever met. She has identified with us. She is interested in us and in Vatican. You know how hard she works."

"Indeed I do."

"When she first came to us," said the cardinal, "she was somewhat less than enchanted. She wanted to write about us, as you

well know, but that we could not allow. For a time I thought that
when the ship next left she would be leaving on it. That I did not
want her to do, for I knew inside myself, well before she demonstrated that I was correct, that she was the capable, devoted histo-
rian we needed and had never found. Tell me, Doctor, if you will,
why simple folks such as we should feel so desperate a need to
have our history written. Not for others, but for ourselves. Jill
would have been glad to write our story for others, but that we
would not countenance. However, we are all too happy to have
her write it for ourselves."

"I am no psychologist," said Tennyson, "so I speak with no
certainty and surely no authority. However, I would like to think
that it might be because you have done a job of which you are
very proud."

"Indeed we are," said the cardinal. "We have reason to be
proud."

"And because," said Tennyson, "you want to solidify your
identity into such a form that it will not be forgotten. So that, perhaps, a million years from now other life forms will know that you
were here, or that you still are here, if, in fact, you still exist a million years from now."

"We will be here," said Theodosius. "If not I, if not my other
fellow robots, at least Vatican will be here. Back on Earth, you humans formed economic corporations that assumed an identity of
their own, persisting as corporate entities over thousands of years.
The humans who formed and carried on the corporations died,
but the corporations did not die. They carried on because they
were ideas expressed in materialistic terms. Vatican is not a corporation but it is akin to a corporation. It is an idea patterned in
materialistic terms. It will endure. It may change, it may have its
ups and downs, it may be forced to evolve, it may face many
crises, but the idea will not die. The idea will go on. Ideas, Dr.
Tennyson, are not easily destroyed."

"This is all fine, Your Eminence," said Tennyson, "and I value
your judgments on this or any other subject, but I came here to
talk of Jill, to tell you—"

"Ah, yes, Jill," said the cardinal. "It was all most unfortunate.

In this saint business, I am afraid, she was caught—how is it you say it?—she was caught in the middle, I suppose. It all must have been embarrassing to her, to have people shouting at her, proclaiming a miracle. Citing her as evidence of a miracle. You are a doctor; can you tell me how it happened? This silly business of Mary performing a miracle on Jill's face is all poppycock, of course, and I cannot believe—"

"Your Eminence," said Tennyson, rudely breaking in, "I came to tell you that Jill has disappeared. I've looked everywhere. I thought, perhaps, that you . . ."

"The poor girl," said the cardinal, "undoubtedly has gone into hiding, fleeing from those fanatic louts out there."

"But where could she have gone? She knew of only a few places she could go to hide. She really had no place to hide."

"Tell me, truly, Doctor, how this so-called miracle came about? What erased the stigma? Not Mary, I am sure of that. It must have been something else. You're a doctor; you must have some idea of what happened. Would you say, perhaps, a spontaneous remission, the body's curing of itself?"

"Dammit, Your Eminence, I do not know. I've come to you for help. I want to know anything you might know that could help me find her."

"Have you looked in the library?"

"Yes, I've looked in the library. I've looked everywhere."

"In the little garden by the clinic?"

"Yes. I've told you. I've looked everywhere. You talk with her a great deal; you go to the library to visit her. Did she ever tell you anything, say anything at all that might—"

A loud hammering on the door interrupted them. Tennyson swung around to see what was going on.

The startled guard opened the door a crack to peer out and whoever had been pounding on it gave it a fierce shove, knocking the guard out of the way. A robot dressed in a monkish habit burst into the room.

"An Old One!" he bawled. "Your Eminence, an Old One!"

The cardinal rose from his chair.

"An Old One," he thundered. "What about an Old One? Cease all this hullabaloo and tell me what you want."

"An Old One is coming," the monk shouted at him. "An Old One is coming up the esplanade."

"How do you know it's an Old One? Have you ever seen an Old One?"

"No, Your Eminence. But everyone says it is an Old One. Everyone is running and screaming. Everyone is scared."

"If it is an Old One," said the cardinal, "they had damn well best be scared."

Through the open door came the faint sound of screaming, a noise that filtered through many corridors.

"Up the esplanade?" asked Tennyson. "Heading for the basilica?"

"That is right, Doctor," said the monk.

Tennyson said to the cardinal, "Don't you think we should go out there and see what the Old One wants?"

"I do not understand it," said the cardinal. "No Old One has ever come to Vatican before. In the early days, when we first came here, we occasionally caught glimpses of them, never very many of them, and always from a long distance off. We didn't try to see them too closely. We had no commerce with them. We never troubled them and they never bothered us. Some terrifying tales were told of them, but that was later on, the length of time that it takes for a myth to build."

"They did kill my predecessor—the young doctor—and the two humans who were with him."

"That is true, but the idiots went hunting them. You do not hunt an Old One. It simply isn't done. That was the first time, and the only time, that the Old Ones ever have committed violence."

"Then it's reasonable to think this one comes with no violence in its mind."

"I wouldn't think he is here to do us violence," said the cardinal, "but who is to know? The people have a right to fear the Old Ones, if only from the stories they have heard, and to flee as they now are doing. It's only common sense."

"Well, are you coming out with me or not?"

"You intend to confront the Old One?"

"Not confront him. Meet him."

"Oh, I suppose I might as well," said Theodosius. "There'll be no one else, I'm sure. I warn you, there'll just be the two of us."

"We will be enough," said Tennyson. "Is there any chance we can communicate with him?"

"There are ancient tales that some communication may be possible with Old Ones."

"All right, then. Let's go out and talk with this one."

Tennyson led the way, with Theodosius at his heels and the guard and monk trailing them at a considerable and, presumably, a safe distance.

As they walked through the corridors leading to the entrance of the papal palace, Tennyson tried to remember what he had been told of the Old Ones. It turned out, it seemed, that he had been told very little. The Old Ones had been here, on End of Nothing, when the robots had arrived. There had been only accidental, glancing contacts between the Old Ones and the residents of Vatican. Over the years a myth of the Old Ones as ferocious killers had grown up, the sort of stories that were told in chimney corners in the dead of night. But whether there might be any basis of fact for such stories, he had no way of knowing. Actually, during the time that he had been here, he had heard very little talk of Old Ones.

They came out of the palace and there, a short distance to the right, stood the massive, soaring basilica, its front facing on the broad, paved esplanade that ran up from the east. The esplanade was empty of either robots or humans—emptier than Tennyson had ever seen it. On top of buildings to either side human and robot heads peeked out, watching what was happening below. A breathless silence lay over everything, broken only now and then by distant shouts and shrieks.

Far down the esplanade a pudgy figure trudged, as broad as it was tall. Viewed from the distance that they stood, it appeared not too large, although Tennyson realized that to loom up as it did from the far end of the esplanade, it must be huge.

He hurried down the steps and along the walk that led to the basilica, with the cardinal crunching along behind him, the monk and guard lagging far behind.

Reaching the flight of wide stone stairs that led up to the basilica, Tennyson and the cardinal climbed them and stood waiting for the Old One.

The cardinal said, in an astonished voice, "Doctor, that thing out there is spinning on its axis."

It was, indeed. It was a huge sphere, standing, Tennyson estimated, some twenty feet into the air. It was spinning slowly, and as it spun, it was moving forward. The surface of the globe was black, and while the surface was fairly smooth, it was pockmarked with numerous indentations. It was suspended in the air, its spinning body clearing the pavement by a foot or more.

"Strange," said the cardinal. "Very strange, indeed. Doctor, have you ever seen anything quite like it?"

"No, I have not," said Tennyson. "You seem astonished. Can it be true you have never seen an Old One?"

"As I told you, long ago, when we first came here. The stories had it that they were globular, but you know how stories are. I, myself, have never seen one until now."

The Old One came up to the foot of the stairs. There it halted and its spinning stopped. It dropped to the pavement and rested there.

"Those pockmarks on its hide," said Tennyson, "must be sensory receptors. Sight, smell, hearing—Lord knows what else."

The cardinal said nothing. He stood erect, no longer muffled by his robes, like a soldier at attention.

The Old One sprouted an arm on his right side. It pushed out of his body and grew in length. At the end of it was what amounted to an outsize hand. It reached the hand into a pocket that had not been apparent before the hand dipped into it. It brought out something clutched in its fist and, lengthening its arm to do the job, laid it on the pavement. It was a human body. Tenderly, the fingers of the massive hand straightened the body and turned it on its back.

"My God!" Tennyson cried. "That's Decker!"

He went several steps down the stairs, then stopped. The Old

One's hand had dipped into the pocket again and now came out. Carefully and neatly, it deposited what it had brought from the pocket alongside Decker's body—a rifle, a rolled-up sleeping bag, a knapsack, a camp axe and a battered coffee kettle.

On the left side it also grew an arm, and with it reached into another pocket on the left side of its body. Out of it it brought another object and laid it on the pavement, alongside Decker's body —a robot with the top of its metal skull torn off, and another rifle. Carefully the fingers straightened out the dead robot and laid the rifle beside it.

The Old One pulled its arms back into its body, became a simple globe again.

It began to hum, like a vibrating drum, and its humming filled the air, as if the air itself might be vibrating. Out of the humming came human words, deep, slow and somberous.

"We are wardens," it said. "We keep watch upon this planet. We allow no killing here. Killing for food to keep life within the body is acceptable, for this is the plan of life for some. But not killing for any other reason."

The humming subsided and the words fell away.

Then the humming began again and more words came. "We have lived in peace with you. We want to keep on living so. Do not allow this to happen again."

"But, sir," cried Tennyson, "you killed three humans only a short time ago."

The humming built up. "They came hunting us. They had it in their minds to kill us. This is not allowed. No one kills us. We killed to save ourselves. We killed because the humans were not desirable—they had no place upon this planet."

The humming died and the Old One began to spin. Once it had started spinning, it began to move away, down the esplanade.

Tennyson leaped down the stairs and knelt beside Decker in hope that there might be life still within the man. Decker was dead, had been dead for hours.

Tennyson looked up at Cardinal Theodosius, who was coming slowly down the stairs. Behind him, Tennyson heard the drumbeat of running footsteps. When he turned, he saw that it was Ecuyer.

"Jill is back," Ecuyer shouted at him.

The running man pulled up in front of him, panting from his running.

"She said she had been to the equation world. She said . . ." He stopped and gazed in horror at what lay upon the pavement.

"What have we here?" he asked.

"Decker dead. The Old One brought him home."

"So that was an Old One," said Ecuyer. "I could not know. One hears so many stories. Jason, do you know what happened?"

Tennyson shook his head. "The Old One brought that other. A robot with the top of its head shot off."

Ecuyer walked over to the robot, stood peering down at it.

"Jason," he said haltingly, "do you know who this is?"

"Just a robot. I can't tell. . . ."

"It's our boy, Hubert," said Ecuyer. "The one that cooked your meals and cleaned up the place, that looked after you."

Chapter Forty-three

"IT SEEMS FAIRLY CLEAR WHAT HAPPENED," SAID TENNYSON. "Decker was hit in the upper part of the chest. One lung was damaged. He probably died soon after. But before he died, he got off one good shot at Hubert. The bullet caught the robot in the eye and took off the top of the skull. The robotic brain is a mess. A tangle of smashed circuitry. He probably died the moment he was hit."

"What I can't get straight," said Ecuyer, "is why the two of them should have been out there, shooting up one another. And Hubert? Why Hubert? He was a scary little creature. He had his faults as a servant, but he did all right. I was really fond of him. He had been with me for years. Decker—hell, I don't think he had ever seen Decker. Knew who he was, of course. Everyone in End of Nothing knew who Decker was."

"The rifle Hubert used," said Jill, "was the one the doctor had

carried when he went out to hunt the Old Ones. It might be interesting to know where and how Hubert got that rifle."

"It might not have been hard for anyone to pick up," said
Ecuyer. "The robots would have made no great fuss about it.
They'd just have tucked it away somewhere when it was brought
back with the men the Old Ones killed. No one would have attached much importance to the rifle. Robots have no use for
rifles."

"One of them had," Tennyson said bitterly. "It's a damn
shame. Decker was a good man. I liked him from the ground up.
He was a friend of mine. The only thing wrong with him was that
he might have known where Heaven is."

"I'd go along with you on that," said Ecuyer, "except I can't
believe Hubert would have been mixed up with the theologians. I
don't know what he thought about the issue. I never talked with
him about it. But he was not the sort of robot—"

"He could have heard us talking," said Jill. "He was always
hiding around a corner, listening. He could have heard one of us
say that there was a chance Decker could show the way to
Heaven."

"Yes, that's true," said Ecuyer. "He was always listening. He
soaked up information. He was hell on gossip, and Vatican is just
one great gossip factory. But he had been with me for years before
I loaned him to you, Jason, and I would swear that he was harmless."

"You were wrong," said Jill. "He was far from harmless."

"You have to look at it this way," said Tennyson. "The two
Heaven cubes disappeared—which, I think, means they were stolen.
Decker had been killed and when we searched his cabin, we found
nothing to indicate he had any knowledge of Heaven. Someone, maybe Hubert, maybe someone else, searched the cabin before we did and either found the evidence or didn't find it. If they
didn't find it, it's probable Decker had hidden it somewhere else.
If he did, there's little chance of ever finding it. If someone else
found it in the cabin, there's no chance it will turn up. It probably
has been destroyed, as the cubes may have been destroyed. With
the cubes gone and whatever evidence Decker may have had gone

as well, and Decker dead, there isn't a chance of anyone getting to Heaven."

"Maybe Mary," said Jill.

"I don't think so," said Tennyson. "She's in a coma. She may not make it through the night. The shock of going out to face that crowd of fanatics—she collapsed and had to be carried back to bed."

"Which leaves us empty," said Jill.

"And plays into the hands of the theologians," said Ecuyer. "Dead, Mary would be more acceptable as a saint than if she kept on living. There's something slightly phoney about a living saint. But once she is dead, they can ram this saint business through to a finish. Vatican will have its first saint and no one arguing about Heaven, for that first saint found it and—"

"But the cardinals can block it, can't they?" asked Jill. "I'm sure not many of them are for it. I know Theodosius isn't."

"I suppose they could," said Ecuyer, "if they were willing to risk a full-scale rebellion. They could oppose it and probably make it stick, but that would leave Vatican in an uproar. That would be unacceptable. Vatican, you understand, must always be a place of perfect tranquility, reeking of sanctity. No matter what else they may do, the cardinals must hold fast to the odor of sanctity."

"If the theologians win," said Tennyson, "and it looks now as if they will, that means the end of the Search Program, and without that. . . ."

"In face of that," said Ecuyer, "your cardinals would take the long view. Always the long view. They'd accept a setback for the moment, then work through succeeding centuries to bring Vatican around again to their point of view. Time doesn't mean a damn thing to a robot. He has all the time there is."

"You must consider," said Tennyson, "that the cardinals who look favorably on the Search Program may never get the Vatican turned around. Not in your lifetime, anyhow. You've got to win now or you, personally, lose forever."

"I know that," said Ecuyer. "I've been thinking. . . ." He turned to Jill and said, "Jason told me something—not much, but something—just a while ago, about this thing called Whisperer and how he went to the equation world. Now I understand you have gone as well. That's where you were when we were looking for you."

"I thought it would be all right to tell him," Tennyson said to Jill. "Decker's gone now and we no longer have to consider Whisperer his secret."

"I suppose that's the way it is," said Jill. "Probably there never was good reason for it to be his secret."

"I think he may have had many secrets," said Ecuyer. "He was a very private man. Since Jason told me, however, I've been wondering . . ."

"If you've been thinking Whisperer could take us to Heaven," said Jill, "I don't think he could. He took Jason to the equation world because Jason had seen the cube. I'd not seen the cube, but Whisperer could take me because he knew the way, having been there once. Jason showed him the way and he remembered it."

"But he doesn't need coordinates."

"No, that's right. There were no coordinates for the equation world, but once he saw Jason's memory of it, he could go there. He must use something other than what we think of as coordinates."

"Then why not Heaven?"

"Because he has to get into the mind of someone who has seen a cube of the place," said Tennyson.

"Into the mind—that's the way he does it?"

"That's right."

"Then why couldn't he get into Mary's mind? Even if she is in a coma."

"Because in a coma she would retain no memories. Her mind's a blank. More than likely, even if she were alert and well, he couldn't get into her mind."

"You mean he can't—"

"Look, Paul, as close as Whisperer was to Decker, he never could get into his mind."

"But he gets into yours and Jill's. What makes you so different?"

"I don't know. I've puzzled over that. Most people can't even see Whisperer. You can't, I know. Whisperer tried to strike up an acquaintance with you. He showed himself to you and you didn't even see him."

"How do you know this?"

"He told me. I have a hunch he tried a lot of people here in End of Nothing, with the same result. He never tried with the robots. They have a different kind of mind, he said, maybe a different kind of senses. He snooped around Vatican a great deal, trying to pick up information. He's gone on information. His task in life is to gain an understanding of the universe. He picked up some stuff from Vatican, but not a great deal. He worked hard for what he got."

"Vatican was aware of someone snooping," said Jill. "Like a mouse nibbling at a ton of cheese. That's the way Theodosius put it. But they never could find what or who it was. It worried them a lot. Apparently they just caught the edges of it."

"So there's not any chance," said Ecuyer.

"I'm sure there's not," said Tennyson.

"Dead in the water," said Ecuyer. "We just sit here and take it. Christ, when I think of all we had going for us. The entire universe out there and us picking away at it. Now it's all going to be thrown away because of an imbecilic search for a true religion."

Tennyson stirred uneasily in his chair. "I wish I could be of some help. I think Jill must wish the same. I have a feeling I'm failing you."

"Not at all," said Ecuyer. "This isn't your problem."

"But it is," said Tennyson. "It's a human concern as well as a Vatican one. Maybe it concerns everyone. I don't know. All life would benefit if we could get some answers."

"We may be able to think of some way to go," said Jill. "I don't think we should give up. I can talk to my own tame cardinal."

"A lot of good that will do," said Ecuyer. "He'll pooh-pooh your concerns. He will say it'll all work out—don't worry about it, child; in the long run, it'll come out all right."

Tennyson rose to his feet. "I should have a look at Mary."

"I'll go with you," said Ecuyer. He said to Jill, "Would you like to come along?"

Jill shuddered. "No, I don't think I would. I'll whip something up for dinner. Paul, would you like to join us?"

"No, thanks. I'd love to, but there are chores to do."

Outside he said to Tennyson, "I didn't want to ask in front of her, but how about her face? What really happened?"

"Someday," Tennyson promised, "we'll tell you all about it."

Chapter Forty-four

"I WISH I COULD TELL YOU," JILL SAID TO TENNYSON, "BUT my mind's all cluttered up. So much strange was happening. As I told you, I looked at that insane diagram with the squiggle to one side and I knew the diagram was me and the squiggle was a question mark. He was asking what I was and I was racking my brain about what I could tell him when Whisperer spoke inside my mind and said he would take over."

"So he did."

"Yes, and I was there with him. He was inside my mind and we were, really, just one mind and I knew what was going on, but I had no idea what it was. Back, millennia ago, they had this device called a telegraph over which men talked to one another with clicks transmitted over wires; you could stand there and listen to all that clicking and not know what was going on because you did not know the code. Or listening to two aliens talking and hearing all the words, all the clatter and the jabber that they use as words, but completely lost because you know nothing of the language."

"You said telegraph. Were there clicks?"

"Some clicks, I guess, and a lot of other things, a lot of other sounds, which I suppose that I was making, not knowing how or why I made them and a bunch of funny thoughts running through my brain, as if they were my thoughts, but they must have been Whisperer's, for they surely weren't mine. At times I would think that I was catching on to what was going on and then I'd lose the thread of it and would be lost again. Ordinarily such a situation would have bothered me; in another situation I might have gone insane wondering what kind of creature I had turned into. But it didn't bother me. It wasn't as if I was in a daze, for I wasn't. My mind was entirely clear, although considerably flabbergasted. At times it seemed to me I was something else entirely and, at other times, I seemed to be standing off to one side, simply looking on, standing outside myself and watching this other self doing all those strange things. All this time the equation person, with a number of others all grouped about him, was slowly running through a number of equations and some diagrams, very simple basic equations and diagrams, not long strings of equations or complicated diagrams, as if he were talking carefully to a child. Baby talk, like one talks to children. And I thought, why, he's as confused as I am. He doesn't know any more about what is going on than I do. For the clicks and grunts and trebles and all the other sounds I was making could not have seemed like a language to him, any more than his diagrams and equations looked like a language to me."

"Whisperer probably was understanding some of it," said Tennyson. "Whisperer was the one in control. He was a sort of double-jointed interpreter."

"He didn't pan out so well as an interpreter for me," said Jill. "Although I think that may have been the case. He was working both sides of the street. We moved up close—I mean I moved up close to this equation person and watched what was going on and every once in a while, I'd point a finger at an equation or a diagram as if I might be asking a question about it, although it wasn't me who was asking the question. It was Whisperer, and when that happened, the equation person would go through all of it again, patient, trying to make us understand. Sometimes he had to go through it several times before Whisperer seemed to understand."

"But you understood none of it?"

"Jason, I think I did—some of it. Not a full understanding, of course, but snatches of it. And some of it I may have marginally understood I plain forgot because I don't think it was the kind of information that the human mind could be expected to grasp the first time around. Some of it, I know, was outrageous—outrageous by human standards. There seemed to be no logic in it. You know what I think, Jason?"

"No, what do you think?"

"I think the equation world operates on a variable logic pattern. One statement can be logical in one context, but not in the next. It was infuriating. I'd grab a piece of it by the tail, then something would come along to make that one piece I had grasped outlandish. I don't know. I really do not know. Some of it I'm sure I caught the drift of at the time, but I don't have it now. Whisperer said he wanted me to go with him because my viewpoint might be different from yours and I guess it must have been. Nothing like this happened to you when you were there—did it?"

"No, it didn't. I was just confused."

"The difference," said Jill, "might not have been with you and me. Come to think of it, I don't believe it was. The difference was with Whisperer. He'd been there twice, you see. He might have been getting the hang of it. On a second trip you, too, might get the hang of it. And he'd probably been thinking about it all the time since he got back with you."

"Jill, I'm sorry you had to go through this. There was no reason that you should. I told Whisperer to leave you out of it. He thought he could work with you as he had worked with me, but I told him—"

"Yes, I know. He told me you had told him."

"Where is Whisperer now?"

"I don't know. I came back. All of a sudden, I came back. Not here, but to my own suite. That's where we started out. Whisperer wasn't with me. He wasn't in the room and he wasn't in my mind. I don't know how I knew this, but I knew he wasn't."

"I wonder if he knows that Decker's dead. That will hit him hard. He and Decker were great pals. Decker tried to pretend that he didn't care one way or the other, but he did. He thought a lot of Whisperer."

Jill picked up the coffee pot and filled Tennyson's cup. "I made a cake," she said. "Do you want a piece?"

"Later," he said. "A little later on. That stew you made. . . ."

"It was good, wasn't it."

"Delicious. Filling."

"Jason, do you think the theologians killed Decker?"

"It all fits together. The cubes gone, Decker dead. They took us out of it. If we could just have held on to the cubes, then Whisperer could have taken us to Heaven. No need for coordinates. He has the ability to follow a very dim trail. Like a dog trailing a fox. If he can take us to the equation world, he could have taken us to Heaven. There's a lot out there in the universe. Many trails for him to follow."

"Jason, could we be wrong? You and I and Paul? Could the Vatican theologians be right? Is a true faith more valuable than knowledge of the universe?"

"Jill, I think that involves a judgment of what comes first. Vatican made that decision long ago and now someone is trying to reverse it. The decision that first you must have knowledge before you can arrive at faith. That may have been a wrong decision. I can't be certain, but I don't think it was."

"Maybe we will never know."

"You and I will never know. Someday someone will."

"What happens now?"

"There's no way right now to know."

"Jason, some bits of it are coming back to me. The bits and pieces I picked up in the equation world."

"Perhaps as time goes on, more and more of it."

"There was a sense of being tired, of resting. Does that make any sense?"

"Not much," said Tennyson. "But take it easy. Your very human mind is trying to translate alien concepts into human terms."

"There is something else. The idea of games and a great excitement that here was a new game to be played."

"It probably was something else entirely, but at least it's a place to start. You picked up far more than I did. Maybe Whisperer, when he shows up, will be able to help out."

"I think so. Whisperer must have understood far more than I did."

A knock came at the door. When Tennyson opened it, Theodosius stood outside.

"How good of you to come," said Tennyson. "Won't you step in. We are greatly honored."

The cardinal came in and Tennyson closed the door. "I'll poke up the fire," he said, "and we can sit and talk."

"I would like to do that," said the cardinal, "but there is no time. His Holiness has summoned the two of you to an audience."

Jill came around the table. "I don't understand," she said.

"His Holiness thinks most highly of you."

"You will go with us," said Tennyson.

"I'll escort you there, but I will not stay. He said the two of you. The two of you alone."

Chapter Forty-five

WHISPERER GAMBOLED. HE WAS GIDDY AND ECSTATIC. HE went skating down a looping bridge of magnetic flux. He danced madly in the midst of a sputtering cloud of ions. He ducked his erratic way through the core of an exploding galaxy. He ran a race with the surging radiation that flared out of a nova. He somersaulted through a field of pulsars.

When it was all done, he hunkered down before a red dwarf and spread out symbolic hands to warm them on the banked fires of the star. The red dwarf, curiously, was the only luminosity in sight. All else was black, although somewhere far away there was the faint hint of high-intensity flickering, as if some great event were taking place beyond the far horizon of deep space. He was penned in by an emptiness and a nothingness and he sensed the loneliness that went with nothingness, although he had no feel for loneliness, for he was a creature of space–time, and in all of space and time, there was no room for loneliness.

He did not know where he was and he gave no thought to it, for wherever he might be, he knew that he was home, although why or how he knew this, he had no inkling and again he gave no thought to it, for it did not matter—he could go anywhere he wished and he still would be at home. Which did not mean, of course, that he'd know where he was.

He crouched before the red-black star and heard the song of foreverness that pulsed in the emptiness in this corner of the universe, wherever it might be. He caught the dim scent of distant life and he thought about the achievements of that life—each achievement peculiar to a certain life form, but all the many achievements of many life forms adding up to a massive reaching out for the incalculable answers that must come about and meld together before the final answer could be known.

This was his heritage, he thought, this the heritage and the task and the striving of his people and perhaps of many other peoples who alone and in the darkness of unknowing clawed toward the light.

Then the star and the darkness went away and again he was in the center of a circle formed by the equation people and he sought out the rose-red one flanked by all the others. The panel of the rose-red one was blank, but as he watched, an equation flickered on it, pale and faint at first, then hardening and becoming sharper. He drove his mind against it and he wrestled with it and finally it became clear and when that happened, the rose-red blackboard was wiped clean of it and again he drove his mind against it and, hesitantly, another equation began to form and finally formed, as hard and solid as had been the first one. But there was a difference: This time the equation was his own, transmitted to the rose-red equation person and now etched upon its blackboard so that it might be seen by all the others.

I am talking to them, Whisperer told himself and felt a surge of pride sweep through him. I am talking to them in their own language and in their own way.

All around the circle, the same equation was formed on the blank surfaces of all the other people and he sensed their wonder and their satisfaction that finally one had come who could talk with them. Probably it was something they never had expected—in this small segment of space–time they had staked out for themselves, they had made themselves content to be alone, divorced and isolated from all other peoples and all other places, not expecting visitors, anticipating no contact with other forms of life, a community that had told itself it was self-sufficient and had settled, in its hearts and souls, for that.

His equation was wiped out and another began to form, not so slowly this time, not so haltingly.

The rose-red equation person was answering him.

Whisperer settled down for a long talk with his new-found friends.

Chapter Forty-six

THE TINY ROOM WAS BARREN, A PLACE OF FOUR WALLS carved from the rock, with the metallic plate set into the wall that faced the chairs on which they sat. The face formed slowly on the plate. For a time after it had formed, nothing happened, then the Pope said, "I am pleased that you could come to see me."

"It pleases us, Your Holiness, to be here," said Jill.

"I have many advisers," said the Pope, "and, at times, they give me much conflicting advice, so that often I am somewhat puzzled as to what counsel I should take. Now, if you are agreeable, I'd like to avail myself of somewhat different counsel. Generally, my advisers give me the benefit of robotic thinking. At times, over the years, there have been some humans, but not many of them and too many of them unwilling to freely express their inner thoughts. I now have Ecuyer, of course, and while he is more valuable than many of the others, he has a tendency to think from a single viewpoint. He is so wrapped up in his Search Program. . . ."

"He is a devoted man," said Tennyson.

"Yes, there's that, of course. May I ask you something? As humans, are you outraged by our calling this place Vatican?"

"Not at all," said Jill.

"Do you happen to be Christians?"

"That is a question we have discussed among ourselves," said Jill. "We are not certain exactly what we are. The two of us happen to have Christian roots. Which is no more than to say that our culture is not Jewish or Moslem or any other of the many faiths developed by mankind."

"We are not *the* Vatican, of course," said the Pope. "Not even a Vatican. We term ourselves Vatican-17, although the numeral is very seldom used. I suspect that at the time this establishment was built, there may have been sixteen other Vaticans, scattered through as many solar systems settled by humankind, although as to that I cannot be positive. I suspect as well that the Old Earth Vatican is still the premier Vatican, if that is the correct way of saying it, and all the others that now exist are subsidiaries, if, again, that is the correct terminology. The subsidiary Vaticans undoubtedly would have had the right to use the name. We did not even ask. If we were to establish ourselves today, I doubt we'd use the name. If I were constructed today, I am certain I would not be termed a pope. When this Vatican and I were built, the robots were fresh from Earth, still starry-eyed and filled with the wonder of the great religions there, especially impressed by the majesty and the tradition of the Catholic faith. Thus, this place became Vatican and I became a pope. You would get objection to what I've told you from many functionaries of this Vatican. There are many who still regard this as a holy place and a holy venture. The terms were used out of the great respect and perhaps even a love of Old Earth Christianity. Despite the fact our founders were denied the privilege of becoming communicants, they still held their love of the ancient faith."

"We understand all that," said Tennyson. "We can understand the robots' reason for the use of the terminology—and sympathize with it."

"As a pope," said His Holiness, "I am supposed to be infallible. I am supposed to know all answers. This community looks to me for guidance. As a sophisticated computer, I am equipped to work out long-range answers; on the short range, more often than not, I find myself fumbling. Ask me for an answer that may be valid ten thousand years from now and, given time, I can come up with the good approximation. Ask me for a decision about tomorrow and I am as uncertain as the next one. You can see my problem?"

"Yes, we can," said Jill.

"The one thing that confuses me the most," said His Holiness, "is this matter of faith. Throughout this galaxy and, undoubtedly, throughout the universe, many different peoples have developed many types of faith, based on widely varying concepts and various kinds of deities. This may seem to you to be a strange way for a pope to talk."

"We are listening," said Tennyson. "Most attentively."

"It is true, as I have said, that throughout the universe there are many kinds of faiths. For sheer diversity, however, no planet that I know of can exceed Earth in the number of its faiths. How many separate faiths would you say that Earth might have?"

"I have never taken the time to count them up," said Jill. "Even if I tried, I imagine I'd leave out a number that were purely local. But there are a lot of them."

"And none agreeing. Each of them arguing, even to the death, that theirs is the one and only faith. There was a time in Earth's history, continuing for centuries, that men of different faiths slaughtered one another to prove their faith was best. A faith based on the letting of blood. Does this seem right to you? To what would you attribute it?"

"To the madness of mankind," said Tennyson. "In many ways we are a vicious race."

"And yet one that is deeply loved by robots. Your people created my people. Out of your minds and skills our people sprang. Out of you came us. You created and developed us. For this reason, if for no other, there must be great good in you. There must be in you an overflowing measure of nobility and love."

"Your Holiness, our philosophers for years have asked the questions you are asking," said Tennyson. "They are not new to us."

"Then what about this matter of faith? You know the problem

that Vatican is facing. As a derivative of a robot, which is a derivative of a human, I am asking you. I do not promise I will accept your advice; I have many factors to consider, but I do need to know how you think about it. That is why I asked you here, alone, unaccompanied by your friend the cardinal. Come on, speak up. Tell me what's in your mind. I ask you as two valued friends."

"We did not come here first as friends," said Tennyson. "Jill came as a writer who wished to tell your story to the galaxy and you were extremely wroth at that. I came as a man fleeing human justice, and while I was given sanctuary, I was tolerated only as a physician, which you needed since your doctor had been killed."

"But since then you both have proved to us that you are friends," said the Pope. "You have become identified with Vatican. There was a time when you resented our implied threat that we would not let you leave; now we would be hard put to drive you off. What have you found in Vatican that brings this change of heart?"

"I am not sure that I can tell you," said Tennyson.

And yet, he thought, perhaps he could. How, he thought, can I count the ways?

"The quietness of it," said Jill. "The quiet way of living and the quietness of the dedication. Although I sense now that the quietness of the dedication is beginning to break up. The little clinic garden, the fields of grain, the mountains. . . ."

"I had the impression," said Tennyson, "that you did not care for mountains."

"I do now. I saw them just the other day. I saw them, Jason, as you have been seeing them."

"Back in the medieval days of Earth," Tennyson told the Pope, "there were many monasteries. Men withdrew to them, spent their lives in them, living Christian lives under Christian rule. They would have told you, had you asked them, that they did it for the love of Christ, that this was their way of serving Christ. I am inclined to think that, deep down, they used the monasteries as refuges against the brutal times. There they found a world of peace and quiet. Which did not make them any less devout, but, without their realizing it, their devotion had less to do with their being there than they might have thought. I think that's what you have here, what I've found here—a refuge from the turbulence of a contending galaxy."

"And that," said the Pope, "is what we wish it to remain. A quiet place in which to go about our work. But the question is: What should be our work?"

"If you are asking me if you should follow faith or knowledge, I'd say knowledge, for it seems to me faith will come out of knowledge, not knowledge out of faith. But that is a personal opinion. Ask a dozen, or a hundred, other humans, not including the indoctrinated humans on End of Nothing, and you would get different answers. Some of them would give my answer, others would plump for faith. Maybe the answer is that there can be no true answer any more than there may be true faith."

"And a true knowledge?"

"I think that somewhere there must be. I know I'll never know it; I'm not certain you will ever find it."

"Perhaps," said His Holiness, "our good robots miscalculated in my construction. Perhaps they failed to instill in me the piety that they felt within themselves. But I am inclined to agree with you. If, however, I make such a decision, Vatican will be torn apart. There'll be contentious arguing for years, and not all of Vatican would follow my decision—which would not do much for the image of the Pope. And whether you may think so or not, the image of the Pope is important to every one of us."

Neither of the humans answered him.

"You humans feel both love and hate," said the Pope. "I can feel neither of them. I think that's one up for me and my fellow robots. You have your dreams and I have mine, but my dream cannot be identical with yours. You have the arts—music, painting, literature—and while I am aware of these, while I recognize the function that they serve and the pleasure to be gotten from them, I cannot respond to them."

"Holiness," said Jill, "faith itself may be an art."

"I do not doubt it," said the Pope. "You may have put your finger on an important consideration. Yet you cannot say that robots are lacking in their faith and their hunger for the faith. It was that hunger which built Vatican and has carried us through a thousand years of searching for a more perfect faith. Could it be that there are many varieties, not of faiths, but of perfect faiths, of truthful and solid faiths?"

"There may appear to be," said Tennyson, "but in the last analysis, I am certain there will be one faith, one faith alone that thinking creatures can accept. There'll be one true faith as there will be one full truth—a final faith and a final truth. I would not be surprised if the two should prove the same, the faith and the truth."

"And this is why you believe we should follow truth, that it provides a better and an easier road to faith than to seek for faith alone?"

"I think so," said Tennyson. "Searching for truth you will have some guidelines. Faith is very short of solid guidelines."

"I have stowed within me so vast a reservoir of knowledge," said the Pope, "furnished by the Listeners through the centuries, that at times I scarcely know where to turn. I must seek frantically through my dustbin of knowledge, hunting for that single bit of information that might fit into a puzzle to which I seek solution. There are many puzzles, and simultaneously I must seek the many bits of knowledge that possibly will give form and substance to the many puzzles. Even while I am doing this, I am haunted by the thought that perhaps the required bits of knowledge for which I seek have not as yet been found by the Listeners. They range far and endlessly and yet they have made only the barest scratch upon the knowledge of the universe."

"Which means," said Tennyson, "that you must keep the Listeners to their tasks. Tomorrow one of them may find one of those bits of knowledge that you need, or it may require a hundred years to find it, or a thousand, but if the Listeners do not continue going out into the universe, it never will be found."

"I know," the Pope said. "I know. And yet there are those who say, with knowing smirks on their metallic faces, that I do not exist in the real world, that in my isolation, imprisoned in the stone of these mountains, I no longer am in touch with reality. I do not think this is true, but I cannot make them understand. I think this real world they talk about is a provincial world, that it is bounded by the areas they know and the peculiar conditions that exist there. What is the real world on End of Nothing and in Vatican would not be the real world on a planet halfway across the galaxy, or even in a planet that was next door to us. Our limited senses, which restrict our understanding and make it limited as well, fences us in against the reality of the universe. I think that I, rather than they, exist in a world much more real than theirs.

"I've outgrown them," said the Pope. "That's what has happened. I have grown beyond them. But that is what they wanted. When they constructed me, they sought infallibility, like the Pope on Earth. But I've outgrown them and disappointed them. Infallibility on a single planet and in the universe are two different things."

Chapter Forty-seven

"WHAT WAS THAT ALL ABOUT?" ASKED JILL.

"Vatican's coming apart," said Tennyson, "and the Pope's the one who knows it."

"We didn't help him much."

"We helped him not at all. He's disappointed in us. The robots still hold the infantile notion that their humans are great men of magic, that we can reach down and come up with answers, that when they get stuck, we'll bail them out. The father image—the Old Man can do anything, he can fix it up. The Pope's the same. Maybe he knew we couldn't do anything for him, but he still held the father fantasy. And now he's disappointed in us."

Tennyson got up and threw a couple of logs on the fire, came back to sit beside Jill.

"It is the Search Program that holds Vatican together," he said. "Ecuyer said something about it, I remember, when we first came here. He told me that Vatican was only an excuse to continue the Search Program. I thought he was simply bragging, trying to impress me with his own importance. But there is a great deal of truth in it. I realize that now. With the Search Program, Vatican is a dynamic operation; without it, it will become a fuzzy fumbling after something that no one understands. There'll be endless empty arguments and much vague philosophizing, and heresies will spring up to fight bitterly with ecclesiastical authority. Without the Listeners, Vatican, in its present form, will not last another thousand years. Even if it does, it will be meaningless."

"But His Holiness told us," said Jill, "that he has a great backlog of knowledge furnished by the Listeners. I got the idea he is nowhere near caught up with it. Couldn't he continue working with what he has? If that's what he wants to do, and I think it is. With all this backlog—"

"Don't you see?" asked Tennyson. "It would be a dead end. A lot of the information that he has never will be used. He can still continue sifting through it, he can sift through it endlessly, still with the greater part of it not being used. To keep his work viable, to keep it moving forward, that backlog he speaks of must keep growing. Like new wood for a fire. This may not be possible, for if the theologians do take over, in a few years the Listeners will be gone. The present Listeners will die off, and if there are no others recruited to take their place and if the clones aren't trained, then the Search Program will die. And that's the end of it."

"And once gone, it can't be started up again."

"That's exactly it," said Tennyson. "Jill, we are sitting here and facing the death of one of the most ambitious research projects the galaxy has ever known. God knows how much will be lost. No one can estimate what the impact of such a failure will be upon the robots and the humans. I include the humans because what the robots have also belongs to humans. We may think of them as two different races, but they're not. The robots have a human heritage; they are a part of us. They belong to us and we belong to them."

"Jason, we have to do something about it. You and I must do something. We are the only ones."

"There is Ecuyer."

"Yes, sure, there is Ecuyer but he's too much Vatican."

"I suppose you're right. He is tainted in a lesser degree than

other End of Nothing humans, but he is still tainted. He is still
Vatican."

"Jason, we have to do something. What can we do?"

"My darling, I don't know. As of now, I'm fresh out of all
ideas. I haven't got a one. If we could get to Heaven. . . ."

"And bring back proof. We'd have to bring back proof."

"Yes, of course we would. Without it, no one would believe us.
But that's something we don't need to worry about. We're not
going there."

"I just thought of something."

"Yes, what is it?"

"What if it was really Heaven? What if Mary had been right?"

"Heaven's not a place. It is a state of mind."

"No, Jason, cut that out. You are mouthing a phrase. No more
than flip judgment. I told you about the equation people. I said it
might be possible they operated on a variable logic pattern. What
if this whole universe operated on a variable logic pattern?
Wouldn't that make all our human preconceptions invalid? Could
we be as wrong as that?"

"If you're trying to tell me there could be a Heaven . . ."

"I'm not saying that. I'm asking you if there was, what would
you do?"

"You mean would I accept it?"

"Yes, that is what I'm asking. If your nose were rubbed in
Heaven—"

"I imagine I would gag a bit."

"And accept it?"

"I would have to, wouldn't I? But how could I tell if it was
Heaven? Not the golden stairs, not angels. . . ."

"Probably not golden stairs nor angels. Those are old tales,
someone trying to make Heaven the sort of place the people of
that early day hungered after. A place they'd want to live. A sort
of eternal picnic. But I think you would know if it was Heaven."

"A good fishing stream," said Tennyson. "Woodland paths to
walk. Mountains to look at. Good restaurants where the waiters
were your friends—not just servitors, but friends—other friends to
talk with, good books to read and think about, and you. . . ."

"That's your idea of Heaven?"

"Just off the cuff. Give me some time to think about it and I can come up with more."

"I don't know," said Jill. "I'm confused by all of it—Vatican and the equation worlds and all the rest of it. I can't help but believe it, and yet there are times when I get angry at myself for believing. His Holiness talked about reality. Living here, I know it's real, but when I get off by myself and think about it, I tell myself it's not reality, it is not the sort of place I could have imagined before I first saw it. It all is so unreal."

He put his arm around her and she came up against him and he held her close. The fire talked in the chimney throat and a stillness they had not noticed before closed down all about them. They were alone and safe in the darkness of the world.

"Jason, I am happy."

"So am I. Let us stay that way."

"You were running from Gutshot when you came here. And I was running too. Not running from anything, not even from myself. Just running. I've been running all my life."

"But not any longer."

"No, not any longer. You told His Holiness about the old medieval monasteries. This is our monastery: good work to do, a hiding from the world outside, a happiness and surety in our hearts. Maybe I don't belong here. There were no women in the old monasteries, were there?"

"Well, only now and then. When the monks could sneak them in."

The firelight glittered on something that floated down in front of the fireplace.

Tennyson sat bolt upright.

"Jill," he said, "Whisperer is here."

—Decker, said Whisperer. Decker. Decker. Decker. I have only now found out.

—Come to me, said Jill. Come to me. I will grieve with you.

—Come to both of us, said Tennyson.

He came to both of them and they grieved with him.

Chapter Forty-eight

ENOCH CARDINAL THEODOSIUS WALKED THE CLINIC GARDEN. There was no one there, not even the ancient caretaker, John. There were few stars to relieve the blackness of the sky, a dozen at most, but widely separated, and here and there the faint luminosities of distant galaxies, fairy hints of myriad worlds very far away. Above the eastern horizon hung the frosty glitter of the Milky Way, the home galaxy, and the dim shimmering specks that were a few of the globular clusters that hung above the galaxy.

The cardinal's feet crunched on the brick pavement as he paced slowly along the walks, his hands clasped behind his back and his head bowed low in thought.

We can be wrong, he thought. We were wrong about the Old Ones and we can be wrong about other things as well. Simply because we believe a thing is so does not mean it's so.

For years we had thought the Old Ones were fierce carnivores. We thought of them as bloodthirsty lurkers in the forest; to meet one of them was death. Jealous of their forests and their world, keeping watch on us, keeping us penned in. And yet one of them brought in Decker, dead, and Hubert, dead as well—he brought them home to us and laid them on the stone before the basilica and straightened their limbs when he put them down so that they lay there in all decency.

And he spoke, saying the Old Ones were wardens and there could be no senseless killings, warning us against further senseless killings.

Wardens? Theodosius asked himself. Wardens of this world? More than likely, he told himself, wardens of this world. All these years watching us and not interfering, perhaps not interfering because we somehow managed to be decent tenants of this world of theirs.

Watching us, studying us far more closely than we knew, for

they know our language. Knowing how to talk, but never talking to us, perhaps because until this moment there had been no need to talk. Talking to us with some effort, perhaps not the way they talk among themselves. Adapting their way to our way because they knew we could not adapt to theirs.

We have lived these thousand years on End of Nothing by their sufferance. They have let us go our way and have made no move against us except for the killing of the humans, which served to reinforce our conception of them as dangerous beasts. But killing the humans only because the humans had set out to kill them. In such a light, their actions can be understood. Humans, even robots, would not hesitate to kill someone who came to them in violence, seeking their death.

There had been stories that the Old Ones could talk in the human tongue, but that had been no more than a part of that myth which had been built around them. Had some human or some robot talked with them? he wondered. He shook his head, doubting it. It was just part of the chimney-corner story that had evolved about them. When a myth is manufactured, there always was the chance that some small part of it might turn out to be true.

The waste of it, he thought, the shameful waste of it. All these years the Old Ones had stood out there as potential friends, as people worth knowing, as people who might have had some impact upon our lives and we, perhaps, on theirs. Certainly when anyone settled on a planet, he should know the wardens of it. So few other planets had wardens; perhaps none at all. So in this sense, End of Nothing would be unique, and we should have known how unique it is. It might have made a difference if we had.

The Old One had brought Decker and Hubert home—and why had Hubert done the deed—why had he killed Decker? Tennyson seemed to have no doubt that Hubert had been the transgressor in the killings. That Hubert had been acting for the theologians was a strong possibility, although now Theodosius found himself reluctant to admit it. That was strange, he thought. He had found no reluctance in believing it had been the theologians who had stolen the Heaven cubes, but theft and killing were two different things, not to be equated. How could a robot, he asked himself, bring himself to kill a human—Decker or any other human? One robot, perhaps, one brain-twisted, deranged robot, but in the Decker killing, if Hubert had killed for the theologians, more than one robot was involved. More than likely a fairly large group—just how many he could not even guess. The thought shook him, that a large group of desperate robots should employ such means to implement their policy. He felt within himself an unaccustomed sense of anger and an unaccustomed fear and the two of them, the anger and the fear, warred with one another.

Tennyson had told him, briefly and in no detail, that there had been a possibility Decker might have held Heaven information and that it was because of this that Decker had been slain. But Decker was a newcomer to End of Nothing, and much as he might admire and even like the man, the cardinal found in himself an unwillingness to accept Tennyson's appraisal of the situation at face value. For Tennyson likewise was a newcomer to Vatican. Tennyson had been a friend of Decker, perhaps the only friend the man had in all of End of Nothing. Decker may have told him, or hinted, that he knew something of Heaven, but how much reliance could be put on Decker's word? The man had been an enigma, popping out of nowhere. He had not arrived aboard the *Wayfarer;* Vatican, early on, had made sure of that. Barring the *Wayfarer,* how could he have arrived? He himself had given no evidence. He had made no friends until Tennyson arrived. He had talked with few; in all his talk he had offered no explanation of himself. There was, Theodosius told himself, something strange about the man.

Yet we have been wrong about the Old Ones, he thought; could we be wrong with Decker, too? In how many ways have we been wrong?

We came here, all the centuries ago, to find that thing the theologians now insist we must look the harder for, striving toward that greater and that truer faith. That was our original intent, that was why we abandoned Earth and now we find ourselves at cross-purposes as to how to go about it. In all truth, he asked himself, have we drifted so far from that original intent? Are we tinged, without admitting it openly, with the materialistic ethics of the humans who built us and trained us and guided us and formed us in their image, not only in the image of their bodies but likewise the image of their minds? And who, having done this, used us unmercifully. Yes, he said, talking to himself, they did use us unmercifully, but despite the lack of mercy, always with an innate kindness. They did this because, deep within themselves, they knew, along with us, that the two of us were brothers, that we were no more, and no less, than extensions of themselves. Looking at us, they saw themselves, and looking at them, we also see ourselves. So we are, in all truth, one race. What we do here in our work, at any time they ask, we will share with them. We go to great care to shield ourselves from the galaxy, but not from the humans in the galaxy. From others in the galaxy, but not the humans who are there. We would give the humans willingly all that we have found, and they, scattered as they are, would share what they have with us. So it is no great wonder that we may find ourselves smeared with their materialism, which in itself is no bad thing, either, for if there had been no materialism in them, if they had not reached hard and far to better their condition, they would, even now, be no more than another species of mammals, sharing their home planet with many other mammals. In such a case, there would have been no robots and no Vatican.

If this is true, he thought, then in our materialism we have been guilty of no sin, as the theologians tell us we have been—unless the original sin of which we hear so much was, in all truth, this same materialism. But it could not have been, for if our brother humans had not attempted to better their condition, they never would have reached the mental capacity to conceive that great religion we admire so much. They still would be worshiping, if they worshiped at all, some nonsense spirit represented by an awkward structure formed of mud and sticks and bones, crouching in their caves against an unreasoned fear of dark, gibbering of omens.

Our human brothers stumbled many times along their way, they followed fearfully and uncertainly that three-million-year-long road—and here we have stumbled along, as bumbling as they, as uncertain as they, for no more than a thousand years. If, at this juncture of our venture and our purpose, we should stumble badly, commit a great mistake, we have done no more than they did many times before and, as was the case with them, we will recover from it.

The task that we must do, that we must work toward with all our strength and faith, is to make sure that Vatican survives, that the structure we built still will stand in place so that, even if we stumble, we can pick ourselves up and go ahead, finally steady to our purpose.

I am aware that many of the humans of Vatican and End of Nothing view with some disdain our robotic inclination to take the long view, to think of a century as nothing, even of a millennium as inconsequential, if such wasting of time (as they term it) will enable us to pick up and carry on.

He halted his walking and stood upon the brick-paved path, lifting his bowed head to stare toward the east, to where the brittle glitter of the Milky Way, so distant from him, yet to which he was so closely tied, the home of Man, shimmered in the sky.

Out there, toward the east, somewhere in those tangled hills above Decker's cabin, he had been told, was a place that was frequented by an Old One. Perhaps the one who had brought Decker home. Perhaps one that had been watching over Decker. Why should one of them, he wondered, watch principally over Decker?

Perhaps, he told himself, it would be only proper for someone from Vatican, perhaps himself, to go out to talk with Decker's Old One. It would be no more than simple courtesy to return a visit.

Chapter Forty-nine

—ALL THIS TIME, JILL ASKED OF WHISPERER, YOU HAVE BEEN in the equation world?

—Yes. I sent you back. I did not come myself. I remained and talked with them.

—You can talk with them? I knew when I was there you were able . . .

—I can talk with them, said Whisperer.

—Can you tell us what they are?

—They are elderly philosophers.

—That sounds familiar, said Tennyson. Earth had its full share of philosophers and I imagine that it still does, and most of them, it always seemed to me, were elderly. Slow-spoken, deliberate men conscious of their wisdom and never allowing you to ignore that wisdom.

—These are used-up philosophers, said Whisperer.

—Used up?

—Too old to be of any further use. Behind the times, perhaps. Mumbling in their beards. No longer with their fellows. Restricted to small space. They spend their days in games.

—Like old Earth codgers, playing checkers or horseshoes—

—No, not like that. Not like that at all. They set up problems and they run them through. Sometimes it takes them long, for the problems are not easy.

—Problems? asked Jill. You say they are given problems. But you also say they are out of it.

—No one gives them anything. They think up the problems for themselves. Hypothetical problems. The kind of problems that no one else would waste their time on. Maybe ethical problems, maybe moral, maybe something else. They tried to explain them to me, but—

—Then all this business of equations and diagrams, those are really problems. Not just talk, but problems.

—They are problems, said Whisperer. Maybe some talk, but mostly problems. They do not need to really talk. They commune among themselves. They know each other so well. . . .

—Wait, said Tennyson. Could these people be retired? You know what retired means?

—I'm not sure I do.

—When a human has worked for the greater portion of his estimated time, he is retired. He no longer has to work. He has time for himself. He can do anything he wants to.

—Yes, that's it, said Whisperer.

—So we found an old folks' home. A bunch of oldsters, fiddling away their time.

—No, not fiddling away their time. In their own minds, they still have work to do. That's why they work so hard. The greatest sorrow for them is that the problems they work on are not immediate problems, not functional problems, not real work. Real work is what they thirst for, but they are not allowed to do it.

—Where are the others of them? Those who are not retired?

—Otherwhere. Near or far, I cannot tell. They work on real problems.

—But the retired ones, the ones you talked with. They do chores as well? They can think as well? They have capabilities?

—They sent me out, said Whisperer. Where, I do not know. No geography. No coordinates. I skated on a magnetic flux and I danced with ions, I warmed myself on a red dwarf star in blackness.

—They really sent you? Not just showed it to you? They sent the atoms of you?

—They sent the atoms of me.

—Why? asked Jill.

—Because they knew I wanted to. They read the wishes of me. Or maybe only to show me the skill of them. This I do not think, for I was made to understand that it was but a small thing that they did. A kindness to me, knowing what I wanted. And I talked to them of Heaven.

—Heaven?

—You want to go to Heaven, do you not? Could I be mistaken?

—No, you're not, said Tennyson. No, you're not mistaken. But there are no coordinates, no data. . . .

—You must talk with me again of it, show it in your minds. You tell me the story that you know. Everything you know of this Heaven place.

—And then?

—I'll talk with them again. Tell them how badly you wish to go. How you so much deserve to go. They'll try, I know. This would be real work for them, not just the games they play. They'll be glad of it. The equations will flash and the diagrams will build and they'll search their data and their memories.

—But even if they found Heaven, if they located it, could they take us there?

—They sent me out, said Whisperer. They sent me many places.

Chapter Fifty

MARY DIED IN THE MIDDLE OF THE MORNING, A FRAIL OLD woman who appeared in death more frail and unsubstantial than she had appeared in life, as if death had subtracted from her a portion of the physical dimension she had held as a living entity. Tennyson, standing by her bedside, looked down on her, the body making only a small elongated mound beneath the sheet. Again, as he had each time before when he had lost a patient, he felt a smudged sense of guilt, not sharply defined, but a vague wondering if he might not better have fulfilled his obligation as a healer, and a dull feeling of blame in having failed. He had saved her life that first time—he was sure he had; the death blow had been struck on the golden stairs of Heaven when the dark man had harried her down the stairs, shaking a finger at her. After that she had not wanted to live, had not fought to live, and by her own acceptance of death had slipped quietly into it.

The nurse touched his arm. "I am sorry, Doctor." The nurse, he told himself, understood. "So am I," he said. "I had a great deal of admiration for her."

"There was nothing you could have done," said the nurse. "Nothing anyone could have done." Then she moved away, and after a moment Tennyson turned about and left.

Ecuyer rose from a chair in the waiting room. Tennyson nodded at him. "It's over."

Ecuyer came up close to him and they stood facing each other. "She was the best of them," said Ecuyer. "The best Listener I ever knew. There is a big crowd outside, waiting. I will have to go tell them."

"I'll go with you," said Tennyson.

"It is strange," said Ecuyer. "Not only was she a good Listener; she was a devoted one. She believed deeply in the program. It was her entire life. And yet she will be the one who will spell its end."

"Have you heard anything? Been given any word?"

Ecuyer shook his head. "It may not happen that way. It all will be smooth and quiet. No big upheaval. Just a steady clamping down. New regulations, quietly inserted into the procedure, a general closing in. One day, without realizing that it has happened, we'll know that we are done, that our work is finished."

"What will you do, Paul?"

"I'll stay here. I have no place else to go. I'll be taken care of; Vatican will see to that. That much at least they owe me. So will the Listeners be taken care of. We'll drag out our lives here, and when the last of us are gone, that will be the end of it."

"If I were you, I wouldn't be so certain," Tennyson said. For a moment he debated with himself whether to tell Ecuyer something of what Whisperer had said, holding out to him one last feeble hope.

"Do you know something?" asked Ecuyer.

"No, I guess I really don't."

There was no purpose in telling him, thought Tennyson. The hope, at best, was a slight one—almost no hope at all. What Whisperer had proposed seemed impossible. On the surface it seemed far-fetched. It was impossible, he told himself, that the equation people could seek and find, with virtually no data, the place Mary had called Heaven. Heaven could be anyplace. It could be in a distant galaxy. It could be in another universe. Although come to think of it, it might not be so far away. Decker had thought he knew where it was; the implication was that he had been there, or very close to it. Although that, he reminded himself, was poor evidence. Decker had not spelled it out and now he never would.

Ecuyer was at the door, holding it open for him, and he went out. The small plaza in front of the clinic was jammed with waiting people. There had been a number of them there when Tennyson had come in; now there were even more. They were quiet—not even the murmur of low whispering that ordinarily was the case with such a crowd.

Ecuyer walked forward and the crowd watched. They know, Tennyson told himself, what Ecuyer is about to say, but they'll wait on his saying it. Human and robot alike will wait quietly for the word—word that Mary's dead and they finally have a saint.

Ecuyer spoke quietly. He did not raise his voice.

"Mary has gone to her reward," he told the waiting throng. "Only moments ago. She died peacefully, with a smile upon her lips. There was nothing that could be done to save her."

A sound swept the crowd, a sound like a monstrous indrawn breath. A sigh of relief? Tennyson wondered. The end of waiting.

Then someone with a foghorn voice—a human rather than a robot voice—broke into formalized prayer, and other voices joined in until the unison of prayer reverberated through all of Vatican. Many knelt to pray, but others remained standing, and a moment later the bells of the basilica began a steady, somber tolling.

Ecuyer came back to Tennyson and together the two of them walked away.

"Shouldn't you be joining in with them?" asked Tennyson. "Don't mind a heathen like myself."

"I'm not—" Ecuyer started to say, but did not finish it. He said something else. "If Mary could only know this, she'd love it. She was a devout person. She went regularly to mass, she spent hours upon her knees, telling the beads. Not for appearance's sake, not for show—she lived her religion."

Which probably accounted, Tennyson thought, for her finding Heaven, but he did not say it.

They walked in silence for a time. Then Ecuyer asked, "How do you feel?"

"Sad," said Tennyson.

"No guilt. You should feel no guilt."

"Yes, guilt. A doctor always feels some guilt. It's a built-in penalty for a doctor, a price you pay for the privilege of being one. It will wear away."

"There is something I must see to. Will you be all right?"

"I'll go for a walk," said Tennyson. "A walk will do me good."

He might as well, he thought. Jill had gone to work, back to the library, saying work would fill her mind and she'd be the better for it. He couldn't go back to the apartment, for without her there, the apartment would be too empty. Anyhow, as he had told Ecuyer, a walk would do him good.

It did him less good than he thought it might. He still felt a vague uneasiness, and the steady, monotonous tolling of the basilica's bells was a disturbing sound.

He walked for fifteen minutes before he realized that he was on the path that led to Decker's cabin. He stopped dead in the path and turned around, began to retrace his steps. He could not go to Decker's cabin, he simply could not go. It might be quite a while before he could visit Decker's cabin.

He took a branching path that led up to a ridge where he often went to sit and watch the eternal shadow show of the looming mountains. The distant tolling of the bells beat at him as he went up the path.

He sat upon the low boulder where he always sat and gazed across the distance to the mountains. The sun was almost at zenith, and the slopes were pale blue with the darker splotches of the forests that climbed them, while the snowy peaks glittered back the brilliance of the sun. They change, he thought—the colors always change and shift. An hour from now they would not be the same as they were now. They change but they endure—in our time reference they endure. But someday they will not be here. Someday they will be worn down to a level plain and the sentient life that still remains here will walk across the plain and never dream there once were mountains here.

Nothing, he thought, ever stays the same.

We grasp for knowledge; panting, we cling desperately to what we snare. We work endlessly to arrive at that final answer, or perhaps many final answers which turn out not to be final answers but lead on to some other fact or factor that may not be final, either. And yet we try, we cannot give up trying, for as an intelligence we are committed to the quest.

He spread his hands before him and looked at them, looking at them with a new perspective, as if they were a part of him he had never seen before. One touch of these fingers, one loving touch, meant as nothing more than a loving touch, and the stigma on Jill's face had gone away. There could be no doubt of it, he told himself; there could be no question. The great, spreading angry scar had been there when he stroked the cheek; when the stroke was ended, the ugly scar was gone. Spontaneous remission? he asked himself. No, it couldn't be, for spontaneous remission did not work that way. Spontaneous remission took at least some little time, and this had taken almost no time at all.

A power, they had said among themselves, perhaps not believing it even as they said it, but needing something to say to one another—a power that had been given him by the equation folk, a gift from one world to another.

He stared at his hands. They seemed to be no different than they ever had been. He searched within himself and could detect no difference there—nowhere within himself.

Could it be possible, he wondered, that through millennia latent talents, or perhaps evolutional talents, had been growing in the human race against that day when they might be needed? Throughout all of history, there had been tales of healing by the laying on of hands. Many claims of this work had been made, but there was no documentation that would bear out the claims. Too, there was the matter of Whisperer. Until Decker came to End of Nothing, there had been no one able to see Whisperer. Decker could not only see him, but could talk with him as well. Decker, however, had been unable to join Whisperer's mind to his. Yet both Jill and he were able to join Whisperer's mind with theirs. Why this difference between Decker and the two of them? Could it mark varying degrees of formerly latent abilities, now developing, but developing unequally from one human to another? Or having the ability and not knowing one had it, thus never making an effort to make use of it?

Yet in the matter of Jill's stigma, it could not be either of these things. Dozens of times he had put out his hand to stroke that scarred cheek and until he had come back from the equation world, the angry scar had stayed no matter how often he might touch it. The reasoning he had outlined might stand so far as Whisperer was concerned, but it failed to explain Jill's cheek. The particular ability or magic or whatever it might be had to be newly acquired, and there was only one place where he could have acquired it.

He looked at his hands again and they were the same old hands he had used his entire life. There was no sign of a fresh ability or magic in them.

He rose from the boulder and thrust his hands into his jacket pockets to get them from his sight. The bells at the basilica were still tolling. He could continue his walk but the walk had gone sour on him. There was no place he wanted to go.

He would go back to the apartment, he decided. Jill would not be there and it would be lonely, but perhaps he could occupy his time by cooking dinner, although it was a bit early to start dinner. He knew what he'd do—he'd tackle an involved gourmet dish that would take a lot of time and keep him busy, although in the end it probably would prove inedible. No, he told himself, that was not a good idea. He wanted to surprise Jill with dinner on the table, and it would do no good to surprise her with a mess she could not eat. It would seem strange for him to cook—Hubert always cooked, with Jill helping out now and then.

Coming around a sharp bend in the path, he came to a halt, staring at the figure striding up the path toward him. The walker wore a purple, belted robe with the skirt hiked up at the belt to keep it from dragging in the dust. It was Cardinal Theodosius, he saw, wearing a brilliant scarlet skullcap.

Tennyson stepped out of the path to give the robot room. When he came up, the cardinal halted.

"Your Eminence," said Tennyson, "I did not know you were a walker."

"Nor am I," said Theodosius. "Although I hear you are."

"Yes, I am. Perhaps sometime we should take a hike together. For me it would be a pleasant experience. I would hope it might be for you. There is so much to see and talk about."

"Beauty?" asked the cardinal. "The beauty of the land?"

"That is what I meant. Far off the mountains and close by the flowers that bloom along the way."

"Beauty in your eyes, but not in mine," said the cardinal. "When your people made us robots, you left out of us certain faculties, and among these is what you call appreciation of beauty. For me there are other kinds of beauty. The beauty of logic, of a magnificent abstraction that one can think upon for hours."

"That is too bad. You miss so much if you do not have our sense of beauty."

"And you, perhaps, from lacking ours."

"I am sorry, Eminence. I meant no offense."

"It is quite all right," said Theodosius. "I took no offense. In fact, I am feeling too well to take offense at anything at all. This walk is a great adventure for me. I cannot recall that I ever was this far from Vatican. But this, I can assure you, is not an idle stroll. I'm off to find an Old One."

"An Old One? Why an Old One?"

"Because they appear to be good neighbors that we have ignored too long and more than likely slandered in our view of them. I understand that one of them may be found in the hills back of Decker's cabin. Do you know aught of that?"

"Decker never spoke of it," said Tennyson. "Are you sure?"

"So it has been said. Through the years. One of the Old Ones keeps watch of us from the hills above Decker's place."

"If the Old Ones have kept watch over you all these thousand years, they must know something of you. Of Vatican, I mean."

"Much more," said the cardinal, "than we may have suspected. But I must be upon my way. The Old One may be hard to find. Drop in to see me someday soon; we could enjoy a few hours in pleasant conversation."

"Thank you," said Tennyson. "I'll do that."

He stood in the path and watched the cardinal until he disappeared from view over a low ridge. Then he turned about and went down the path toward Vatican.

Reaching his apartment, he put out his hand to the knob, then pulled it back, shrinking from entering the emptiness and loneliness he would find there. He stood there, with his hand pulled back, raging at himself for his lack of courage. Finally he reached out again, turned the knob, pushed the door open, and stepped inside.

There was no emptiness or loneliness. The fire was blazing brightly and Jill was rising from the couch to greet him. He rushed across the room, seized her in his arms, pulled her tight against him, clinging to her. "I'm so glad you're here," he told her softly. "I was afraid you wouldn't be."

Gently she pushed him away. "I'm not the only one who's here," she said. "Whisperer has come back."

He looked quickly about the room and saw no sign of him.

"I don't see him."

"He's here inside my mind," she said. "He wants to be in yours as well. He comes to take us back to the equation world."

"Heaven!"

"Yes, Jason. The equation folk have found the way to Heaven. They can take us there."

Chapter Fifty-one

LATE IN THE DAY, THEODOSIUS FOUND THE OLD ONE THAT he sought.

He walked up close to it and waited for it to notice him. It made no sign it did.

Finally Theodosius spoke. "I've come to visit you," he said.

The Old One began its vibrating, drumming sound, and after a time words formed in the vibrations.

"Welcome to my place," it said. "I seem to recognize you. You were standing on the steps, were you not, when I brought the Decker home?"

"Yes, I was. I am Enoch Cardinal Theodosius."

"Oh, you are that cardinal. I have heard of you. Tell me, could the organic being that stood on the steps with you have been the Tennyson?"

"Yes, it was Tennyson. He was a friend of Decker's."

"So I understand," said the Old One.

"You said you had heard of me. Do you know many of us? Or have you heard of many of us?"

"I know no one," said the Old One. "I observe. That only."

At first, the Old One had seemed to talk with effort, but Theodosius noticed that after a few sentences, he now was speaking more easily and fluently.

"We have been unneighborly, I fear," said the cardinal, "and I beg your pardon for it. This visit should have been paid centuries ago."

"You were afraid of us," said the Old One. "You feared us greatly and we did not correct the fear. You feared us out of the figments of your mind and not because of anything we did. We did not correct the fear, for we have no real concern with you. Our concern is with the planet, and you are but a passing phase upon the planetary surface. What small concern we have with you regards how you treat the planet."

"I think we have treated it rather well," said the cardinal.

"Yes, you have, and for that we give you thanks. Perhaps we owe you more than thanks. We may even owe you some assistance. Do you know a Duster?"

"Duster?"

"The Decker called it Whisperer. Perhaps you know it by that name."

"I have never heard of it," said Theodosius.

"Once there were many of them here upon this planet and then they went away. They left one of them behind. They left a runt behind."

"The runt is Whisperer? Decker's Whisperer?"

"That is right. And now the runt that was left behind in such disdain by his fellow Dusters begins to show great promise. We are becoming proud of him."

"I'd like to meet him," said the cardinal. "I wonder why I haven't. Nor heard a mention of him."

"You cannot meet him now. He has gone away. With the Jill

and the Tennyson he has gone away. Together they go to find the Heaven."

Theodosius gasped. "Heaven! Did you say Heaven?"

"This Heaven you have heard of? It means something to you?"

"It means a great deal to us. Can you tell me what Heaven is?"

"All I can tell you is that the three of them have gone to find it. They have help from others who are called equation folk. People the Listeners found many years ago."

"You surprise me by how much you seem to know of us and our operation."

"Our concern for the planet," said the Old One, "made it seem wise that we keep marginally informed."

"Heaven!" said Theodosius, gulping slightly.

"That's right—Heaven," said the Old One.

The cardinal found he could stay no longer. Abruptly he turned about and went plunging down the hill, tearing his way through low-growing bushes, his purple vestment catching on the bushes, torn to shreds as his headlong flight tore the fabric free.

At the foot of the hill, he came to a shallow ravine paved with huge flat stones that through the years had fallen from the hillsides. A small, shimmering sheet of water slid among the stones.

Here Enoch Cardinal Theodosius dropped to his knees. He clasped his hands together and held them on his breast. He lowered his head to rest against the clasped hands.

"Almighty God," he prayed, "let it come out right! Please, make it come out right!"

Chapter Fifty-two

IT WAS EXACTLY AS HE REMEMBERED IT—THE PEA-GREEN carpet of the surface ran out to the distant horizon to meet the pale lavender of the shallow bowl of sky. The cubes were there, the same as ever. . . .

And yet it was not the same as ever, and the difference lay not in where he was or where the cubes might be—the difference lay within himself. He was not himself, not himself alone; he was himself and someone else, himself and others.

On his first trip to the equation world, he had sensed Whisperer only marginally; the greater part of the time he had not sensed him at all. Too scared, perhaps, to be aware of him, too taken up with all the rest of it. He did sense him now, he knew that he was here, the soft, almost fairy touch of him. But it was not Whisperer; it was someone else that he felt closer to.

—Jason, said Jill, speaking as a part of him, the two of them inseparable, as if their minds had become one mind and their bodies one as well. Jason, I am here.

He had felt some of it the night before when the two of them had joined, opening their minds so that Whisperer might join with the both of them that they might grieve with him. There had then been the touch of two minds becoming one, but its effect had been softened and obscured because the sharp, keen memory of Decker had been there. But now it hit him full force. He and Jill were together as never before, closer together than when their bodies had been locked in love.

—I love you, Jason, she said. I do not need to tell you now. You know how much I love you now.

And she was right, as she was always right. There was no need for her to tell him and no need for him to tell her, for they were together and could not help but know what was in the other's mind.

Five cubes stood apart and closer to them than the other cubes. The others had pulled back, forming a large circle in which stood the nearer five.

—These are the ones, said Whisperer, who will be our guides.

Among the five, Tennyson saw, was his old friend who was deep purple with the equations and diagrams glowing in brilliant orange. There were, as well, the one who was startling pink with the equations all in green and the extrafancy gray one with copper spots and the equations in startling lemon yellow. The fourth was a rose-red creature with equations in showy damson plum and its diagrams in sulphur yellow.

—That one's mine, said Jill.

The fifth one was a sickly green with both its equations and diagrams in a somber golden brown.

—How can they be sure? Tennyson asked Whisperer. Are you sure they know where Heaven is?

—They do not know of it as Heaven. They know it by another name. In a distant sector of the galaxy lies a famous place. Unknown to us, of course, but famous.

—And this famous place is Heaven?

—They're quite sure it is, said Whisperer. It has the shining towers and the noise that you call music and steep stairs leading up to it.

They had been moving toward the five cubes. As they moved toward them, the cubes had been moving, too, so that when they came close to them, the cubes had spread out and now closed in to form a circle with the two of them in the center of it.

The rose-red cube was facing them, and now that they were close to it, it wiped away the equation that it had been displaying and began replacing it with another, forming the new equation slowly so that it could be read even by one who was unfamiliar with that kind of communication.

—We welcome you, the equation said. Are you ready for our venture?

—Whisperer, said Tennyson. Whisperer!

There was no answer; there was no need of one, for it was quite apparent that it was not they who were reading the equation—it was Whisperer and because Whisperer was there, linked with them, they understood it, too.

—You do nothing, said the equation, flowing smoothly. You will simply stand where you are. And do nothing. Is that understood?

—We understand, said Whisperer, and as he spoke the words, the answer he had given appeared as a brief and simple equation on the surface of the rose-red equation person, printed there, thought Jill, so that the other cubes might know the answer that Whisperer had made.

It's all damn foolishness, thought Tennyson, but he had no more than thought it than both Jill and Whisperer came swarming in on him, burying his mind so he could think no further, extinguishing the cynicism and the doubt that had come welling up in him.

Now another equation was forming slowly on the rose-red blackboard and Tennyson caught the beginning of Whisperer's translation—then they were in Heaven.

They stood in a central plaza, and all around them reared the soaring towers. Celestial music came down upon them from the towers, enveloping them so that all the world seemed music. The paving of the plaza was gold, or at least gold color, and the towers were shining white, so shining and so white that they seemed illuminated by a light within them. There was a holiness, or what appeared a holiness, and it all was sanctified.

Tennyson shook his head. There was something wrong. They stood in the center of the plaza and the music filled the place and the towers were white and shining towers, but there was no one there. To one side stood the five equation people, and Whisperer, a small globe of glittering dust, was floating there above them, but there was no one else. The place was empty; they stood alone within it. Heaven, to all appearances, was uninhabited.

"What's the matter?" asked Jill. She stepped away from Tennyson and turned slowly to look around the plaza.

"There is something wrong, isn't there?" she asked. "For one thing, there is no one here."

"For another," said Tennyson, "there aren't any doors. None in the buildings. Not what we think of as doors. There are only holes. Round holes. Mouse holes. Eight feet or so above street level."

It was true, she saw. And there weren't any windows. In all the soaring height of the towers, there weren't any windows.

"There are no windows," she said. "You'd think there would be windows."

A chill breeze came blowing down the plaza and Tennyson shivered at its touch.

There were, he saw, between the towers, what seemed to be narrow streets. Here, he thought, they must stand at the heart of the city, if it was a city. He looked up at the towers and realized that they were much taller than he at first had thought they were. They rose high into the blue, so high that the last glitter of them was lost in the blueness of the sky. At first, too, he had thought that there were many buildings, each one supporting its individual tower, but now it appeared possible that there might be only one building, enclosing the sprawling square in which they stood, with the towers placed at regular intervals. What he had thought of as narrow streets between the separate buildings might be no more than tunnels, cut at street level through the massive structure.

The building (or buildings) was of flawless white that did not have the look of stone. It had the look of ice, ice frozen from the purest water, ice with no air bubbles or other imperfections in it. That couldn't be, he told himself. If this great structure was not stone, neither was it ice.

All the time the music poured in upon them, engulfing them, seeping into them—an indescribable music that made one think it was more than music, or music raised to a poignancy no human composer had ever quite achieved.

Whisperer spoke to them.

—This place, he said, is not as empty as it seems. There are many here. This place teems with life.

As if on signal, life appeared.

Out of one of the narrow streets (or tunnels?), a massive head pushed out. It was a worm head. The front of it was flattened and heavily armored, a thick and heavy carapace covering the entire front part of the head. Behind the carapace, on either side of it, huge compound eyes looked out. Antennae sprouted from the top of the head. The head stood tall. Tennyson, gagging in distaste, estimated the top of the head stood a good six feet above ground level.

The worm emerged—it continued coming out, the long, thick body tracking behind the armored head. Once a fair length of it was out, it began to elevate its front end higher off the ground. Slender jointed legs that had been flattened to enable it to pass through the tunnel began to straighten up, lifting the body until it stood two feet taller than it had before.

As more of it emerged, it began to turn toward those who were standing in the plaza. Tennyson and Jill began slowly backing away, but the five equation beings stood their ground. Their blackboard sides were blurring in flashing colors as the equations raced.

Then all the worm was out of the tunnel, at least thirty feet of it, standing tall, well supported by the close-set legs.

The worm changed its direction again, angling away, back toward the structure of towering white. Its movement appeared to be purposeful. It gave no indication it had noticed those who were in the plaza.

It came to a halt under one of the eight-foot-high mouse holes and reared up. Its forward legs caught hold of the edge of the hole and began to lever itself into it. They watched as the worm drew its entire body through the hole and disappeared.

Tennyson let out his breath in relief.

"Let's have a look," he said. "Let's see what we can see."

They found out very little. The narrow streets did turn out to be tunnels, set at intervals along the structure, which turned out to be one building rather than many separate ones set together. But the tunnels were closed. Inside of them, thirty feet or so in from the opening, the way was blocked by doors. The doors were not white but blue. They filled the tunnels, wedged close against the tunnels' curving sides. There seemed no way to open them. Tennyson and Jill pushed hard against several of them and failed to budge them. It did seem, in a couple of instances, that they could feel some give, but that was all.

"They're tension doors," said Tennyson. "I'm almost certain of that. Push against one of them hard enough and it will open. But we haven't the strength."

"The worm came through it," said Jill.

"The worm probably is much stronger than the two of us. They may be exclusively worm doors. The worms may be the only things that have the strength to open the doors."

"We're fairly sure," said Jill, "that this place is not Heaven. But we have no proof. We can't just go back and say it isn't Heaven. Before we go back, we must have proof. If I only had a camera."

—We had to hold down weight, said Whisperer. We knew not what we'd find. We travel light and fast.

—What think our equation friends of this? asked Tennyson.

—They stand much amazed.

—So do we, said Jill.

"Maybe photographs alone," said Tennyson, "would not be acceptable proof. Photographs you can get anywhere at all. We have to do better than a handful of pictures."

They made a circuit of the square and found nothing else.

"We're trapped in here," said Jill, "with only one way out, those mouse holes that the worms use. We could have Whisperer float over all of this and see what's on the other side. There must be another side."

"So could the equation folk," said Tennyson. "They can float in the air, but at the moment I would hate to have us divide our forces. I have a feeling we should stick together."

Far down the plaza another worm came out of a tunnel and came straight toward them, but it swerved to pass them by to reach another of the mouse holes. Rearing, it passed through the hole and disappeared.

"I'm not certain I would want to use one of those holes," said Jill. "All that ever seems to go through them are worms."

"The worms seem to have little interest in us."

"Not while we're out here. They might pick up an interest if we went inside."

"I wonder," said Tennyson, paying no attention to what she had said. —Whisperer, could you ask one of our equation friends to squat down a bit so I could climb up on him. Then he could float me up to one of the holes.

"If you are going, I am going, too," said Jill. "I'm not going to be left out here."

—Any one of them would be happy to, said Whisperer. Which hole do you have in mind?

—Any one of them, said Tennyson. I wouldn't ask it, but those holes are out of reach for us.

—Would that one just behind you be all right?

—It would do just fine.

"I have a feeling," said Jill, "that we're quite out of our minds."

The rose-red cube had moved up close to the wall, below the indicated mouse hole. The cube began broadening out, spreading itself, squatting down so they could reach its back.

"I'll boost you up," Tennyson told Jill.

"Okay," she said. "I hope this won't be as bad as I think it will."

He boosted her up and she scrambled to the top of the cube.

"It's ishy," she said. "It's terrible. The thing is like a mound of jelly. I'm afraid I will break through it. And it's slippery as hell."

Tennyson made a running leap and landed spread-eagled on the quivering surface of the cube. Jill reached down a hand and helped him scramble up beside her. They sat together, clinging to one another to retain their balance. The cube ceased some of its quivering and seemed to harden slightly, offering more support. It began to rise slowly in the air, not really rising, but assuming its normal shape, rising from its squat.

The mouse hole was in front of them and Tennyson made an awkward leap for it. He landed on his hands and knees, swiftly scrabbling around to reach out a hand for Jill, but before he could extend his help, she was there, sprawling beside him.

They rose to their feet and looked about them. The mouse hole was another tunnel, but a short one and there was no door.

At the end of it blazed a brilliant light. The floor was solid underneath their feet and they moved toward the light. Looking over her shoulder, Jill saw that the five equation folk had entered the tunnel behind them, with Whisperer scintillating above the foremost one.

When they reached the other end of the tunnel, they saw that the tunnel floor connected with a broad white road, apparently constructed of the same materials as the walls and towers. It led off into the distance, finally blotted out by the glare of light. It was suspended in midair, with dizzying heights above it and dizzying depths below.

The interior was vast, but its vastness was masked by columnar structures that rose within it, spearing from the depths into the upper reaches, both the depths and the upper reaches being blotted out by sheer distances. The columns basically were of the same white material of which the rest of the structure was made, but little of the white showed through the blinding, crazy flickering of the lights that ran all around them. The lights took no particular pattern and their flickering had no rhythm. They were of every color.

The entire place, Tennyson told himself, was a massive carnival, a riot of dancing color, a gaudily decorated Christmas tree multiplied a million times.

"Look," said Jill, jogging his arm. "There is one of our friendly worms."

"Where?"

"Right over there. On one of the columns. Look where I'm pointing."

He looked but it took a while to see what she pointed at. Finally he made it out. One of the worms was clinging tightly against one of the columns, hanging straight up and down the column. But not using all its feet to maintain its grip, for it was using many of them in a manipulatory way, working on the circuitry or the lights or whatever the column held.

"Maintenance men," said Jill. "Maintenance worms, that is. Jason, they are the things that keep whatever this is running."

"It makes sense," he said.

"Let's get out of here," said Jill. "All this makes me dizzy."

They hurried down the whiteness of the road, although the road no longer was entirely white. It shimmered with the many colors of the flashing lights.

Far ahead they glimpsed the opening of another tunnel. When they came up to it, four creatures were waiting for them. The creatures were black cones, dead black, with no highlights in the black, as if the blackness sucked light into it, leaving none to be reflected. They were broad-based and stood five feet high, moving easily but with no hint as to the mechanism that made it possible to move.

At the mouth of the tunnel, just inside it, stood a platform, also black, mounted on wheels.

Three of the cones stood at the back of the platform and, as Jill and Tennyson and the equation folk came up, effectively herded them, without a sound or signal but by some judicious shoving, onto the platform. When Jill would have walked over the platform and back onto the roadway, the fourth cone blocked her doing so, keeping itself in front of her no matter where she turned.

"I guess they want us to stay here," she said to Tennyson.

When all of them had been herded onto the platform, the cones stationed themselves at each corner, and the platform and the cones began to move down the tunnel, the cones apparently furnishing the motive power.

The platform shot out of the tunnel into another vast space in which there were no columns. A number of roadways, a three-dimensional roadway system, ran in all directions, crossing over one another, looping around one another. Some of the roadways were for vehicles only, most of them platforms powered by the cones, although now and then other vehicles, some of them beetle-shaped and others shaped like flying open arrows, also shared the roads. Other roads seemed to be for pedestrians only. Along these crawled and hopped and skipped and walked and jumped and shambled an array of life. Looking at them, Tennyson remembered the *Wayfarer* captain and his loathing of all alien forms. Seeing some of those that traveled the pedestrian ways, he could understand something of the captain's loathing. In his time he had come into contact with varied alien life, but never in such horrifying forms as he now was seeing.

In between the roadways, set at every angle, each surrounded by small courtyards, were buildings of every shape and size. These were not formed of the same material as the larger structures, but were of every color. It was, thought Tennyson, as if one were looking at tabletop models of many villages, but with all the table-tops haphazardly slung together with no regard to their relationship to one another.

The platform took a sudden curve, almost throwing them off their feet, changing from one roadway to another and almost at once entering another tunnel. When it emerged from the tunnel, it was in what appeared to be the interior of one of the larger buildings they had been looking at. Gently the platform came to a halt in what could have been a parking lot, for there were many other vehicles there.

Jill and Tennyson stepped off and the equation folk floated off the platform, with the four cones herding them down a path between the cars.

They entered a room. At the farther end of it a bubble sat on a dais ranged against the wall. Other cones were there in groups around the dais, and to one side of it sat a small haystack that had eyes peering from the hay, while an octopuslike creature hopped back and forth before the bubble. Each time it landed on the floor, it made a squishy sound like a large chunk of fresh liver hurled against a solid surface.

The cones herded them forward until they stood before the bubble, then fell back and left them there.

The bubble was more than just a bubble. It had a dimple in the forefront of it, and inside the dimple was what might have been a face—the sort of face that one could not be sure was there. One second you could see it and the next moment it had dissolved into drifting smoke.

Jill gasped. "Jason," she said, "do you remember that memo— the memo that Theodosius wrote. The one I found in the wastebasket in the secret closet."

"My God, yes!" said Tennyson. "The bubble is one of the things that the cardinal described. A face like drifting smoke, he said."

Noise came from the drifting smoke, a grating, scraping noise. The noise went on for some time. In a little while, it became apparent that the noise was the bubble talking to them.

"I can't make out a word of it," said Jill.

—It is trying to communicate, said Whisperer. That is evident. But unintelligible.

—It sounds as if it might be shouting at us. Is it angry, Whisperer?

—I think not, said Whisperer. It projects no sense of anger.

One of the cones came scurrying up and stood before the bubble. The bubble grated at it, and it turned and scurried off. The bubble fell silent. It was still looking at them, although at times the smoke would obscure the face, but even then they felt it still was looking at them.

—I think, although I cannot be entirely sure of this, said Whisperer, that it has summoned someone that may be able to translate the conversation it essays with you.

The bubble stayed silent. The cones were silent, too—if, in fact, they ever made a sound. The only sound was the squishy-liver sound of the octopuslike creature that kept hopping back and forth. The eyes of the haystack creature to one side of the dais watched them unblinkingly.

Silence, except for the liver plopping, held the room. Then there was a new sound—the unmistakable sound of someone walking, of bipedal human walking.

Tennyson turned toward the sound.

Thomas Decker was striding purposefully across the room toward them.

Chapter Fifty-three

"Ecuyer, this time I want you to come clean with me," said Cardinal Theodosius.

"Your Eminence," protested Ecuyer, "I've always come clean with you."

"If by that you mean that you have told me no lies," said the cardinal, "you may be right. What I'm talking about is that you have not always told me all you know. You've concealed facts from me. For instance, why did you never tell me about Decker's Whisperer?"

"Because the subject of the Whisperer never came up in any conversation with you," said Ecuyer. "That, combined with the fact that I did not hear of it myself until just a few days ago."

"But Tennyson knew about it. Well before you did."

"Yes, that's true. He was a friend of Decker's."

"How did he get mixed up with the Whisperer?"

"The way he told me was that the Whisperer sought him out."

"But when he told you it was considerably after the fact."

"I gather that it was. He had the feeling that he owed it to Decker not to tell me, or anyone. He told me only after Decker had been killed."

"Except for the matter of the Whisperer, you and Tennyson were very close. By which I mean that he told you everything."

"That was my impression."

"Did he happen to tell you that he was going to Heaven?"

Ecuyer jerked upright in his chair. He stared at the cardinal for a moment, trying to read his face—but no one ever read a robot face. Then he slumped back again. "No," he said, "he didn't. I had no idea."

"Well, it happens that he has. Gone to Heaven, I mean. He's either on his way or already there."

"Eminence," said Ecuyer, "you can't possibly know that."

"But I can," said Theodosius. "An Old One told me. I thought about it for a while before I summoned you. We have plans to make."

"Now, wait a minute," said Ecuyer. "You say you heard it from an Old One? Where did you find the Old One?"

"I went visiting. I found one in the hills above Decker's cabin."

"And he told you Tennyson was about to go to Heaven?"

"He said he was already on his way. Tennyson and Jill. The Whisperer, he said, had found a way to take them."

"We talked about it—"

"You talked about it? And not a word to me?"

"There was no point in saying anything to you. All of us agreed it was impossible."

"Apparently it was not impossible."

"It's true that Tennyson has been missing for a day or two, but that doesn't mean—"

"Jill has been missing, too. If not to Heaven, where would they have gone? There's no place on End of Nothing that they would be going."

"I don't know," said Ecuyer. "It seems impossible they could have gone to Heaven. For one thing, no one had the least idea of where to look for it. Maybe if we could have found the Mary cubes. . . ."

"The Old One said the people of the equation world had given them some help."

"Well, yes, that might have been possible. Both Tennyson and Jill had been to the equation world."

"There, you see," said Theodosius, "that's something else that you never told me. Didn't it ever occur to you that I might like to know what is going on?"

"How sure are you that the Old One knows what he is talking about? And how come you went visiting an Old One and—"

"Ecuyer, all these years we have been wrong about the Old Ones. They are not the ravening horrors that the myths have told. That's what is wrong with myths, they so seldom tell the truth. The Old One I talked with was the one that brought Decker home, and Hubert. Standing on the esplanade, he talked with me and Tennyson. We owe them an apology for all we've thought of them. We should have become friends with them very long ago. It would have been to our advantage if we had."

"Then you're fairly sure about the Heaven visit?"

"I'm sure," said Theodosius. "The Old One seemed to have no doubt, and I believe he told me true. It was an act of friendship, his telling it to me."

"Christ, it seems impossible," said Ecuyer. "Yet, if it was done, Tennyson would be the one to do it. The man is remarkable."

"When Tennyson and Jill return, we must be ready for the word they bring."

"You think they will be back?"

"I'm certain that they will. They do this for Vatican. Despite the shortness of their stay with us, they—the two of them—have become one with us. Tennyson told His Holiness the other day something that the Pope passed on to me. He was quite tickled with it. About the monasteries of Old Earth. . . ."

"What do you propose to do? If they have gone to Heaven, if they really find it, if they do come back—"

"For one thing, I am fairly certain I know now who has been behind all this theological nonsense. John, the gardener in the

clinic garden. I have a fairly good idea that he has been working
for the Pope, an undercover agent for the Pope, although why the
Pope should think he needs an undercover agent is more than I
can figure out. But that will make no difference. I'm about to
make certain that our friend the gardener becomes a piddling little
monk and stays a piddling monk forever. And there are others of
them. . . ."

"But you have no power structure within which to work."

"Not yet, but I will have. Once I talk with His Holiness and tell
him what I've found. Once he knows that I know about his undercover agent, once he knows that Tennyson and Jill will be coming
back from Heaven. If it weren't for the fact that Heaven will be
unmasked, the Pope would be reluctant to take action. Once he
knows, however. . . ."

"What if this story of yours, Eminence, should prove to be flat
wrong? What if—"

"In such a case, I will be sunk," said Theodosius, "and so will
you. If we don't act, we'll be sunk anyhow. We have nothing much
to lose."

"You're right on that point," said Ecuyer. "You are absolutely
right."

"So will you go with me to see the Pope?"

"Yes," said Ecuyer, rising from his chair. "Let us see the
Pope."

The cardinal also rose.

Ecuyer asked another question. "You said that now Heaven
was about to be unmasked. How can you be sure that it will be
unmasked?"

"Oh, that," said His Eminence. "Well, that's a gamble too. A
calculated risk. If it turns out that I am wrong, I'll probably become a piddling little monk."

"You take the gamble willingly?"

"Indeed I do," said Theodosius.

Chapter Fifty-four

"UP TO A POINT I CAN REMEMBER SOME OF IT," SAID DECKER. "I remember being plastered against the hull of the ship, trying to dig my fingers into the metal of it, looking out and seeing the hub of this place spearing up at me and the roads that ran into the hub like so many spokes. I don't remember running for the lifeboat because it wasn't me who ran, not me, this Decker II who sits here and talks with you, but the real, the first, the original Decker who was the pattern for me."

"It all checks out," said Tennyson, "with what little the original Decker, as you call him, told me. He didn't tell me much. He was a tight-lipped man."

"So am I," said Decker II, "but the shock and I might say the joy in meeting people of my kind has knocked some of the reticence out of me."

They sat in a pleasant room, high in one of the many towers. Thick carpeting covered the floors and paintings hung upon the walls. Comfortable furniture stood about.

"I'm glad," said Jill, "that you were able to find this place for us. In all the alienness, it is a touch of home."

"It took a bit of doing," said Decker, "but the Bubbly was insistent that I find a proper place to put you up. He's gone on hospitality."

"The Bubbly?"

"The bubble with the funny face," said Decker. "He is only one of the many who are here. Out of my irreverence, I call them Bubblies. They have another name, of course, but it's well-nigh unpronounceable in the human tongue and a literal translation of it sounds ridiculous. This particular Bubbly that you met is what might be called a friend of mine, although perhaps more than an ordinary friend. It's hard to explain. I call him Smoky, from that face of his, although all of them have the same kind of faces. He doesn't know what Smoky means, although I call him it to his face. He thinks it's an affectionate human name. If he knew its human meaning, he might get sore at me. You saw the Haystack that was there with him?"

"I noticed it," said Tennyson. "It was watching us."

"He is Smoky's first friend—first because he has been with him longer. I am his second friend, second because I've not been here that long. We make up a triad. Among the Bubblies, no Bubbly stands by himself. There must be two others with him. It's a sort of brotherhood, a blood brotherhood, but that's not exactly it, either, but it's as close as I can come. Old Haystack must have given you something of a start. He's a strange-looking critter."

"He certainly is," said Jill.

"Haystack's not too bad a sort," said Decker, "once you get to know him. For one thing, he's not the kind of slobbering horror that you meet so often here."

"You take all of it very well," said Jill.

"I have no complaint," said Decker. "I've been treated well. At first I wondered about my position—captive, refugee, exhibit? I guess I still don't know what I am, but I don't worry about it any longer. The Bubblies have done well enough by me."

"The Bubblies took what amounted to a picture of you, out there in the ship; not of you, but of the original Decker," said Tennyson, "and used it to recreate another Decker, which is you. From that distance, with you behind the hull of the ship—"

"You have to understand," Decker told him, "that far more than a picture, as you term it, is involved. I'm not sure about the technique. I understand the principle but not how it works. The nearest I can come to explaining it, and it's a feeble explanation, is to compare it with the body scanner that was developed on Earth a long time ago. First it was called a brain scanner because it was used principally on the brain, usually to detect tumors. But later it was used as a body scanner. It could take a picture of cross sections of the body. It sort of peeled the body, speaking photographically, which is an awkward way of saying it, taking X-ray pictures at different depths. The term 'picture' is not right, either. The data was fed into a computer that put together the findings so they could be read. Well, this is what the contraption used by the Bubblies can do. But it can operate over considerable distances. Its data can be used to reconstruct any sort of matter, anything on which the data has been obtained. I was told that in my case, in addition to the data on my body, it also had data on a cross section of the ship. But they only used my body data. I suppose the specifications on that cross section of the ship is still somewhere in the files and that it could be recreated if there was any point in doing it."

"But Decker, the original Decker, was two hundred years or so out of his time," said Tennyson. "That's what he told me. The lifeboat held him in suspended animation while it searched out a planet where he could survive. The search took some two hundred years. Yet your best estimate is that you have been here only a hundred years or so."

"This is the first I've known of that," said Decker. "But I can make a guess. It probably took the Bubblies a hundred years before they got around to me. They have a lot of data piled up. Sometimes they have to pick and choose what they want to re-create. Some of the data they have here may have been in the files for several hundreds of years. Some of it they may never get around to."

"You say a hundred years. How old were you when this happened—forty years or so? You don't look a hundred and forty to me. You don't look a day older than the Decker that I knew."

"Well, the way it goes," said Decker, "is that they improve upon the data. When they turn out an organism from the data, they try to spot the weak points. I suppose that when I was built from the data, the data provided for that useless human organ, the vermiform appendix. Noting it was useless, they'd have probably left that out. I'll make you a wager I have no appendix. A weak or malformed heart valve—they'd fix that up as well. A missing tooth would be replaced, one that had caries would be replaced as well. A bad kidney or a suspect length of gut . . ."

"You sound as if you could be immortal."

"Not immortal, but I'll probably last awhile. If something went wrong and there was any need of saving me, they probably could do something about it—replace a heart, perhaps, or a liver or a lung. That's the way it is with everything. I'm the only human they have and they had no idea of my life style. But when I explained, once I'd learned their language, what I needed, they came through with—carpeting, paintings, furniture, the kind of food I required. They even made a few extras, more than I needed. That's what you have here. Give them the specifications and they'll come up with anything. They have matter converters of a sort. Not a dingus that you shovel sand into and out comes bouquets of flowers or ice-cream cones or decks of playing cards or whatever you may ask, but efficient machines, terribly efficient."

"There are no other humans here?" asked Jill.

"A few other humanoids, but they aren't human. On a number of counts they aren't. Two legs, two arms, two eyes, two ears, a mouth and nose, but they aren't human. Which is not to say they are any less than human, for they aren't. Some of them may be a cut above a human. I know all of them and all of them know me; we all get along together. We do have a few things in common. For any one of us, it is better than associating with a brainy spider or a blob of pulsating intelligence."

"But what's the point of all of this?" asked Jill. "It sounds like a sort of galactic zoo."

"It's that, of course. But it's something else as well. My best translation, which is far wide of the mark, of the term used to describe this place would be the Center for Galactic Studies. The basic operation is very like your Vatican, although from what you've told me, the approach is somewhat different and the motives somewhat different, too. The Bubblies were the ones who started it, perhaps close to a million years ago, but they're only part of it now. Top dogs, of course, but along the way they picked up partners from other cultures oriented to research. Taken all together, it is an impressive operation. The entire undertaking is based on going out into the galaxy, going physically, and bringing back data. Once the data are in, life forms can be recreated and studied. It's not only data on life forms that they bring back, but artifacts from other cultures—machines, buildings, vehicles, toys, foods, crops, you name it. In this respect, the method would seem to be somewhat better than the Vatican approach; a more solid approach, but the area is restricted to a single galaxy, although there has been some noise over the last century or so about developing a technique that will make it possible to go farther out, to some of the nearby galaxies perhaps."

"How about security?" asked Tennyson. "It would seem to me a place like this would be a treasure trove. Once some of the races out there learned what you are doing, they might consider some judicious raiding. Vatican achieves some security by being in a remote location and keeping a low profile. Here you're sticking out, wide open."

"My crew, or rather the original Decker crew," said Decker, "was scared off by a psychological weapon. A sense of terror was broadcast and I honestly can't tell you how it was done, the terror mixed with a booming voice that told them, though they couldn't understand the words, to get the hell out. The crew was so scared and so was I that no one made a move to veer off; they simply ran in terror, anything to escape. The ship crashed fifty miles beyond this place. Even your Listener, Mary, was effectively scared off. I didn't know about this until you told me, but it's apparent to me that she was frightened off. Even if she was not in the flesh, she still was detected. Somewhere in our files there is some data on her. Nothing done with it yet, I would imagine. Probably it didn't seem all that important."

"It brought us here," said Jill.

"Yes, it did. How much are you going to tell the Bubblies?"

"We've told it all to you."

"Yes, of course you have. And I'll tell it to Smoky. Is there anything in particular you'd like me to say nothing about?"

"Not a thing," said Tennyson. "We are an open book."

"My best advice," said Decker, "is to make an open breast of it. The Bubblies will be intrigued enough that they will start some digging. I doubt there is anything to fear from them. They're really fairly decent, even by human standards. Alien as all hell, of course, and hard at times to figure, but they're definitely not ogres. This is the first time in all their history that anyone has sneaked up on them. That is guaranteed to catch their attention. These equation folk of yours must have plenty on the stick."

"They're good at what they do," said Jill.

"I would guess that from the interest Smoky showed in them they're new to the Bubblies. Have you any idea where they are located?"

"Not the faintest," Tennyson told him.

"You mean that, not knowing their location, you still could contact them?"

"That's exactly right."

"But how?"

"Look, Decker, we've told you almost everything. Leave us one trade secret."

"That's fair enough. It seemed to me that I saw a Duster with you. Could that be correct?"

"Duster?"

"A Duster. A fuzzy ball of glitter."

"One came along with us," said Jill. "He seems to have disappeared."

"Could he have had something to do with it?"

"Decker, I said one secret, didn't I?" asked Tennyson.

"Yes, you did. I'm sorry."

"How about the equation folk?" asked Jill. "Do you know where they are?"

"They're clustered in Smoky's parking lot," said Decker. "All bunched up together and the equations and diagrams flickering so fast you can barely see them. But, now, I'll have to say good night. You people want to get some rest. And I have work to do tomorrow."

"You have a job?"

"Certainly. Almost everyone does. You are allowed to pick what you want to do—that is, if you're qualified. My specialty is interpreting. Strangely enough, I found that I had an ear for alien tongues. I can manage with quite a lot of them. But basically I'm a sort of curator. I make a valiant effort to classify all the junk from distant worlds that finds its way into this place."

"You know, of course," said Jill, "that we don't intend to stay long?"

"Protocol, if nothing else," said Decker, "demands that you talk with Smoky and perhaps some of the other Bubblies. They'd take it rather badly if you didn't. I would guess they have a lively interest in you. I'll go along with you to act as interpreter."

Chapter Fifty-five

PLOPPER KEPT PLOPPING ALL ABOUT, MAKING HIS SQUISHY liver sounds. Plop, he went, plop, plop, plop. . . .

"Can't he rest awhile?" asked Haystack. "Can't he stop that hopping all about? Can't he sit and rest awhile?"

Plop, went Plopper, plop, plop, plop. . . .

"Leave him alone," said Smoky. "You're always after him. You're always criticizing."

"He drives me nuts," said Haystack.

"Decker doesn't mind him," said the Bubbly. "He never complains about him."

"Decker's not with him all the time," said Haystack. "Decker's not as close to you as I am. I'm your constant companion. At your eternal beck and call. Decker runs around a lot. If Decker had to live with Plopper, the way I do. . . ."

Plop, went Plopper.

"He never quits it, day or night," said Haystack. "He's hopping all the time. We are supposed to be a triad, aren't we? Where does he fit in? All the rest are three; how come we are four?"

"We are a triad," said Smoky. "Don't try to get cute with me. Don't say things that aren't true, thinking you can catch me in a lie. You know Plopper is not one of us. He is nothing but a pet. Perhaps if you weren't grumbling all the time and Decker spent more of his time with us, I wouldn't need a pet. But I have found a pet and have grown fond of him and—"

Haystack grumbled without saying anything.

"What was that? Speak up."

"I said you were more than fond of him. You put up with him, which is more than I am able to do, and Decker too. Decker runs around so much because he can't stand all the plopping. Plop, plop, plop all the blessed time. Not a moment's peace."

"He'll bring us good luck," said Smoky. "He is more than a simple pet. He is a talisman, a good-luck charm. . . ."

"You have no need of a good-luck charm," said Haystack. "I tell you and I tell you and you keep on pushing. You don't let up a minute. Everyone is sore at you; you haven't got a friend in all of Center. You're pushing to hard, and when I try to tell you, you pay no attention to me. Once you have control of Center, what will you do with it?"

"It's not only Center, Haystack. It's much more than that. You and Decker stick with me and—"

"There you go again," said Haystack. "I don't know why I put up with you. You're heading straight for trouble. You and your impossible dreams. If Decker didn't go along with you. . . ."

"Decker has vision," said Smoky. "He sees eye to eye with me. While you—"

"Decker may have vision, but I have common sense. I know what's possible; Decker doesn't."

Plop, plop, plop went Plopper.

"No one has ever dared to reach out for Center," Haystack said. "You're sneaky about it, of course. You move in devious ways. You think you're being smart. But the others know. They are waiting until you make a tiny slip, then they'll be down on you. They'll crush you without mercy, without a second thought."

"When three beings form a triad," said Smoky, "which is the logical condition of our way of life and which from observation has proved to be the best mode of existence, they are loyal to one another. They do not bicker among themselves. They do not—"

"I am being loyal to you," said Haystack, "the best way that I know. I am trying my level best to keep us out of trouble. Why don't you listen to me?"

"I do listen to you, Haystack. I listen endlessly."

"You listen but you pay no attention. You are maddened by

your dream of glory. You've reached a point where you recognize no reason. Even now you are plotting how you'll use these new arrivals to the best advantage. Don't tell me that you aren't."

"It takes so long to reconstruct them," complained Smoky. "It would seem there should be a faster method."

"The procedure is long," said Haystack, "because there are so many factors that must be considered and worked with. There can be no mistakes, and in almost all of them that one might want to use, there are revisions to be made."

"I had given thought to making use of the originals," said Smoky, "and not waiting for the recreations. But that could be dangerous. The others, the cubes, I know not of, but the humans are hair-triggered creatures. It is strange that after all this time, with Decker being the only one we have, two more humans should show up. And yet I am tempted. . . ."

"You are counting on the fact that they'd be identical to Decker? You can't do that. You'd be taking a long chance. Individuals within the species may vary and, besides, with Decker there were revisions made."

"You advise caution?"

"Yes, indeed I do."

"You always advise caution. I'm sick to death of your endless caution."

"Even if you had two more humans," said Haystack, "you could not be certain they would complement Decker. They might be of differing temperament and intelligence. Decker happened to turn out to be the sort of creature you could work with; these other two might not."

"Well, we'll wait and see," said Smoky.

Plop, plop, plop, went Plopper.

Chapter Fifty-six

"I DON'T KNOW," SAID JILL. "THIS DECKER PERSON . . ."

Tennyson put a finger to his lips, cautioning her. She looked about the room. There was nothing there. Decker had left and they were alone.

"I wonder where Whisperer went," said Tennyson. "It's unlike him to desert us."

"Maybe he found old friends," said Jill. "Decker said there are Dusters here. He may be hobnobbing with them."

"I wish he would come back," said Tennyson. "We should talk with him."

"So you feel it, too."

"Yes, Jill, I feel it, too."

They sat together on the sofa, looking about the room. It had familiar furniture. The carpeting was all right. The paintings on the wall had a familiar look to them. The room could have been transported back to Vatican and it would not have seemed out of place; it would have seemed all right. But despite this, there was a haunting, a frightening sense of alienness.

Tennyson reached out a hand and Jill took it. They sat side by side, holding hands, like two apprehensive children, alert and unsure of themselves, stiff and stark against the menace of a haunted house.

Jill began to speak, but Tennyson tightened his hand on hers and she gulped and said nothing.

Then: "Jason, Whisperer is here. He's come back to us."

—Whisperer? asked Tennyson.

—I am here, said Whisperer. I'm sorry that I left you. But I found Dusters. There are Dusters here.

—Whisperer, come to us, said Jill. We should talk among ourselves.

Whisperer came to them. They sensed him in their minds.

—We think there is something wrong, said Jill. Decker isn't right.

—I wasn't sure that you noticed it, said Tennyson. But, then, I was the one who knew Decker back at Vatican. He is not my Decker. How about you, Whisperer?

—He is not the Decker that I knew, said Whisperer. A Decker, but a different Decker.

—He lied to us, said Jill. He said he had not known of Mary until we told him. And that makes no sense. This place, this Center, is sensitive on the matter of security. Mary tried twice to sneak in on them, not knowing she was sneaking in, of course. Just doing her job. They might have missed her the first time, but they must have known about her the second time, for they employed their psychological defense system to drive her away. Not knowing what she was, for no one would be afraid of Mary.

—They probably picked up some data on her, said Tennyson. Maybe not too much. Not satisfactory data, for they were dealing with whatever a Listener is when it goes out to another place. But you are right, Jill. They knew about her and I'm sure they got something. Whatever they got, they must be very puzzled with it and, from my judgment of Decker's position here, he certainly must have known about it.

—Did we tell Decker too much, Jason? Did we tell him more than we should have?

—Maybe. I don't know. We had to tell him something. Maybe we did tell him too much at first. It was a while before I sensed the wrongness in him. The word "sensed" is right, for it was only that. He held up well otherwise, but there was a wrongness to him. Something that was not the old Decker. Can you remember all we told him?

—I can remember best what we didn't tell him. We never mentioned the robots. So far as he knows, Vatican is a human institution. We never mentioned the religious angle. We never explained why the name Vatican was used. We did not tell him that Mary thought she had found Heaven. So far as he is concerned, he does not know that Vatican is anything other than a research center like this one.

—Even so, said Whisperer, it shook him up. I think it shook this Center up. It must be a shock to know there is another Center in the galaxy.

—Do you happen to know, asked Tennyson, if we really penetrated this Center without their knowing it—not knowing until we were actually here?

—I am sure we did, said Whisperer.

—Once we got here, though, said Jill, they must have known. They must have all sorts of sensors out, tuned to pick up any kind of life. In any case, the first worm would have reported us.

—That's what worries me the most, said Tennyson. There is no doubt they took pictures of us—whatever you call the kind of pictures that they take. They must have data on all of us, maybe even Whisperer. By now they may have recreated another Jill and Jason, other equation people, recreated from the data.

—Could they be listening to us now? asked Jill.

—I think not, said Whisperer.

—But there are Dusters here. They know how Dusters operate.

—There are only a few here now, said Whisperer. At times there are none at all. My people are not a part of Center. They drift in and out. They keep a check on Center, checking back on occasion to learn what has been found, if there's anything here that they can use. And so far as recreating one of us, I doubt that they could do it. We are, after all, little more than a mass of molecules and atoms.

—You mean the Dusters are using this place?

—Well, yes, you might say they are. There has been no cooperation. My people are scattered very far.

—I put too much faith in this Decker to start with, said Tennyson. I was glad to see him. Like meeting an old friend in an unexpected place. I was blinded by my memory of the first Decker. I may have been too open. I may have said too much. It was too late to unsay it when I began to feel that he was a different man. There was a different texture to him. He was too smooth. The old Decker was never smooth. Decker II lied several times—I am sure he did. He lied about never having heard of Mary until we told him. He lied about his own data lying around for a hundred years before he was recreated. I am convinced the Bubblies would have processed his data immediately. They would have wanted to find out what it was that had come tearing down out of space straight toward them.

—You can understand the differences that are in him, said Jill. He has been subjected for at least a century—more than likely two centuries—to the influences of this place. He has come to identify with it. He accepts its viewpoints and absorbed its philosophy, if it has a philosophy and I assume it must. He seems to have it good, has made a place for himself. He is a part—a triad, is it?—with this Bubbly he calls Smoky. He and Haystack. Decker II is not the same man he was. He has changed. He probably had to change to survive. You can't blame him too much. He did what he had to do. And this is not like the old Decker at all—not like the man you described to me, Jason. Your Decker never conformed, never even tried to conform. He didn't give a damn. He lived his own life, the way he wanted it, with no notice of what others might be doing.

—You said a triad, said Whisperer. That means three, doesn't it?

—Yes, it means three.

—There are more than three, said Whisperer. There are four.

—Four?

—There is Plopper.

—Plopper? You mean that thing that was jumping all around?

—That is the one I mean. He is a part of Haystack and Decker and the Bubbly.

—Well, I'll be damned, said Tennyson. How do you know this?

—I know. I know not how. But the Bubbly and the Plopper are very closely related.

—Let's try to sum it up, said Tennyson. We are here. We found this place and it is not Heaven. We should be getting back to Vatican with the word it isn't Heaven. But how can we prove it isn't Heaven? We can't just say it isn't. No one would believe us. And we haven't much time to hunt around for proof.

—We should be leaving now, said Jill. Whisperer, could you take us home?

—I can take you home.

—How about the equation folk?

—No need to worry about them. They can find their way back. If they want to go.

—You think they may not want to go? Oh, yes, I see what you mean. They were put away in an old folks' home and now they've broken free of it. . . .

—So we have only ourselves to think of, said Tennyson. What worries me is how much time we have to try to pick up proof and how much danger we may be in by waiting. Once the Bubblies recreate the new Jill and the new me, they might just put an end to us. They could use the new ones of us to try to weasel their way into Vatican.

—Why do we feel this way? asked Jill. Here we are, assigning the Bubblies an adversary role. Maybe it won't turn out that way at all. This Center and Vatican are engaged in the same activity. They might want to be cooperative. They might want to join in with Vatican. . . .

—Which is the last thing Vatican would want.

—I can't help it, said Jill. I think the same way you do—that the chance is they are adversaries. But we can't be sure of that.

—For one thing, said Tennyson, Decker showed far too much interest in the Listeners. He asked a lot of questions. In their data-gathering capability, Vatican is light-years ahead of this place. This gang would dearly love to get their hands on the Listeners.

—But they must have known about Vatican long before we came here. Remember the Theodosius memo. A survey party of the Bubblies did visit Vatican.

—Yes, I know. I have been wondering about that. Also what Decker said about the data piling up. A Bubbly survey sweep might take centuries, might cover a lot of planets. They'd come back with tons of data. They'd be forced to pick and choose. They'd study only what seemed the most important. Maybe the Vatican data still is in the files untouched. Vatican's not too spectacular. It might not have made much of an impression. Perhaps the Bubblies never had run across robots before, would not even guess at their capabilities. So far as we know, the human-made robots are the only ones in the galaxy. To the Bubblies, a robot might seem to be nothing but a lump, a chunk of metal, a machine. They stayed only a few minutes, not much more than a fly-over. Remember what that memo written by Theodosius said— that the one he saw clearly looked down upon him with enormous disdain.

—Theodosius couldn't be sure of that. It was only his impression.

—I'm not certain of that. A robot cardinal can be pretty damn discerning.

—Well, maybe so, said Jill. I hope you're right.

—Do you now, asked Whisperer, wish to go back home? I am ready to transport you there. I'd not mind going back myself.

—We can't, said Tennyson. We simply must have proof. Otherwise, all this will have been for nothing. What we must have is some sort of iron-clad proof.

—You endanger yourselves, warned Whisperer. I know of danger in this place.

—I wish we could pin down, said Tennyson, some idea of what this place is all about. Decker called it a study center, and I'm inclined to believe it is. But the motive is the thing. Most research centers—human research centers, that is—are aimed at knowledge for the sake of knowledge alone. In Vatican, the acquisition of knowledge is aimed at the acquisition of a faith, in the belief that faith will come through knowledge. Another motive might be power, using knowledge as a power base. I fear that this may be the motive here. Decker spoke of a move to extend this Center's research to nearby galaxies. Could this be a reaching out for power—for power rather than knowledge?

—It could be, said Jill, but the exercise of power must presuppose a political organization. Does this place operate politically?

—There's no way we can know, said Tennyson. We haven't the time to find out. It might take a long time to find out.

—I know, said Jill. I know what we could take back as proof. One of the worms. If we took back a worm, the theologians would have to agree that this is not Heaven. There are no worms in Heaven. There simply could not be.

—I sorrow to tell you this, said Whisperer, but I cannot transport one of the worms. There would be too much mass for me to handle. I do not have the energy.

—Now that we know where Heaven is, said Jill, could we send out other Listeners? They could bring back proof imprinted on their cubes.

—It wouldn't work, said Tennyson. It may be the Bubblies missed Mary the first time. She came and saw Heaven and was so impressed and captivated by what she saw—or by what she thought she saw—that she returned a second time. She only caught a glimpse of it that first time. The second time she tried to enter Heaven, perhaps intent, as we are now, to bring back proof of it. The second time this place knew that she was there and they scared her off. But now that they know of the Listeners, another Listener wouldn't have a chance.

—If we, said Jill, could only take back a cube.

—We can't, said Tennyson. We aren't Listeners.

—They let us in, said Jill. They must have let us in. They could have stopped us or driven us off as they drove off Mary.

—In that you're wrong, said Whisperer. The equation people do not operate as the Listeners operate. The equation people did get us here without detection. We were here before Center knew of us. Having done it once, however, I'm not sure we could do it a second time. The people here, now aware of the chink in their defenses, will take steps to insure it won't come about a second time.

—So that's it, said Tennyson. There is no way we can come again. There is nothing we can take back as proof. Our word is all we have, and that will not be accepted by the theologians. No matter what we might take back, they could always say it was something we'd picked up along the way.

—Do you mean to say, Jill asked, that we have made this trip for nothing?

What was the answer to that? Tennyson asked himself. Could what little they had to tell give Theodosius and those who supported him the resolve to fight a little longer? Would what they had to say give the theologians some pause, stave off a little longer their take-over of Vatican and the Search Program? There was, he told himself, a bare chance that it might, but more than likely not for long—at best a short breathing spell.

Why, he wondered, had he (or Jill) not been able to foresee this situation? They had talked about it, of course—the necessity of returning from Heaven with some proof, one way or the other. But they had given no adequate thought to what such proof must be. Why had they not realized the near impossibility of obtaining unquestioned proof?

If they only had more time, they could work it out. It seemed, however, that they had little time. There was a danger here, a danger that he could not define, but a danger that every fiber of his being insisted that they faced. And Whisperer agreed.

Failure, he thought. They had accomplished their mission and still they faced failure.

What the hell could he do, or Jill, or the two of them together? One thing, he knew, they could not do. They could not turn tail and run, not for a while at least.

—If we could only get word back to Theodosius, said Jill. Word that we are here and it isn't Heaven.

—I can take back word, said Whisperer.

—But who could you tell it to? There is no one on End of Nothing you can talk with. Not Theodosius, not Ecuyer. . . .

—There are the Old Ones, said Whisperer. I can talk with them. The Old One above Decker's cabin could take the message to Theodosius.

—But we need you here.

—It would only take a while.

—No, said Tennyson, we do not want you to leave, even for a while. We might have great need of you.

—Then I can send another Duster. One of my flock brothers would carry the message for me. I told you, didn't I, that there are Dusters here?

—Yes, you did, said Jill.

—Then not to worry, said Whisperer. I'll ask one of them.

Chapter Fifty-seven

WHEN A MONK BROUGHT WORD THAT AN OLD ONE WAS COM-ing up the esplanade, Cardinal Theodosius went out to the basilica to meet him.

The Old One spun sedately up to the steps, halted his spinning and settled to the pavement. He instantly began his vibrating drumming and finally he managed words.

"I return your visit," he said.

"I thank you for it," said Theodosius. "It is gracious of you. We should get together often."

"I also bring you word," said the Old One. "I have a message for you, brought me by a Duster."

"Whisperer? Decker's Duster?"

"No, not the Whisperer. One of our long-lost Dusters, happily home again. Once there were many of them here, then they went away. We had despaired of ever seeing them again. We thought of them, strangely enough, as our special children. Now one of them came back to us; we hope that others may."

"I feel happy for you," said Theodosius. "You said the Duster brought a message."

"A message for you, Cardinal. The Tennyson and the Jill reached Heaven, but it is not Heaven."

"Thank God for that!"

"You did not wish it Heaven?"

"Some of us had hoped it would not be."

"Also," said the Old One, "that the Jill and the Tennyson will be returning."

"When?"

"Soon, the Duster said. They'll be returning soon."

"Fine. I shall be waiting for them."

"I suggested," said the Old One, "that when they did return, they arrive upon this esplanade."

"How will they know?"

"The Duster went back to this not-Heaven to tell them. I had it in mind that the two of us might wait here to greet them."

"We may have to wait awhile."

"I have patience for long waiting and I think you as well."

"That is fine. We both are full of patience and we have much to talk about. We can talk away the hours."

"Your pardon, please," said the Old One, "but talking in your method is laborious for me. I cannot talk for long."

"In that case, we shall share a mutual silence. Perhaps the two of us may find we have no need of talk. Perhaps we can commune together."

"That is a noble thought," said the Old One. "We'll attempt communing."

"If you don't mind," said Theodosius, "I think I'll get a stool. It is silly that a robot should ever need a stool, but I have become accustomed to a stool. When I visit Jill in the library, I always sit on one. I know it is a ridiculous habit, but. . . ."

"I'll wait for you while you go to get it," said the Old One.

He waited on the esplanade while the cardinal went to get his stool.

Chapter Fifty-eight

HAYSTACK WAS ASLEEP AGAIN. HE SLEPT A GREAT PART OF the time, or perhaps he only closed his eyes, all thirteen of them. Haystack didn't move around a lot, and if his eyes were closed, there was no way to tell if he was asleep or only shutting out the world. Haystack more than likely was bored, thought the Bubbly that Decker had named Smoky. There were times when Smoky had been convinced that he should get rid of Haystack, but on more deliberate consideration had always kept him on. Despite his slothfulness and his unkemptness, Haystack was a wise old bird. It would be hard to get another like him—impossible, more than likely. Also, once one had taken on another as a triad partner, the relationship was such that one shrank from disrupting it. It took a long time to build up a smoothly operating triad, and Haystack had been with him longer than he could remember. One would think, Smoky told himself, that in all that time the two of them should have become so accustomed to one another that they would be inseparable as a result of the close personal ties that entwined them both. They were inseparable, all right, thought Smoky, but not because of any strong ties—close only because Haystack would not allow himself to be pried away. There was some psychological factor that made Haystack, in spite of all his wisdom, an insecure personality. He must have someone to hang on to, someone to shield him against the world. He might complain and fulminate about the racket that Plopper made, he might even threaten to take off, to break up the triad, but he would never do it because he knew that safety and security lay within the triad.

Plop, plop, plop, went Plopper.

Haystack was asleep (or maybe only had his eyes shut) and Decker was not around. A lot of the time, Smoky grumbled to himself, Decker was not around. At times he could be an amusing and entertaining creature, and there was no question that he had an audacious imagination, and all in all had been loyal enough, but there were times when one could not help but have certain doubts of his devotion to the central triad theme. Decker, Smoky admitted, was an opportunist, albeit a most engaging one. So long as no greater opportunity presented itself, Decker would stay, and, Smoky told himself with some pride, there was at the moment no better opportunity than to be with him. There was no other Bubbly in all of Center that had more clout than he had, and that clout had been generated by the wisdom of Haystack and the audacity of Decker. In his triad, he knew, he had chosen well and wisely. How, then, did it come that at times he felt irritation and downright disaffection for the two of them? Would it be possible, he asked himself, once the recreation of the two newly arrived humans had been completed, that he could add them to his triad and make of it a quintet? Would he dare? Could he get away with it? It ran counter to all tradition and right thinking and there would be fierce criticism, but he could withstand some criticism if that was all it was. Would it be wise? he wondered. Three Deckers would be a bit lopsided, but there was strength in these so-called humans. With the wisdom of one Haystack and the sharp opportunism of three humans. . . .

It was something, he decided, that he must think about, think very hard about.

Plop, plop, plop, went Plopper.

Why, Smoky asked himself, should he hesitate? He already was a tetrad, although no one was aware of it, or he hoped no one was aware of it. He had concealed it rather effectively (at least so far he had) by making out that Plopper was no more than a passing pet, when the fact of the matter was that if it came down to a pinch, he would let go the other two if necessary to keep Plopper with him. He had worked it very well, he thought—no one had suspicion.

Why was it, he wondered, that he valued Plopper so? Plopper had no wisdom, like Haystack, and he had no audacity and imagi-nation like Decker, but he did give him deep moral strength and a sustaining comfort, qualities that so far as he knew no other member of his race had ever had before.

Haystack was still sleeping and Decker still was absent and all the cones had drifted off, so he sat alone, almost alone—the only thing that showed any signs of life was the bouncing Plopper. The silly cubes that had come along with the two humans and the Duster (he had not seen the Duster, but Decker said he had) were out in the parking lot, roosting in a circle, yelling at one another with the flashing, skittering symbols they paraded across themselves.

The diversity of the galaxy, he thought, the utter unending diversity of its life forms and the diversity, too, of the concepts that they had developed, some of them making not a single bit of sense, others pregnant with awe-inspiring possibilities. Yet there was in them all a certain logic if it only could be found—and all of these, all the concepts and the logic, could be adapted to sure and certain use if they could be puzzled out. This Center was the place where they could be puzzled out—that was the purpose of it. But once they were puzzled out, there was yet another step, and that step was to put the logic to a proper use—to selfish use, perhaps, but selfish use, he told himself, was better than no use at all. Of all of them, of all the others of them here, he was the only one who had the wile and craft to put them to that use. With the aid of Haystack and Decker, and the close support of Plopper, who never failed to assure him that his course was right, he could put to proper (and to selfish) use all the concepts and the knowledge that had been harvested through millennia. The others, in their arrogance and pride, who in their self-deceit thought they were the ones who might accomplish it, were not the ones who would accomplish it. He was the one, the only one who could manage and turn to his own good the possibilities and the promises. He thought, hugging the thought against himself, of the expressions he would see upon their shocked and incredulous, their ridiculously surprised and beaten faces, once the knowledge of his actions finally burst upon them.

First the galaxy, he thought, and then the universe. First the galaxy, then the universe.

Those others, sitting smug within their restricted orbits, secure in their associations with their triad fellows, had missed the one bet that he had not missed. They had missed because of their misplaced arrogance and their fatal smugness, their failure to recognize a simple truth—that they could be wrong.

Over the millennia, Center had come upon hundreds, perhaps thousands, of faith systems. Difficult as they might be to study, they had been studied and after being studied tested and in every instance had failed the tests; all of them, every one of them, had been judged meaningless. Not only was it concluded that all gods were false gods; the judgment had been carried one step further: There were no gods at all, either weak or strong, true or false. The faith systems had been pegged as no more than self-delusions, willing self-delusions sought after and propounded by weak people who felt compelled to erect shelters for themselves against the bitter truth of existence, against the overwhelming evidence that there was nothing within the universe that cared.

Plopper landed directly in front of him and now, instead of

plopping off in a new direction, it jumped in place, straight up and down in front of him. Plop, plop, plop it went, going very fast.

Watching it, half hypnotized by the straight up and down, by the steady rhythm of the plopping, he felt the wonder, the never-ending wonder, enter him; he felt the piety, the passion, and the power, all welded together, the piety to the passion and both of them welded to the power. All of the three equally sanctified so that the power was no whit baser than the piety. And gripped by all of this, he thought, marginally, that all was as it should be, that the power was equally sanctified with the piety and passion. That pleased him, for it was the power that he cared about. There were those who said that power was evil and the use of it was evil, but that was not so, for those who said it were in error. As they had been in error when they had said there were no gods. Wrong because he had found a god and it was his own—along with Haystack and Decker, it was his very own. In time, it would give the power he needed to carry out his plan. When the time came for him to move, he would hold the power.

Worship me, the god commanded.

So he worshipped it, for that was the bargain he had made with it.

Plop, plop, plop went Plopper.

Chapter Fifty-nine

SMOKY SAT ON HIS DAIS. LOOKING AT HIM CLOSELY, TENNYSON saw that he was a rather splendid creature. Now that some of the unfamiliarity had fallen away, the outer beauty of him was revealed. He was egg-shaped rather than globular, and his outer shell, if it was a shell, had a pearl-like sheen with iridescent highlights. The dimple in the egg was cloudy, like a small area of gray woolen clouds, with the hint of clouds still remaining when they cleared away to some extent to reveal the face, which was a cartoon face, the sort of face that a human child, scribbling with crayons, might have drawn in its first attempt at art.

To one side of Smoky squatted Haystack, more like a haystack than a living creature, with the occasional twinkle of eyes glinting through the hay. Standing on the other side of Smoky was Decker II. Looking at him again, Tennyson sought some feature that would distinguish him from the authentic Decker. There was none; he was Decker come to life. In front of Smoky, Plopper was plopping all about, but covering not too great an area, simply plopping back and forth.

All about the room stood the cones, sinister in their stolid blackness. Functionaries of some sort, Tennyson wondered, or were they guards? That was foolish, he thought, for against Jill and him there was no need of guards.

Whisperer spoke to Tennyson.

—Don't look around, he said, but the equation people have just now arrived.

—Do you have any idea of what is going on? asked Jill.

—I do not, said Whisperer. It is an audience, of course, but its purpose I fail to catch. The Bubbly, I am certain, is up to no good, and watch out for the Plopper.

—The Plopper?

—The Plopper is the key.

Decker spoke to Tennyson. "Smoky greets you and wishes to know if you have been well treated. Is there anything you wish?"

"We have been well treated," said Tennyson. "There is nothing that we wish."

The Bubbly spoke in his grating guttural tones.

Decker said, "Smoky says the Duster must go. He has an antipathy to Dusters. He does not want it here."

"You tell the Bubbly," said Tennyson, "that the Duster stays."

"I warn you, friend," said Decker, "that this is most unwise."

"Nevertheless, please tell him that the Duster stays. He is one of us."

Decker spoke to the Bubbly and the Bubbly answered, his eyes gleaming out of the cloudy dimple straight at Tennyson.

"It is against his wish," said Decker, "much against his wish, but in the hope of harmony and a fruitful conversation, he concedes the point."

—Mark one up for us, said Jill. He is not so tough.

—Don't kid yourself, said Whisperer.

"I thank you," said Tennyson. "Tell the Bubbly that I thank him."

The Bubbly spoke again and Decker translated. "We are glad that you came to us. We are always glad to meet new friends. The Center's aim is to work cooperatively with other life in the galaxy."

"We are glad to be here," Tennyson said shortly.

The Bubbly spoke, Decker translating, "It would be proper now for you to tender us your credentials, with a statement of why you came, so kindly, to visit us."

"We have no credentials," said Tennyson. "We are representing no one. We came as free members of the galactic society. We came as travelers."

"Then, perhaps," said the Bubbly, "you would not mind telling how you came to know of us."

"Certainly," said Tennyson, "all in the galaxy must know of the greatness of the Center."

"This one mocks us," Smoky said to Decker. "He would make sport of us."

"I doubt it," said Decker. "It is just his way of speaking. He is a rank barbarian."

The Bubbly said to Tennyson, "Then your purpose. You must have had a purpose."

"We were looking around," said Tennyson. "We were no more than giddy tourists."

—You're pushing it a bit, Jill said to Tennyson. You best ease off.

—He's fishing for information, said Tennyson. I'm not about to give any. It's apparent he doesn't know who we are or where we came from, and it's best he remain in ignorance.

"Friend," said Decker, "you are going about this wrong. It would be only common courtesy to give us some straight answers."

—They have not as yet finished the reconstruction of the two of you, said Whisperer. If they had, there would be no questions asked of you. The answers could be gotten from the recreated humans. It seems, however, that this one is in something of a hurry. He does not want to wait for answers.

"I can tell you honestly enough," Tennyson told Decker, "that I have been giving answers as straight as you will get. If your friend wishes to know where our home planet lies, tell him to seek it out by other means, for I am not about to tell him. If he wishes to know how we got here or why we came, then he can learn it later from our recreations, but from us he will not get it. Or he might try talking with the cubes. Maybe they will tell him."

"You are deliberately making it difficult for me," said Decker. "You know very well we cannot converse with the cubes."

"What is this all about?" grated Smoky. "Tell me, Decker, what is going on."

"Just a matter of semantics," Decker told him. "Give me a little time and I'll get it all worked out."

Plop, went Plopper, plop, plop, plop.

"I do not like this," said Haystack. "Dammit, Decker, there is something going on. Tell us what it is."

"Be quiet," said Decker. "Keep your fat mouth shut."

"I've told him and I've told him," wailed Haystack, "and he pays me no attention. Decker, you and I are reasonable beings. Let's give ourselves a little time to work it out. Let's drop the matter for the moment; we can pick up later on."

"I will not drop it for the moment," yelled Smoky. "I want the answers now. There are ways that we can get them."

—I cannot catch the thoughts complete, said Whisperer, but I would judge it is getting slightly sticky.

—Let it get sticky, then, said Tennyson.

—I could jerk you out of here.

—Not quite yet, said Tennyson. Let us see what happens.

Plopper had positioned himself directly in front of Smoky and was jumping now in place, straight up and down, going very fast.

Plop, plop, plop, plop, plop, plop . . .

—We still have no proof, said Jill. If we go now, there'll be no proof. We must get some proof.

"I'll tell you man to man, human to human," Tennyson said to Decker, "something that you can understand. Being human, you can understand it; no alien could. We made a bet, you see. We bet that we could come here and bring back proof that we had been here. Give us that proof—proof that no one could question—and let us go. Should you do that, we'll return—on our honor we'll return and answer all your questions."

"You're mad!" yelled Decker. "To expect me to believe that kind of story. You cannot bargain—"

"Decker!" screamed Smoky. "Fill me in. I command you tell me."

"They refuse to answer questions now," said Decker. "They have proposed a bargain."

"Bargain! They would bargain with me?"

"Why should we not bargain?" piped Haystack. "As creatures of reason—"

"I will not stand for this!" raged Smoky. "I will not be defied by supercilious barbarians."

"It would be better if you accepted some defiance," counseled Decker. "I know humans because I am a human, and I stand here to tell you that you cannot shout them down and further-more . . ."

Plopper's plopping now became so rapid and so loud that it was almost continuous, drowning out what Decker was saying. He was bouncing up and down, straight up into the air and down, main-taining his position in front of Smoky, and now Smoky was begin-ning to bounce, too, not as high or as energetically as Plopper, but jiggling up and down at a fairly rapid rate.

—I think, said Whisperer, that it may be time for us to go.

—We have to have some proof, said Tennyson. We can't go back with nothing. . . .

—You'll get no proof from these maniacs. Any minute now they'll explode right in our face.

"Smoky!" yelled Decker, trying to raise his voice so it could be heard above the racket. "Smoky, you are out of line. You are—"

"Anathema!" screamed Smoky. "Anathema! I call down anathema!"

—Now, said Whisperer, and Tennyson tried to cry out a protest, but there was no time to protest.

But before the scene cut out before him, he caught a glimpse of Plopper exploding in his face—a flare of light and fire that was not fire, but cold. . . .

Chapter Sixty

THE RUMOR THAT SOMETHING WAS HAPPENING QUICKLY spread in Vatican. There was something happening or about to happen. Cardinal Theodosius and an Old One were out at the foot of the basilica staircase, waiting for something that they must know was about to happen. And did you hear the latest—Jill and Tennyson are in Heaven and now they're coming back? Just like Mary went to Heaven and came back. They'll be bringing good word. They'll bring word that it is really Heaven. They'll tell us that Mary was right in what she told us.

Or at least that was what some of them said. Others had a different version. You're wrong, they told the believers. To believe that Heaven is a place you could go to in the flesh is at variance with the tenets of Vatican. Heaven is a mystery; it is not of this world, but of some other and some better plane. There were still others who also disputed what the first group said on the grounds that Jill and Tennyson were creatures of Theodosius and other cardinals who did not believe in the finding of Heaven, or who would not allow themselves to so believe, for if it was determined that the place Mary found was Heaven, then they must abandon their search for knowledge, since Heaven would wipe out any need of knowledge; if Heaven was found, then there would be no need of knowledge, since faith would be all one needed.

John, the gardener, came striding down the steps of the basilica to confront Theodosius.

"I understand, Your Eminence," he said, "that you have been to see His Holiness."

"That I have," replied Theodosius, "and who has a better right?"

"And that in your audience with him, you accused me of treachery to Vatican?"

"I accused you," said Theodosius, "of interfering in matters that were none of your concern."

"The preservation of the faith is everyone's concern," said the gardener.

"But the murder of an esteemed human and the theft of Listener cubes is not," said Theodosius, speaking bluntly.

"Did you accuse me of that?"

"Do you deny that you were the instigator and the leader of the theologian movement? Do you deny that you are the one who stirred up the stink about canonizing Mary?"

"It was not a stink. It was an honest attempt to haul Vatican back to the course it should have followed all these years. The Church had need of a saint and I supplied it one."

"To me it was a stink," said Theodosius. "It was a stench within the nostrils of the Church. You used the story of a deluded woman to bring all this about."

"I would have used," said John, "anything at all to bring Vatican to its proper senses."

He turned on his heel and started up the stairway, then turned about and spoke again.

"You demanded of His Holiness that if there should prove to be no Heaven I'm to be demoted to a piddling monk."

"That I did," said Theodosius, "and I mean to see it done."

"You have first to prove it is not Heaven," said John. "Should you fail, the same to you."

"I would think," said the cardinal, "that you have it twisted all around. I would argue that the onus lies with you—not that I must prove this place of Mary's is not Heaven, but yours to prove it is."

"Why is it, Your Eminence, that you are so hostile to Heaven?"

"I am not hostile to it," said Theodosius. "I would much hope that there is a Heaven. But not the kind of Heaven you dreamed up."

John turned about and this time he went up the stairs, saying nothing further.

Still the rumors ran.

Did you notice that Theodosius is sitting on a stool? No robot before him has ever sat so long upon a stool. Someone told me that it is a punishment—that His Holiness has told him that, in all humility, he must perch upon a stool.

And the Old One? What's the Old One doing here? He has no business here. Do you notice how he and the cardinal stick so close together, as if they were firm, fast friends? What business has a cardinal of Vatican to be friends with a ravening beast such as the Old Ones are? I tell you there is more to all of this than meets the eye.

But another objected, saying you must remember that an Old One, this same Old One, some say, brought the dead Decker and Hubert home to Vatican, a neighborly and compassionate thing to do.

Brought them home! exclaimed another. It was the least that he could do, since more than likely he was the one who killed them in the first place.

These and other rumors. Vatican went wild.

No work was done. Crowds gathered along the perimeter of the esplanade, leaving the central area free since, by some kind of popular osmosis, it seemed to be understood that whatever was about to happen would take place out in its central area. The basilica stairs were jammed with watching robots. Wood-cutting crews, harvesters, cowherds, haulers, steam-engine operators, all dropped what they were doing and came trickling in. End of Nothing humans left their jobs and businesses and zeroed in on the basilica. Someone began ringing the bells, and this continued until Theodosius got up from his stool and went storming up the stairs and put a stop to it. Even some of the Listeners, who rarely mingled with the Vatican hosts, came out to see what was going on. A hastily put-together corps of technicians, wholly without authorization, installed a huge video screen on the basilica's facade

and hooked it up to one of the papal audience panels. Within minutes after the hook-up had been made, the cross-stitch visage of
His Holiness appeared upon the screen, saying nothing, but joining the watch.

Nothing happened. Hours went by and nothing happened.

The crowd that had been noisy with constant chattering grew
quieter as the sun went down the western sky. The tension grew.

"Could you have been mistaken?" Theodosius asked the Old
One. "Could the message have been wrong?"

"The message was as I gave it to you," said the Old One.

"Then something has gone wrong," said Theodosius. "I just
know something has gone wrong."

He had counted too much, he told himself, on everything going
right—on his two human friends returning with word that would
set Vatican on its proper track again, putting an end to the prema-
ture, infantile infatuation with Heaven and with saints.

He tried to console himself. If, in fact, everything went wrong,
it would not be forever. He and some other people in the Vatican,
perhaps not many, but a few, would keep the flame of hope alive.
Vatican would not go down to a saintly darkness that would last
forever. It would not dream the remainder of its life away. Sometime, centuries from now, people would weary of the sterile saint-
liness and would turn back to the search for knowledge which, in
time, might lead to the true faith. And if, sometime in the far future, it should be determined that there was no true faith, that in
fact it was an uncaring universe, it would be better to learn this
and face it than to go on pretending that there had to be a faith.

Thinking all of this, he had bowed his head in a prayerful attitude and now he heard behind him a sudden rustle of attention.
Jerking up his head, he saw what the others saw.

Jill and Tennyson stood on the esplanade, no more than a hundred feet away. Above them he caught a glimpse of a momentary
glitter, as if a patch of diamond dust were shining. He wondered
momentarily if the glitter might be Whisperer.

He started to rise from the stool, then sat down again with a
weak-kneed knowledge something had gone wrong. For out in
front of Jill and Tennyson hopped a strange monstrosity. It looked

like an octopus standing on its head, and as it hopped, it made a plopping sound.

Out on the esplanade, Tennyson spoke to Whisperer.

—What the hell is going on? he asked. You brought along the Plopper.

—I just sort of grabbed hold of him at the last second, said Whisperer. When he exploded in our faces, I somehow got inside his mind, something I had not been able to do before, although I'd tried. I don't think I planned to bring him along with us, but he just sort of came.

—The last time I saw him, said Jill, he was big and fiery.

—Well, said Whisperer, it seems he got over that.

—Do you know what he is? asked Tennyson.

—I'm not entirely certain. It becomes slightly complicated. Smoky thinks he is a god, a god that he could use. Worship him and use him, paying for his help with worship, which, after all, is what you humans do as well, but in a slightly different way. Not quite so cynically, perhaps, as Smoky.

—And is he—a god, I mean.

—Who's to know? Smoky thinks he is. He figures he has gotten hold of something none of the other Bubblies have and that he can use it to achieve his ends. Get the right god, you know, and you can do anything. Near as I can make out, Plopper thinks he is a god as well. Which makes two of them thinking it, and where does that leave us? How many people must think a thing's a god before it truly is?

Plop, plop, plop, went Plopper.

Theodosius had risen from his stool and was walking out to meet them. The Old One, spinning slowly, moved along beside him. Behind them the people clustered, the robots and the humans. They jammed the staircase that ran to the basilica, they perched on every roof, they spread out as flankers on both sides of the esplanade. On the facade of the basilica, the cross-hatched face of His Holiness stared out at them.

Theodosius held out his hand to them, first to Jill, then to Tennyson.

"Welcome home," he said, "and our heartfelt thanks for the journey that you made for us."

Plopper, bouncing madly, hopped an intricate fandango around Theodosius and the Old One.

"You," said Theodosius, speaking to Tennyson, "have met Decker's Old One, but I doubt that Jill has met him."

"I am pleased to meet you, sir," said Jill.

The Old One wheezed and hummed and finally he said, "It is my privilege and pleasure to have met the two of you and to welcome you back to End of Nothing."

The crowd had started slowly edging in, a close-packed semicircle about the four of them—five, if one counted Plopper.

"First of all," said Theodosius, "out of sheer curiosity, what is this bouncing horror you brought along with you? Does it have significance?"

"Your Eminence," said Tennyson, "I rather doubt it does."

"Then why is it along?"

"You might say it got caught up in a traffic jam."

"Our intelligence is that you reached Mary's Heaven."

"Yes, we did," said Tennyson, "and it is not Heaven. It is a research center similar to Vatican. We did not have the chance, however, to explore it. It seems we got entangled in local politics."

A robot elbowed his way through the crowd and came up to stand alongside Theodosius. Tennyson saw that it was John, the gardener.

"Dr. Tennyson," asked John, "what proof can you offer that it is not Heaven?"

"Why, no proof at all," said Tennyson, brazening it out. "No documentary proof. Can you not accept our word? I would have thought a human's word would be enough for you."

"In a situation such as this," said John, "no unsupported word is good enough. Not even a human's word. It seems to me you humans—"

"John," said Theodosius, "where is your respect?"

"Your Eminence, respect is not a factor. We all are in this together."

"The Tennyson speaks the truth," said the Old One. "He radiates the truth."

"You thought, perhaps," said John to Tennyson, ignoring the Old One, "that this bouncing betsy you brought might serve to support your story. Pointing to it, you would ask if such a thing would be found in Heaven."

"I thought no such thing," said Tennyson, "for if I should do that, then you would ask that I prove it was, indeed, from Heaven, and not picked up otherwhere."

"That I would have done," said John.

The crowd cried out in a single voice and thereupon surged back, still crying out in wonder and in terror.

"For the love of God!" exclaimed Theodosius, standing straight and rigid.

Tennyson spun around and there they stood: Smoky and Haystack and Decker II, huddled in a row, with the equation folk standing guard on them.

—The equation folk must have understood what was going on, said Whisperer. I wondered if they did and felt certain that they didn't. Could this be the proof you need?

Decker II was walking down the esplanade toward them.

"Why, that is Decker," said the cardinal. "And it cannot be. Decker's dead. I said a mass for him. . . ."

"Later, Your Eminence, I'll explain," said Tennyson. "This is a different Decker. Another Decker. I know it is confusing."

They stood and waited for Decker II. Tennyson stepped out several paces to meet him.

"I suppose," said Decker, "that this is Vatican."

"Yes, it is," said Tennyson. "I am glad to see you."

"I don't mind telling you," said Decker, "that back there, at the end, it was getting very hairy. You damn near got us killed."

"I almost—"

"You were dealing with a maniac," said Decker. "An alien maniac. Aliens alone are bad enough, but—"

"Yet you were one with him. You seemed to be his man. What was it you called it—a triad?"

"My friend," said Decker, "in that hornet's nest back there

your first thought is survival. To survive you do what you must. You have to be fast on your feet and shifty in your attitude and you must go along."

"I can understand," said Tennyson.

"And now I must speak to the man in charge," said Decker. "You're not the man in charge, are you?"

"No, I'm not," Tennyson told him. "The man in charge is His Holiness, on the wall up there. But I think you had best speak to Cardinal Theodosius. You'll get along with him better than you would with His Holiness. When you speak to the cardinal, you address him as Your Eminence. It's not necessary, but he likes it."

He took Decker by the arm and marched him up to Theodosius.

"Your Eminence," he said, "this is Thomas Decker II. He desires to speak with you."

"Decker II," said the cardinal, "you drop in on us unceremoniously and with no warning whatsoever, but I'll be glad to listen."

"I speak for an alien being who is a fugitive from his home planet, Your Eminence," said Decker. "He is that egg-shaped bubble out there and I call him Smoky, although he has a more proper name."

"It seems to me," said Theodosius, "that I have seen this Smoky, or one of his fellows, a number of years ago. And now, please, eliminate all the palaver and get on with what you want to tell me."

"Smoky throws himself upon your mercy, Eminence," said Decker, "and begs sanctuary of you. He can't return to Center, for if he did, his life would be forfeit. He is truly a homeless creature and fallen from very high estate. He is quite humble now."

"He sounds in bad shape," said Theodosius.

"He truly is, Your Eminence. He petitions you—"

"Enough of that," said Theodosius. "Now, tell me, is this place he fled from known as Heaven?"

"Not to my knowledge. I have never heard it called that."

"Are you aware that one of our Listeners made an attempt to visit your Center—is that what you call it?"

"Yes, Your Eminence, that is what we call it, the Center for

Galactic Studies. And, yes, we are aware that someone or something that fitted the description given me by Tennyson of your Listeners had tried to infiltrate the Center, but we frightened it away."

Tennyson glanced over his shoulder and saw that the equation people had spread out so that Smoky and Haystack stood relatively alone. Hopping frantically toward them was Plopper, making straight for the Bubbly.

It reached a position in front of Smoky and began hopping up and down in place, going very rapidly.

"Oh, my God," cried Tennyson, "not again!" He lurched around and started running toward the two of them. Behind him he heard the pounding of feet and Decker yelling at him, "Get out of the way, you damn fool! Get out of here!"

Tennyson kept on running. Decker came up beside him and reached out an arm, thrusting at Tennyson, hitting him on the shoulder and sending him sprawling. Tennyson tried to keep his feet beneath him, running hard and sidewise to regain his balance. But it was impossible to stay upright, and he went plunging to the pavement, striking on one shoulder and skidding, finally coming to a stop piled up in a heap.

Decker was yelling at Smoky in the Bubbly language. "No, Smoky! Don't try it. Haven't you had enough? You're finished, I tell you. You are all washed up; you haven't got a chance."

Haystack also was bawling at the Bubbly. "You and your goddamned pet! You'll be the death of us."

Haystack yelled at Decker. "Get out of the way! The fool is going to do it."

Decker hurled himself to one side, running desperately.

Plopper blazed. He became a circle of brilliant fire, but the fire was cold. Even where he lay, fallen off to one side, Tennyson felt the bite of it.

But even as this happened, an awful silence fell, cutting off the screaming of the crowd—a silence and a darkness. Tennyson, lying on his back and looking toward the basilica, saw the shaft of darkness projected from the vision plate that had been installed for His Holiness. The shaft of blackness extended out over the esplanade, and within it lay the deepest night. The brilliance of Plopper blinked out and the darkness went away. Plopper was no longer exploding. He lay sprawled on the pavement and did not stir. Haystack had been tipped over on his side and Smoky tipped as well, lying on his face. As Tennyson watched, the Bubbly began a slow crawl up the esplanade, painfully hitching his way along. Theodosius and the Old One stood waiting as Smoky crawled toward them. Decker strode across the pavement and picked up Haystack, setting him on his feet. Plopper was stirring feebly and Decker, going over to him, picked him up by one tentacle and walked slowly down the esplanade, dragging Plopper behind him.

Tennyson hauled himself erect. One shoulder, the one he had fallen on, was sore and there was a throbbing pain in it. He hobbled along lopsidedly as he walked over to join Decker and Haystack.

"He just wouldn't give up," said Decker, making a thumb at Smoky. "He is one of those fanatics who never know when they are licked. Even when he was flat on his butt and knew it, he still had to make another try. You know what his motto is? First the galaxy, then the universe."

"He is mad," said Tennyson.

"Of a certainty," said Decker.

"But you stayed with him."

"As I told you, friend. Survival."

By now Smoky had reached a position in front of Theodosius. He stopped his crawling and remained face down on the pavement.

Decker spoke to him and Smoky answered in a muffled voice.

"I told you, Eminence," said Decker, "that he was humble when I spoke to you before. I missed a lick, it seems. But he's humble now. He's truly humble now. Take the bastard and lock him up, as tightly as you can. The best way would be to put an end to him."

"We do not put an end to life," said Theodosius. "With us, all life is sacred. But we have a place for him. How about the hopper?"

"Throw it in with him. It's not likely it will live."

"And the other?"

"You mean Haystack, Eminence?"

"Yes, I suppose I do."

"Haystack's all right. Harmless. Even decent. I'll vouch for him."

"All right, then. We'll take care of the other two. And please accept my gratitude."

"Your gratitude?"

"For telling me that one of our Listeners was frightened from your Center."

The crowd was buzzing again, beginning to pick up steam.

A voice boomed above the chatter.

His Holiness was speaking.

"These proceedings," he said, "are ended. In due time all the facts in this situation will be taken under careful consideration. The results will be announced at a later time."

Chapter Sixty-one

THEY HAD GATHERED IN TENNYSON'S SUITE, IN FRONT OF THE blazing fire. Tennyson got up to refill Ecuyer's glass. He said to Theodosius, "It seems to me, Your Eminence, to be inhospitable to be able to offer you nothing while the rest of us chomp down sandwiches and slosh down the booze."

The cardinal hunched down more solidly on the stool that Jill had brought in from the kitchen. "It is sufficient," he said, "to be here, in this circle of friendship before this warming fire. You remember the night I came and you invited me in?"

"Yes, I do," said Tennyson, "and you couldn't because you were bringing a summons from His Holiness."

"That is right, and I have looked forward ever since to an invitation."

"There is no need to await an invitation," said Jill. "Drop in any time. You'll always find a welcome."

"It seems to have turned out all right," said Ecuyer. "It looks as if we can pick up where we left off. The Listeners can settle down and start going out."

"His Holiness said an announcement will be made at a later time," said Jill. "Do you think there is any chance . . ."

"None at all," said Theodosius. "After listening to what the second Decker had to tell us, especially about the Center having been aware of Mary's visits, I would think there'd be no question. His Holiness, as a matter of fact, would accept lesser proof than what we have. He was more upset than any of us knew by the Heaven business and the proposal to make a Listener a saint. You must remember that he is, basically, a computer, although a most sophisticated one. None of us should have had any doubt where his interest lay."

"Yet, had it come to a pinch," said Ecuyer, "he would have ruled against us."

"He would have done anything to hold Vatican together. And so, I think, would have all the rest of us."

"There's still one thing that worries me," said Ecuyer. "The Bubblies, so-called, did survey this planet. Some centuries ago."

"There is little need to worry about it," said Tennyson. "Decker assures me that portions of every survey record still lie in the files and, with new data flooding into the Center all the time, there's not much likelihood any of them will go digging back. They have no way now of knowing they have a record of the planet."

"But there are your recreations, Jill II and Jason II. They could tell them the record is in their files. They could tell them where we are."

"It is a danger, surely," said Theodosius. "It is a wonder that someone has not nosed us out before. It is a situation that we must accept. We are not entirely defenseless. We don't talk about it or flaunt it, but you saw what His Holiness did to quell the Plopper. A damping effect. A rather humane weapon, as a matter of fact. It simply squelches everything in its path. We have others. . . ."

"I was not aware of this," said Ecuyer.

"Few are," said Theodosius. "We would use them only under the greatest provocation. From what Decker tells us, the Bubblies must be a vicious race. Each one of them a little island to itself, waiting for the chance to move up a rung or two."

"Smoky had plans to take over the galaxy and then take aim at the universe," said Tennyson. "He was mad, of course. He had found this feeble little god and planned to use it as a secret weapon."

"Only he used it too soon," said Jill. "Jason, you goaded him into it. Did you have an inkling of what was going on?"

"No, I was just smarting off. I was determined he'd get no information from us. I guess I carried it too far."

"A good thing for us you did," said Ecuyer.

"A little god, you say," said Theodosius. "There are no little gods. There is only one God, or one Principle, whatever you may call it. I am sure of that. One must beware of little gods. There are no such things."

"The thing we don't understand," said Jill, "is that finding, or thinking he had found, a god of any sort would have loomed very large to Smoky. He ascribed it much greater power than he would have otherwise because the Center had become convinced, through its studies, that no spiritual values existed—that all religion and all faith had no basis whatsoever."

"How true," said Theodosius. "How true. Always there are those who think that. They stand naked before the universe and glory in their nakedness. Even when we find the true faith that we seek—if we find it—there'll still be those who will deny it. They will be those who cannot subject themselves to discipline or restraint."

"How about Decker II?" asked Ecuyer. "What will happen to him?"

"He and Haystack," said Theodosius, "are being held in house arrest. They seem harmless enough, but we have to be sure. The only one we need to worry about is Smoky and, where we have him, he'll not be going anywhere."

"He wouldn't go anywhere anyhow," said Tennyson. "The other Bubblies know by now what he was planning and he wouldn't dare go back. It was a stroke of genius when Whisperer grabbed hold of Plopper and brought him along. Even if the equation folk hadn't brought us the other three, Smoky probably would have had a try to seek out Plopper. I don't know. When I try to think about it, it gets all tangled up. Whisperer maybe has it clear in his mind, but I haven't, not yet. Whisperer claims he didn't actually intend to haul Plopper along, but I can't be certain of that. Whisperer's thinking can get complicated."

"It worked out well for us," said Ecuyer, "that the equation people brought the other three to us. Why do you think they did it?"

"Who can say?" said Jill. "The equation folk are faster on their feet than we ever dreamed they were. I have a feeling—well, I have a feeling. . . ."

"Go ahead and say it," said Ecuyer. "We won't hold you to it."

"Well, I have a feeling they can look a ways ahead. Into time, I mean."

"I wouldn't doubt it for a moment," said Tennyson. "I wonder if they're still around. I lost track of them."

"No, they left," said Jill. "I don't know where they went. I'm sure that if we ever need them, Whisperer can sniff them out again."

"It seems to me," said Theodosius, "that once again we are back to the Vatican of old. We can take up our work and carry on again. I wonder, Jason, if you'd pour me a glass of booze so we might drink a toast."

"But, Your Eminence. . . ."

"I'll pour it on my chin," said Theodosius, "and pretend I am drinking it."

Tennyson went to get another glass and brought it back, filled to the brim with Scotch.

Theodosius took the glass and rose. He held the glass on high.

"To those of us," he said, "who really kept the faith."

The others drank the toast.

Theodosius tipped back his head and solemnly poured the liquor on his chin.

About the Author

CLIFFORD D. SIMAK is a newspaperman, only recently retired. Over the years he has written more than 30 books and has some 200 short stories to his credit. In 1977 he received the Nebula Grand Master award of the Science Fiction Writers of America and has won several other awards for his writing.

He was born and raised in southwestern Wisconsin, a land of wooded hills and deep ravines, and often uses this locale for his stories. A number of critics have cited him as the pastoralist of science fiction.

Perhaps the best known of his work is *City*, which has become a science-fiction classic.

He and his wife Kay have been happily married for some 50 years. They have two children—a daughter, Shelley Ellen, a magazine editor, and a son, Richard Scott, a chemical engineer.